CONTENTS

Acknowledgments	3
Prologue	5
Chapter one	8
Chapter Two	29
Chapter Three	51
Chapter Four	59
Chapter Five	79
Chapter Six	99
Chapter Seven	140
Chapter Eight	160
Chapter Nine	189
Chapter Ten	202
Chapter Eleven	208
Chapter Twelve	244
Chapter Thirteen	263
Chapter Fourteen	307
Chapter Fifteen	321
Chapter Sixteen	343
Chapter Seventeen	363
Chapter Eighteen	371
Chapter Nineteen	378
Chapter Twenty	395
Chapter Twenty One	409
Epilogue	421

ACKNOWLEDG-
MENTS

Firstly a massive thank you purchasing and reading my first novel, it means the world.

I kept this a secret from almost everyone, but there is a few people I would like to thank in helping of the making of my first novel.

I would like to say a special thank you to Anika Tunstall for making my beautiful cover, taking my photos and for proof reading. You have been a truly amazing friend.

I would also like to thank Eve my book buddy, for proof reading and supporting me along the way.

To my few friends that knew, thank you so much for all your love and support.

To my dad, thank you for my laptop when my old one was close to exploding. But not only that thank you for believing that I could do this.

Not forgetting my husband, you've been my number one supporter. You've been with me every step of the way. I love you.

Without out all your help, encouragement and believing that I could do it, I probably wouldn't have.

Thank you all for putting up with my crazy neurotic behaviour while writing my first novel. I will try and die down the crazy when writing my next novel. I love you all.

Please take at look at my truly talented friends art on her website anikatunstall.co.uk or follow her on Instagram.

To all my family and friends that didn't know I was writing a novel, surprise!

PROLOGUE

Things that happen in our life don't always change us. But they do shape us to the people we are today. What we choose to let shape us it determines our life choices and who we become. Sometimes you need to let go and rise above.

11 years old my world came crashing down. 11 years old I had to grow up. 11 years old anxiety took control over my life.
I stand at my best friends' grave side. Clutching a single lily in my hand. I had failed my best friend, he took his own life because he felt like he had no one. He needed me and I wasn't there for him.

It's been 4 weeks since I found Cameron dead. Today is my first day at a new school. It was supposed to be me and Cameron starting together. I can feel the stares, I can hear the whispers. They blame me. I blame me.
I sit down at my table in class, my head down. Someone comes to sit next to me.
"I wouldn't sit next to her. I've heard she's a jinx. Her best friend killed himself because of her."

I hear a girl sneer behind me.

I don't react I just carry on staring at the table in front of me. They couldn't cause me any more pain than I am already in.

"Shut up Gemma, go be an evil bitch somewhere else. You pick on her again and I will tell Mr Marks."

To my surprise I feel the person continue to sit down next to me after defending me to Gemma.

She nudges me and I look up in to her kind face. She smiles.

"Don't listen to her she's just a stinky bag of dog crap. You can be my new friend. I am Bex."

Bex smiles at me. I smile a small smile and nod in return.

Break comes and Bex introduces me to Rachael as we sit down to eat our lunch. I excuse myself to ring my mum.

Mum picks up on the third ring.

"Hello."

"Hi mum its Lily. You okay? Dad okay?" I ask.

"Yes, sweetheart we are okay. How's your first day?"

"It's alright, is Axel feeling better? Does he need a doctor? I could come home and look after him for you so you could go to work." I ask concern and worry running through me.

"Sweetheart we are all okay please don't worry just enjoy your first day in big school, we will see you later I love you."
I nod biting my nail anxiously.
"Okay mum. Love you bye."

I'd ring my mum every day checking in on her, my dad and my younger brother and both my sisters. Just in case they needed me. When they each got themselves a mobile phone I would text. The same with my new friends Bex and Rachel.

I promised I would never miss any friend or families cry for help again. I would always be there for them, whenever they needed me. I wouldn't let what happened to Cameron happen again. I will never fail anyone again.

CHAPTER ONE

Sometimes I think that I could just jump on a train and see where it takes me. To go on an adventure to live life like I know I should, like everyone keeps telling me to.

Then real life comes crashing down on me. What if I am away and nan has a fall? What if something happens to anyone in the family or they need me, and I can't get to them in time? What if something happens to me? It's just a few things that run through my head on a daily basis.

My family doesn't know the full extent of my anxieties. They just think I am just stuck in my ways. It's amazing what one person can cover up with a smile or by cracking a joke. I may have my anxieties but I'm one good actress.

I do try to make the most out of my boring everyday life.

I work for a magazine company called "Crop a feel" magazine. A magazine for growing crops, for the modern-day farmer.

Rise Above

Thanks to ex rock stars and boyband members are retiring buying a farm to live a calmer life. A lot less sex, drugs and rock n roll.
It's made it the 'in' thing to do and apparently there's a market for it.
It's not what I dreamed of doing when I was a little girl. But it's safe, it's close to home and the people that need me.
I work with a mixture of people, and I believe there are always people that fit their names perfectly.
Malcolm my chief editor is one of them.
He is the beige king of everything beige. Beige cord trousers, beige shirt, and patterned cardigan with different beige shades. Oh, and not forgetting dress down Friday, he goes all out and wears brown cords.
There is only 4 of us "reporters". I say reporters lightly as how many times can I interview the latest yuppie couple who recently retired from bond street or the fashion industry and have all these magical and wonderful ways to grow bloody fields of carrot.

Things do get a bit more exciting come early summer when we write and interview people about growing the perfect strawberries.
Now I love strawberries in prosecco that is.

So I am sat here with the 3 other reporters of our little magazine.
You have Wendy who is a late 50 something who

is stuck in the 70s hippy phase of her life and grows her own food. I think she grows more than a bit of fruit and veg. Her motto is "a brownie a day keeps the arthritis at bay."

While Wendy makes some days interesting in the office, like the time she rescued a rat from a trap we had set up in the kitchen.

That little fella jumped straight from her arms, runs across the office floor straight under Malcolm's desk. To which he jumped on his chair and screamed like a girl.

My other colleagues aren't as laid back as Wendy and me.

There's Jim in his forties, he takes his job very seriously. He went out and rented an allotment so he can get a feel for the environment, a feel for what it's like to grow crops. I swear most days his cologne is "Au de cow shite". I mean he must have access to water.

Then there is Rebecca, an early thirties mum of twin toddlers, who lives and breathes anything organic, no toxins, no sugar, no chemicals Just no to anything man made, that sometimes makes some crap food taste great.

She brought them into work once, they are two and a half years old and they sat there quietly drawing. I didn't hear a peep.

That was until I gave them some of my skittles. Let's just say the kids went so high I think they did taste the rainbow, met a leprechaun and found the pot of gold at the end of that rainbow. Also it made for an interesting photo day at their nursery. Their eyes rabid, hair wild and smiles crazy.

Rebecca hasn't spoken to me much since that eventful day, apparently they were rocking and shaking from the come down of the sugar.

Now see just a little treat is good, keep them from it and all hell breaks loose, it was like those kids were tripping out on acid.

So anyway meeting is finishing up, and we've all been given our next stories to report on. All I can think is thank god it's Friday.

"Lilly are you with us? Are you on board with your story?" Malcolm asks.

Hey, what? Oh bugger I zoned out again, bugger just smile and nod.

"Um yes sure Malcolm no problem."

"Great you leave first thing Monday. You can leave early today as you'll be working away and need to pack and prep for your trip. Now the magazine has paid for your ticket, and sorted accommodation. I am really trusting you to represent our magazine and this is the biggest article we've ever had, don't let us down." Malcolm continues while I stare like a stunned fish.

What the bloody hell have I agreed to? Where am I going? What the what??? And he's still talking, I stop zoning out. I give myself a Mental slap,

I retune into Malcolm.

"So you'll be our eyes and ears to what is coming from the big old USA farming, all the nitty gritty. I want you there for a month to start with, see what comes from that. I want your article emailed to me once a fortnight on Friday am our time, pictures also if you can. Gives me time to go over it before Monday.
Read the file it's got all the details of travel and accommodation. Good right off you pop, I am sure you'll have to sort out few things. Safe travels."
That's it? I grab my folder and mumble a goodbye.
Rebecca is giving me an evil smile and Jim looks sick with jealousy and I stare back in a daze. I wander over to my desk grab my bag and head for the tube home.

On my way to the station, my anxiety starts.
Why America? That's thousands of miles away. They have guns over there. Why couldn't it have been Cornwall or Wales somewhere that doesn't have a different time zone.

While I am sat on the tube I look at the folder to see where the hell it is they're sending me. There's a plane ticket to Texas??! But what?! My breathing becomes erratic, my chest feels tight. I am struggling to breathe, I am having a panic attack. I go through my breathing techniques I

Rise Above

was told to do by my doctor.

Calm, I need to calm myself it could be a trip of a life time. Nice hotel maybe? Maybe a nice hunky cowboy? Like on my calendar.

I carry on reading

"nnnnnnnnnooooooo!!!"I shout. I quickly cover my mouth.

I am staying with a family on their farm in a small town in the middle of no-wheres-ville.

Mr Stan Merrick and Mrs MaryAnn Merrick. Oh sweet mother of shitting Christ. Hill billies they sound like hill billies.

Texas chainsaw massacre.

It Says I am to live with them, work and learn how they grow their crops. They are known from starting from a small amount of land and now sell home grown organic veg and fruit.

I put my head between my legs. As a damp cold sweat of panic takes hold.

I am shaking, I feel sick. People on the tube don't notice a hyper ventilating gagging woman.

It's an unwritten law on the London tube, no eye contact, don't get involved. But I really think i am going to be sick. My stomach is churning with dread, the anxiety I feel. My stomach is in knots and probably ever so slightly out of date supermarket sushi isn't helping.

I cover my mouth with my hand and try to take slow deep breaths. Nope not working I am now making that awful retching sound when you try

to fight it. Like a cat with a hair ball or a dog that's chucking up the grass he's just decided was a good idea to eat. I turn and before I can stop myself, I am emptying my stomach on a nice gentleman sat reading his paper next to me.
Oh holy shit!
The gentleman just stares at his lap hands in the air, then looks to me. He does this a few times mouth open and eyes wide in shock.

"I am terribly sorry." I try to apologise, but I can feel myself becoming light headed.
My breathing is still erratic. The next thing I know I'm falling face first into another poor man's crotch.
The man simply stares at me as I'm on my knees trying to push myself off his crotch.
"I'm so dreadfully sorry." I mumble.
He does hold a hand out to support me into standing. But other than that he continues to avoid eye contact and pretend like the whole thing of my face being in his crotch never happened.
I turn slowly to sit back down and see the other gentleman whose lap I've just been sick on. This day couldn't get any worse.
The gentleman looks at me then down at his lap.

"Here, I carry wipes." I say, reaching into my bag I pull out a pack of wipes, and proceed to wipe my sick off his lap, I am now scrubbing with force. Who knew salmon would stick like wallpaper paste?

Oh why am I feeling a hard lump? Oh I hope he's not allergic, it really is starting to swell.

Then I freeze and stop what I'm doing, realising I am wiping up his crotch. I am rubbing at it. Kill me now. Kill me now.

"Oh my god I am so, eww um, so sorry here you might be better wiping that than me." I hand him the packet of wipes mortified.

He wipes his crotch, With blushed cheeks. I can't believe I gave the guy a bloody hard on by rubbing sick off his lap.

I sit down again mortified.

He may not be thankful now, but it could have been worse. I am on one of my fad diets. Coffee and some herbal shake are all I've had for breakfast and healthy sushi for lunch. The shake looks exactly the same going in as it did coming back up.

I'm so embarrassed. I keep apologising. The gentleman in true British form quietly grunts "its fine." not wanting to cause a scene any more than what I already have, and he swiftly jumps off the tube at the next stop.

I massage my temples, I feel a headache coming on.

Soon I'm getting off the tube. Keeping my head down, walking to my flat that I share with my sister Rose and nephew Caden.

My mum named us after flowers she is obsessed

with them my other sister who leads a lovely life with her husband Tony, being a lady of leisure, is called Daisy. Love my mum but she's slightly bat shit crazy.
I stop off at the off-licence for emergency supplies, its nearly 3 pm In the afternoon perfectly fine and totally a crisis. So alcohol is a must.

I grab vodka, peach schnapps, cranberry, cherry energy drink and amaretto liquor. All I need for home-made woo woos cocktail and cherry bombs. I also make a grab for large bag of crisps and dip. And lots of chocolate.
There goes my diet but to hell with it right now! I get back to my flat grab a jug and one of my special bomb glasses. I make up a jug of woo woo, and quickly make up a couple of cherry bombs and knock them back.
I grab the jug put a straw in it and grab my bag of goodies. I curl up on the sofa and soon everything seems a lot better after nearly half a jug of woo woo and a couple of cherry bombs.

At around 6pm my sister and my nephew arrive home, to me singing and dancing around the lounge with Dolly Parton blaring out my nephew's karaoke machine.

My sister turns off the karaoke machine and I turn around wondering what the hell made my music stop?
"Hey!! big sis come dance with me I am learning

Rise Above

line dancing.

Caden!!! come line dance with auntie Lily! Woo-ooo working 9 till.."

I start to sing but my sister interrupts me.

"What for the love of Christ are you doing?" Rose shouts.

She turns to my nephew.

"Caden sweet, here take this bar of chocolate and go to your room. You can play video games early while I make auntie Lily better."

Rose gently pushes Caden in the direction of his room while giving me daggers.

"Cool oh and I think you might need coffee and water mum, as granddad would say she's two parts pissed to the wind."

Caden says and hurries to his room, that kid knows when he's on to a good thing. Chocolate before dinner and computer games it's like Christmas for the little guy. I head to the karaoke machine ready to start up my Texas dance routine. But Rose stops me and pulls me to the sofa.

"Why did you pull me on the sofa? I was nailing dolly, and what's that even mean anyway? You know I love you my skin and blister!"

Rose looks at me with a slightly pissed off look on her face, she sighs and rolls her eyes.

"You've had enough dolly, and what does what mean?" Rose asks frustrated.

"What does two parts pissed into the wind mean? Dad uses that saying all the time, I was sick on the tube, I was sick on a dick! Hey that rhymes! And my face was in another man's crotch and not in a fun way." I laugh.

"Shut up Lily, number one why were you sick on the tube, number two why the hell were you sick on a dick? And number three why was your face in a man's crotch? And to answer your question dad is just dad." Rose replies looking more annoyed.

I focus my eyes on my lovely sister, well as best as I can. I take a deep breath and prepare to fill her in on today's events and that she will probably never find my body as it will be part of their organic fertiliser in Texas.

"Well I was sick on a guys lap on the tube on the way home, because of what happened at work got me so worked up I mean, Texas. Then because I couldn't control my breathing I started to get dizzy and lost my balance and fell face first into another man's crotch. All because of my stupid boss. I've seen chainsaw massacre Rose! I'm going to die I know it, or they'll feed me road kill and then they will make me marry their cousin Merle who has 6 toes and only 4 fingers and spits tobacco!" I wail, I slobber a full on snot fest. And blubbering things that even I don't understand what I'm saying. Until my bitch of a sister slaps me.

"Now Lily stop being a dick, you are not making any sense, I have just got in from a long day dealing with an alcoholic pensioner who also overdosed on Viagra and looked like he pitched a tent in A&E. He tried to cop a feel when he got the chance. I swear if he asked one more time to suck the poison out of his todger to make it go down I was going to snap it!" Rose rants.

"Now calmly and slowly tell me what the hell you're on about and I swear on that old man's dick if you get hysterical again I will slap you upside the head."

I blink and nod, my sister is a mean cow.

"Okay so I am sat in the meeting at work and Malcolm is handing out new articles for the upcoming magazine issue, I kinda zone out its so boring. Anyway next thing I know he is handing me a folder with my new article, he wants me to write and says about a plane ticket and how I can go home early to prepare for my flight Monday. And it's a ticket to Texas!!" I wail but soon stop when my sister gives me a look, that's says don't you bloody dare, and believe me you don't bloody dare.

"Wow that's awesome Lily. So you get to live it up in a nice hotel in Texas, what is it a 2 week thing or just a week? Oo you might meet Mr may from our calendar. No wonder you threw up and got dizzy from excitement, your so lu.."

I interrupt Rose.

"Will you shut up and listen! No swanky hotel, no not 2 weeks it's at least a month, and not cool Houston Texas or even Austin Texas. It's a

little town called Mufftown, in the middle of nowhere, and I will be living and learning with a family on their farm.
Mr and Mrs Merrick are who I will be staying with in Mufftown, I repeat Mufftown. A town called muff, i am going to live in a pussy!!!!"

Rose stares at me blank face mouth open very much like my stunned fish face I did earlier. She leans over and grabs a bomb glass and makes a cherry bomb. She downs it, breathes out a slow steady breath.
"Really that could be good. I mean, I'm sure they are nice people. You'll be like a foreign exchange student. And you never know maybe you'll meet a nice cowboy?" She shrugs.
"Oh shut up you're just trying to be nice, you're thinking the same as me chainsaw massacre, and hillbillies and pussy. Don't lie I can see it in your eyes."
"Will you stop saying pussy!" Rose whisper shouts at me. "I don't want Caden hearing that!"

"Anyway, let's not judge them, they could be lovely and I'm sure your magazine wouldn't send you to some random hillbilly hell. Let me go jump in a shower and get my pj's on. Then we can look over the info they gave you and then let's order takeaway and do some research through the good old internet."
I nod my head, damn my sister is so sensible. She never used to be, maybe it's a sensible chemical

that gets released when you give birth to a child? As Rose gets up to shower and get changed, I get ordering the takeaway. Once that's done I make up another jug of woo woos and grab an extra glass for Rose.

Caden comes wandering into the lounge, switches on the TV and sits next to me on the sofa.

"Hey Caden, how was school?" I ask.

"It was so boring, and I hate my teacher she blames me for everything, even when I don't do anything wrong." He whines.

I look at my lovely little nephew and raise my eyebrow, he may be a picture of innocence with his dark brown hair and big brown eyes with eyelashes any woman would die for, but I know he is a cheeky little bugger.

"So what happened then for the teacher to think it was you?"

Caden lets out a sigh and starts telling me with a very serious look on his face and big hand gestures.

"Well we had show and tell, so I took in this awesome big glittered rubber worm, Louis said it was a snake, but I told him it's too fat, short and it's all bendy with ridges on it. So it can't be a snake plus there was no eyes or tongue he really is silly sometimes. So I take my turn at the front of the class, Mrs Dickerd..."

I choke on my drink and start coughing.

"What's your teacher called?"

"Mrs Dickerd, pay attention aunt Lil'." Caden chastises me.

Poor Mrs Dickerd no wonder she teaches infants rather than secondary school teens. She wouldn't survive. Poor woman what an unfortunate name.

Caden continues. "I go to the front of the class to take my turn at show and tell, I lift up my giant worm and wave it above my head so all my class can see it. I start telling people that my mum is so cool to have this giant worm I found and that I think it will be a birthday present for me because she tried to hide it in one of her draws."

"Um Caden what colour is this giant worm?" I interrupt him. Dread creeping in on the thought of what he took into class for show and tell.

Please don't say purple please god no.

"Purple, don't know why mum would buy me a purple one when my bestest colour is red."

My 7 year old nephew took in my sisters dildo that I got her as a welcome to singleton gift when she got divorced, to his school for show and tell. She is going to fucking kill Caden and die with embarrassment.

Its already hard enough on her because of some of the clicky stuck up bitchy mums, that constantly look down their nose at her and Caden. Just because she's a single mum working full

Rise Above

time and she doesn't follow them licking their arses.

Caden does what he wants and always has. He doesn't follow what's cool he does what he likes and what makes him happy I've always admired that in him.

So when one of the clicky mums son pushed Caden. He kept picking on him for always wearing his coat like a cape and always being the evil baddy, like Darth Vader. Instead of being cool and being the superhero.

The slimy little snot bag then told Caden that he was a weirdo always wanting to be the bad guy and that's probably why his dad left him.

Caden only took so much, snapped and punched him right in the face.

When I asked him why he always liked being the baddy, he said "Because the baddies are always, evil geniuses, I am also a genius and they always have a good reason to why they turned evil."

I couldn't argue with him on that.

I try to think of a way to help Caden.

"Okay buddy here's what we are going to do, I will go speak to your mum, give me the dil', uh I mean worm. I will sweet talk your mum and we will say no more about it." I offer.

"But I don't have it! Mrs Dickerd put it in her draw and I'm not allowed it back until mum goes into talk to her!" He wails.

Caden's eyes starts welling up, his bottom lip starts wobbling. God damn it, he knows it's my weakness I can't see him crying. He really is an evil little genius.

"Okay, okay don't cry I will sort it, happy?" I try to soothe.

Tears gone and a smile on his face he nods no sign of tears, little shit gets me every time. With that Rose comes out of her bedroom pj's on.

Caden scoots over so she can sit down on our big comfy crappy sofa. He then cuddles in, being all sweet. When Rose finds out, I will get the blame as I brought it for her.

"So what are you guys chatting about? Rose asks looking from me to Caden then back again.

"Oh just telling him I've ordered Chinese for dinner." I say grabbing my drink, hiding behind the glass from Caden I mouth talk later to Rose and she nods.

"Okay then, so what shall we watch? It's Friday night so what about a movie, Caden?" Rose asks.

"Um yeah okay mum, can I pick?"

"No please no, I can't stand to sit and watch one of those crappy sing song happy kids films, if I have to sit through that again I'm going to bleach my eyes and cut off my ears!" I beg. And giving Caden and you owe me boy Look.

"Um, can we watch Labyrinth?" Caden asks sweetly.

With Rose's back to me I give him the thumbs up.

After we've eaten our Chinese, Caden soon falls asleep. Rose picks him up and takes him to bed. I look around our miss matched not perfect big old flat. I realise how much I'm going to miss my home. Sure it's only for a little while but, I've never been away for more than a week's holiday, and that was a school trip.

I feel my chest tighten as worry creeps in my mind.

Rose comes back in and I quickly bury my worries. She sits down on the sofa and pours us more cocktails.

"So how long do you reckon you'll be gone?" Rose asks.

"Um well Malcolm said I would be over there at least a month and to see how it goes, maybe two or three months. It could be more I don't know." I say, emotion in my voice.

I know it's silly, but I'm used to seeing my sister pretty much all the time, we live together now and have done since the giant tit dick face left. I'm going to miss her and Caden.

"Hmm, Okay well let's look through this folder then." Rose says avoiding looking at me I know she's fighting back the tears. Just as I am.

After going through my folder with all my travel information and tickets, where and who I will be with and what I am expected to report on. Rose and I pour our third jug of cocktails, and I lost count of how many cherry bombs.

I feel now is a good time to tell her about Caden taking the giant dildo into class. Surprisingly Rose takes it rather well. That may be the alcohol talking.

"I'm sooo guna miss you sooo much, I, I, I, I love you my skin and blister!" I wail, sniffle and slosh my glass everywhere hugging with my swaying sister.

"So we have this weekend to get you packed and ready to go go go. You're going to have to ring mummy and daddy in the morning and tell them." Rose drunkenly states.

Oh crap mum's going to panic and worry and want to do a big family send off.

"You need to ring Daisaaay too, And I'm sure Mumma will let Ax know if he's not out on manie-euvers menn maneuvers fuck it!" Rose slurs.

My baby brother Axel.

He doesn't have a flower name like the rest of us. He's named after the lead singer of guns and roses because dad chose his name for him and my dad is a huge fan.

Of course, it was always funny to other kids in school when my mum would shout us over.

"Lilly, daisy, axel, rose, time to go!"

Anyway our baby brother Ax is in the army, he's away a lot. Which means we worry a lot. He doesn't tell us a great deal as he knows it will only worry us more. Especially mum.

"Do you fink mum will invite the whoooole family to a fair well buff,buffeeet party?" I ask downing the last of my cocktail. I go to pour more but the jug is empty. It really is a crap day.

"Of course the whole crazzzzieeee claaaaan will be there, even aunt Brenda." She giggles then frowning at the jug that is sat there empty. Staring at it hoping her magic stare will refill the jug. Now is a good time to stop drinking when the booze runs out and the effort to make a normal sentence is an almost impossible task.

"Oh fuckity fuck not aunt Brenda, she will just go on and on and on that I'm still not mar-mared-married and that my womb is shrivel shrivelling up. God ramn it what's why can't I talk?!"

I'm now getting angry with my tongue, poking it out of my mouth giving it the death glare.

"Stop stwaring at your tongue like a twatsicle. I'm off's to my bed and so should you, its nweary 2, or is that 3? fuck a duck I need my bed."

With that Rose stands and walks off to bed, but it's more like watching Bambie take his first steps.

"Nighty night twat face!" I sing.

I sit there for a bit thinking about my trip, I am crapping myself. I've never been on a plane before either, and it's not exactly a short flight. I'm also worrying about what the Merrick family will be like. Are they going to be old fashioned

big Christian believers?
Nothing against Christians but you here those stories from deep down south in USA. Small towns that think modern living, like women wearing a skirt above the knee, and are against homosexuality and cradle snakes in churches?
I don't think I could handle that.
With that awful thought I head to my bed, I land with a belly flop and pass out.

CHAPTER TWO

I wake up to the feeling that I'm being watched. I turn my head slowly thanks to my pounding headache, and squint as my eyes don't want to fully open.

As I turn I find Caden's face is literally an inch from mine hovering over me.

"AARGH HOLY SHIT CADEN!"I scream now fully awake and my head screams at me in protest of my shouting.

"That's a bad word auntie Lily. Do you know you look like that scary clown from Scooby doo, who wasn't really a clown ghost but Mr Whitlock the light-keeper. He just put on a suit. I think I might like to be a light keeper. What's a light keeper auntie Lily? Do they keep everyone's lightbulbs? Because I'd keep all the peoples lightbulbs that are mean and smelly, so they had to stay in the dark and be scared because the dark is scary." Caden rambles.

"God make him stop! Please!! Please Caden stop talking so loud auntie Lily's head hurts."

Caden looks at me for a minute and carries on

bloody talking.

"Grandad says I have to wake you up and get your booze head out of bed and not to stop talking until you do. He also said that you'd have stinky breath and he was right, he said that the tooth fluff monster would have taken a poop in your mouth, so you need to brush your teeth before you go in the lounge or everyone will be sick."

After his long rambling he finally stops. I stare at him giving him my best evil eye. Which I probably look like a pirate in drag after a bad storm.

It takes a while for my brain to kick in, my dad is here?

"Wait, granddad is here?"

"Yup! And nanny too, she's tidying up the hell hole and says she didn't raise ogres and that you and mum are slobs." Caden informs me.

Oh god not mum too, I can't handle them both this hungover. And to tell them I'm leaving in 48 hours to Mufftown. All this on a hangover someone must really hate me.

"Okay snot face get off and move I'm getting up." Caden jumps off my bed, and runs out of my bedroom, shouting.

"Grandad you were right, that tooth fluff monster must have done a real big poop in aunt Lily's mouth, she really stinks!"

I do a quick breath smell check, yep that kid is right cocktails and Chinese doesn't make for good morning breath!

I shuffle slowly to the bathroom, do my business and brush my teeth. I make the mistake of looking in the mirror.

I forgot to take my make-up off last night, and although my dad would be proud as he would think I'm doing a tribute to kiss. looking like this my mum would be mortified. I wash my face, trying to power on through my pounding headache.

I leave the bathroom and walk into the lounge, to find Rose slumped over a cup of coffee looking slightly green. Dad sat reading the paper with a coffee. Mum is with a cloth in her hand which I swear is a permanent part of my mum, I'm surprised she doesn't have a deformed wrinkly claw for a hand.

I stumble to the kettle and make myself a coffee then search the cupboard for painkillers. Finding them and knocking them back and then i take the packet of painkillers to my semi living sister.

"Well good morning sleepy head! Don't you look like death, you girls shouldn't really drink like that, know your limits!"

My mum tells us with a pointed finger at me like I forced cocktails down Rose.

This coming from the woman, who at our cousin Danny's wedding drank so much free wine and prosecco, she was up dancing on tables to Acdc and tried to crowd dive. There was no crowd.

To this day she denies all knowledge of it and

therefore in her mind it never happened even though there is photos, and a video online titled Brit gran rocks out. That has over 100,000 views.

My brother posted it, my mum of course has no idea. He would be dead by now otherwise.

"Morning mum, morning dad why are you here so early?" I ask in confusion.

I flop down next to my sister and Caden who's sat glued to his tablet.

"Early? It's almost 9:30, its Saturday family breakfast day! You know that. So you girls better hurry up and get showered and dressed or we will be late getting to Daisy's."

Arrgh I forgot it's the end of the month. We take it in turns to do a family breakfast once a month, this month its Daisy's.

It was mine and Roses turn last month, let just say ours isn't appreciated. I ran out and got a giant load of fast food breakfasts.

I buy a range of breakfast muffins, bacon rolls and pancakes. What more could you want? Caden loves it.

"Fine I will jump in shower first, Rose can finish her coffee,"

Rose doesn't lift her head, she just gives me a thumbs up. Obviously incapable of speech this morning.

I get up give dad a kiss on his head, as he hasn't put down the paper to join in the conversation and head to the bathroom.

After my shower I'm looking at what to wear for the day.

I'm not your average wear what's in fashion type of girl I'm more of a rock/retro type girl. I have a few tattoos, only 2 can be seen when wearing clothes, the rest are covered by clothing.

I decide on wearing my high waisted deep red pencil skirt, its stretchy, and today is a need for stretchy clothes for breakfast, I plan on eating to get rid of this hangover.

I grab a v neck long sleeved black fitted yet also stretchy top.

I grab my low heel comfy black pumps the have big red bow on them to finish off my outfit.

Quickly I put some basic make-up on mascara, eyeliner with a flick, and my deep red lipstick. which always stands out against my pale complexion and dark brown hair.

I think sod it and just put serum in my hair and leave it to dry naturally, and just hope for minimal frizzy waves.

That's one of the good things living in London with my anxieties. I can wear whatever I like and be comfortable. As with the diversity of people no one is the same and no one seems to care, I can blend, and no one pays me much attention. Its why I love living here.

I walk into the lounge once I'm ready to see mum, dad and Caden coats on waiting for Rose and me.

"Oh sweetie, are you not going to do your hair? And maybe put on some tights? Its chilly this morning."

"No mum I'm not going to do my hair as that would take longer and you will moan that I made us late. Also what you mean is I should wear tights to cover up my tattoos on my legs. Which I will not do."

I stare back at my mum. It's the same thing all the time.

Whenever we go to Daisy and Tony's my mum likes us to look presentable as it were, she has no problem with tattoo's she has a few herself you just can't see them.

Daisy and Tony live in a posh middle class apartment building. As much as Tony is an okay guy he is a bit of a snob. Women with tattoo's, he thinks is just for bikers or rock stars.

I on the other hand love my tattoos, I have them on the back of each of my legs, long thin corset type seam line which looks like it's been threaded with red ribbon and they run right from the back of my ankle to the top of my thighs just few inches below my bum. At the top of them is a beautiful red bow.

"Oh will you leave the poor girl alone she looks fine, everybody has tattoos these days Penny. That boy needs to grow some balls and stop being such a bloody snob." My dad rants to my

Rise Above

mum and gives me a wink and a smile.

I love my dad, don't get me wrong I love my mum too. But I am more like my dad, he has tattoos all over his arms and back. I have his dark hair and deep blue eyes.

He's a handsome man always kept himself in shape. Especially being a builder so he has big strong arms. That give the best cuddles and make me feel safe.

"Fine ben but if one more of my friends from book club asks me if she's a lesbian, I shall say yes." Mum says on a huff. Dad rolls his eyes.

"Penn, you only joined that book club so you could get to know Tony's mum. You hate those up tight snobs. Who gives a crap if they think she's a lesbian?"

"What's a lasbeing?" Caden asks looking up at mum.

I try not to laugh but can't keep it in and a giggle escapes me.

"Um well, its um Ben you want to help me explain?" Mum asks dad desperate for him to rescue her.

"Ha! Not a chance this is all you, carry on."

Dad motions for mum to continue, while mum gives dad the ultimate death glare. So okay maybe I am a lot like my mum too.

"Well sweetie you see, its uh, uh."

With that my sister walks in and saves mums arse.

"Caden a lesbian is a woman who loves another woman, like Zack's mum." My sister says straightforward, with a big eye roll at mum. My dad and I just smile at each other, enjoying the moment with mum flapping.

"Oh okay can we go now I'm hungry," Caden says taking my dad's hand dragging him to the door.

"Oh well glad that's that then."

Mum says while blowing out a big sigh of relief.

"Seriously mum its 2018, we live in London a big city, lots of different people. It's not a big deal."

My sister grabs her bag and coat, she heads out the door following dad and Caden.

"Oh yes I know love just put me on the spot is all, let's go."

I follow mum and lock up. We squeeze into dads car and head off to my sister Daisy's house. She lives just only a 20 minute drive away.

"You going to tell them you're leaving over breakfast?"

Rose whispers over Caden's head.

"I don't have much choice I fly out at seven in the morning on Monday." I sigh.

"I'm glad I took the painkillers because mums going to lose her shit and be all dramatic."

Rose tells me this like I don't know that.

"Yes I know that stupid. Will you shut up your making it worse!" I seethe.

"Hey, don't call me stupid, your stupid with a bat cave fanny." Rose spits back at me. That's it this bitch is going down.

Rise Above

"Ha my fanny is not a bat cave! You've had a kid, your vagina is probably like the black hole. ECHO, echo, echo, echo!!! hell I can hear some poor bastard calling for help from your vagina, he's lost and all he wants is to see is the light of day! What's that he's saying? Duh-n uh-nuh-nuh-nuh-nuh-nuh-nuh bat cave!" I fire back at her.

"Yeah well at least my vagina isn't like the fucking Sahara Desert!!! You cough, and puffs of dust come from your crotch and tumble weed just rolls on passed your bedroom. We all choke on your vagina dust every time you walk past!" Rose says and mock coughs.

"GIRLS!!! I will pull this car over right now and you can go bloody hungry. Now stop talking about your Mary's! I don't want to hear any more! Am I clear?! My dad shouts while gripping the steering wheel tightly.

Oh and Mary is my mum and dads name for your fanny, clunge, mini, muff, vagina.

Whatever you call it, they called it that as my dad says, because of the virgin Mary and ours better stay that way until we're married.

I look at my sister and she looks at me then we both burst out laughing. We are laughing so hard my side hurts and I have tears in my eyes. Which soon turns into a quiet a sob.

"I am really going to miss you big sister." I say grabbing her hand giving it a gentle squeeze.

"And I'm going to miss you too my crazy baby

sister," Rose replies squeezing my hand back.
We both gather ourselves as we pull up to Daisy and Tony's flat. And thank god that Caden had his headphones in the whole time glued to whatever is on his tablet.

"So mum can you take me to the bat cave one day mum? it sounds cool was it in the movies?" Caden asks jumping out of the car.
We all stop what we are doing and stare at each other. The little rat bag was listening the whole time!
"Uh, no its uh a type of alcohol! Yes that's it a type of alcohol so sorry bud you can't have it." Rose answers him and we are all hoping he takes that answer.
"Oh that's boring."
He skips off up the steps of the big manor type house that's been converted into flats.
We all let out a breath, mum gives me and Rose death glare for corrupting her grandsons brain.
We all follow Caden up to Daisy's flat. She is there to greet us looking lovely and perfect I don't know how she does it. She never looks like crap. So annoying.
"Hey guys breakfast is nearly ready, we've got eggs Benedict, fruits and crepes. Oh and brioche fresh from the bakers." Daisy sings as we walk in.
"Oh sweetheart you didn't need to go to all that trouble, you are so good." My mum coos giving Daisy a kiss on the cheek.

I roll my eyes and lean in to give Daisy a hug and a kiss.

"Hey skin and blister how's you? You pregnant with my niece yet?" I ask because her and Tony have been trying for a few months now.

"I'm good, and no I'm not. We will get there it just takes time sometimes."

Daisy answers with a smile that doesn't reach her eyes. Looking at her I notice there are bags under her eyes, and she looks like she's lost some weight.

I know she really wants a baby. Ever since she was little she wanted to have a big family. It's something she dreamt of.

And she would be an amazing mum. but something's not right with her. I'm going to have to ask Rose to keep an eye on her while I'm away.

I give her an extra squeeze.

With that we walk into the lounge, where we find Caden running around the sofa shouting.

"duh-nu-nuh-nuh-nuh-nuh-nuh-nuh bat cave!"

I freeze and look over to Rose who has her head in her hands shaking her head back and forth. I turn to look at my mum and dad. My dad has his hand over his mouth shoulders shaking from silent laughter. Whereas my mum looks like she's about have a heart attack or kill me and Rose, I can't tell which.

Then I spot Tony in the doorway to the kitchen, spatula in hand wearing Daisy's floral apron with a very confused look on his face. He looks like

he's got a sharp stick shoved up his arse.
I start giggling at the scene in front of me. Slowly so does Daisy raising an eyebrow in question as to what the hell is going on. Soon we are all laughing apart from Tony who's looking at us like we have lost the plot.
"Ah that boy is going to age me badly!" Rose states, coming to stand next to me and Daisy.
"Yeah but at least he will make you laugh while getting the grey hair and wrinkles"
I chuckle. Rose gives the famous mum evil eye.

"Okay you guys let's get you fed, and caffeinated." Daisy gently pushes us toward the kitchen diner.
She may be my younger sister, but she always has been the most grown up. And always the peacekeeper between me and Rose.

We all sit down around the table. I dive for the pot of fresh coffee.
"Well this is just lovely Daisy and Tony, just wonderful."
My mum beams with pride, probably thanking god that at least one of her offspring can hold a civilised meal.
"Well tuck in everyone, we don't want it getting cold"
Tony sings bringing in some fresh toast.

After downing some coffee I dive for some toast,

Rise Above

the thought of eating eggs Benedict makes my stomach roll. Looking at Rose she's feeling just as fragile. Slowly nibbling a piece of toast.
"So Lily how's the fast paced life of the world of journalism going?" My dad asks with a mouthful of breakfast.
"Uh dad I write about crops. It's hardly fast paced, but uh yeah its um going okay same old same old."
I shrug a reply while stuffing toast in my mouth and avoiding all eye contact.
With that Rose gives me a swift kick under the table, with what I know will be her evil mum stare looking back at me.
I slowly swallow my toast, eyes down at my plate well here goes, I take a deep breath and on a rush exhale of breath I let it all out.
"Um I'm flying out Monday morning to Texas will be gone a month maybe more, staying in Mufftown, Mr and Mrs Merrick."

The table is silent, I look around my dad has his mouth open with a forkful of eggs Benedict mere inches from his mouth. My mum has wide eyes and doing the fish thing with her mouth, huh must be a family trait. All eyes are on me apart from Caden who's emptying a whole jar of chocolate spread on his toast. The little genius knows when to take his opportunities.
"What do you mean you're going to Texas? And what is Mufftown and who are the Merrick's?"

My mum squeals. Her eyes are so wide she looks like a pug.

"Mufftown is a small town in Texas, I have been assigned to go there and stay with Mr and Mrs Merrick to report on their organic crops, I will be there at least a month maybe more, depending on what I can report." I say while still staring at my plate like it can help me get out of this situation.

My mum doesn't like the thought of us living far away, even if it is a short period of time. She likes to keep us as close as possible, when my brother axel joined the army she didn't talk to him for 2 weeks. She always had her family close and wanted the same for us. She's not up in our personal lives or anything but, likes to know she can pop by or like today monthly family breakfasts.

" But do you even have a passport?! I mean you've never been on a plane and I'm sure I read an article on the high date rapes in Texas, something about under their Stetsons, and well you're so pale what with the sun and heat you won't cope, you'll burn which can cause skin cancer. Not just that there's that awful man! You know the one with that awful flappy comb over, puts too much fake tan on, makes your skin crawl, oh what's his bloody name?!" My mum rants on tapping the side of her head trying to remember.

"Mum that is president Trump, she will not be nowhere near him, and you need to stop reading those stupid made up articles on the internet. Remember last time you read one that said that all London cab drivers are part of a sex cult. That they sniff back seats after you've been in their cab. And as for her skin, she can wear sun cream mum." Rose states trying to help correct my mums frantic over active imagination.

"Now calm down Penny. This could be an amazing career opportunity for Lily. I mean think of future references." My dad says ever the optimist.

I sigh, rest my head in my hands dealing with my mums over active imagination, with a hangover is not fun. Not at all.

"I think this will be great for you Lily, I have contacts in the states. One is a millionaire from turning his ranch into an exclusive resort for the celebs and other high profile people. He said that me and Daisy could go and stay anytime. Not sure how close his place is to where you are, but I could contact him for you, see if I can get you a stay there for a couple of days at least? Of course you'd have to make an effort with your hair and clothes as it has a certain standard there." Tony offers.

He can be a nice guy but a total douche at the same time. All about who he knows and the amount of money they have. I'd love to bring him down a peg sometimes, make him take a step in the real world. But I keep quiet for my sister. Like I said not a bad guy just not my type of guy.

"Hey! Your leaving? But you said you would sort Mrs Dickerd. And get my worm back." Caden wails his bottom lips wobbling, eyes wide and filling with tears. Looking all cute and sad like someone has told him Santa isn't real. This look kills me.
"Caden honey, its sorted aunt Lily spoke to me last night, I have it covered." Rose reassures Caden.

"Hehehe Dickerd." My dad chuckles to himself.

"Grow up Ben. What's this Caden are you in trouble at school?" Mum asks staring at Rose and I like it's our fault. I jump in to try and explain for Rose.
"Okay fine just promise you won't go mental, or put me on a time out again, I'm 28 damn it!."

I stare at mum waiting for that agreement from her. Time out was not fun last time, I mean it was totally uncalled for. I was only teaching Caden the cling film over the toilet prank. How was I supposed to know she would get a stomach bug?
"Fine." Mum says through gritted teeth.

"Right, so it was Caden's show and tell at school, he found uh something in roses draw. A giant purple worm and took it for show and tell. Mrs Dickerd has confiscated the worm and won't give it back until she speaks with Rose."

Mum is looking at me eyebrows drawn together confused. God damn it please just take what I'm saying because I really don't want to mention the giant purple dildo in front of her and especially not in front of dad.

"What purple worm Caden? is it a toy your dad got you?" Mum asks looking at Caden.

Rose has just face planted the table and I don't blame her. I might join her. No one wants the discussion over family breakfast to be about your giant purple dildo.

"No nan, I found it in mums bedside draw, it was with some funny slimy stuff that when I put it on my finger they went all tingly. Oh and a weird little thing that made a funny humming noise when I push the on button." Caden states so innocently while my mum chokes on her coffee, and dad starts to cough loudly followed by whistling and looking around the room for something, anything to take him away from the thought of his daughter and sex toys.

I look at my sister through my fingers it's like watching a horror movie.

"Oh um well um, I will sort it. They are not mine they were a friends. I was looking after them for her, her err, her hen party, was just keeping them safe until then." Rose rushes out while turning beet red.

"Well there you go your mum will sort it Caden no worries there. She will need to give her friend back her um things, so we will get it back. My mum flusters almost as red in the face as Rose.

"Oh bummer I thought that awesome worm was a surprise for me. Your friend is sooo lucky mum. It's got real ridges on it and everything, and it's so thick I can't get both hands around it. Can you buy me one like that for Christmas but in red because red is my most favouritest colour." Caden pleads by this point I'm crying tears, they're run down my face where I'm trying not to laugh and have my sister kick my arse for it.

"I swear to Christ I could kill you sometimes Lily, if we weren't at Daisy's I would kick you so hard in the crotch right now!" Rose seethes.

"Hey, I didn't tell him to take your giant dildo in! And it seems you've upgraded since I brought you that toy! I wondered why the batteries kept going missing from the remote control. No one goes through a set of batteries in a month in their TV remote I was going to go buy a new remote I thought it was broken!" I rant back to her! There's silence around the table, looking at my dear sister Rose she has steam coming off of her and a face that says I'm going to get my arse kicked.

My dad is now looking at the table legs giving a shake,

"Ah these are Allan key screws, good stuff, sturdy,"

Daisy's shoulders are shaking with silent laughter, Tony's jaw is on the table and he has a strange look on his face staring at Rose.

As for my mum she is looking back and forth between me and Rose mouth open doing her stunned fish face.

"What's a giant dildo?" Caden asks innocently.

"Aargh I'm going to kill you!!!!" Rose screams as she launches herself across the table at me, glasses get knocked over in the process, Rose grabs some scrambled eggs from the serving dish and shoves them in my face shouting.

"You idiot saggy twat face, now my son wants to know what a giant dildo is you, you stupid bellend!"

"mmmphfhh" I reply trying to fight off the scrambled eggs being shoved in my face.

"ENOUGH!" My dad bellows standing at the head of the table, hands on his hips and a scary look on his face.

"Now you two will stop this stupid idiotic argument, you will apologise to Daisy and Tony for causing such a scene and as punishment you shall clean up the mess you have made. Do I make myself clear?!"

Rose and I nod, eyes cast down. We apologise to

Daisy and Tony and start to clear up while mum, dad, Daisy and Tony take Caden to distract him in the lounge.

"I'm sorry skin and blister" I say to Rose while scooping up scattered scrambled egg.
"I'm sorry too. You're not a saggy twat face, but you can be a stupid bellend. Rose replies wiping up spilled coffee and orange juice.

Once all is cleaned up we meet everyone in the lounge, mum, dad Daisy and even Caden don't bat an eye when we walk in. They are immune to mine and Roses outbursts towards each other. It was an everyday occurrence in our house growing up. Not so much anymore as we're adults and have matured. Well at least a little bit anyway. But still every month or so we get into a spat, but the name calling is every day.
Tony however is not sure how to deal with us after that outburst.
"Err all okay?" Tony hesitantly asks.

"Yeah all good and it's all cleaned up for you guys."
Rose replies while sitting next to Caden who's glued to his tablet watching some American kids open toys no doubt.

On the journey home mums organising my leaving party. And not listening to me at all.
" Ben you'll have to get the big gazebo out of the

garage, and the fairy lights, and after we dropped the girls off we will have to make a stop at the shops to get all the bits for a buffet, table cloths and napkins. Oh and I shall do one of those online event thingy's to let all the family know. It will be a rush, it doesn't leave me a lot of time. Are you sure you fly out early Monday Lily? could you not rearrange it?"

"Mum, I told you I don't have time for a party I have to be at the airport by the crack of dawn Monday., I have to pack and sort all my stuff out. And no I can't rearrange it."

I rub my temples I feel another headache coming on.

"Now Lily stop that, my baby is leaving and not just leaving to move to Essex or Bristol, you are leaving for Texas USA! And I will throw you a leaving party. It's a mothers right!"

My mums voice is getting higher pitched and wavering slightly. I see dad put his hand across the car and give her hand a gentle squeeze.

I sigh, I should just let her have her moment, I can't handle mum getting emotional on me. Peoples tears are my kryptonite, I have an overwhelming need to comfort and do anything to make them happy again.

"Sorry mum your right it will be nice to say goodbye to everyone, I just need to make sure I'm not up late okay?"

"Yes, yes of course. We will set the time for midday then at least I know you won't be up late

partying."
Mum pulls out her pad and pen and starts her shopping lists.

CHAPTER THREE

7 hours later my suitcase is full. My biggest handbag is packed for on flight. Including my kindle not going anywhere without that.
Passport and ticket are on my dressing table.
Spending most of my day washing and drying clothes was not on my list of fun times. But it's done I'm organised. With a heavy sigh I flop on my bed. I could go to bed now I'm exhausted.

My overthinking mind kicks in. I have never flown before, what if the plane crashes? What if I get there and I don't blend in and what if people don't like me? That's what I like about living in London I can wear what I want and be me and no one pays you any attention. Small town Texas I imagine there aren't many girls like me there.

The room fills with sounds of Motorheads, ace of spades, sitting up I grab my phone and see who's calling me with a big smile I answer.
"Hey my favourite brother!"
"I'm your only brother, so your leaving for Texas tomorrow?"

I sigh.

"You spoke with mum; how did she even contact you? I thought you were out training new recruits or something?"

"She rang headquarters told them it was a family emergency and they pulled me off exercise." He chuckles.

I cannot believe she did that. She is definitely a woman on a mission.

"Oh god! Ax did you get into trouble, you know mum she's a force of nature when she's got her mind on something."

Laughing axel replies.

"No its fine, they've met mum, the time I got my medal and she made sandwiches for everyone and started wiping Sarge's blazer after he spilt some egg and cress sandwich down himself. They know what we deal with when it comes to mum."

Axel is still chuckling down the phone. clearing his throat he continues.

"So Texas, you all set for your first trip on a plane big sis?"

"Yeah all packed and ready to go, I'm shattered if I wasn't so tired I'm sure I would be nervous as hell. You able to come to my leaving party tomorrow afternoon? I'd love to see you before I go you could show me some killer moves to defend myself in case its hill billy hell over there."

Crossing my fingers hoping he can come and not

just to teach me some super awesome ninja killing skills.

"Yeah I've been given a day leave as you know family emergency. that and I have a list of mums sandwiches and especially her cakes I have to bring back for the boys."

"Yippee!!!! oh I can't wait to see you little bro. Been too long. Just shame won't be able to see you for longer. I've Missed you."

I can feel myself getting emotional.

"Missed you too skin and blister, be good to catch up with you and Rose, Daisy and my man Caden. Listen I got to go I will see you tomorrow. Get a good night's sleep sis you'll need it for your long travels and of course surviving the party."

"Yeah don't I know it, see you tomorrow little bro."

I disconnect and take a big deep breath. My stomach growls reminding me I have yet to have any dinner. Getting up I walk down the hall, the smell of garlic making my mouth water.

Walking into the lounge/kitchen area, I see my beautiful sister Rose dishing up dinner. Not just any dinner one of my favourites.

"Please tell me that is steak with garlic butter served with stuffed portobello mushrooms with chunky chips?" I ask practically drawling.

"Why yes it is. Skin and blister take a seat I made you your favourite farewell dinner." My sister states while placing my plate on our little dining table where she set the table all nice with a candle and a bottle of my favourite wine also there.

"You even remembered the peppercorn sauce, you my dear skin and blister are the flipping shit!"

I dive in to my food like some starved animal.

"Caden. at dickheads?" I ask around a delicious mouthful of steak.

"Yeah dropped him off a few hours ago, they are taking him with them to the charity fundraiser. That dick has to attend with Barbie of course. As I was leaving Caden was demanding to wear his shredder costume to it. I left wishing him luck."

Rose is chuckling, god I'm really going to miss that kid.

"So what's this big charity thing that is so important they just have to attend?"

"Something to do with raising money for less fortunate, who can't afford plastic surgery."

I pause my fork an inch from my mouth staring at Rose.

"What like victims of assault. Like acid attacks or fire, that need reconstruction skin grafts that sort of thing or is more or breast cancer survivors?"

Not a bad cause if that's what it is even for.

"Umm no its for aspiring models/actresses that don't have that perfect nose or perfect breasts. I stopped listening to Barbie at that point it just turned into white noise."

It still baffles me that my dear sister Rose was

married to that dick Aka Richard. Peterson. They were happily married for 2 years until Rose walked in on him banging Barbie over his desk. He's a private plastic surgeon and Barbie aka Vanessa was a client of his.

Caden was 6months old at that point. Turned out Barbie wasn't his first. He'd been banging most of his clients from before he even married Rose. Pure arsehole. Barbie was apparently the love of his life and he's been with her ever since.

"You have got to be fucking kidding me?! And people are actually raising money for this?!" I ask stunned because it sounds like the most outrageous charity appeal I've ever heard of and can't believe anyone with at least a single braincell would give money too.

"Nope I'm not joking all the Barbies will be there. Including her plastic fantastic crew. And off course dick, the charity is called cocoon their slogan is everyone deserve to be beautiful. So of course the who's who of yuppies and beautiful people are all for this charity."

"Good god this charity function is going to be filled with wrinkled willies, fake tan and plastic! Surely that comes as some sort of fire hazard. Poor Caden. having to put up with that tonight." laughing Rose replies.

"Yup,Caden. will be fine. He's already asked Barbie before now why she's so shocked all the time. He will make a presence like no other tonight you know that kid has no filter."

Of course how could I forget. I almost wish I could be there to witness it.

"Caden will be back in time before the party ends tomorrow though won't he?"

"He will, I told dick to drop him to mum and dads for 1pm sharp. He wasn't pleased at the possibility of seeing dad. I didn't mention that Axel will be there, or he wouldn't drop him off."

Dick would shit his pants seeing Axel, he's already scared of dad, but Axel is trained to kill and has made that point to dick before.

"he-he awesome, well I shall make sure I have my camera ready to capture that moment." I say raising my glass to toast with Rose.

We finish up dinner, clear up and flop onto the sofa.

"You spoke to Rachel and Bex and told them your off?"

Rose ask flicking through the channels on the TV.

"Yeah rang them earlier, they are excited for me and told me to find my cowboy." I laugh, my two oldest friends they are all settled down and married now. Rachel moved up to Scotland with her husband because of his work and she is due to pop any day now. Bex already has two girls and lives in Devon she moved there after her and her partner split, to be close to her folks. I miss them like crazy.

"So you all packed, passport and tickets? Oh!

And have you checked in online?" Rose lists off. See sensible.

"No haven't checked in online and yes to the rest."

I reply.

"Well go on, go get your laptop, we will check you in and pick you a window seat."

Rose says practically pushing me off the chair.

I go grab my laptop, ticket and passport not knowing what I need to check in online. And sit back down on the sofa.

"Umm Rose I don't think a window seat will be a great idea as I've never flown before and I am already crapping my pants." I say watching Rose type away on my laptop.

"Nonsense, you wait it's amazing looking out the window. Besides worse case pull the little blind down if you don't like it. Oo look here now pick a seat"

Rose hands me my laptop and I pick my seat that is as close as I can get to the exit. I hand my laptop back to Rose and take a big swig of wine.

"There all done that will save you a bit of time at the airport." Rose states as she shuts down my laptop.

"Now I'm thinking Jack Sparrow or Brad Pitt, which do you fancy?"

Rose asks flicking through the movies on TV.

"Well I actually fancy both, but I'm in the mood for either Tom Hardy or Gerard Butler. As I'm off to the states lets stick with UK hotties on my last night."

"Good choice how about Krays and then follow that up with PS I love you?"

I nod in agreement as Rose selects the movie. She then the crafty minx pulls out bags of sugary goodness from behind her cushion.

"Surprise! I got all your favourites." Rose smiles as she plonks them in between us on the sofa.

"God I flipping love you!"

I dive in, grabbing the bag of pick n mix sweets. We watch the movies drinking wine and stuffing our face with sugary goodness. Best last night ever. Just what I needed.

CHAPTER FOUR

The morning turns into a flurry of panic and chaos. Making me panic more. I worry on what to wear. It's a lot hotter in Mufftown than here, so I don't want to be sweating my arse off when I get there. It's a good five hours travel by bus from airport to Mufftown so need to make sure I'm comfortable and cool.

After a lot of flapping and nagging Rose on what I should wear, I decide to go with my long floaty wrap maxi dress. Its black with little colourful flowers on it, has a V-neck thin strap and it wraps at the front around my waist. It Shows a little cleavage and a little leg not slutty but its thin cotton and will keep me cool. I pair it with my simple flat tan with sparkle sandals to match my tan handbag.

I keep my make-up simple but apply my deep red lipstick and leave my hair down in waves.

I put on my little crop denim jacket and gather my suitcase and handheld, making sure again I have my ticket and passport.

I dump all my stuff in hall by the front door. Grab

my phone and charger and place them in my handbag.

Rose walks out a moment later.

"Right are you ready for the nightmare that is your leaving party at mums and dads? You know you don't have to stay at mum and dads, I don't mind getting up early to take you to the airport."

"As ready as I will ever be. There's alcohol there right? I know but it's not fair making you and Caden get up at like four in the morning. Its fine mum and dad said they will do it." I reassure Rose.

"Of course this is mum we are talking about she wouldn't dream of having a party without alcohol, come on or we will be late. You grab your hand bag and hand luggage I will get your suitcase."

I grab my sunglasses, put them on and grab my handbag and hand luggage. While Rose grabs my suitcase and head's out the door.

We arrive at my parents' house an hour later, pulling onto the drive way, we get out of the car and you can hear my parents blaring out the classic rock music and the chattering of people coming from the garden.

I take a deep breath, family parties tend to turn a little crazy, I'm just hoping that because I'm leaving for the airport in the early hours they will miss the crazy part.

"You ready to face the crazy?" Rose asks with a raised eyebrow.

"One can never be ready for our families crazy. You just have to smile and ride that crazy train to where ever it stops."

Rose and I laugh linking arms walking up to my parents side gate to the garden.

My parents' house and our childhood home is 1930's semi. We loved growing up here. With its big bay windows and arched porch. It was spacious yet homely.

As we walked through the gate and rounded the side of the house into the rear garden. I'm greeted with cheers, raised glasses and my nan blowing vuvuzela? See crazy.

Mum had gotten the gazebo up, which inside contain the buffet table. There was garden lights strung from the trees, and my dad was on the BBQ with a beer in hand.

My parents may be nuts, but I love them because they done this all for me. My eyes swell with tears and I take a few deep breaths and wave and smile at my family as they all come to greet me one by one.

My nan got to me first squeezing my cheeks. My nan who I swear is no more than 4 foot tall, has little round cheeks and a blue rinse perm, with deep warm brown eyes that sparkle with mischief.

"My beautiful granddaughter is leaving me for an

adventure!"

My nan smiles big.

"Nan its hardly an adventure, I'm staying on a farm studying and reporting on crop growth. Not like I'm going to Vegas or New York."

I try to dial it down not for my nan but for my own nerves.

"You are off to America, you will of course have an adventure. Maybe it will be an adventure with a few hunky men. Just be careful always carry protection. I have a box of Johnny's in my bag dear. Never trust a man, they like to make a mess but never like the clearing up after ha-ha"

" NAN! Thanks but I don't think I will be meeting anyone over there I'm staying with an older married couple the Merricks. In a place called Mufftown. That is a small town only a few hundred people live there. No hunky men I'm sure."

"Well what a way to put out an old ladies fire dear. I live precariously through my grand babies. Your trip sounds as boring as my knitting club. Although with a name like Mufftown it could signal you're in for a bloody good time dear! Ha-ha!"

I chuckle at my nan who on first appearances is a sweet old lady that would make you cakes and knit you jumpers. But as soon as she starts talking you know that is not the case, that indeed she is a real live wire and who is always up to mischief.

She lives with my parents now that we've all

moved out. And just one incident that happened at a neighbours BBQ last summer. My nan spiked the punch, flashed her knickers and fed everyone pot brownies. Safe to say my parents haven't been invited over to any neighbours since.

"Nan your terrible. You look nice though nan very 1950s Hollywood, loving the red lipstick." I compliment.

"Thank you angel, I try my best. I like to wear what I want and look good too!"

The sadness creeps into my nans eyes she takes a deep breath and smiles at me and holds my face again.

"You look stunning as always. An effortless beauty, your smile makes even the darkest days lighter." I swallow a lump in my throat.

My grandad was violent and controlling towards my nan until the day he died 20 years ago of a heart attack.

I don't know the full history, but my dad only got back in contact with his mum after his dad died. My grandad never hit my dad, but my dad witnessed it and when he left he tried to take his mum too. But she'd been too scared he would find her. She was a shell of the woman she is now. It's why my nan is the way she is now all those years being trapped and controlled when she finally broke free it was her mission to enjoy every day and live her life doing exactly what she wanted.

I adore my nan she is the strongest person I know

and loves us all so fiercely. I am going to miss her and her antics.

"Love you nan I'm going to miss you" I say trying to hold back the tears that are welling up.

"Hush now none of that It won't be long, and you'll be back, plus I got your brother Axel to put me on that faceybook. So we can stay in touch on there and I've made Axel promise me that he will help me update my news on there so you can see what I'm getting up to and you must do the same! It will be such fun!"

Oh Christ my nan and tech do not mix well, she accidently text a picture of herself in front of her bedroom mirror in only her bra and pants once with message "look I took a selfie". She didn't realise we could see her bra and pants. I hope Axel has put blocks on there in case same thing happens and some pervert starts messaging her.

"Yeah that will be great nan, friends request me, and I will add you before I leave."

With that she kisses my cheek, turns and shouts.

"Axel help Faceythingy Lily! What do I press?"

I laugh to myself watching her drag my brother to help her.

"Lily!!! come her my darling niece and show your favourite auntie some love!"

Smiling I turn around to my auntie standing with a drink in one hand cigarette in the other. I walk to her and give her a big hug being careful not to burn my hair or spill her drink.

"Hey auntie Brenda how's you?"

Rise Above

Auntie Brenda is my mums younger sister and is the life and soul of any party, but mainly she has a big heart. And helps anyone out that needs it. But she also wants to see us all married off too.

"I'm good thank you baby girl, no ring on your finger yet then? Maybe you'll find yourself a husband over there."

Brenda doesn't even give me a chance to reply she carries on chatting.

"Been busy helping out at the dog rescue place, oh sweeties there's this one poor pup I just couldn't leave him, so I adopted him. He'd been starved and tied up outside the local supermarket. I've called him Gary, he's only 5 months old. Want me to show you a picture?"

She asks already reaching into her bag pulling out her phone. I love dogs just as much as my auntie, but I don't want to see an abused pup. It will break my heart.

Brenda scrolls through some pictures and finds the one she's looking for. And turns her phone round to show me. I take her phone and look at the picture.

"That's a puppy?! He's huge! I thought you said he was five months old?" I ask in shock because in this picture is a slightly small bear.

"Oh he is. The vets think he's a mix between a great Dane and newfoundland. He's beautiful isn't he?" She asks.

I look, he is beautiful and a lot to handle I'm sure. I dread to think the size of his poop. She must use bin bags to pick it up.

"He is beautiful auntie, I will have to meet him when I come back I'm sure he will be even bigger by then."

"Oh you don't have to wait sweetie he's here, your mum made me put him in the dining room. I need to take him for a walk around the block now anyway. Wait here I will bring him out."

My auntie hands me her empty glass and puts out her cigarette and swans off to get Gary.

My mum walks over to me.

"Where's Brenda going?"

"To get Gary to meet me then she's taking him for a walk around the block."

My mum turns quickly to me.

"Shit I better hide your dad, Gary has taken quite a liking to him. He pounced on him earlier, humped your dad like his life depended on it. Gary look so satisfied after I nearly handed him a cigarette. Your dad on the other hand did not, he was mortified and later told me he's never felt so violated." My mum chuckles.

"I blame your dads new aftershave that your nan got him. She got it from the Sunday market. Brought him out in a rash as well. I had to dash to the pharmacy to see if they had a cream that was okay to use on his neck, face and his balls."

My mum loud whispers to me, while I try to hold back the vomit that is crawling up my throat at that horrific thought of my dad's balls.

"Mum! Too much information, I do not need to know that. And for future reference I don't need to know any intimate details, involving you or dad." I shudder at the thought.

"Well sorry darling but you should be proud that your dad likes to be clean and smelling fresh for all occasions. It makes our nookie that much more fun. Sometimes I like to guess the scent, especially when your dads used the scented oils I got him for Christmas."

My mum carries on blabbering on about her and dad, while I've gone pale and near doubled over ready to bring up my breakfast. I'm saved by my auntie Brenda bringing out her puppy Gary or should I say he's dragging her out in the garden nearly knocking over people on their way over.

"Oh auntie Brenda he's adorable!" I say while giving him lots of head scratches, although he seems more interested in my dad.

My dad has his back to us chatting away and hasn't seen that Gary has been released from the dining room. It's then as if my dad senses someone watching him, he turns his head and catches Gary's staring at him. My dad tenses, his eyes wide, Gary lets out a loud deep woof! And makes chase over to my dad with my auntie Brenda trying to hold on to the leash. All I can do is stand there and watch as my dad lets out the most girlie scream I've ever heard, and he starts to run.

"Ben stop running you're making it a game for Gary, of course he's going to end up chasing you!" My auntie Brenda shouts while still trying but failing to control Gary.

"I will not be violated again by that beast! I had to throw away my favourite jeans because of him!"

My dad shouts not stopping. Still running around like a crazy person. Eventually with the help of mum and a dish of cocktail sausages Gary soon calmed down and he lapped up all the sausages. Then my auntie Brenda took him for his walk.

Of course I then burst out laughing as did the rest of the family at my dad's girlish and dramatic act.

"Shut up all off you have no idea what that beast did to me!"

My dad shouts waving his BBQ tong at all of us. My mum puts her arm around him and guides him back to the BBQ rubbing his back soothingly.

"Shhhh now Ben I know what you went through its all okay now."

" This bastard family are laughing at me Penny, I had to throw out my favourite jeans I wore them to the rolling stones concert, where I shook Mick Jagger's hand! They were my lucky jeans." Dad carries on wailing.

"Well Gary certainly got lucky on them jeans!"

my brother chuckles to himself

"I heard that boy! Just because you can shoot a gun, just remember I can still kick your arse!" My dad threatens as my mum is handing him a beer. I turn to my baby brother Axel who's come to stand beside me.

"See you're getting a leaving party you will never forget." Axel smiles, eyebrows raised.

"I wouldn't have it any other way. Wish you would all stop acting like I'm going forever, I could be back in less than a month and it will be like I've just been on an extended holiday."

"Oh come on Lil, you've never left London. Never been away from the family for more than a week and that was school camp. Even then mum had to force you. You've always been to scared of change and what might happen to nan, mum or dad. If you're not here when they need you. But all they want for you is to live your life and be happy. Stop worrying about everyone else or what anyone else thinks. Have confidence in yourself and enjoy this opportunity. Who knows this could be a trip that changes your life."

I stare up at my little brother, blurry eyed and wondering when he became so wise.

"What if I get there and no one likes me and I'm all alone. Or what if my plane crashes or what if something happens to one of you and I'm not here?" I ramble on with tears in my eyes. I know I sound silly and stupid to some people, but I have anxiety when there are things out of my control. "Look Lil, I know what you went through loosing Cameron growing up, but you can't let that determine your life, you were 11 years old, just a kid, stop blaming yourself."

Cameron was my best friend at preschool and primary school, we were in our final year when his parents went on a weekend break away to France. Cameron stayed with his grandparents.

His parents tragically got mugged and shot dead. Cameron a few months later, still suffering in the loss of his parents he killed himself. I was the one to find him. I blame myself for not being there enough for him. For not noticing he needed help. I didn't notice and I was his best friend.

"I guess, you're right." I say not truly believing those words, I failed my best friend and I shall always carry that with me.

Axel shakes his head knowing that his words have no effect on me and that I will live with Cameron's death on my shoulders until the day I die.

Axel clears his throat, puts his arm around me in a side hug.

"Well what are you going to do if they ask you to ride a horse? You're shit scared of them, and you're going to be in Texas after all." Axel asks. I love my brother for changing the subject.

"Well I shall politely decline to ride a horse. They do have cars there you know, not everyone travels on horseback. Plus I have these things called legs that are pretty good for walking. Unless I'm drunk then they are useless and uncoordinated." I state this but I'm now actually thinking and hoping they don't want me on a horse. They are scary hoof kicking machines!

"Being drunk has nothing to do with it, you're always uncoordinated. I've seen you trip and knock things over so many times when your sober. Being drunk might actually coordinate you a little more."

Axel nudges me smiling.

"Ha-ha very funny dip shit."

Someone calls my name from across the garden, I turn and son of a biscuit eater. It's only bloody veronica my old friend from school and her husband who's a slime ball, he makes my stomach turn.

At school she went by the name Ronnie, since she married and had two perfect little children and moved to a middle-class estate she now likes to go by the name veronica. And seems to forget we all know where she came from and that she always used to steal peoples pens and tease the teachers and act as the class clown. I groan because who invited her?! Rose walks up next to me spotting veronica.

"Oh for the love of saddle bags who invited the stepford wife and slimy weasel?!" She whispers a hiss in my ear. I shrugged my shoulders in response

"Oh my gosh Lily, congrats on the promotion. It's not New York but still. Jon went to New York on a business trip and surprised me by taking me too. Oh it was wonderful. We are so lucky that are parents let us have a weekend off each month for a bit of us time I feel that it is so important don't you Rose?

"I wouldn't know veronica." Rose replies in a shut the fuck up tone of voice. Or It could have been I really want to kick you in the vagina type tone. I can't really tell.

"Oh silly me, I forget you're a single parent now. Well anyhoo, just thought we would swing bye and send you are well wishes and all that. As this is our weekend break from the children, Jon has booked us in for a spa day. Safe travels."

With that she pulls me into a stiff hug and air kisses both cheeks, turns and leaves waving her hand over her shoulder. Her slime ball husband Jon turns looking up and down my body and giving me a wink. He is such a prick.

"Why are you even still in contact with her? She has a stick so far up her arse. She forgets I saw her giving Sammy Dillet a blowy on prom night." Rose states scrunching up her face in disgust.

"You never told me that, why don't I know about this?"

I ask because Sammy Dillet was my date, I didn't fancy him or anything he was a spotty computer nerd who loved gaming. And he was a little on the large side. Nice lad, I asked him just so I had someone to go with. And he wasn't a complete jerk, we were friends.

"Saw them behind the school hall by the wheelie bins, when I came to pick you up and you'd got drunk, rang me to come get you so mum wouldn't find out. I walked around to try and find you. You were puking your guts up literally on the other side of the wheelie bin. Sammy and Veronica didn't seem to bothered by the retching noises you were making." Rose shudders.

"Oh my god, what a cow, he was my date. I know I didn't like him, and we went just as friends but still. She was supposed to of been a mate. Did she see you? Ewww did you make eye contact while she was sucking him off?"
"No after I got you up off the floor and was helping you walk to the car, we passed them just after he was finished. Veronica was stumbling to her feet. I may have said something to her." Rose shrugs taking a sip of her drink.
I don't remember any of this at all. Blimey, it's a good job i never mix cheap cider and vodka any more.

"What did you say?" Axel asks smiling, knowing our foul-mouthed sister offends most people on a daily basis, and sometimes what she comes out with is hilarious.
"All I said was that I hope this makes her final

school report, because Sammy dick is the smartest thing I've ever known to come out of her mouth. And that she should add some sand to her knickers to make the crabs feel more at home."

Axel and I burst out laughing, while Rose just smiles and shrugs her shoulders.

"Hey where's Daisy? her and Tony aren't here yet."

I look around the party for them.

"She text saying they were on their way ten minutes ago so shouldn't be long." Rose replies.

"Oh good, right then I'm getting some food. Then I shall go speak to the rest of the family until Daisy gets here."

After getting a burger and speaking to the rest of the great aunts and uncles that I only ever see at family occasions. Daisy and Tony arrive twenty minutes later complaining about traffic and apologising for being so late.

"I'm so sorry Lily, I was ovulating, so we had you ... you know and then the traffic. I'm just glad we didn't miss you." Daisy apologises.

"First off, I hope you enjoyed yourself and glad you got yourself some. I Swear I think my hymen has grown back it's been so long. second stop apologising your here now so it's all good."

I give daisy a wink and a smile, while she laughs and pulls me into a big hug.

"I did not need to hear that Lily, there are some

things a brother really should never hear his sister say." Axel says while making gagging noises.

"Oh pipe down there Shirley, when you lived at home with mum and dad you were going at it with that girl from Elliott's horse riding school in the lounge, she was riding you like sea biscuit, boots and all! Swear I thought she was going to give you a sugar cube for being such a good boy! Ha-ha!" Rose says doubled over laughing. Of course me and Daisy all join in the laughter too. With Axels stunned face it's hard not to laugh. But Tony is not seeing the funny side at all.

"How in the hell did you know that? You weren't even living at home then you were at uni."
"Mum and Dad were away for the weekend and mum asked me to come check on you, to make sure you weren't having any wild parties. As it was the first time you've been left without one of us around as Daisy was on a college trip. I nearly bleached my eyes after walking in on that. Thank god I could only see your legs. You know I wanted to do horse riding up until that point. She was in full canter I thought she was going to shout yeeha!" Rose shouts raising her hand in the air.

Daisy and I are crying with uncontrollable laughter. Axel has the decency to blush and look mortified.

"I love riding Bobbie, I ride him so fast and hard it sometimes hurts my bottom."

We all freeze, stop laughing and turn to my nephew Caden who at some point decided to creep up on us.

I start to chuckle as does Daisy and Axel. Again Tony just smiles looking uncomfortable. My sister Rose is not finding it that funny.

"Um Caden honey how long have you been stood there listening to our conversation? And where's your father? Also Remember what I told you about listening to other people's conversations it's rude."

"Dad just dropped me off at the front, I walked in with great auntie Brenda and her dog."

Caden continues.

"Sorry mum, I heard you talking about my friends riding school, and I went there once. I don't remember there being a horse called sea biscuit though."

God this kid. I'm really going to miss the weird little bugger.

"Come on cades, let's go have a kick around with a football for a bit."

Axel puts his arm around Caden and takes him out the front to play. Caden's face lights up because he thinks his uncle Ax is the coolest.

"Hold up and I will join you." Tony says catching up with them, shortly followed by my dad, all the great uncles and cousins.

Soon the whole family are playing a big game of football in the street, jumpers are used as goal posts, mums the referee and me and Daisy are the linesman. Everyone is having fun and no broken bones so all in all great times. Caden's team wins thanks to my mum being a bias nan. And all too soon the uncles and aunties are saying their goodbyes.

Not long after it's just me, Rose, Caden, Axel, Mum and Dad. Daisy and Tony just left, and I've already started to cry. I blame Daisy she started it.
Dad always said and still does that he will punch the bastard that ever makes us cry. And when its more than one of us and no one has made us cry he doesn't know what to do with himself.

"Come here sis and give your little brother a hug."
Tears in my eyes I squeeze my baby brother Axel in a tight hug. He kisses the top of my head and releases me to Rose who is also crying.
Axel picks up Caden and puts his little arms around me and Rose.
"Going to miss you aunt Lily will you bring me back a real cowboy hat?"
"Of course I will buddy."
I kiss his chubby cheek and Axel takes him off to give me and Rose a minute.
"Going to miss you skin and blister. Bring me back a real sexy cowboy. Caden can have his hat and I will settle for the cowboy instead." I chuckle and give Rose another squeeze then step

back wiping my cheeks.

"Not sure I can kidnap one, but I will do my best. Right I will message you when I arrive and will call to speak to you as soon as I can. I Love ya."

Rose turns and jumps in the car. I stand on the drive waving at Caden and Ax as they pull off the driveway.

Mum pulls me into a hug, smiling a teary smile trying to reassure me.

"Come on sweetheart lets go pour a large glass of wine. Think we both need it."

I smile and nod at mum.

CHAPTER FIVE

My alarm wakes me at 4:30 am. I must be at the airport in two hours. There's a heavy feeling in my stomach, my nerves are in knots. I take a deep breath closing my eyes. After giving myself a mental prep talk. I get up and shower, putting on clean undies I also put on the same outfit as yesterday. Not wanting to mess up my packing.

I grab my handbag and head down stairs. My mum is already up and dressed pouring me a cup of coffee. I take a seat at the kitchen table, mum joins me.

"You all ready?" Mum asks sipping her coffee.

"Got everything in my bag ready to go, my stomach is in knots. I don't think I'm ready but i don't have much choice do I?"

I drink some coffee, probably not the best thing to be having when I'm already anxious.

"Here take a couple of calming tablets, you'll be fine sweetheart, this will be the best thing for you. I promise."

Mum hands me some tablets I take them and smile a tight smile not sure that what my mum says is true.

"Right come on then, let's get going it may be the arse crack of dawn, but this is London, there is bound to be some kind of traffic or a road closure." Dad bellows from the hallway. Smiling at mum, we head out to the car.

After checking in my luggage, I say my goodbyes to my mum and dad.

"Now make sure you call or at least email me when you've arrived. So I know you've got there safely." Mum demands.

"I promise mum."

My mum pulls me in for a tight hug, nearly cutting off my air flow.

"Alright Penn easy, your crushing her lungs."

Mum lets me go as dad makes a grab for me pulling in for a tight hug.

"Now you listen to your old man, go out there don't even think about us lot or worry. We will be all fine. Also if some American twat upsets you or makes you cry you tell me, and I will be on the first plane over there to kick their arse. Don't give a shit if they have guns or not. No one makes my girls cry."

Smiling I wipe my few stray tears.

"I love you dad, love you mum."

I kiss both their cheeks and turn to walk through to the departure lounge. I wave over my shoulder. Mums crying and dads rolling his eyes waving at me.

I'm on the plane, ready to take off. I grip the seat

like my life depends on it. Eyes closed trying to concentrate on my breathing. Soon I feel the plane pick up speed and then we're up in the air. I brave peeking out the window. And what I see takes my breath away. The view of London getting smaller and smaller, soon the plane is surrounded by clouds and it feels like I'm flying.

Just like how you imagined it when you were a kid. It's beautiful. I can't help but take a deep breath and smile from ear to ear. I can do this.

So after a very long nearly 10-hour flight, I'm in Houston Texas. My journey isn't over yet, I have a bus to catch to a town called Shelby.
I get my suitcase and wheel it as best as I can to the bus terminal on the other side of the airport. It's like a sea of Stetson hats. It's probably not but when you come from England it really seems like it.
Eventually I find my bus, I hand over my ticket and suitcase to the driver. He gives me a smile and a nod with a tip of his Stetson. I feel like I stand out not having one.
On the coach it's me and around 10 other people. So I put my bag on the seat next to me. And I stare out of the window of the bus and the new scenery passing me by. I drift off to sleep the long journey and time difference finally hitting me.
I awake to someone having a coughing fit behind me. Dazed and confused it takes me a few

minutes to realise where I am.

Pulling out my mirror i check what state I'm in making sure I don't have a crease on my face looking like I've been slashed and no dry crusty dribble at the corners of my mouth.

Thankfully apart from looking dead tired, no crusty dribble or slashed face look.

I pull out my concealer trying to cover up my black bags under my eyes and apply my blush and lipstick to freshen myself up.

I don't want to scare the poor family on the first time they meet me. Running my fingers through my hair that will have to do. For all I know they will be tobacco chewing hillbillies.

But mum always said first impressions stick. I can never leave the house completely make up free. I must have at least concealer on.

5 hours after leaving the airport at Houston I'm off the coach getting my suitcase off the driver. I look around at the deserted small bus station. Its late at night and there's no one around. No one waiting for me like there was supposed to be.

I see a bench just up ahead, so I walk towards that to sit and wait. Maybe the Merricks forgot? Or changed their mind? Oh god what if I'm not in the right Shelby town. America is huge maybe there's two of them. I pace up and down by the bench.

The bus then pulls away, I am really on my own. I know no one at all in this town and I have no idea where anything is.

I pull out a bag of sweets I picked up at the airport and sit down on the bench and start eating them thinking about what I am going to do.

I look at the time on my phone it's the only thing its good for, it won't be any good for calls until tomorrow. I set my time and see its nearly midnight. If no one arrives to get me in the next 30 minutes I will take a walk into the town and see if I could find a hotel or a taxi service, luckily I have some dollars on me.

12:30 comes and goes and still a no show, so I get up and take a big breath. I hope that this is a nice town with no rapist or Murderers in.

I start to walk towards where I can see building lights, hoping that this is the correct way. Lugging my suitcase even though it has wheels as the pavement is uneven. I can hear music coming from a bar just up ahead. So I pray that it's not some scary dive bar and aim for that. If there's a bar, there could be a hotel or taxi service.

As I get closer I can see it's a biker bar with a load of bikes lined up outside and a couple of guys stood just by the entrance smoking. They are both looking my way. Oh shit I really hope that these were the good kind of bikers the ones that do charity runs. Not the type that do illegal stuff. I've seen the tv shows, I know what happens.

Pulling back my shoulders and raising my head

as not to appear scared, I approach the guys standing outside.

"Umm hello I was supposed to be picked up at the bus station around 30 minutes ago and no one has arrived. I am staying and working in the next town over I think, Mufftown. With the Merrick family do you know them or know how I could contact them? Or even a hotel I could stay until morning then maybe get a taxi over there?" I rush out on a breath.

When I finally stopped talking I noticed both men are staring at me. One is smiling, he is as big as a bear with a big long beard that is plaited down to his chest. He has kind blue eyes, yet I could imagine him being a scary guy if crossed.

"You're British? Shit and you're a hot piece too, guys are guna be swarming to you like bees to the honeypot." The big guy states while still smiling.

I blush taken aback from his forwardness. My heart is thumping, and my palms are sweating. I probably look like a deer caught in headlights.

"Err um yes I am from London England. Err, thank you for the compliment it's kind of you, umm could either of you possibly help? or in the bar maybe someone there could help?"

Its then I notice the leather waistcoat with patches on. Their bike club is called Satans Outlaws and they have the 1% . My stomach plummets knowing that means they are proper outlaw bikers, Shit. I haven't even made it to where I'm supposed to be, and I could end up raped and murdered. Awesome. I suck at this travelling shit.

"Deep breaths there darlin' you look like you're about to pass out on us. Now let us take you in the bar get you a drink and call the Merricks, I'm Mammoth, this here is Rubble." He says jerking his thumb towards the quiet guy with tattoos, that is stood next to him. Who just gives me a cool guy nod.
"Um hi I'm Lily, nice to meet you. Uh um okay if you're sure?"

"Christ you aint gotta worry we'll make sure you arrive safe we aint the type of guys to ever lay a hand on a lady. Follow me flower let's get you a drink you look like you could use it. Don't worry about your luggage Rubble will put it behind the bar for you."
Mammoth puts his big hand on the small of my back and holds the door open for me, I'm hit with the sounds of ACDC blaring out. At least the music is familiar.
The bar is full of bikers and I'm guessing locals. Mammoth guides me to the bar and orders me a tequila shot. Without wanting to be rude and I never shy away from a drink, plus I could really do with it. I down the shot. I can feel eyes on me, but I try my best to avoid them. I look up at Mammoth, he's got a big grin on his face which

makes me smile too.

I feel myself relax a little, this big guy's warm smile and tequila is helping.

He asks what I would like to drink so I tell him a vodka lime and soda. He orders our drinks then he guides me over to a table with really good looking men sat around it. There's a couple of girls sat with them and I swear I just saw a nipple pop out, they are in tiny clothes that barely cover their bodies.

I feel the stare of a guy looking at me, so I look up into a pair of ice blue eyes, my god he is stunning. Dark hair almost black long enough to run your fingers through, a couple of days' worth of stubble, strong jaw and lips that I want to nibble on. My eyes stay focused on his lips, without thinking I lick mine wondering what he tastes like.

Laughter breaks through my daze and I feel a blush hit my cheeks. Looking back up into the Adonis's eyes he's smiling and gives me a wink, he knows exactly what I'm thinking. Damn, I blush more if that's even possible.

Mammoth starts to introduce me, so I avert my eyes smiling politely at each one he introduces me to.

"So from left to right that there is Khan"

I put my hand forward in greeting and it gets engulfed in another very handsome guys hand.

Khan is olive skin with green eyes, and long hair in top knot on his head and trimmed beard. He gives me a cheeky smile and a wink.

"Then there's Rip."

That's the Adonis. Christ I'm going to be a puddle of goo in a minute. I can feel my blush on my cheeks creep up again, as he stands with my hand in his and kisses the back of my hand. Oh nice, the smooth bastard. God is its getting hot in here?

"And this here is big papa"

Mammoth finishes his introductions. He's an older guy I'd say in his fifties but still good looking and obviously in good shape too. I wonder if these bikers own a gym coz these guys are clearly ripped.

"Hi, I'm Lily it's nice to meet you all." I say while smiling as I sit down on a chair mammoth pulled out for me.

Taking a sip of my drink I notice that a few of the women here are giving me funny looks. Oh I hope I don't have anything on my face, or has my hair gone unbelievably frizzy?

"Christ darling with that face, tits and ass you have every man looking at you and all the women envying you. But add your sweet and shy nature with that British accent, you're a walking wet dream!" That came from the Adonis , I mean Rip. Again that bastard has made me blush. I notice he has a patch that says president on his waistcoat.

" Umm thank you I guess, umm I notice you have a patch that says president on your waistcoat. I'm guessing you're in charge of the club?"

I take a sip of my drink while the table starts laughing at what I just said. I don't understand why they are laughing I was only asking a question.

"First off, it's a good job I like you and your all cute and innocent. Because if you were a dude I probably would have knocked you on your ass for that comment. It's not called a waistcoat it's called a cut." Rip says while giving me a smile, but I have no doubt him and his men probably would have given me a kick in for that comment. I don't think I've ever been happier to have a vagina, than I am right now.

"I am sorry I didn't mean to cause offence. It's just in England we call them waistcoats. Generally there not leather but still."

I shrug suddenly feeling myself beginning to ramble on. I grab my drink and down the rest that's left which was nearly all of it. I lick my lips having rather enjoyed that and very much needed it. I look up to all the guys watching me.

"What? Is something on my face?"

I start to blush immediately I grab my bag and pull out my compact mirror. Nothing on my face thank god and no lipstick on my teeth. All good. So I put my mirror away and turn around to see if someone is stood behind me. Nope no one there, so I turn back to face the guys all are still looking at me. Mammoth is smiling wide and so is Big Papa.

Khan and Rip are looking at me in a scary way. I

can't tell if I should be turned on or start running away. This must be what books mean when they say about smouldering looks. I've just never seen it on a guy before. Hell I've never seen men like this before.

"Christ she's killing me, swear to god the things I could do with that mouth." khan says to Rip and as soon as he says them Rip turns to him giving him a look that would make anyone shit themselves, but instead khan just gives him a cocky smile in return.

"Gottcha pres, all yours."

I sit there mouth open eyes wide. Did they just have a little spat about who gets me? That's stupid. I've seen some of the girls here tonight and although on the skanky side they are half my size and probably a few years younger too. I need to get out of here and to the Merricks.

"Excuse me I'm going to get myself a drink and see if I can use the phone. I should be thinking about getting to the Merricks. They are expecting me."

I quickly stand to leave, and I sway lightly on my feet jet lag, and spirits on an empty stomach clearly don't mix. Mammoth reaches out grabbing my hand to steady me. I smile and nod once thanking him. When I know I'm okay. I walk to the bar without trying to embarrass myself further.

Once at the bar I order another vodka, lime and soda. I ask if there's any food available even a snack.

"Sorry sweets kitchens closed, but I can make y'all a grilled cheese sandwich. You look like you could do with some food especially if you've been travelling for so long."

The barmaid smiles kindly at me, she's a few years older than me, jet black hair that falls in soft waves down her back. And she has olive skin and eyes so dark they're almost black. I notice she too is wearing a cut that says property of Big Papa.

"Thank you that's really kind of you, I know it's so late. But I am starving. The plane food was tasteless. I'm Lily by the way."

I put out my hand in introduction. She puts down her cloth wipes her hands down her jeans and shakes my hand smiling.

"Good to meet you I'm Raven, old lady to Big Papa. And it's no sweat I will get right on that."

"Oh so your part of the club too, married to Big Papa? Sorry to ask for something else but is there any chance I could use your phone I will pay of course, but I was supposed to be picked up by someone to take me to the Merricks as that's where I'm going to be staying and working. But when no one turned up after I waited nearly an hour I gave up and walked down here."

"Yeah I'm married to Big Papa, have been for 15 years now. He's the best just don't go telling him that or it will go straight to his head. Yeah of course you can use the bar phone sweets no charge not sure you'll get an answer though. Merricks went away last night to look after MaryAnn's sick sister. They left Blake in charged while they were away. I'm sure they would have told him you were coming."

"You know the Merricks?" I ask hopeful.

" Yeah everyone knows the Merricks who live in the neighbouring town they sell the best fruit and veg and deliver to us. Been doing it for generations. Blake helps them out from time to time as they're getting older and so they need the help."

Flipping great! where in the hell am I going to go now? What a disaster.

"Um do you by any chance have this Blakes number? And maybe he has a contact for where the Merricks are at her sisters that I can get hold of them. If all else fails is there a motel near here where I could stay?"

"Sorry sweets I don't have Blakes number and honestly if I was you I wouldn't stay in the local motel. That place has some big ass cockroaches."

I can feel my nose beginning to tingle and tears start to fill my eyes. I blink rapidly and take a deep breath to try and hold back from bursting into tears in the middle of a biker bar surrounded by strangers.

"Um ok, well in that case keep the tequila coming."

At least if I'm drunk, I won't care that I'm sleeping on a bench or in a cockroach invested motel. Raven gives me a sympathetic smile hands me the bottle salt and slices of lime.

"I'll just get you your sandwich sweets, your guna need that to line your stomach."

I smile while already on my second shot, twenty minutes later I'm eating my grilled cheese sandwich and I'm about four shots into my American meltdown.

"Oh shit! Raven what time do you shut? What time is it now? Oh bollocks I just dropped some cheese. This sandwich is awesome."

I sway on my stool a little smiling at Raven, she's so cool I want to be like her.

"Its 1:30 am and I shut at 3:00am sometimes closer to 4:00am by the time I get these lot to leave. And thank you it has three different types of cheese in it, my mum used to make it for me."

I smile nodding my head then downing another two more shots, I head to the juke box. I avoid looking over to Rip and the guys table not that I can focus much anyway. I look at the jukebox songs and put in my money and pick my choices. Turning and walking back to my seat at the bar the speakers start blaring out my choice of zz tops la grange. As soon I hear it I smile it's one of my all-time favourite songs, a comfort reminding me of home. I down another shot at the bar smiling at Raven, I start to move my hips to the music. Raven laughing just shakes her head at me like I'm a bit batshit crazy.

Rise Above

I start dancing more and I'm getting hot in my cropped jacket so of course in my drunken state I strip it off, I lasso it over my head and let it fly. Still dancing around not caring that anyone could be watching. I put one leg up on my stool which makes my dress expose pretty much my whole leg. I start moving my hips and doing air guitar and head banging. Raven who by this point is doubled over laughing. I start laughing too. I can't help it I always want to dance when I've had a drink.

Leg still up on the stool I make the mistake of looking over at the guys and Rip is watching me. All the guys at the table are looking at me apart from Big Papa who is smiling while taking a pull on his beer.

Soon the next song I chose starts up, I've downed another tequila and I start dancing again. This time to Bad Company's feel like making love.

Dancing this time I get lost in the music, tequila clearly gives me balls to dance like no one is watching. I'm shaking my ass, I'm grinding, and I think I may have even done a slut drop.

I'm so busy dancing I didn't notice the tap on my shoulder. I step back and stumble because I didn't know anyone was stood that close behind me.

Hands grip my waist to help steady me. I turn and look up into a pair of the bluest eyes I've ever seen, they are blue like the sea but with little flecks of green through them. My eyes travel over his face, perfect nose that leads to a perfect kissable mouth surrounded by dark brown closely trimmed beard. I can't tell what his hair is like as he's wearing a Stetson, but I can see dark brown flicks of hair around the base of his neck.

I'm vaguely aware that his hands are still on my hips and my back is still pressed up against him. I lick my lips because my mouth seems to of gone very dry. His eyes watch my tongue and I swear I feel his chest rumble.

"Hey Blake! Glad you came." Mammoth states clapping him on the shoulder, that breaks his and my attention. We both move to face Mammoth.

Blake shakes mammoths hand and smiles. Ah shit if I wasn't in a puddle on the floor before I am now. Dimples as well. This guy doesn't fight fair. It's any wonder this guy doesn't have women constantly following him humping his leg.

"No problem, after you rang I spoke to MaryAnn and she confirmed it and felt awful that she forgot to tell me."

"Well Blake this is Lily, Lily this is Blake he's here to take you to the Merricks place."

Now if I was in a sober state of mind I would have thanked him shook his hand and I would have done proper introductions, but I wasn't sober I was drunk oh so very drunk. So what I said was.

"Yeeha I'm guna ride me a cowboy!" Then I high fived Raven over the bar who again was laughing her ass off. I then turned and walked up to Rips table leaned over in front of him and said.

"Sorry biker boy I'm off, you're still hot, well you all fucking are it's like a model agency threw up in this town!"

I give Khan a wink who lets out a deep throaty laugh, then I grab Rips face in my hands and kiss him. I went in for a quick kiss on the lips but as I went to pull away he stood and put his hands on my face and pulled me in for more. And boy was it more, that guy could kiss. He stop's kissing me and pulls away a fraction. I slowly open my eyes to find him staring at me intently. In a quiet growl across my lips Rip says.

"In a different world you'd be mine," He growls.

He pulls away and sit's back down in his chair. I find myself dazed and still leaning across the table with a small smile playing on my lips. If I wasn't pissed out of my head I probably would have noticed that most of the bar had stopped talking and watched the show.

I would have definitely appreciated that kiss a lot more.

I give Rip a wink and lick my lips still tasting him. He graces me with a panty melting smile.

I turn around smiling only to be faced with an angry looking cowboy with his arms crossed across his broad chest.

"What's up Mr handsome? Here have a shot of tequila it might put a smile on your handsome face."

Mammoth lets out a bellowing laugh which

makes me chuckle. To my surprise, cowboy takes the shot down's it and slam's it down on the bar his eyes never leaving mine. And still looking pissed off.

"Huh that didn't work. Maybe I should stay with these biker guys I got tats I could fit in." I state swaying on my feet.

"Flower you got tattoos? I can't see one on ya anywhere!" Mammoth asks, as I give him a wink.

"Under the clothes my biker buddy!" I reply.

"Yo pres flower got tats!" Mammoth shouts across the bar.

"Come on then show us what you got." Khan says approaching us with Rip.

"Well I can only show you a little bit coz well I not the flashing type of girl."

I swear I didn't pick it when I went to the juke box earlier but Warrants cherry pie comes over the speakers. Of course in my already drunken state I think this is a good idea to stand on the nearest table.

Raven hands me another shot laughing. I down it and my hips start to move in a seductive dance. Well I think I look seductive but I'm that drunk I could look like I'm doing the truffle shuffle from the Goonies.

I point my leg to my side and slowly lift my dress, exposing more leg a little at a time. They will start to see my stocking seam tattoos. I'm looking over my shoulder, thinking I'm sexy again in reality I'm probably dancing like a mum at a wedding.

I can hear Khan and Mammoth whooping and cheering. My dress is literally only just above my knee, when then next thing I know I'm being picked up and I'm over someone's shoulder hanging upside down.

" Ahhh put me down, help! Someone's kidnapping me!"

I try wiggling but that just earns me a smack on the arse.

"Shut up I'm not kidnapping you, I'm taking you to the Merricks."

"How dare you smack my bloody arse!"

I smack his back as its right there. Wow that's a firm arse. I poke it and grab it some more. Oh yeah that's a well-toned arse right there.

"Woman will you stop grabbing at my ass."

Opps that will be the tequila. Before I know it we are outside, and I'm still slung over cowboys shoulder.

"All her bags are in your truck, good luck buddy."

I hear Mammoth chuckle. I push up and look up smiling and waving to Mammoth, the guys and Raven stood just outside the bar doorway as cowboy walks across the car park to his truck.

"Thanks hot biker guys! You fucking rock!" I shout doing the devil sign with my fingers. I hear them all laughing as they start to pile back into the bar. I'm then dumped on a seat in cowboys truck.

He leans across me to buckle me in. I notice he has taken his Stetson off. He has messy dark hair. God I bet it feels great running your fingers through it.

"Hey, you wana stop playing with my hair."

"You have really nice hair Mr handsome."

I let out along yawn and start close my eyes, I see a small smile on his face, just as my eyes close. I mumble sleepily giving in to the jet lag and alcohol.

"See I can make you smile."

CHAPTER SIX

I awake with a headache from hell I can barely open my eyes. Who the hell turned on the sun?! I groan pulling the cover over my head. Its then I remember I'm not at home. I force my eyes open and look around the room. It's a light an almost rustic room, I'm in a black iron double bed, and there's flower print walls and flowers on a vase next to me. There's a cute vintage white wardrobe and matching dressing table and chair across the room.

Slowly, I sit up my head is spinning. I get up and head to what I assume is the door to the bathroom. I take care of business then wash my hands and face. I make the mistake of looking in the mirror. My god I look like utter shit.

Its then I notice I'm in just my strapless bra and knickers.

I rack my brains trying to remember what happened last night. It slowly comes back to me. I put my face in my hands groaning. I'm such an idiot. I bet that cowboy Blake gets me fired. I deserve it what must he think of me. Some slut from England probably. Wait a minute did he undress me?! Did we have sex?!

I splash more water on my face and rinse my mouth.

I walk back into the room and can't see my suitcase anywhere or my dress from yesterday, there's a man's shirt hanging on the back of the door. I grab it and put it on, it will have to do.

I open the door to the sound of a deep male voice talking I'm guessing on the phone as I can't hear anyone else. I follow that sound downstairs, I keep following the sound until I hit an open door way and see its Blake with his back to me, shirtless.

If I wasn't awake properly before, I am now.

Blake has broad shoulders and a well-defined muscled back. God he really is perfect.

His body turns and I carry on staring. Holy shit he has a strong chest , a perfect four pack stomach not a six pack but I never did like too much muscle he's more solid than slender. Oh and there's the happy trail that disappears into low hung jeans.

He lets out a cough, making me jump. Oh Christ I've just been caught eye fucking him and I'm sober no excuse of tequila now.

I look up into his eyes and he's smiling, I feel a blush creep over my cheeks, and there's those bloody dimples again.

"Yeah she's awake, I will don't worry about it MaryAnn it's all good. Send my best to your sister. Yeah bye."

"Umm morning. Sorry is this your shirt I couldn't find my stuff, so I just grabbed it."

Blake's eye's travel down my body. I feel myself blush again and goose bumps break out across my skin and my breath quickens. His lazy gaze comes back to my eyes and I swear if he can make me feel like this just by looking, fuck knows what he's like with actual touching involved.

"It's fine, your case is through there in the living room. I was going to bring it up for you in a little bit. Just fixin' some coffee you want one? There's some Tylenol in the cabinet in the bathroom for your head."

"Um thanks I could use some paracetamol my heads a little fuzzy.

I want to apologise for my behaviour last night.

You see I was waiting at the bus station for nearly an hour I was jet lagged and exhausted. Mammoth and Rubble were friendly and took me into the bar, and when I thought I had nowhere to go or stay apart from a crappy sounding motel full of cockroaches. I thought well to hell with it. So I started to down shots of tequila. Which I might add I'm regretting now. And um well I want you to know I don't normally behave like that. So I am sorry for that."

I look up after my rambling and fiddling with my hands to see him still looking at me like he's bored.

"So did you want a coffee or not?" He asks.

I can feel myself getting annoyed, putting my hands on my hips.

"Yes please 2 sugars and dash of milk, and for future reference it is rude to dismiss a person when that person has just apologised. The polite thing to do is to accept the apology."

Blake just shrugs.

"Don't care what you get up too, aint none of my business. So you don't need to apologise for nuthin."

I don't know what pissed me off more, the fact he hadn't accepted my apology or that he didn't care what I got up to.

"Whatever, did we have sex last night?!" I blurt.

He stops what he's doing and looks up at me angry.

"First of I am not the type of man who would take advantage of a woman who was in no fit state. Second I like my women to be awake and screaming my name when I'm fucking her, writhing beneath me, and taking everything I am giving her. So no we didn't fuck last night."

He growls angrily at me.

Christ I'm surprised my knickers aren't melting off me. But I will be damned if I'm going to let him know that.

"Pffft blimey you're arrogant. Think a lot of yourself to make that statement."

With that I spin on my heel and storm off to the sitting room to find my suitcase and grab my clothes. I'm bent over looking through my suitcase when I hear a low growl. I turn my head looking over my shoulder and see Blake stood there with two cups in his hand and his eyes are on my arse.

I immediately reach round with my hand to pull down his shirt that had risen exposing the bottom part of my arse.

I stand and cough crossing my arms.

His eyes meet mine then drop down to my chest. This man is unbelievable what a pervert.

"Excuse me! Eyes up here. You may like your women awake but here's a tip don't be a pervert and stare at women's arses and breasts! Because funnily enough we don't like it."

Blakes eyes meet mine as he holds back a smirk.

"You might want to cover up if you don't want me looking."

he nods towards where the shirt I'm wearing has come unbuttoned all the way to my belly button, well that's just fan-bloody-tastic. Now he's going to think I'm definitely a slut.

I'm mortified, I quickly grab the shirt close and pick up my clothes and my wash bag and run past him upstairs.

As soon as I get in the shower. I let the tears fall. This has been such a disaster already. I've made such a tit of myself.

On top of that Mr handsome downstairs has seen most of my body. All my wobbly bits. God he was probably looking at me in disgust. Especially if the girls at the bar are anything to go by with their tiny perfect waist, all firm and nothing wobbles. Even if they were a little on the skanky side.

I get out of the shower and look at myself in the mirror. Yep there's no chance any one like Mr handsome would look twice at the likes of me. Hell I bet Rip kissing me last night was a dare of who's going to kiss the chubby Brit.

But at least if Mr handsome isn't going to be looking at me like that, then I can relax and not get all flustered. I can be me and no one will stare as I'm sure there's plenty of stunning looking girls here that I can keep under the radar.

Nobody ever notices a pale plain wobbly jane when all I've seen is tanned and toned. That thought makes me feel a little more relaxed, I like going unnoticed. Although apparently when drinking I'm the polar opposite.

I get dressed, I can already feel the heat of the day and the house clearly has air con. so I put on my cut off high waisted jean shorts, there not ridiculously short they come to about mid-thigh and have a couple of rips through them, but you don't see much skin. I wouldn't wear them if they did. And I pair that with a loose white vest top that I think is a man's, but I have on my bright red halter bikini top on underneath. I've technically not started working officially yet and it seems so hot out that I just want to stay cool. I tie the vest in a knot at the side of my waist. I put on minimal make up. Brush my hair and put frizz treatment through it and leave it to dry naturally.

I check the cabinet for medicine for my head, I find it quickly taking some hoping that will shift my headache.

I grab my stuff and walk out of the bathroom to see my suitcase and my other bag on my bed. Blake must have brought them up while I was in the shower.

I walk over to my hand bag and grab out my phone plugging it in and putting it on the bedside table to charge.

I sit down and send a quick email to my mum. Telling her that I have arrived safe.

I put on the same sandals as yesterday and head downstairs.

I turn and head for the kitchen. No sign of Blake but I spot the coffee pot on the side with a mug. I pour myself a cup and have a look around the kitchen. It is huge, modern farm house style kitchen. Cream cupboards, thick rustic oak work tops. Big basin sink and a huge oven.

I walk over to the big glass door at the back of the kitchen and I look out, the view is stunning. I notice decking with a seating area.

So I step out into the warm sun and take a seat. I can see fields upon fields of crops, it's not something I'd ever notice before. But with the sun and blue sky right then it was stunning. For the first time since I arrived I felt a little bit of hope that I may enjoy my time here.

I curl up on the chair with my coffee in my hands smiling enjoying the peace. You would never get this in London. I close my eyes enjoying the feel of the sun on my face.

Someone lets out a gentle cough, that makes me jump and let out a girlie squeal, making me spill hot coffee on my bare leg.

"Son of a donkey dick!"

I jump up doing a weird like hop while fanning my leg with my hand trying to cool the burn.

"Jesus wept that hurts. Why would you creep up on someone and scare the shit out of them?"

I look up at Mr handsome still fanning my leg with my hand like it's helping.

"Sorry I didn't mean to. Come with me let's put a cold cloth on that to stop it blistering."

With that he turn's and walk's back into the kitchen. I follow noticing that he has gotten changed and is now in a fitted grey t-shirt that clings to his broad shoulders and chest. And jeans that make me want to bite that arse like it's a juicy peach.

I lean up against the counter while he dampens a cloth.

He walks towards me with the cloth I go to put out my hand to take it off him, but he drops to his knees in front of me. And place's the cloth on my thigh over the burn while holding my leg with his other hand.

My body immediately covers in goose bumps

and I swear I am panting like a dog in heat. He may not notice plain old me, but god I'd have to be blind not to notice him. I have no control over my bodies reaction to him.

He looks up at me those deep blue eyes holding me in place. His thumb rubbing soothing circles on the back of my thigh.

"how'd that feel now? Helping?" He asks his voice gravelly.

I snap out of my fog.

"uhh yup great thanks."

He stand's and takes the cloth over to the sink.

"If you're ready I thought I'd take you out to get some breakfast and show you the town."

"Yeah that would be great thank you, I was going to take a walk to explore but would be easier you showing me around."

Blake turns and grabs his keys.

"Get your bag, and I will meet you out front."

with that he walks past me and puts on his black Stetson and walks out the front door.

I run upstairs to do a quick check of myself, I apply my nude lip gloss. Spritz on some perfume. And grab my bag.

I run back downstairs and out the front door to Blake sat waiting on the porch swing.

He locks up the house, then walks to his truck and opens the door for me.

Huh I suppose he can be a gentleman when he wants to be. I hop in as he rounds the truck and gets in.

Soon we are travelling down a dirt road.

"So how far is town from the house?" I ask.

" By car it's only a 15 minute drive."

Wow so the house really was in the middle of nowhere. I love that. In London everyone was on top of everyone always busy, always rushing around never a quiet moment. I love that I can hear myself think without the sounds of sirens.

"I just want to say thanks for coming and getting me last night and staying to keep an eye on me. Also for this, showing me around. I appreciate you giving up your time." I say while fiddling with my hands.

"It's no problem, MaryAnn asked me to watch out for you." He shrugs.

Ah so he wasn't doing it to be nice and kind to me he was doing it for Mrs Merrick.

"Oh of course, how long are they going to be away?"

"Not sure her sister has cancer and has just had op to remove the tumour. She won't want to leave her sister until she is back on her feet."

"Oh that's awful, I would be the same. So is there anyone that tends to the crops if they are away? I only ask as my boss will be wanting my article soon so need to get going on that in the next day or so."

He looks over at me briefly, hand draped over the steering wheel god he even drives perfect. All manly.

I wonder if there's a place I can get a vibrator or at least order one online discreetly. If not I'm going to be having very long cold showers or finger cramp while I'm here.

"Yeah cancers a bitch. But she is fighting it. Yeah there's me and sometimes my brother Wes will help me. It's not harvesting season yet so there's no panic. They have pickers for the fruit and veg. Oh and Sam the Merricks nephew is manager. So you could speak to him."

"Oh okay great. When will he be in?"

"Tomorrow morning any time around 8am. I will show the business entrance on our way back, so you know where the office is and where to find him,"

We soon turn down a road that slowly starts to show houses and more signs of life. Houses that are next to each other but still loads of space. So different to London.

Soon we pass a small school, a library and police station. My face is pressed up against the window loving the small town and how pretty it is with hanging baskets. There's no gum stuck on the pavements, no dog shit, no rubbish.

"This town is adorable!" I'm smiling as I turn to Blake, he smiles back.

"Yeah it's a pretty great town."

Soon we are on the main high street.

We pass a salon, chemist, restaurant, what looks like a hunting shop, a florist and a small supermarket.

I must look like a crazy person my face pressed up against the window smiling.

We pull into a parking spot just in front of a small diner called Jeanie's. It looks just like something you'd see on the tv.

I was so busy looking out the windscreen I didn't even know Blake had gotten out of the truck and had walked around to open my door.

"You wana get some food or just look out the window of my truck?"

Blake says smiling at me. I'm smiling from ear to ear with excitement and the fact there's no scary hillbilly with a chainsaw. It's a normal cute little town.

"Keep your cool Mr handsome, I'm from London this is just a little exciting for me. I've never seen a place like this. It's so cute."

I jump down from the truck and smile up at Blake.

"Mr handsome huh? Come on let's get you some proper American food."

I blush, at letting slip my little nickname for him, then shrug I'm sure he knows how handsome he is.

He places his hand on the small of my back, which gives me feelings that I choose to ignore. We walk into the diner which is just how I imagined it would be. Booths along the walls and windows small two seater tables down the centre, and a bar with stools all along.

Blake guides me to a booth, and I take a seat and Blake sits opposite me and hands me a menu.

It's only then I notice that people have stopped talking and are looking over at us.

"Hey, Mr handsome, everyone is looking at us." I whisper over my menu.

"Just ignore them, it's because your new they will soon carry on when they get their gossip of who you are."

I look back around the diner giving everyone a small smile.

All but one table smile back politely. That table has three women sat on it and all of them look like they just entered a beauty pageant. I mean how is their make-up not melting off they don't have a hair out of place they look perfect. Only thing I notice that isn't perfect is there manners. The filthy looks they are aiming my way now makes me look down and check my outfit.

"Ignore them honey, they're just jealous. Now welcome to Jeanie's, I'm Jeanie and what can I get y'all?"

I look up to see a cute woman in her 50's with her hair up in a twist, bright pink lipstick, and a pair of kind blue eyes. She's filling up my coffee cup while smiling down at me.

I immediately feel at ease with her, so I smile brightly back.

"Hi, I'm Lily. I'm writing about the Merrick place for a while and staying there. I just arrived late last night. You have a lovely diner." I say in greeting.

"Well aint you the cutest, Blake son, you can bring her in here any time. I like her." Jeanie says with a wink she sets down her coffee pot and pulls out her note pad and pen.

"Right what will y'all be having?"

"I will have the usual and the same for lily please Jeanie." Blake replies.

"Blake I don't know what your usual is and If I will like it."

He raises one of his perfect eyebrows at me.

"Fine, are you vegetarian?"

"No" I reply.

"You like eggs and pancakes?"

"Yes."

"Then you will be fine."

I stare at him. I've never had a guy order for me before, and he doesn't know me, so I find that even stranger.

"Right, be back in a jiffy with your food. Welcome to Mufftown honey."

Jeanie gives me a wink then walks away behind the bar to the kitchen.

"Okay, I know I'm going to be embarrassed asking but I have to know. I don't remember getting back last night from the bar. The last thing I remember is you man handling me into your truck. So um well how did I get from there and into bed and to be just in my underwear?"

I look up at Blake, pink hitting my cheeks. Biting my lip I wait for his reply. His eyes drop to my lips.

"You were completely passed out in my truck, I carried you up to your room and put you on the bed. I went to turn and leave, but you got up mumbling to yourself in a semi-conscious state. Something like bloody perfect people, and that you felt stickier than a prostitutes vagina. And took your dress off then face planted the bed."

Oh dear god, I cover my face with my hands.

"I am sorry. I am so embarrassed. I wish I never asked. In fact I wish I never drank that tequila."

Blake reaches over and pulls my hands away from my face smiling at me.

"Hey, it's cool, we've all done stupid shit when we've been drinking. Once I got so drunk on moonshine that I streaked across the football field at school as a dare."

"How old were you when you did that?"

"It was my last year of school, so I was 18"

"See exactly 18! I'm 28. I should know better."

Blake chuckles a deep throaty laugh. I immediately want to make him laugh more often. Soon Jeanie brings our food. All I can say is wow it is huge, two pancakes, bacon, scrambled egg, hash browns, and French toast on the side and a jug of syrup.

"I know I'm a big girl and I like my food but in no way am I going to be able to eat all this!" I say eyes wide pointing to my plate.

Blake looks up at me already with a mouthful of food.

"Firstly I was planning on you not eating it all, it means more for me. Second you're not fucking big, you're perfect the way you are."

He says that in an angry tone.

I shut up and tuck into my breakfast, its delicious. I can only manage about half and I'm stuffed. I lean back in my seat patting my belly.

"I can't eat another bite I'm stuffed. But that was some of the best food I've ever tasted. Never have I put bacon, syrup and pancakes together. But it tasted flipping amazing."

Blake laughs at me, he finished his just before me and has a clean plate. I have no idea where he puts it all.

Jeanie comes over to our table.

" You folks enjoy that? Can I get y'all anything else?"

"Thank you Jeanie that was delicious, and no I couldn't eat another bite I am stuffed!" I smile up at her.

"Was the best as usual Jeanie thanks." Blake states.

"I will just get your bill."

Jeanie leaves going to the till. I push my plate towards Blake raising an eyebrow in a challenge.

"No way aint got no more room in my gut."

"Ha I knew it! No way anyone could eat that much and still function having a normal day, this would put you in a food coma." I chuckle, reaching into my bag to get my purse.

"Don't even fucking think about it"

I look up at Blake.

"What? I can't expect you to pay for me. After all you've done ferrying me around. Please let me pay as a thank you." I beg.

"Not a chance my uncle max would kick my ass if he knew I let a lady pay."

"Ughh fine but what about I pay the tip then?"

No reasoning with a stubborn gentleman.

"That's fine although I will already cover the tip, if you want to put in extra you do that."

Jeanie places the bill on our table, Blake reaches for it and places the money down, I decide to put an extra ten dollars for tip. It was nice food and good service after all.

Blake shakes his head at my defiance. As we stand up to leave the three beauty queens from the other side of the diner are suddenly in our way.

"Howdy Blake, you going to introduce us to your new friend?"

I swear I've never seen a smile so fake in all my life and that's not because of her veneers, or her collagen lips.

"Fine Elise this is Lily. Lily this is Elise and her friends Melanie and Kaylee."

I put my hand out to shake.

" Hi there, I'm Lily I'm staying at the Merricks. Just arrived last night. It's nice to meet you." I greet.

My hand is just left hanging there in mid-air as I wait for Elise to shake my hand but instead she just turns her nose up at it.

"Well enjoy your stay there. If you find our summer too much being a fuller lady the chemist does a chub rub ointment that will really help." She sneers.

Smiling an evil smile at me, while her friends snigger behind their hands. Then she turns dismissing me completely, leaning into Blake, putting her hand on his arm.

"Blake honey, I will see you at the den at 8 o'clock."

She gives him a squeeze on his bicep followed by a wink then turns and leaves.

I stand there slightly stunned anyone could be so bloody rude. And I feel embarrassed. The diner has gone quiet, the people near us would have heard. And comparing myself to them girls and standing next to Blake makes me feel insecure about myself more than I already am. It was like I was back at school, the chubby girl being picked on all over again.

I push my shoulders back, flash a fake smile at Blake and continue towards the door. The fact that Blake hadn't even said a single word to her to defend me or at least stop her being so rude meant that deep down he must look at me the same way she does. The chubby Brit. I just wanted to go back to the Merricks and shut myself in my room.

We get outside and walk to his truck, the silence is awkward between us.

Blake brakes the silence when we get to his truck.

"Listen, you need to ignore Elise she can be a bit of a spoilt brat sometimes."

I look up at him open my own door and reply.

"Don't know what you mean she seems lovely. If it's okay with you I want to go back to the Merricks now, all that food and jet lag I could use a nap."

I give him a small smile and jump in his truck.

On the drive back I rest my head against the window, looking at the town and scenery passing me by. Not saying a word.

The only person or people to truly make me feel welcome is Jeanie and in the other town the Satans Outlaws. Ironic that the people I should fear welcomed me with open arms.

Blake pulls up at a gate further down from the house and puts the truck in park.

"That there is the business entrance and if you walk just down there you see the small out building and greenhouses. That's where you'll find Sam tomorrow morning."

"Great thanks for showing me. Can I get back to the house from here by walking?" I ask looking around.

"Yeah just through the bushes there, see it?"

Blake points to a small gap in the hedges that if you weren't looking for it you wouldn't know it was there.

"Fab, thanks can you give me the keys? I will walk back from here I'm sure you have things to be getting on with and plus you're out meeting Elise tonight."

I put my hand out waiting for him to pass me the keys. When he doesn't hand me them I turn and look at him.

Blake is staring at me intently like he's trying to figure out a big maths problem.

I wave my hand in front of his face.

"Hello anyone in there?!"

Blake smiles a small smile at me then reaches in his pocket for the keys.

"Are you sure you don't want me to take you to the door? It's no problem." Blake offers.

"Nah it's fine be good for me to see where I'm going, plus my head could do with a little fresh air. Your babysitting duties have way over run."

I give Blake a cheeky wink then open the door to his truck and hop down.

"Thanks for the breakfast. I will see you around I guess."

Before I can hear Blakes reply I shut his truck door and start walking towards the path. I wave over my shoulder, soon I'm out of sight. I hear his truck pull away, I let out a long breath and take in the fields around me. I can see the house up ahead. It really is a beautiful house. A wrap around porch, I counted 4 bedrooms, and 3 bathrooms, a big farm house it is just stunning.

Rise Above

I get to the house when I realise I didn't have any food or drink in. I am going to have to walk into the town a little later. Or maybe I wondered if there was a bike I could use to cycle. First things first I want to lie down for a nap. I set my alarm on my phone for 2 hours' time. So I don't over sleep, I would still have time before dinner to go to the supermarket. I lay down and think of home. Soon my tiredness takes over and I am out like a light.

After my nap I take another shower and I get changed into fresh clothes. This time I have on my simple cotton, lemon summer dress. It is thin strapped with a sweet heart bust, it is fitted to the waist then it flows out down to the knee. Still wearing the same sandals. But this time I put my hair up in a messy bun letting bits fall. As I know this walk would take me a little while and although it is 3 in the afternoon, it is still very warm. I grabbed my bag and keys. I'd written a list of things to keep me going for a few days.
I put in my headphones and press play on my phone and i start walking. There was no bike I could see, and I didn't want to be rude and go snooping too much.
Now this I could get used too, the warmth and the quiet roads. I smile to myself as I make it on to the main country road leading to the town.
Soon I can see the start of houses up ahead and I

know I didn't have much further to go.

Taking the turning down to the main high street, I see its quieter but still a couple of people about.

As I make my way past the salon I look in the window and see an elderly lady with a head full of rollers. And I'm guessing the hairdresser Amy as the place was called Amy's was smiling down at the lady fondly. Amy looks up as I am passing and gives me a smile and a wave. I return the wave and carry on walking. See why can't they all be welcoming like that?

As I enter the small supermarket I grab a trolley and start looking down the aisles, a few people smile politely at me and I've had a couple of ma'am's with a tip up of their Stetsons. which caused me to giggle like a school girl.

I finally make it to the checkout and load my groceries. There's a young lad packing at the end.

"Howdy and welcome to Kelley's Market I'm Evelynn."

I look up and smile at the lady at the checkout. She has deep red hair, kind blue eyes and a warm welcoming smile.

"Hi, I'm Lily nice to meet you."

"Oh I know who you are. You've been in town for a good few hours now and word travels fast. You're the talk of the town." Evelynn says smiling at me as she processes my groceries.

That can't be good after that Elise chewed me out at the diner. I bet she's spread around I have crabs or something. Evelynn sensing my thoughts carries on.

"It aint in a bad way or nuthin', all good Jeanie said how nice you were." Evelynn reassures me smiling.

"That and you were all cosy with Blake Stone."

"Um that's good to hear I suppose, I wasn't cosy with Blake Mrs Merrick asked him to keep an eye on me and show me around that's all."

"Uh huh, you know no one would blame you getting all cosy with Blake. He's a whole lotta cowboy. So how you finding it so far?"

Evelynn asks , having finished with my groceries. I turn to the que of people behind me and offer an apologetic smile. I receive smiles in return and think they are quite happy waiting to listen in on the gossip of the new girl in town.

"It's a lovely town and a big change from London. And most of the people I've met have been more than welcoming."

"Uh huh I heard about Elise. Ignore her she's all big hat and no cattle."

I look at Evelynn confused.

"It means all talk no action Hun."

I chuckle as does Evelynn. She hands me my receipt and I thank her and the lad who packed my bags. Just as I'm pushing my trolley to the exit Evelynn shouts.

"Hey Lil' good to meet ya, I will see you around." Evelynn waves and smiles which I return.

I walk over to put my trolley away looking at

the bags of shopping I have to carry back. Maybe I should have just got a small bag of food bits rather than 4.

I load myself up with the bags, and it's still hot. I'm going to be sweating buckets by the time I make it back. What makes it worse is that they are brown paper bags that have no handles. So I look like a waddling penguin from behind. I make it to just outside of the main high street near a small park area with a bench. I decide to take a break, the heat is crazy.

Thankfully I brought a bottle of water, sitting down I take a long pull.

Getting back up I grab the bags and load myself back up and start the walk back to the Merricks. I'm just passing the last of the houses, thankful that I'm about half way there. When I hear a car approach from behind. I stop and turn. A new looking black shiny truck stops just next to me.

The window slides down and I am faced with a guy I've never seen before.

"Howdy ma'am, you look like you could use a lift and some help with those bags. I'd be honoured if you let me help you with that?"

He flashes me a charming smile. He's good looking, blonde and blue eyes. The all American boy next door type. Not my type but still a handsome guy.

"Hi, I'm Lily thank you, but I was taught never to get in a car with strangers. Very kind of you though thanks."

I smile and start to walk. He jumps out of his car and stops in front of me.

"My name Is Ven, its a pleasure to meet you miss Lily."

He takes 2 of my bags and takes my hand and kisses the back of it, giving me a wink.

"Now we aint strangers and I can help you."

I chuckle because this guy is smooth but there is something that doesn't sit right. Maybe it's just because I am tired and hot. He has been polite and kind I should give him the chance.

"Okay fine but show me your id so I know who you are in case you plan on kidnapping me." I say with a smile. He puts his hand in his back pocket and pulls out his wallet showing me his Id.

"See miss Lily. I am Ven Johnson. And I am at your service."

He flashes me another charming smile and a wink and puts my bags in the back of his truck.

He holds the passenger door open for me and I climb in. Once I'm in the truck I am thankful for the air con.

Ven starts up and pulls away.

"You at the Merricks place right?" He asks.

"Yeah that's right."

Ven nods and smiles at me.

"So miss Lily how are you finding our little town?"

"I'm finding it lovely and that word gets around incredibly fast."

Ven lets out a laugh, it's a nice deep rumble. It

doesn't have the same effect on me as another certain cowboys laugh but still I can't deny Ven is an attractive guy all the same.

Soon he's pulling up at the Merricks. I turn to thank him, but he already hops out of the truck and is round at my door opening it for me.

Say what you like about American men, but they sure have manners.

I go to grab my bag's, but he has already beaten me to it and tells me to open the door and he will carry the bags in for me.

Inside he places my bags on the kitchen counter.

"Thanks so much, can I offer you a cold drink or something? I don't have any beers or anything, but I have juice and water."

I look up from unpacking the bags and find him watching me. I smile politely.

"No thanks miss Lily, but I sure would like to take you out tonight for a drink, what do you say?"

Ah shit I am not really in the mood to go out, but he was really kind helping me and maybe I will meet some more locals that are friendly. What the hell, I am supposed to be living life right?

"Umm sure okay, but I will warn you if I yawn don't take it personally. It's the jet lag."

"Great I will be back to get you at 8pm."

I smile.

"Fab. Where are we going is there a dress code?"

"Anything you wear will be just fine miss Lily, it's just a bar nothing fancy."

Rise Above

"Okay great and please just call me Lily and drop the miss, it makes me feel like an old lady."

I say smiling at Ven he gives me a wink. Walks towards me until I am looking up at him.

"I shall see you tonight then Lily."

He then bends down and lightly kisses the back of my hand while looking at me in the eyes. I am not going to lie It makes me feel nice. Can't say many British men act so gentlemanly.

Ven then turns and leaves. I look at the clock it's just coming up to 5pm. Gives me enough time to grab a quick bite to eat, ring mum and get showered and changed.

I'm sat on the back porch having just finished my food and now video calling my mum. Who still doesn't get that she needs to move her face back so I'm not having a conversation with her nostrils.

"Mum for the last time move back a little, all I can see is your nose hairs!"

Mum pulls her face back and frowns at me.

"I do not have bloody nose hair!"

laughing, she soon smiles back at me rolling her eyes.

"So tell me darling have you got a hot cowboy boyfriend yet?"

"Bloody hell mum I've only been in America for 2 days. So no I haven't. I am however going out with a guy called Ven who helped me with my groceries today. As friends only, I thought maybe I might meet some more new people."

125

I didn't tell my mum about the biker bar and I didn't tell my mum about Elise having a dig at me. She would only worry.

Dad came on and said hello and that I already looked tanned. And that mum had drove him bonkers worrying that I'd arrived safely.

As I was just about to end the call with them my sister Rose literally pushed them out of the way to talk to me.

"Hey skin and blister!!! what's happening and why are you speaking to these old folks rather than ringing me, your favourite family member?"

I burst out laughing. I do miss her already. I had gotten used to seeing her and my nephew every day.

"Hey big sis, how's you and my nephew?" I ask.

"Same old, kid drives me nuts. But enough about us, I want to know what's going on with you?"

With that mum pipes up.

"Rose she has a date with a cowboy tonight. She won't tell me nothing you drill her for information."

"Mum just because you are not in front of the camera, doesn't mean I can't hear you!"

My mum then tries to crawl pass the camera so not to be seen, yet I can see the top of her head as she scurries passed.

At this point I am holding my stomach from laughing at her.

"I swear Lily we will have to look at putting her

in a home soon she's losing the plot!"

Quietly in the distance you hear my mum shout.

"Oi! Rose I heard that!! And I can hear you both laughing! That's it Daisy is now my favourite daughter!"

Me and Rose carry on laughing.

"So come on then spill, what's this about you are already going on a date with a cowboy?" Rose asks.

"Arrgh, it's not a date Ven helped me with my food shopping and then asked if I wanted to go for a drink tonight just for a couple of hours. I thought It would be good to go meet some more people. that's all it is."

Rose is smiling big at me through the camera.

"Yeah ok sure he doesn't sound interested in you at all. What are you going to wear?" Rose replies sarcastically, rolling her eyes.

"I'm not sure. It's just a local bar so nothing dressy, not that I brought anything dressy. What do you think?"

I wasn't worried before but now I am starting to think I need the perfect outfit to make a good first impression if I meet any more people.

"Wear your red cold shoulder wrap dress with the flowers on it. Cork wedged sandals and take your denim jacket"

"You sure that's not to dressy?"

"No not at all its a colourful summer dress, with a denim jacket. Plus your boobs look fab in that dress."

I look at the time crap I have less than an hour until Ven arrives.

"Listen rose, I got to run and get ready I am leaving in less than an hour I will call soon I promise."

"You better, and nan says you need to faceybook her."

Rose says laughing.

"I will, right give Caden a big kiss from me love you lots skin and blister."

I quickly close down my tablet then run in to shower and change. I don't have time to stand around deciding if I should wear something else, so I go with what Rose said. It's not slutty and it flatters me. Or as Rose says my boobs look good in it.

I do a quick run with straighteners over my hair just to tidy it up a bit. I apply plain make up but add my blood red lipstick. Spritz some perfume on and put on my cork wedged sandals. They have thin black straps crossing over my feet. And are not too high and are comfy so I shouldn't fall over, hopefully.

I am just putting my bits into my bag when there's a knock at the door. I look at the time its 8:01pm. Ven is bang on time.

I quickly check myself in the mirror and run to the front door.

I swing the door open with my head down double checking I have the keys for the house.

"Hi Ven, just give me a second I need to find the

house keys to lock up."

"Lily you look beautiful."

I stop searching my bag and look up at Ven, he's holding out a single rose for me. Huh maybe he thinks this is a date after all. I smile up at him and take the rose.

"Thank you Ven you look very handsome too."

finally I find the keys and we are soon on our way.

"So Ven, where is it we are going tonight?"

"We're going to the Den. It's our local bar and dance hall. They have a live band playing tonight. A few of my buddies will be there too. I will introduce you."

Ah wasn't the Den the place Blake was meeting that Elise? Well hopefully the place is big enough I can avoid her. Plus she will be on her date with Blake she won't notice me.

"Hey Lily, you ok? You look uncomfortable all of a sudden."

I turn to look at Ven and try my best to give him a reassuring smile.

"I am alright, just a little nervous I guess."

" Aint got nuthin' to worry about. All will be fine you will have a great time." Ven states.

A little while later we are pulling into a car park at the den. It looks like a huge barn with coloured lights strung around it. I can hear music from out here. Of course its country and western. Hopefully the more fun upbeat country music. I am not a big fan of this type of music, but I do love a live band.

I hop down from the truck and start walking in with Ven. As soon as he opens the door the music becomes louder and a bustle of people chatting and dancing. Ven walks toward a table of people me trailing behind him, looking around.

"Yeehaaa boys! Ven is here now the party can begin!" Ven shouts to the three other guys sat around the table. Who all cheer back raising their glasses. All the while I'm just stood behind Ven like a complete plum.

After Ven greats his buddies, he finally remembers I'm there, turns and puts his arm around my shoulder and brings me forward to meet his friends.

"Hey y'all this is Lily, Lily that there on the left is Jake, Middle is Cole and on the end is Troy."

I smile and do a little wave. The way Cole and Troy smile and look at me is making me feel a little uncomfortable. Jake just gives me a polite smile and nod.

"Well aint she a looker, nice to have a nice piece to look at." The one Ven introduced as Cole says smiling and giving me a wink. Ven isn't listening he's too busy chatting to Jake about something sat in the chair next to him while I'm still stood there like a prat.

These guys are making me feel uncomfortable. Or maybe it's just the different culture over here. I need a drink. It's probably just my nerves meeting new people.

Rise Above

I tap Ven on the shoulder, and he turns to look at me.

"Um I'm going to get a drink do you want one?"

Ven smiles at me then back to his buddies and pulls out some money.

"Sure honey, I will take a beer and so will these guys, you can get yourself whatever you like."

Ven hands me the money and I stare at it. A little shocked gone is the well-mannered guy from this afternoon. But he is paying, I did offer to go to the bar. So I smile and nod and head over to get the drinks.

The bar is crammed with people and eventually I manage to squeeze in. I am literally sandwiched between two big guys both have their backs to me chatting to their friends. I am not a tall person but I'm not tiny either and I have on my wedged sandals, yet these guys are still unaware of my presence.

I try leaning over the bar waving the money around to try and get the barman's attention. But he is too busy chatting up his co-worker by the look of it. After that doesn't work I pull myself up a little on the bar. So my top half of my body is laying across the bar and my legs are off the floor dangling. I am still waving the money around calling the barman.

"Yoo-hoo! Over here!" I holler.

The bastard barman still ignores me! This is crazy, I have been waiting 20 minutes to try and get served. I look over my shoulder at Ven to see if he's looking for me but he's not. He's still chatting away to his buds. Figures I knew coming was a mistake I could be sat on the porch having a glass of wine in peace and quiet and it wouldn't take 20 minutes to pour it either.

I'm still leaning right over the bar legs dangling and I've had enough at this point. So I put my fingers in my mouth and do a loud whistle to get his attention. Only it doesn't get just his attention, but everyone stood at the bar too. I am at a point where I just don't give a crap.

"Oi You! Barman stop chatting up your co-worker, don't you know you should never bonk where you work. Stop thinking with your dick and come here, serve me and do your bloody job. I've been stood hear for over 20 minutes now, and I've had enough! Now let me tell you I'm English and we are the bloody best at queuing but that only applies when someone is doing their job. And you sir are not." I rant.

I let out a long exhale as the poor barman who now looks a little terrified of me and a little embarrassed I just called him out chatting up his co-worker. Walks over to me.

He looks at me frowning then his eyes focus behind me and then goes wide eyed and puts on a smile.

"Evening Mr Stone, is there anything I can get you?"

You have got to be fucking kidding me. Is it because I am a woman?! Or because I'm not from here?

I turn around ready to lay in to this Mr Stone.

"You can bloody well wait your-"

As I turn I slide back down to my feet and come face to chest with Blake.

I look up to see his smiling face looking down at me.

With his eyes and those dimples I think I have lost all brain function.

And of course he's wearing a white shirt that he has rolled up to the elbows and tucked into a pair of nicely fitted jeans.

I am vaguely aware of the fact that I am staring and not saying anything hell I might even be dribbling.

"Uh hi Blake, what you doing here?" I ask nervously, and embarrassed he's just heard me go off on one at the barman.

"I work here, I am sort of the boss." He replies.

My head snaps up to look him in the eyes sure enough he's not joking he's deadly serious. God is he going to throw me out for verbally abusing his staff?

"Jack, get this lady what she wants please."

I turn around and order the beers and a double vodka soda for myself. I earned it.

"Who are you buying beers for?" He asks frowning, crossing his arms across his broad chest.

"Oh I am not paying this is Ven's money. Funny thing, he helped with my food shopping earlier

today and asked me to come out for a drink tonight. He's over there chatting with his buddies. I said I was going to get a drink and he gave me the money to get them all including me a drink."
I shrug.
I look up at Blake and see his eyes are on Ven and his buds. He looks angry. His jaw is set and that little jaw tick thing that hot guys do is going.
Suddenly Blake turns and demands.
"Jack take those beers over to Ven's table."
"Yes sir." The young barman obeys.
I take my drink and take a very long glug. I really needed that.
"Lily, you should have said. I would have taken you to get groceries. You need to watch Ven and his friends, Ven can be an asshole. He doesn't treat women right."
I wave my hand dismissing Blake.
"You had stuff to do, you didn't need to babysit me further. Don't worry it's not like that. He's been kind and helpful it's just as a friendly welcome from him. It's not a date or anything."
Taking another sip of my drink I down the rest. Waiting nearly 30 minutes for a drink will make you thirsty.
"Well you might see it like that, but I bet Ven doesn't."
I look up at Blake confused, no one has shown any interest in me in that way since I arrived. Well apart from the president of the Satans Outlaws, but that was bikers they aren't fussy when

it comes to getting their leg over.

"Honestly it's fine, anyway I'm going to get another drink and you should get back to your date."

I turn and because Blake is stood directly behind me I order another drink straight away, no waiting around this time.

"What date? I'm not on a date I'm working." Blake states.

"Elise said at the diner this morning." I reply taking my drink and when I go to pay the barman is already gone. Oh well maybe it's a complementary freebie.

"She's here yes, having a drink with her friends and I'm working. She said that to make you think she was on a date with me."

"Why would she do that? And why would you not correct her?" I ask confused by the whole thing, I've literally just arrived in town, of course nothing is going on with me and Blake. Why on earth would she act like that?

"I used to date her about 3 years ago, only for 6 months. It didn't work out. She's been trying to get me back ever since. And I did just chew her out 10 minutes ago. I didn't in the diner because I didn't want to cause more of a scene than she already had, especially on your first day in town."

Oh well there you go that made a little sense. Elise sounds like a crazy bunny boiler.

"Oh okay. Listen I best get back to Ven's table he will be wondering where I've got to. And I don't want him to worry that I'm lost or something. Thanks for the free drink and I will see you around."

I smile and lift my drink, and squeeze past him to get back to Ven.

I don't make it that far as Blake grabs my arm. Leaning in close he whispers in my ear.

"You look beautiful tonight. Remember what I said. Be careful." He warns.

The smell of him and the feel of his face against mine, having him so close I swear my lady parts were doing a Mexican wave of excitement down there.

Straightening myself, I carry on to Ven's table. When Ven sees me coming he gives me a big smile.

"Hey darling I was beginning to wonder where you'd got to."

Ven pulls me out a chair, then puts his arm around me.

Feeling a little uncomfortable at the closeness of Ven I try to pull away a little, but he just pulls me in closer.

"Aint she a hot piece, you seen these tits guys?"

With that Ven gropes my breast, I freeze, I look to Ven's friends they are all just smirking, watching. I push his hand away and move to stand. Ven just grips my arm painfully tight.

"Now then darling I'm only giving you a little cuddle you need to relax. Plus I seen you talking with Blake. You came here with me I will not be disrespected by having you getting cosy with fucking Blake Stone. You owe me, and I take what's owed." He growls in my ear.

Ven's hand on my arm is really starting to hurt me and his whole change in demeanour is freaking me out and pissing me off all at the same time.

Someone starts shouting my name a few feet away and waving me over. It's Evelynn from Kelley's market. Thank god. I smile and wave with my other hand. I then turn around on Ven, gritting my teeth as I yank my arm from his grip. I then grab my bag and my drink and start to walk away.

"Don't you walk away from me! You have any idea who I am in this town? It's a fucking privilege to be out with me." Ven seethes. Standing from his chair, he grabs my arm and yanks me backwards I stumble towards him. I turn around to face him.

"Go fuck yourself Ven, don't speak to me or come near me ever again."

I step back and throw my drink all over him. I storm over to Evelynn's table now aware that quite a few people were listening and watching.

"Stupid fuckin' fat bitch, I took pity on you it's the only reason why I brought you here. Cover yourself up the sight of your fuckin' fat body is making us all feel sick." Ven spits.

I hear giggles and see Elise and her friends watching, finding the whole scene amusing.

With tears in my eyes and feeling pure humiliation I run out of the bar. I have only been in this stupid fucking town two days and I already want to go home. Why did I even think for one second that I could be confident and try and meet new people. I guess I really am a stupid fat bitch.

Tears are running down my face when I feel a pair of arms come around me.

"Hey there sweet girl, don't cry over that weasel he aint worth your tears."

I wipe my cheeks and look up to see Jeanie from the diner. I give her a weak smile and nod.

"Um is there any chance you could give me a ride back to the Merricks place? I don't really feel like being out now."

Jeanie hands me a tissue.

"Of course honey, my car is just over there,"
we get into Jeanie's car and head off to the Merricks.

"Thanks so much for dropping me back, I didn't mean to ruin your night." I apologise.

"Don't be silly now, I was going to leave soon anyway. I have a diner to run. I can't be out partying all night." She kindly replies.

I smile at Jeanie and look back out at the passing

scenery.

Soon we are pulling up outside the Merricks house. I thank Jeanie and run inside. As soon as I'm in I get changed into my pj's and take off my make-up. I climb into bed eager to forget the day. And hoping tomorrow is a better day.

I have enough food in to last a few days so I can just focus on work and stay here at the house. Avoiding the town and certain people in it.

CHAPTER SEVEN

The next morning I'm up and dressed ready to meet Sam the Merricks nephew. And I plan on burying my head in my work as much as possible.

Walking up to the office building where Sam would be, I knock on the door but there's no answer. I check the time it is nearly 9 am, I thought he would be in by now.

I turn and start to make my way back to the house when a truck pulls in.

A guy I'm guessing jumps out. He's an attractive looking guy short, stocky build with kind brown eyes and a warm smile.

I walk over, wiping my sweaty palms and put my hand out in greeting.

"Hi sam is it? I am Lily I'm staying at your aunts and uncles place I work for the magazine crop a feel. I'm hoping to do some research on how things run here and gather any tips for our readers." I splutter nervously.

"Howdy Lily, yeah I'm Sam, it's nice to meet you. It's a bit of a boring time here, until the main harvest comes in that's when it gets crazy. I shall do my best to help in any way I can though."

Sam shows me to the office and then takes me on a tour of the farm. His warm and welcoming personality eases my nerves. I actually think I might like working here.

Over the next couple of days I learn that Sam is really a lovely guy, he's married to a woman called Louisa with their first baby on the way in three month's time. I contact my editor and send him pictures and notes I've written.

I'm thankful for being buried in work and not facing the gossip I'm sure is going around the town.

Sam brings Louisa with him the next day, as she is dying to meet me and of course she is just as lovely as Sam.

Louisa tells me she's heard a couple of the locals talking about what went down at the Den between me and Ven. Apparently most of the locals weren't surprised it happened.

"It's been a long time coming, the way Ven throws his weight around n' all because his daddy is sheriff. And the way he treats women, it's no wonder he hasn't had a kicking yet. No one will though because of the repercussions." Louisa states, as she absently rubs her baby bump.

Louisa is little and a cute looking woman, she has light golden blonde hair and has a young and innocent face with big round doe eyes. She's adorable. I just want to put her in my pocket and take her home.

"Well I've been avoiding going to town as I just don't want to face all the gossip. But I am running low on food, so I know I'm going to have to head there later today." I sigh dreading the thought of running into Ven or Elise.

"You don't need to hide away, but I can see why you'd be worried about running into gossip. I guess in London you don't really get that being a big city n' all."

I laugh because there's always gossip. It's just I am a nobody in London I can go around, and no one will notice me amongst all the different people that are in the city. I miss being me without judgement.

"Oh there's gossip, but it's more the type of gossip you get in the newspapers about famous people. Sometimes there's dramas I just like to stay away from it all. I'm no one special or different in London, no one notices what I do or don't do, apart from my family. So yeah it's a little strange being thrust in the main spotlight in a small town." I shrug.

Louisa is watching me closely.

"How about I come with you to the market store and we can go in get your shopping and get out, that way I can drive you too. Save you carrying all your bags all that way. What do you say?"

Sighing I relent. I'm going to have to go out at

some point may as well get it over with. At least I won't be on my own.

I nod and Louisa smiles.

"Sure okay just let me get my bag and I'll write a list."

"Oh thank goodness, it gives me something to do. I am so bored since stopping work, Sam won't let me do anything. I love him but he's driving me a little crazy."

I smile up at Louisa as I finish my list and put it in my bag.

"He's only being protective because he loves you. Come on let's get this over with so I can get back here to hide some more." I say, helping Louisa out of her chair.

Louisa are in Kelley's Market chatting away. Louisa, I think is doing her best to keep me from worrying if people are looking and talking about me as we pass them. Its sweet, but she's talking that much that I'm worried she might pass out from lack of oxygen.

I grab her arm.

"Louisa I get what you're trying to do, and I think its sweet, but please slow down and come up for air I'm worried you will pass out and then Sam will be mad at me for not looking after his very pregnant wife."

Louisa lets out a laugh, which makes me laugh because this sweet and innocent looking woman has a really evil sounding laugh.

We carry on our shop until we are down the sweets and chocolate aisle where Elise and her friends are stood. My steps falter and Louisa notices and looks up.

"Oh not Elise, my nana said that girl has been nuthin' but trouble since she opened her mouth. She's a bully, always has been. My nana also said if people are trying to bring you down its only because you're above them." Louisa states trying to reassure me.

Louisa gives my hand a squeeze as we carry on down the aisle like she isn't even there. Of course Elise can't let us pass without comment.

"Well it's nice to see you Lily, stocking up are we? They have a sale on salad here which would probably suit you better." She says with a false smile.

"Hello Elise, if you would excuse me I have to finish my shopping."

I try taking the high road, still being polite. Even though that's the least she deserves after being so rude to me.

"Of course I wouldn't want to get in the way of your food."

Her twat friends giggle. What is wrong with them we're not in a playground anymore.

I continue to walk past them, when Elise declares.

"Oh and make sure you leave enough food for the rest of the town won't you, I am making dinner for Blake tonight, his favourite. Can't have you eating it all." She boasts.

I stop and take in a deep breath, trying to hold back my emotions and from giving Elise a piece of my mind. I don't want to cause another scene. But I shouldn't have even tried because Louisa has spun around hands on her hips looking furious at Elise.

"Y'all better mind your manners. Especially you Elise. How dare you treat Lily this way she hasn't done nuthin' to you."

Louisa is even more cute when she's mad and its lovely she has my back. I just don't want her getting too excited and going into early labour.

"Quit it Louisa this aint nuthin' to do with you. We don't like strangers in this town and she aint welcome. Coming here with her English accent thinking she's cleverer than all of us. Flirting with my man and even he wants her gone."

Louisa goes to speak but I interrupt her.

"Blake wants me gone?" I ask.

I don't know why that upsets me more than it should, I barely know him. Maybe it's because I thought we got along and that he liked me. Even if it was just as a friend.

It makes sense I suppose in the time I have been hiding at the Merricks place he hasn't once stopped by, and I'm sure he would have heard about the drama between Ven and me.

"Finally I'm getting through that fat head of yours. Yeah he wants you the hell out, most of the town do. Just that Blake is too much of a gentlemen to tell you." Elise shrugs and smiles she's enjoying every moment of this. I grab my trolley and start walking away. Soon Louisa is walking right next to me she places her hand on mine.

"Don't listen to her. Blake and she haven't been an item in ages. She's just a raging b-i-t-c-h."

I burst out laughing because just hearing her spell that word is ridiculous coming from her. I may have known Louisa just a day, but I just know that she never swears. She really must be angry.

Louisa giggles next to me and bumps my shoulder with hers.

We make it to the checkout thankfully no more dramas along the way.

Evelynn is there and immediately gives me and Louisa a big smile. Louisa fills her in on the showdown with Elise.

"That stupid bitch tits, I can't stand the girl. Now I aint calling her a slut, but I swear I've seen her vagina on hoarders: dicks edition." Evelynn states smiling.

My eyes are wide, and I may look like a fish. I cannot believe she just said that in the local market. What's weirder is I look over to Louisa who's smiling like she just made a comment about the weather.

"Don't worry honey, my uncle owns the place,

family run. Job for life."

Evelynn gives me a wink.

It's then that I burst out laughing.

"I cannot believe you just said that, although thanks' for making me laugh."

"Anytime honey, say we should have drinks, what do you reckon? You too Louisa although virgin cocktails for you."

"I'm not sure, last time I went out for drinks it didn't end well, and there's a few people that don't like me much in this town. I'm probably best just laying low."

"Great I will pick you up at 7 tonight. Louisa we will swing by yours on the way. Oh and wear whatever you like just be comfy it aint fancy where we are going."

I stare at Evelynn, she's just completely ignored me, and I admit part of me is happy she did. I just hope that this night doesn't turn into a disaster.

"Fine I will be ready, come on Louisa I'm going to have to stop at a cashpoint and take some money out for tonight."

Leaving the market we hear Evelynn shout.

"See y'all later be ready!"

When we arrive back at the house I offer to cook something for Sam and Louisa for tea. They accept so I just make some quick chicken fajitas. Taking care not to make them too hot in case they don't like spice. I have hot salsa if they do. After eating an early dinner they head off home so Louisa can get showered and changed and I do the same.

I am stood there going through what clothes I've got, that are not dressy and are also comfy, as I'm sure it will be a warm night.

In the end I decide on my dark skinny high waisted jeans. These have the purpose cuts in them one is fairly close to the start of my arse, but I love them. I put on my loose red cami top that has red lace at the bust. Then I put on my comfy wedge sandals, and a long thin silver necklace and some silver bangles.

I keep my eye make-up light with winged eyeliner and wear my bright red lipstick. My hair again is left loose in waves down my back with serum in to control the frizz. It's just too hot to blow dry and straighten.

I'm just putting my money in my bag when I hear a car horn outside. I grab my little black cardigan in case I'm cold later and head out locking up.

I smile when Evelynn is still honking her horn and flashing her lights.

I climb in the front music blaring out of the speakers.

"You ready to party Texan style?" Evelynn sings excitedly.

Chuckling I nod.

"You look nice Evelynn, love the red lipstick." I compliment.

"Thanks honey, can't go wrong with nice black

top and jeans and my red lipstick to dress it up a bit."

A little while later we are pulling up to Sam and Louisa's place I get out to go and ring the bell. They live in a nice quiet street ideal for families. So I don't think they'd appreciate Evelynn honking her horn.

The door opens and Louisa is in her pj's ready for bed.

"I'm so sorry Lily, I am just too darn tired. Please don't be mad but I just want to sleep." Louisa sobs.

"Oh Louisa I'm not mad at all. My sister was the same in the final few months, so don't worry. Just rest up."

Louisa gives me a hug.

"Oh you and Evelynn must come to my baby shower at the Den, I will let you know the details."

"The Den?" I ask dreading that I could possibly bump into Blake.

"Yeah we got a great deal. They are doing all the food and decorating. Please say you will come and make sure Evelynn comes too."

I nod and give her a quick hug promising I will be there.

When I get back into the car I explain to Evelynn and tell her about the baby shower.

"Silly girl of course we understand. And I will be

there for her baby shower. Free food and a bar, just try and stop me."

I laugh. We start on the road again.

We stop off to pick up Evelynn's friend Suellen, who has awesome rainbow hair and is just as funny as Evelynn.

We park up at the Den. I was hoping we would end up at a different bar, but I guess this is the only one in this small town.

Once inside I notice it's not as busy as it was the other night I was here.

We order a couple of jugs of cocktails and take a seat in the corner of the bar. No live band tonight and I notice the juke box to the side.

The conversation flows easily between us, chatting about anything and everything. Evelynn fills Suellen in on the gossip of what went down with Ven and I.

"I swear he's so country he thinks a seven-course meal is a possum and a six pack." Suellen states with a dead pan face. Me and Evelynn on the other hand are in hysterics.

"Well he is, he's stuck in the 50's thinking women should be in the kitchen and run around after their man. And let me tell y'all he's so crooked if he swallowed a nail he'd spit up a corkscrew."

More laughter and more drinks carry on through the evening. I am really enjoying myself.

"Excuse me lovelies, I am in need of f-f-p." I say

standing and swaying a little from the alcohol and the head rush.

"Well what in tarnation is an f-f-p?" Evelynn asks.

"Fatal-first-piss. Once you've gone for that first pee when drinking, you need to go more frequently."
Evelynn and Suellen chuckle while I stumble to the ladies.
On my way back to the table I stumble again, this time I come face first into a hard-solid wall. Except it's not a wall but a wall of a hard chest.
My eyes travel up into a pair of familiar deep blue eyes. But not the same face or hair that would match those eyes.
"Sssoo, sorry, you're not Blake." I drunkenly state.
I am gifted with a handsome smile.

"Howdy there ma'am, I am guna guess you're the famous Lily I keep hearing about."
I take a step back and put my hands on my hips. Giving him my glare. Although in my drunken state I probably look like I have something in my eye.

"Now listen here Mr i-don't-know. Whatever you've heard around this town of from that knobhead Ven about me is a lie. Just know he deserved it speaking to me like that and man handling me. Bloody tosser bruised my arm, look!" I say swinging my arm up, pointing to the finger shaped bruise marks that are on my upper arm.

I look back at this stranger with the familiar eyes. And he has an angry look on his face.

"Annndd who are you twat face with the familiar beautiful eyes?"

Soon his face changes and he gifts me with that smile again.

"I'm Wes, I believe you know my brother, Blake. It's a pleasure to finally me the girl that my brother cannot shut up about."

My face makes a slightly stunned expression. Then when I've gotten passed the knowledge that this is Blakes brother, it sinks in what Wes just said.

"Blake talks about me?!"

Wes lets out a deep throaty chuckle.

Must run in the family the ability to make a woman want to hump your leg.

"C'mon I will escort you back to your table. And will join y'all for a drink. I'd like to get to know the beautiful girl that has my brother all riled up."

Wes gives me a wink and walks me back to our table.

Evelynn's and Suellen's jaw drop as we approach the table.

"Holy shit he's as hot as a two-dollar whore on the fourth of July." Evelynn blurts out.

"You can say that again Evelynn." Suellen

eagerly agrees.

I burst out laughing and so does Wes.

"And now my draws are as hot as Hades." Suellen states.

Still laughing we sit down.

"Now ladies what are y'all drinking?" Wes asks.

"Now we like you even more, we are drinking jugs of cocktails but just a single glass will be fine." Evelynn replies.

Wes signals the barman over and asked us to order what jugs of cocktails we wanted.

"That's very kind of you thank you. We will chip in and pay for your next few rounds of beer at least."

I say and get greeted with laughter from around the whole table.

"What? Why are you all laughing?"

"Lily I am Wesley Stone, I own this place with my brother Blake." He informs me.

Wide eyed looking to Suellen and Evelynn for conformation. When they both smile and nod their heads in agreement I turn back to Wes.

"I had no idea, wait a minute if you guys own this place, then why do you guys help out at the Merricks?" I ask.

"We do it because the Merricks helped us out a lot when we were young so it's our way of repaying them."

I smile and nod taking a sip of my drink.

"So hot guy, why's your brother not snapping our girl up? Way I see it she's been here near 'nuff ten days, and he aint even taken her dancing. He's burning daylight!" Evelynn hollers while I choke on my drink. Wes laughs while patting my back.

"No idea, he's an idiot for wasting even a second. Hell I've known Lily five minutes and already I can see she's the real deal. My brother would be a fool not to claim Lily as his."

I'm blushing now, I know I am. Its sweet that Wes has paid me this compliment.

"That's sweet Wes thank you. You Texan boys know how to pay a woman a compliment. You won't see manners like that in London."

Wes is laughing shaking his head.

"Jesus, you have no idea do you?"

"Sss-she has absolutely none! She is comp-p-p-pletely blind." Evelynn slurs sloshing her drink around the table.

The evening carries on. Until I'm well and truly pissed out of my face. And I'm telling them the story of my first night at the biker bar.

"So I'm there, and ch-cherry pie comes on aa-nn-d I'm up on the table and I start dancing s-se-se-ductivy I then start lifting up my dress!"

I fling my arms wide spilling my drink everywhere but I'm too drunk to care.

"Then yoooouur brother flluung me ovra his shoulja and and carrweed me to his truck! Why can't I spweak pwopraly?" I slur.

Evelynn, Suellen and Wes are all doubled over laughing at me.

"You are a commode-hugging, knee-walking drunk! That's why your mouth aint working." Suellen points out with Evelynn nodding into her drink.

Wes stands, pulls out his phone to make a call.

"Oi! You ring Bwake? Where is he any hoo?"

"I met a guy who was a biker once, he was sooo nice and man he had a mon-ster cock! It was huggee. Best god damn night I ever had."

Evelynn still making large gestures with her hands just to emphasize how large he was in case we missed that part of him being hung like a horse.

Wes returns to our table.

"Right ladies I've sorted a lift for Evelynn and Suellen. Also leave me your keys Evelynn and I will make sure your car is there at your house ready for you in the morning.

"Whaaat 'bout me?" I ask raising an eyebrow.

"You can crash at mine, I'm planning on visiting the Merricks place tomorrow anyway may as well drop you back then. And don't panic I have a spare room, you can sleep in there."

I shrug and yawn, I'm at the point I'm beyond caring where I sleep. I could crash down anywhere.

Soon Evelynn and Suellen are in their car to take them home. Evelynn shouts out the window, as the car pulls off.
"Remember to keep your fucking knickers on! Or don't Yeehaaa ride that cowboy!"
All I hear after that is them pair cackling away. Laughing I shake my head.
I head back inside the bar to find Wes shutting down the tills and switching off the lights.
"Give me a few minutes while I shut everything down and check takings in my office."
I nod with a smile to Wes, I go to grab my bag off my chair. I head over to the door to wait for him. I sit down and lean my head against the wall closing my eyes.
Soon I am vaguely aware I'm being lifted. I open my eyes slightly and look up expecting it to be Wes. Except it's not its Blake.
Without my control my body snuggles in closer and I press my face into his neck breathing in his scent. The alcohol giving me the courage that I wouldn't normally have.
"You smell really yummy." I mumble into his neck.
I then start to gently kiss his neck and my tongue can't help but want a taste.
"Mmm you taste just as good as you smell."
Blakes hands tighten their hold on me and his body tenses.
Soon I am being deposited on my feet. I wobble slightly and Blake's hand reaches out to steady

Rise Above

me.

Suddenly I'm not so sleepy and I'm wide awake. Blake opens the truck door.

"Get in the car I will take you back to the Merricks, Wes is busy." Blake says his voice gruff and avoiding looking at me.

My heart sinks. I've done it again and made a complete fool out of myself.

I nod, now avoiding even looking at Blake and climb into his truck. He shuts my door, rounds the truck and gets in.

The drive is silent and awkward, it seems to take forever, when all I want to do is shut myself in the house and hide again.

Soon Blake pulls up outside the house.

I open the truck door and hop down turning to Blake but not making eye contact.

"Thanks' for the lift, um and sorry about earlier." I mumble.

I shut the door before giving Blake time to reply, I practically run in to the house slamming the door shut.

Leaning against the door I close my eyes and let my tears fall.

Tonight has proven that I need to keep avoiding Blake because clearly I can't control myself around him and I seem to make a fool out of myself every bloody time.

I need to stop being so stupid to think that a man like Blake, would even want to be with someone like me. The type of women he would go for wouldn't have anything that wobbles when it shouldn't.

Taking a deep breath I head upstairs. Go to the bathroom and take care of business, I wash off my makeup and brush my teeth.
I climb into bed and no matter how hard I try my mind won't shut down.
Frustrated I get up and get a drink of water and sit on the back decking. Looking up at the stars.
Hoping the peace will quieten my over thinking brain. But it doesn't.
I decide to get some work done.
After finishing up my article I email it to my boss, also with a brief note asking when I can come home.
I then look at my nan's page and Instantly laugh. My sister Rose took her to a male strip show. And they only got my nan up on stage.
Her eyes are wide as she stares at the man's crotch. There's also another one of her with two hot strippers either side of her, arms round them both smiling big. And another where she appears to be tweaking a guy's nipple.
I wish I could be as care free as my nan. I send her a private message asking her if she got lucky after the show. And sending her my love.
Soon I've sent an email to my mum and my two sisters as well just to check in with them.
I look at the time and its nearly 4:30 am. Shaking my head I shut everything down and bring it all

inside. I head up the stairs to bed. Hopefully no one expects me up early tomorrow so at least I can get a few more hours sleep.

I close my eyes and immediately Blake appears. Groaning in frustration. I eventually manage to fall asleep with Blake invading my dreams.

CHAPTER EIGHT

The next morning I am woken up to a banging on the door.
Groaning I turn over looking at the clock, I see its only 7:30 am.
I groggily get up and shuffle my way down stairs to the door.
I am tired and I am pissed off.
I swing the door open to be greeted by a smiling Wes.

"Well good mornin' beautiful." He greets.

His eyes scan me from head to toe. Its then I realise I'm in my little satin and lace nightie that just finishes below my bum.
When Wes's eyes glide back down and linger on my chest for a brief second that's when I realise I also have no bra on. Apparently my nipples have a mind of their own and just wanted to pop up and say hello.
I quickly cross my arms over my chest. I feel the heat rise on my cheeks. Christ I may as well be stood here naked.
Just to make my morning even better I of course

have major bed head. The only saving grace is I had taken my make up off, so I don't look like something from a horror movie.

Wes lets out a whistle and gives me a wink.

At this point having had bugger all sleep I am not in the mood for any of this.

Putting my hands on my hips I frown. Wes also gets to witness my short temper when I am tired.

"Now why on earth would you come banging on the door at 7:30 in the frickin' morning? I have had bugger all sleep. And now you've just basically violated me with your eyes. And again waking me up. I was asleep!" I fume.

By this point I have slightly pushed Wes backwards by poking him in the chest while giving him what for. So much so the front door has shut behind me.

I turn and stomp my foot as I go to flounce off back into bed. But come face to face with a shut locked door. Letting out a long sigh I let my head fall against the door. And slightly headbutt it.

"This may not be the best morning for you darlin', but it certainly is for me." Wes says chuckling.

I swing round and lean against the door crossing my arms over my chest.

"Please tell me you have a spare key?" I beg.

Smiling Wes shakes his head.

"No I don't, I would say I am sorry, but that would be a lie. I am enjoying the show too much."

Covering my face with my hands I try to think of a way around this that doesn't end up in me breaking a window to gain entry into the house. "I do know someone who does have a spare key, let me give them a ring see if they can get here to let you in."

I immediately jump up and wrap my arms around Wes's neck.

"Oh thank god, please call them."

I step back and Wes is smiling big. Shaking his head.

"Damn brother is a fool, he's guna love this."

After Wes makes the call, we both sit on the steps to the house waiting for the spare key to arrive.

"So come on then why are you here so early? You must have known I'd be at least a little bit hanging from last night."

I'm trying to sit as demurely as possibly so not to flash or have an accidental boob pop out.

"I brought stuff to make you breakfast figured you'd need it. And I did say I was coming to the farm to help out anyway. Sam and Louisa have a hospital appointment so I said I would cover for him." Wes states.

"That's kind of you Wes. Umm I suppose I should say sorry for making a fool of myself last night and well right now too. I swear I don't normally.

Well not this often anyway but it seems it's a daily occurrence here."

Wes let out deep throaty laugh. That if I was wearing knickers they'd probably be wet.

"Aint got nuthin' to apologise for, you've been yourself nuthin' else. I do have to ask one thing though, what you said last night when you thought I was a friend of Ven's. Was that true what he did?" He asks.

I think about answering with a lie, but I don't want Wes thinking I'm the type of girl that would make up drama. So without going into details I just nod.

"Shit, why didn't you tell the staff at the Den they woulda' kicked his ass out."

I shrug, looking down at my hands in my lap.

"I don't know, it was my first proper night in this town I didn't want any trouble. Also he's a local and I'm a stranger. It's his hometown not mine. At some point I will be on a plane back home. No need to have attention turned my way and it's better to not cause a mess while I'm here." I state fiddling with my hands.

Wes shakes his head.

He opens his mouth about to speak when we hear a truck near the house.

Wes stands up and smiles down at me giving me a cheeky wink.

As soon as I see who's truck it is my stomach plummets. Bloody Blake. It comes to a stop just in front of us. I'm still sat down and can't see into the truck, but Wes is standing arms crossed and he's laughing.

Blake jumps down from the truck he's in jeans and a fitted army green t-shirt that is stuck to him in sections and his hair is damp. Clearly he woke up showered and came straight here.

His eyes are on me, ignoring his brothers laughter.

I slowly stand, and Blake stops in his tracks. His eyes do a very slow sweep from my head to my toes. I can't help my bodies reaction to him. My skin pebbles and my nipples harden from his intense stare.

Blake lets out a low growl, which I swear with the look in his eyes and that sound, if he ask me to strip naked right now I would.

"Yeehaaa! Brother I knew it." Wes hoots.

Moment broken as Wes claps Blake on his shoulder still laughing, still finding something amusing. I quickly cross my arms over my chest and then comes the familiar pink blush I feel creep up over my cheeks that always seems to happen around Blake.

"Why are you out here dressed like that?" Blake asks, now looking irritated.

"Because, your bloody brother woke me up!" I snap.

Blakes gaze swings to Wes. Wes puts up his hands surrendering.

"Hey man I'm here to take over for Sam for a while. Thought I'd bring her breakfast. Aint my

Rise Above

fault Lily here is not nice when you wake her up." Wes says smirking.
Seriously I can't believe he just blamed me.

"Hey! I've had three and a half hours sleep. You were pounding on the bloody door. I don't know anyone that would wake up in a good mood from that. And it isn't my fault the door slammed closed on me! Actually Blake while I'm on it what do you mean with the comment dressed like that?!"
By this point I've had enough I just want to crawl into bed and go back to sleep. My hands on my hips and as Rose calls it my mum face. As it's the same face our mum used to use on us when we were in a shit ton of trouble.
"See what I've had to face brother, do not annoy the beast when she has not had enough sleep?"
My eyes widen as I look at Wes.
I then look to Blake to see he's fighting back a smile. A bloody smile.
"The beast? Really Wes. And I don't know why you are bloody smiling, for god sake unlock the door so I can go back to bed!"
With that both Wes and Blake laugh. I swear it's the sexiest sound I've heard. I find myself fighting back my own smile as theirs is so infectious.

"You aint going back to bed I'm making breakfast remember. Now go put on a robe so I can concentrate on making breakfast without you distracting me."

Wes walks passed me whistling to his truck.
I turn and walk up to the house to wait for Blake to follow. I don't realise he's on the bottom step while I am on the top, Until I hear him growl.
"Jesus Christ." He growls.
I turn to look at him and his eyes are on my arse. I quickly step to the door. Embarrassed again as that the second time now I've accidently flashed Blake.
He comes close and leans across to put the key in the lock. His chest brushing up against my side. I get a waft of his scent. Fresh clean manly smell. That has me closing my eyes and letting out an involuntary moan.
I feel Blake pause next to me. I quickly open my eyes. And he is mere inches away from my face looking deeply into my eyes. My mouth has gone dry, so has my lips. I run my tongue along my bottom lip and his eyes follow.
Blake starts moving in slowly as if he's going to kiss me. I can feel his breath on my lips. I close my eyes.
Suddenly Wes's whistling becomes louder and his footsteps start up the steps. Blake immediately pulls back unlocking the door I run inside, and I run up the stairs.
"I will be down in a minute let me jump in the shower and put on some proper clothes." I shout.

I'm out of the shower and I quickly moisturise then get dressed. I am just in my coral wrap maxi skirt and black loose hanging vest top. Underneath I have my bikini on again as I plan on sunbathing on the deck a little while later and catching up on some sleep.

I just have a little bit of concealer on to cover my bags under my eyes. My hair is still wet, but I don't care. I can smell Wes's cooking and it's made me realise how hungry I am.

I make my way down the stairs and round to head to the kitchen. I stop dead when I hear both Blake and Wes talking.

"She likes you man, why are you being an ass to her? She's a mighty fine girl."

"Wes just drop it. She aint my type ok?" Blake replies.

" Ha yeah right, you gotta dick? She's every man's type. But she only has eyes for you." Wes states.

"I mean it, she drives me crazy. She'll be gone soon 'nuff, so aint no point going on so just leave it Wes."

"You're full of shit. But fine I will take your word for it. So you won't mind If I take her out on a date tonight then?"

"Yeah Wes, go have at it." Blake shrugs.

Seriously have at it. Like I'm some fucking ride to have a go on!

I can't deny I'm hurt over what Blake said, I'd be lying if I hadn't hoped he felt just a tiny bit of the attraction I feel for him in return.

But he doesn't, I drive him crazy and I'm not his type. I feel tears sting my eyes and I quickly blink them back. Taking a deep breath and plastering on the best fake smile I can muster I walk into the kitchen.

Instantly both brothers turn to face me Blakes making coffee while Wes is at the cooker.

"You feel more awake now darlin? You look beautiful as always."

Wes lays on the charm with what I've come to realise is his signature cheeky wink.

I smile at Wes trying my best to shut out Blake.

"Thanks Wes do you always charm the girls with that smooth mouth of yours?" I tease.

Wes throws his head back and laughs.

"Darlin' this smooth mouth is only reserved for the ones who truly deserve it."

It's my turn to burst out laughing as Wes makes kissing duck face at me.

Blake lets out a loud cough and my gaze automatically swings to him.

"You want some coffee?" Blake asks holding out a mug. I nod and give him a small smile as I reach out to take it. His fingers gently brush mine. Just a simple touch like that sets my body alight.

"Err thanks Blake." I mumble.

I brake contact taking a sip of my coffee. Closing my eyes enjoying the caffeine fix I've been craving.

"Mmm, god I needed that." I moan and open my

eyes to find both Wes and Blake staring at me.
"What?" I ask.
"Fucking clueless, absolutely clueless." Wes keeps saying while shaking his head at the frying pan.

I decide to set our cutlery for breakfast outside as it's so nice. Soon Blake, Wes and I are tucking into a delicious breakfast.
"How did you learn to cook Wes? The scrambled eggs taste amazing." I ask around a mouthful of food.

"We both know how to cook thanks to our mamma, when things were good home. Mrs Merrick taught us a lot when we were here too." Wes replies.
"Oh so you both know how to cook, that's great. My dad can't cook unless giving step by step instructions. My mums always cooked though. Good home cooked meals that add on 20 lb."
Wes chuckles and to my surprise I find Blake smiling back at me.

"So come on then Lily, you got a man back home waiting for you? Although I will say if you have, he's an idiot and you should dump his ass for even letting you outta his sight." Wes asks.

"Nope, no man waiting been single a while now, last relationship wasn't great, so it put me off."
I give a small smile and a shrug. It's Blake that speaks up next

"Why wasn't it great? did he hurt you?"

I look up into Blakes eyes and he looks angry, the ticking in his jaw is going.

"No not physically just well, he was over honest I guess you could say. Would say things like. why are you wearing that? When it makes you look even fatter. telling me I needed to watch what I eat. Things like that. Then one day I came back early from work and he was shagging my friend. Obviously not my friend anymore."

I shrug.

"Of course he blamed me saying it was my fault I pushed him to do it by being fat and not attractive enough for him.

It knocked my confidence in men and myself.

I've since learnt that it was never my fault I am who I am. I like to eat normal food not live off of lettuce leaves. I know I'm chubby, but it's me I've always been plump." I finish, cutting into my food and smiling as i take a big bite of pancake.

I stop smiling because both are staring at me like I've grown a second head.

"What? Have I got syrup on my face?" I ask.

I grab a napkin and wipe my face just to make sure there's nothing there at least I don't think there is.

"See man, clueless and sweet. Mamma didn't raise us to be fools and you're being the biggest fool I know right now." Wes states grabbing his plate and mug from the table taking it in to the kitchen.

"What's he on about?" I ask looking back and forth between the kitchen and Blake.

"Nuthin' he's just being a jackass." Blake mumbles in response.

I shrug and carry on with my breakfast.
I offer to clear up as Wes cooked the breakfast, but he refuses.
Insisting I go lay down on the sun lounger outside and relax.
I don't need telling twice so I dash off outside with my sun cream and strip off down to my bikini. I only ever wear this bikini for sunbathing as it shows more than I am normally comfortable with. With Blake and Wes clearing up and then they will be gone and no one around to see me so I don't care.
It's a bright red halter, and the bottoms are high waisted and high rise on my legs. I put cream on especially over my tattoos, so they don't fade too soon, I lay down face first with my arms crossed underneath my head.
Soon I'm sound asleep the warm sun on my skin.
I am woken to the feel of a hand gently stroking the hair out of my face.
I blink several times trying to adjust my eyes to the brightness.
I see its Wes crouched down in front of me.
"Go away, I'm sleeping"
Wes chuckles.
"I am darlin', heading over to the farm now. All

cleared up for you. Get some sleep but be careful not to burn this beautiful skin. I will set your alarm on your phone to wake you so you can turn over."

I'm nodding with my eyes closed, I am struggling to fight to stay awake.

"And Lily?"

"Hhmm"

"Just so you know, you have a fucking great ass." With that he slaps my ass.

"WES!" I shout practically throwing a temper tantrum. All I can hear is him laughing in the distance.

I lie back down and soon settle back into a sleep.

This time I feel a hand slowly trailing up my leg following the line of my stocking tattoo.

In my sleepy state I let out a moan. Enjoying the feeling. The hand carries on past where my tattoo finishes at the top of my thigh. It carries on travelling so slowly over the swell of my arse.

It then carries on its slow moving path up my side passed my waist and slowly touching the side of my breast.

It feels like blissful torture. My breathing has become heavier, my is body wanting more.

My eyes still closed as the hand moves across my back up to my neck sweeping my hair to one side.

Soon I feel a mouth on my neck trailing kisses

across to my shoulders. I can't help but whimper wanting and needing more.

I feel and hear the rumble from his chest.

I know by his scent and that sound that its Blake. And that makes me want this even more.

I knew that from his touch it had to be Blake my body hasn't reacted like that to anyone else's touch.

Blake still kissing and nipping across my skin. His hand trailing down to where my bikini ties up across my back. With a simple pull it becomes undone. His hand moves round the side of my breast.

Needing him I arch to give him better access. He slowly moves his hand over my breast slowly circling my already hardened nipple.

"Mmm Blake please"

I need more. I turn my head in Blakes direction blinking out the sun.

He's sat next to me leaning over. I lift my head and look at Blake in the eyes.

His pupils are dilated and he's breathing deeply too.

Biting my bottom lip, using every ounce of courage I have. I push up on to my knees still staring into Blakes eyes. Never breaking contact. I lean forward slowly worried I will lose this moment, I want to savour it.

I stop just and inch from kissing him. Looking into his eyes, for any sign he's about to pull away. Before I can close the distance, his hand cups the back of my head crashing my mouth to his. I moan as his tongue slides with mine. I grab at the base of his head running my fingers through his hair

Blake lets out a throaty moan. Which only drives me more.

I straddle his lap and as soon as I do I can feel just how much he's turned on. By this point I've lost all control of my body and I am shamelessly dry humping.

I let out a moan as he takes my nipple into his mouth. His hands on my arse, making me ride him faster. My body feels like it will combust.

I'm close I can feel it building within me.

"Oh god, I'm going to come." I moan.

With that Blake moves one of his hand around and circles his thumb on my clit and takes my nipple in his mouth.

I lose it and I come hard.

"Oh god Blake."

"Fuck your beautiful."

My head drops to his shoulder as he slowly stops circling my clit making me shudder. I kiss his neck. Slowly lifting my head I look into his eye's. And the blush take's over my cheeks embarrassment taking over I look down.

Blake takes my chin in his hand making me face him.

"Don't do that, you've got nuthin' to be embarrassed about. That was fuckin' hot. And I swear I nearly came in my pants like a teenager."

I laugh kissing him.

"Your beautiful and your especially beautiful when you come."

I lean in kissing him again letting him know what his words mean to me.

"What about you?" I ask wiggling slightly over his extremely hard bulge.

Blake grabs my hips to stop me moving.

"That wasn't about me, it was all about you. I'm guna do this properly, well I was. Tonight I am taking you out. And when the time is right it will be us coming together, with me buried deep inside you." Blake promises.

I feel my nipples harden and my breath quickens. Christ he's turning me on again. Blake runs his thumb across my hard nipple.

"Christ, babe you need to get off me and cover up before I lose all the self-control I have."

I lean in kissing and nipping at his neck.

"Maybe I don't want you to have self-control." I whisper in his ear.

I have no idea where this bold and confident person has come from. Crikey I can't even get changed in the changing room at the local swimming pool, without hiding behind a towel.

Blake lets out a groan. His grip tightening on my hips.

He lifts me like I weigh nothing off his lap so I'm standing. He slowly stands up too.

Taking my ties from my bikini he leans in wrapping it around my back and ties them up. While kissing my neck and shoulders.

Titling my head back holding on to his shirt I let out a moan.

If this is his way of stopping it isn't working.

Slowly Blake pulls back slightly keeping me wrapped in his arms.

"I will pick you up at six tonight. Be ready. Make sure you wear shoes you are comfortable to walk a little in."

he leans in kissing me again.

"Blake if you want to do this right then I suggest you stop kissing me, or I will tackle you to the floor right now." I state.

Blakes head falls back and he lets out a throaty laugh. I smile big looking up at him.

"Umm Blake I'm not joking."

"I know darlin'. But I am doin' this right. And we need to talk properly first okay?"

His hands cup my face while he looks into my eyes.

"Okay, but I have to know what made you change your mind about me so suddenly?" I ask confused.

Blakes thumb strokes my cheek.

"I never changed my mind about you, I wanted you the moment you gave me your drunken sass trying to make me smile. And then of course when you started to strip in the bar, that sealed

the deal for me."
Blake laughs as I slap his chest.

"But you stopped me from stripping, which I thank you for that by the way. But you have avoided me and made it clear for Wes to have at it."

"Shit, I'm sorry darlin' I didn't mean for you to hear that, I didn't mean it. Wes knows I was full of shit. He knew I liked you and that I've had my head up my ass. He did it to give me the kick I needed." He apologises.

Blake puts my hair behind my ear. And leans in kissing me so softly I feel like I am floating away. "I promise I will explain all tonight okay. We will talk."

I nod with that he leans in giving me one last fucking awesome kiss, before he does leave.

I stand there sighing like a love struck teenager and walk into the house. I immediately email my sister Rose. Telling her all about Blake and asking if by chance she should see this what the ever loving fuck should I wear?!

I shower and potter around for a while still wondering what to wear. Rose hasn't replied yet. I pull out most of my clothes that I have brought with me, laying them out on the bed. It takes me over an hour to narrow it down to two outfits.

I can't deny my brain has been on overdrive. This has come out of nowhere. I honestly thought he wasn't interested. I am Just praying my heart doesn't get broken.

My tablet starts ringing with an incoming video call, it's my sister Rose thank god.

"So flipping happy you rang which outfit?"

I don't even give her the chance to say hello before I turn my camera round to show the outfits laid out on the bed.

"Definitely the black wrap dress, its cap sleeves will keep you cool. Its low cut but not slutty and its form fitted. Plus it has a nice split up the side to show a bit of leg." Rose states.

I'm nodding biting my nail.

"Now what undies are you wearing with it?"

"Umm Rose I didn't really think about undies it's our first date."

Rose starts laughing.

"Little skin and blister, when I get an email like that from you and you already hinted at what already went down on the sun lounger. By the sounds of it you can't keep your hands off each other.

So yeah pick some good undies and make sure you shave your bikini."

"Fine I will wear my red lace undies they always make me feel sexy. And for your information I had it waxed a few days before I left so all good in that department."

I put away my other outfit while answering my nosey sisters questions.

Rise Above

"Right I'm going to go, I better start getting ready its 4:30pm. I don't want to rush around and end up all sweaty."
"Yes fine go, but I want full details and a picture of him soon. Relax enjoy yourself. And remember he's lucky to be going out with you not the other way around."

"Okay I will I promise loves ya skin and blister."
I disconnect butterflies in my belly as I run to go get ready.

After showering for the second time today, I moisturise all over and I'm stood there in my red lace matching bra and French knicker set blow drying my hair, so I don't get to hot and sweaty again.
I've put my music on and hooked it up to my Bluetooth speaker.
I'm dancing away swaying my hips to the funk of Average White Bands Pick Up the Pieces. With my music and the hair dryer I don't hear anyone come in.
I bend over and blow dry my hair underneath wiggling my bum to the music. When suddenly the music stops.
Hair dryer still in hand and still bent over I look over my shoulder to where my tablet is.
Except I don't see my tablet I see a pair of dark denim jean clad muscular legs.
I let out a scream and jump up dropping my hair

dryer.

Clutching my chest above my crazy beating heart I see its Blake stood their arms crossed. His eyes alight, looking at me.

"Jesus bloody Christ! You scared the ever loving shit out of me Blake!"

His eyes cut to me after doing a sweep of my body. My skin heats from his intense gaze.

"You left the door unlocked, anyone could have been stood here now. You should always lock the door." He says deadly serious.

"Most people knock and there's no one around here so I am fine stop being overprotective."

Blake stalks towards me I swear he looks like he's going to pounce. And I don't care if it makes me a slut he won't have to chase me I would happily just jump him now save him the effort.

Blake keeps walking to the point I'm having to walk back until my legs hit the back of the dressing table. My hands grip to hold on as I lean back to look at him.

His hand traces along the edge of my hairline and tucks my hair behind my ear. He then cups my face. Staring at me so intently.

"When I'm not with you, lock up ok?"

I nod all my brain function has gone, he's used his magical hot guy powers on me. If he said drop to your knees and suck me off I wouldn't hesitate. Just the thought has me licking my lips wanting to taste him.

"What are you thinking about that has you licking your lips like that?"

I bite my lip and shrug.

"Nothing."

"Nuthin' my ass, I have an idea, but I will get it out of you later.

But first let me say how fuckin' hot you look in this underwear its taking everything in me not to throw you on that bed." Blake says while slowly running his finger over the edge of the lace on my bra, instantly my nipples harden, wanting more.

I look up to find him watching me not my breast and looking at my reaction.

"Now I'm guna go and wait downstairs for you to finish up because I am early. I will leave you to get ready because I can't trust myself. and I am doing this the right way we need to talk first. I plan to treat you the way you deserve to be treated."

"I don't mind if you can't trust yourself. We could talk later?" I inform him.

Blake lets out a throaty groan and looks to the ceiling.

He then slams his mouth down on mine. The kiss is hungry like he can't get enough of me and I return his kiss just the same. It's frantic, it's wild and I love it. slowing down he stops and is slowly kissing and nipping at my lips.

He leans his forehead against mine both of us breathing deeply. His eyes are closed.

"Get dressed I will be downstairs."

Blake gives me a gentle kiss on my nose and walks out the room, closing the door behind him.

Still clinging on to the dressing table calming my breathing. I can't help but smile. I have never felt like this before, surely it's too soon for him to make me feel this way?

Just the looks he gives me makes me feel beautiful, sexy and as if I have all the power to bring him to his knees. No one has ever looked at me the way Blake does.

I finish my hair and make-up. I keep my eye make-up simple and apply my red lipstick.

I slip on my dress and look at myself in the mirror.

Taking a deep breath I decide Blakes already partially ruined seeing my nice underwear. so I take off my knickers and throw them on the wash pile.

This is something I've never done before but I want to tease Blake and bring him to his knees. I just need a few glasses of wine for the courage.

I slip on my flat sandals and head down stairs.

Blake is sat on the back decking. I walk out to him. He turns and smiles when he sees me. Looking me up and down. He runs his tongue over his lower lip, and instinctively I clench my thighs together at the thought of his tongue on my body.

Blake gets up and smiles knowingly at where my

thoughts are taking me.
"You were killing me in your underwear, now your killing me with this dress and I know what it looks like underneath which is even more teasing."
Loving the power Blake makes me feel. I smile and wink grabbing his hand and pull him along.
"Come on your supposed to be taking me out. Also you don't know exactly what it looks like under my dress." I tease.

He stops which makes me come to a stop, I turn and look at him over my shoulder. He turns and locks the back door. And then grabs my hand pulling me along we reach the bottom of the stairs he stops and turns to look at me. The look in his eyes are hungry and I am sure my eyes are reflecting that look right back at him
"Fuck it!"
Blake takes off his Stetson and chucks it on the floor, turns and grabs my face, and crashes his lips to mine.
He steers me back to the stairs where he lowers me down.
Both our hands are all over each other frantic, I'm undoing his buttons on his shirt, getting frustrated when I can't get them undone fast enough.
Blakes kissing and nipping down my neck over my collar bone.
I can feel Blakes extremely hard through his

jeans and with no underwear on I am shamelessly moving my hips for friction.

Blake lets out a low growl. And leans back slightly panting.

"Tell me to stop now, because I don't know how much longer I can hold back."

I'm panting, looking into his eyes. I take his hand and lead it slowly up my inner thighs, until I reach my bare pussy.

"I don't want you to stop."

Blake lets out a deep growl watching me as his fingers trace over my sensitive area. I push my hips up into his hand needing more.

Blake slides his finger inside, circling where I need it.

I can feel my orgasm starting to build. When suddenly he removes his hand. I whimper in frustration at being so close. My eyes shoot open and I look up to see him suck his finger.

"Just as I thought, you taste fucking sweet. I will get a proper taste of you later but now I want to feel you come with me buried inside you."

All I can do is nod and watch as he undoes his belt and jeans, pushing them down his thighs exposing his long thick cock. I can't take my eyes of it. Beautiful.

Blake takes out his wallet and pulls out a condom. I watch as he glides it down.

"You keep looking at me like that baby I aint guna last."

I look up at Blake and feel the blush hit my

cheeks.

"Don't be embarrassed, its fucking hot the way you look at my cock like your desperate for it."

Blake leans over me positioning himself at my entrance. Kissing me he slowly fills me.

I suck in a breath at the feel of him stretching me, Blake stops moving waiting for my body to accommodate to his size.

"You okay? Fuck you feel incredible." He says his voice strained.

"Yeah I'm good." I breathe.

I move my hips up inviting him to start moving. He does slowly while kissing my neck. He leans back slightly and pulling my dress down over my arms along with my bra straps exposing my breast's. He takes a nipple in his mouth and I cry out the feeling going straight to my core. Blake lets out a groan at my reaction.

I'm building again close to coming. Blakes hips speed up hitting the spot over and over.

"Hold on baby don't come yet."

I try to hold it at bay, but a wave of pleasure takes over my body.

"Oh god I can't hold back Blake I'm coming" I cry out as I climax.

Blake let's out a growl and starts pounding me faster his hands gripping my hips. I watch as he climaxes the muscles in his neck tighten and he lets out a deep low moan.

Leaning forward so his head is in my neck slowly trailing kisses. I cup the back of his head running my fingers through his hair. Slowly we both steady our breathing.

Blake leans back moving my hair from my face. His eyes searching. I don't know what for.

"God your beautiful you know that?"

I look away, as a blush heats my cheeks. Suddenly now feeling nervous and exposed. I've never known how to take a compliment. Never had many from people that I'm not related to.

"Um we could still go out you know, I mean if you wanted to?"

I ask looking anywhere but in his eyes. What if he immediately regrets what we've done? Or what if that I am like a challenge around this town? I come under the category slept with a foreigner or shagged a chubby brit?

"Lily, look at me."

Blake takes my chin forcing me to look in his eyes.

"I don't know where your mind was going just then but wherever it was I can tell it wasn't good. This is why I wanted to do things right by you, treat you the right way. Now if you're still up for it and hungry I will still take you out. Otherwise I am going to be hard again and we won't get anywhere other than the bedroom."

My cheeks heat and I feel myself clench at the thought of me and Blake in bed upstairs.

"Hell don't do that to me again darlin', or I will do as I promised. Now let's go out and get something to eat then we can spend the rest of the night in bed if you still want to by then, that sound good?"

I smile and nod.

"Yeah babe that sounds good too."

Blake leans down giving me a gentle kiss and slides out of me I whimper in protest. Missing the connection already.

"Go get cleaned up while I sort this condom out." With a quick peck on my nose he stands pulling me up with him.

I am not going to lie my back and bum are aching from having sex on the stairs. But it's so totally worth it.

I get cleaned up, touch up any make up that needs doing and head back downstairs smiling to myself. Never would I have thought I'd be lucky enough to have sex with someone like Blake, so handsome and kind. Let's just hope I am not wrong, and he turns out to be an arsehole because after my ex I don't think I could take it.

As I make it to the bottom step I notice Blake on the front porch waiting for me. I close the front door and lock up, he takes my hand and we get in his truck.

Soon we are on our way.

"So where are you taking me?" I ask looking over at Blake and I smile, then he briefly looks over at me taking my hand and kissing it then placing it on his thigh.

"Making a quick stop as I need to pick something up then we will be on our way, it's a surprise."
Soon we are pulling up outside Jeanie's diner.
"Won't be long."
Blake leans in giving me a kiss then jumps out the truck. I can't help but watch him as he walks. His fitted black shirt sleeves rolled up to his elbows, dark navy jeans that fit him perfectly showing his firm thighs and arse. Then there's his black Stetson who would have thought I'd find a man attractive that wears a cowboy hat?
I sit there waiting and soon Blake returns with a cooler and picnic blanket. He gives me a wink and I smile.
Soon we are off driving a way I am not familiar with. But I don't care as I am with Blake and he's holding my hand on top of his thigh. I can't help the happiness I am feeling right now with the butterflies in my belly. It feels good to feel this happy and carefree.

CHAPTER NINE

Blake has taken me to a beautiful spot right up on top of a ridge to watch the sunset.

Jeanie had made a delicious picnic, of sandwiches and pasta salad and even some homemade chocolate brownies, which were amazing. And Blake brought the strawberries fresh from the farm and a bottle of bubbly to drink for me and beers for him.

Sat on the picnic blanket with this view and the man sat beside me I feel like I am in a dream. Like something out of the movies.

I took a picture of the view and a selfie of Blake and I to send to my sister later.

After we've eaten Blake moves to sit behind me. So I am nestled, my back to his chest in between his legs. I let out a long sigh.

"Thank you for the most amazing date I've ever had."

Blake squeezes his arms around my chest kissing my neck.

"Glad you're enjoying it. I am only giving you the date you deserve."

I lean my neck to give him more access.

"So come on then you wanted us to talk, so Mr handsome get talking."

I feel Blake smile against my neck he gives me a teasing bite back for my sass.

"Okay darlin', well as I said you had me with that sass and wanting to make me smile. And well I've been holding back fighting my desire to take you out and to get to know you more because I kidded myself I didn't want anything to do with a relationship.

I've been screwed over by a woman before and since then I like to keep myself to myself. And well no one had even caught my attention to make me want to try again.

Well until you."

"I umm glad you caved in. what happened to put you off wanting a relationship again?" I ask.

Blake lets out a long sigh.

"She cheated on me. I didn't know she was cheating on me. She got pregnant tried to pass the baby off as mine. I was happy as a hog in mud. Until I found out about the cheating and that the baby was the other guys and then she had an abortion.

I was dumb as a box of rocks.

They were having an affair right under my fucking nose and I had no idea. Promised myself I wouldn't let any woman play me like that again. " Blake says it so coldly and matter of fact, but there's a dead sadness and bitterness there. I immediately turn and straddle his lap. Taking his face in mine. I kiss him and rest my forehead against his.

"I am so sorry that happened to you. I understand that you'd want nothing to do with a woman again. I am pretty sure I would understand if it made you hate women.

But I will say this, that stupid cows loss is my gain. And she must be really bloody stupid because why would she risk losing you for a second. You're really hot!"

Blake throws his head back laughing. I can't help but smile feeling oddly proud that I can make this beautiful man laugh.

Blake stops laughing and looks at me he runs his finger gently over my smiling lips.

"Kiss me beautiful." He demands.

I lean in and kiss him. We make out like a couple of teenagers. eventually we manage to control ourselves, as we lay down, me cuddled into Blakes side on the picnic blanket looking up at the stars.

"So come on Mr handsome what's your favourite movie?"

"Hhmm, that's a tough one it will have to be either Con Air or Die Hard. What about you?" Blake replies.

"Die Hard really?" I roll my eyes. "Is that like a must be favourite movie for all guys or some-

thing? I've never seen it."
Blake chuckles.

"I guess your right it was one me and Wes watched repeatedly. So come on what's yours? And there's no way you haven't seen Die Hard."

"Okay well I have three favourite movies, Some Like It Hot, Blues Brothers, and Con Air. I swear I haven't seen it!"

"No you're definitely lying everyone has seen Die Hard.

"I am not!" I affirm.
Blake sits up and leans over me.

"Fine, just means we will have to have another date, and I shall introduce you to all the Die Hard movies."
I laugh.
"Oh god really? I can't promise I won't fall asleep watching them."
Blake throws his head back laughing.
"Fair nuff', I shall find ways to keep you awake. What about music then any favourites?" Blake asks wiggling his eyebrows making me laugh.
"I look forward to it. And as for music I don't really have any favourites I like too many different bands or artists to have a favourite. Too much great music to like just one or two.
What about you? Country music?"
Blake smiles and winks.

"Now that is judging a book by its cover. Just because I'm Texan and wear a cowboy hat you think my favourite would be Country music. No darlin', I like lots of different types too. And here's the big secret but you can't tell anybody."

Blake turns looking over his shoulder as if to make sure no one is listening. He lean's in close to my ear and whispers

"I don't like Country music!" Blake loud whispers in my ear.

I burst out laughing.

"You're a fraud! You're a cowboy that doesn't like Country music." I say in mock horror.

Blake joins in laughing with me.

"Nah my pa didn't like Country music either. We grew up with rock music mostly maybe a bit of soul."

"Us too well my dad is a massive Guns and Roses fan. My brother is called Axel and my mum loves flowers, so my younger sister is called Daisy, and my older sister is called rose."

"It's just occurred to me Lily I don't know your last name, what is it?" Blake asks.

I grimace I hate my surname, my dad of course loves it. And according to my mum it ties us all together as a family theme.

"Fine my full name is Lily Anne Rocke."

Blake chuckles slightly.

"So I bet your dads happy that he is the rock

music?"

"Ughh yep he told us that every day, that it's in our DNA. My mum on the other hand sees it as we are all, well apart from Axel are flowers with our surname Rocke she says our family is a beautiful garden theme. They are a little nuts, but I love them."

Blake leans down kissing me tenderly. He leans back slightly, looking into my eyes. He always looks into my eyes, like he's reading into my soul or searching for something. I want to look away, but his eyes are so damn pretty I can't.

"Let's get you back. It's startin' to get cold."

I nod and help Blake load up the bits onto his truck soon we are on the way back to the farm.

Pulling up to the Merricks house, Blake parks up and walks me to the door.

He leans in kissing me tenderly, my hands start to roam from his broad chest down over his stomach, I reach the hem of his shirt and slip my hands underneath feeling the heat of his skin.

They move of their own accord feeling his hard abs.

Blake lets out a moan deep in his throat.

"Open the darn door darlin, we aint doing this here. I am guna' take my time with you."

At that promise I quickly turn and unlock the door as fast as I can, feeling Blake wrap his arm around my waist pulling me flush to his back. Feeling every hard inch pressed up against me.

Once inside I turn and start kissing Blake my hands are unbuttoning his shirt, my hands shaking from a mixture of nerves, excitement and anticipation. Blakes walking me backwards toward the stairs.

I feel the bottom step at the back of my heel and carefully step backwards still kissing Blake.

Before I know what's going on I'm being flung over Blakes shoulder in a fireman's lift and being carried up the stairs. I squeal in surprise and Blake slaps my arse.

Laughing I lean forward straight for Blakes toned arse and I bite it. I've being dying to bite that arse.

Blake throws me down on the bed and looms over me.

"Did you just bite my ass?"

Smiling and nodding in reply.

"Um yup I did."

"Right then darlin, my turn."

My eyebrows draw down questioning what he means. He's going to bite my arse?

Soon I feel his hand slip my dress up to my waist, Blake lets out a hiss.

"Jesus darlin' you aint been wearing panties this whole time? I coulda' enjoyed this out on the ridge."

He runs his finger slowly down my centre, making my hips buck wanting more.

His hand moves up over my waist lifting my dress over my head, so I'm soon just led in my red lace bra.

Blake leans over kissing me and removes my bra. I'm completely bare to him. Blake leans back looking at me taking in every inch of my body.

I instinctively place my hands over my stomach. I feel exposed and vulnerable to him. I don't want this beautiful man seeing my most hated parts of my body. In my previous relationship I'd usually cover it somehow during sex.

Blake notices straight away and places his big hand over mine on my stomach.

"Don't do that darlin', you don't ever have to be embarrassed about any part of your body in front of me. Do you understand?"

I watch as Blake leans down moving my hands to either side of my body and he kisses my stomach.

"Beautiful."

Blake looks at me in the eyes as he moves kissing me lower on my stomach.

"Fucking perfect."

Never loosing eye contact with me he moves lower again just above my bikini line I suck in a breath at the feel of his mouth and his words.

"Fucking gorgeous."

With that his mouth hits my centre. I cry out and my hips buck at the sudden feel of him there. He kisses all over my sensitive spots. I feel him pushing my legs wider apart completely exposing all to him. He doesn't give me long to think about it before his mouth is on me licking and sucking.

I grab hold of the sheets, moaning enjoying the feel of him there.

He slowly slides in a finger while his mouth continues, my hips buck wildly as he curls his finger up reaching the perfect spot.

With his tongue and his finger I am soon falling apart.

"Shit, Blake I'm going to come!"

All this does is make Blake hum in approval. I am falling over the edge in an amazing orgasm. Blake moves his finger and is slowly licking, tasting all that is me.

Slowly he kisses his way up my body, taking my sensitive nipple in his mouth.

"Taste so sweet darlin'." Blake hums in approval.

"wow, that was just wow." I sigh, smiling.

"It's just the beginning darlin', now kiss me."

I lean up to kiss him, pushing up so I am sitting, Blake is standing in front of me, his shirt undone hanging open stood there in just his jeans.

God he's perfect. Butterflies swarm my stomach. I swallow down my nerves.

Looking up at him I lean forward and place a gentle kiss just above his jeans. I slowly undo his belt and jeans still kissing his lower stomach, pushing his jeans down to his thighs, leaving him in just a pair of fitted boxers. I can see his hard length bulging its almost teasing me, I lick my lips.

Reaching forward I kiss down that beautiful trail

of hair men have, slowly pulling down his boxers as I go.

His hard length springs free and I slowly curl my hand around the base gently stroking.

Slowly I lower my mouth and take in the tip, swirling my tongue.

Blake lets out a deep moan of appreciation that only spurs me on more.

I take him further into my mouth sucking and swirling my tongue.

Blake holds the back of my head as I take as much of him as I can.

I find myself getting wet and moaning enjoying having this power to make him loose control.

Blake moans gripping my hair tighter.

"Christ darlin' I am guna' come in that mouth of yours if you don't stop."

Wanting exactly that, I carry on until I feel him pulse in my mouth, his hand gripping the back of my head tightens. Watching as Blake moans leaning his head back and I feel him spill down my throat and I swallow every last drop.

Blake moves us up further on top of the bed, where we kiss, and Blake starts kissing me all over, he's already hard again. I can't help but be impressed.

"Thought you might need a few more minutes."

"Not with you darlin', I can't get enough of you."

Blake leans over to reach for his jean pocket for a condom.

"I am on the pill Blake, and um well, if you're you

know err good. I haven't been with anyone in a really long time, you don't have to if you don't want to that is -."

Blake puts his hand over my mouth stopping my babbling.

"Darlin'." Blake groans.

Blake without warning he fills me. I hold my breath waiting for my body to accommodate to him.

" God damn darlin you feel fucking amazing. Like you were made for me. Breathe darlin'."

Blake stops all movement until I'm ready. I rock my hips and moan.

Blake starts takes over and moves slowly taking his time.

He takes my nipple in his mouth and I feel myself start to build.

I moan lifting my hips.

"Come for me darlin, let me feel you."

Blake still moving, he slowly takes my nipple in his mouth and grabs under my arse tilting me hitting that perfect spot.

"Oh god!"

I shatter, feeling myself tightening around him. Blake kissing me groans feeling it too.

Blake brings up my legs wrapping them around his waist making him feel deeper, his thumb circles over my clit making me jolt from how sensitive it is.

Blake picks up his speed pounding into me repeatedly his thumb still moving over my clit. I can feel myself building for another orgasm.

"Oh god Blake"

"Come for me again darlin."

Blake moves his hand from my clit to my breast slightly pinching my nipple, as he leans forward still pounding into me our skin slapping at the sound, he gently bites my neck. I'm calling out his name coming so hard, like I've never felt before.

Blake lets out what sounds like a manly roar, he spills himself deep inside me.

I take his weight as he leans on me both of us trying to control our breathing.

Blake rolls to his side taking me with him, staying connected.

Blake kisses my head I'm already falling asleep smiling to myself.

I've never felt so happy and relaxed. And that scares me. One date and this man already holds the power to hurt me.

"you feeling okay darlin'?" Blake asks.

Blake asks rolling me to my back leaning over me looking into my eyes.

I smile.

Never felt better, I don't want this night to end and well um I hope it was okay for you?" I ask nervously.

"Are you kidding me? That was incredible why would you think different?"

"Well my ex, he said I wasn't very good at it, being a lover that is." I say looking down at my hands.

Blakes pauses for a minute, then leans in kissing me.

His hips start moving, I can feel he's hard again.

"You feel that darlin'?" Blake breathes.

All I can do is nod in response.

"I cant get enough of you, your ex was a fuckin' idiot. And Darlin' the night isn't ending yet."

He's right, it didn't. Blake made love to me again until my mind and body was too exhausted to think or move. I fell into the most blissful sleep.

CHAPTER TEN

The next morning I'm woken to kisses trailing up my back.
"Mmm morning." I say sleepily with my eyes still closed.
"Mornin darlin, tell me about these tattoo's."
Blake kisses down my back until he's reaching the curve of my behind.
I smile lazily enjoying being woken up this way.
"Huh?" I ask confused and still half asleep. Blake chuckles.
"Tell me about your tattoo's darlin', damn your sweet when your sleepy."
Blake bites my arse cheek. Causing me to jolt.
"This one the devil, tell me about it."
"That's my naughty little devil, it was a dare from my sister Rose to get a trashy tattoo. So I chose a naughty little devil bending over saying spank that."
I feel Blake run his fingers over the outline of another one of my tattoo's that's on my hip.
"What about this one?"
"That's a rose for Rose, a daisy for Daisy, a Lily for me. All wrapped around a rifle which repre-

Rise Above

sents my brother Ax who's in the army. It's silly really he's the baby of the family so us three have always looked out for him growing up, we still do now. And of course we worry about him a lot while he's in the army."

Blake places a kiss on the tattoo.

He rolls me so I'm led on my back and I know the one tattoo he's going to ask me about. My first tattoo I ever got and it's on my right rib cage.

"What about this one?

Taking a deep breath I blink back the wetness in my eye's, I struggle to talk about Cameron without getting upset. Even if it was 17 years ago.

"It's um for Cameron, my best friend when I was younger, he passed away."

Blake squeezes my hip gently, while I focus on the ceiling.

"Darlin' you don't have to tell me anymore it's okay." He soothes.

"It's fine Blake, you'll find out eventually anyway."

I concentrate on a spot on the ceiling and continue.

"Cameron lost both his parents in an armed robbery while they were abroad, he was staying at his nans at the time.

He didn't handle their death at all. We thought he was getting a little bit better, he started to smile more and slowly began getting back to himself. Or so we thought.

I went to call for him one day and his nan said he

was out in the garage. He liked to tinker on his dads old Harley.
I went to the garage and he was there hanging, by his belt. I screamed and I screamed over and over. I tried lifting him, but it was no use he was too heavy. His nan came in and rushed over to him, both of us lifting him together but it was useless he was already dead."
I have tears streaming down my face. My eyes blurred I can't see through them.
Blake cups my face kissing my tears away.
"Darlin, I'm so sorry you had to go through that, how long a go did this happen?"
"17 years ago, I was eleven and so was Cameron, we were best friends, Inseparable. He needed me and I let him down. Your supposed to go to your best friend when no one else will listen or help you. I failed massively. I should have made sure he was okay, I should have been there for him. He needed someone and I wasn't there."
I can't control my tears, the pain still feels as strong and raw as it did the day I found him.
Blake moves quickly grabbing and wrapping me in his arms, stroking my hair. I slowly ease up crying, Blake soothing me and being wrapped in his arms makes me feel safe.
"I'm sorry, it's just something that I've found has never gotten easier and it's a guilt I live with every day." I admit.

"What in the hell have you got to feel guilty

about? You were a kid, it was not your fault, not ever. He kept them demons locked in tight darlin'. It sounds like he didn't want to let anyone in.

He didn't have the right professional help, they failed an eleven year old boy! not you! Not his poor family they were dealing with their own grief too. You are never at fault do you understand me? You were probably the only light in his life at that time. It's just that he couldn't handle the darkness that he was living in. The pain of losing his parents."

Blake wipes my tears away his eyes caring, making sure that I am truly okay.

"My family say the same, but I can't help feel what I feel. Friends tell each other everything. Maybe he tried but I didn't listen hard enough, it's something I will never know."

I trace the outline of the tattoo with my fingers.

Clearing my throat I continue to tell Blake about my tattoo.

"Anyway his dad owned a Harley, Cameron loved it, said he want to be a proper biker when he was older.

So I got his dad's Harley tattooed in the clouds and had them surround it with vines with Lily's. Representing me obviously, showing I will never leave his side. And the words broken hearted, ride free, be free, love you always. Because when I was little I said he was going to be my husband when I grew up. And we were going to start our own biker club, with the words ride free, be free on the patch."

I shrug smiling at the memory. We were naive believing we could take on the world and do anything.

Blake kisses my forehead, not releasing me and keeping his arms still wrapped around me.

"Again darlin' I am sorry you had to experience that, especially as a child. I am sure Cameron is at peace now and he's with his folks, it's where he wanted to be. It's good you had your family around you, looking out for you." Blake says his voice soft and caring.

"I grew up pretty quick from that moment, it made me more into looking out for my family. Never being far from them just in case one of them needed me. Drove my family potty. This is the furthest I've been away from them and the longest too."

Blake rolls over me, stroking my hair.

"Is that why you try to contact them as much as you can while you've been here?" I nod.

"Darlin' you've only been here a couple of weeks, I'm sure your family just want you to relax and enjoy yourself."

I nod again because that's exactly what my family want for me, but I still need to contact them to touch base. Make sure they are all okay.

I am surprised at how much Blake has paid attention to me and what I do when I thought he wasn't interested. I have never told anyone that much about myself before. Sure I've told people about Cameron, but never about my insecurities. I just keep up pretences that I am all okay. But I get the impression if I was to try that with Blake he would see right through my bullshit. He already seems to know how I tick and what runs through my mind without me even telling him. I feel exposed.

"Come on darlin' let's go get you something for breakfast then I have to head home and get to work."

Blake leans down kissing me it turns hot and heavy, fast.

"How about a shower before breakfast?"

I ask biting my lip.

Blake doesn't even answer he just picks me up over his shoulder.

"I have legs you know? You don't have to go all cave man and carry me."

With that Blake slaps my arse and proceeds into the shower.

That morning I found out that I really liked showers with Blake, and I wouldn't mind starting every day like that.

CHAPTER ELEVEN

The next week goes by slowly, Blake had to go away for some work thing the following day. I spent it with my head stuck into my work writing for my next article, hanging out with Louisa and Sam. I had sent Rose the photo of me and Blake. She had in her word's 'had an on the spot orgasm just looking at him. And that if I haven't already rode that cowboy like red rum she was jumping on the next flight to do just that.'

Clearly Rose was going through a long dry spell, hopefully she would resolve that situation soon for the goodness of mankind. Goodness knows what she would behave like if she came here to visit.

Three days after Blake left for work, Evelynn and Suellen had messaged saying about meeting for lunch later that day. So I had something to do outside of the house instead of hiding away at the farm.

I could do with some laughs, I was slightly sulking missing Blake. And weirdly confused at why I was missing him so much when really we barely knew each other and only been on one date.

Evelynn picked me up with Suellen meeting us at Jeanie's as she was working, and this was her lunch break.

Sat in the booth having just ordered. Evelynn and Suellen turn both their attention on me.

"Come on spill those beans are you and Blake an item?" Evelynn asks smiling. I can't help but smile back.

"I wouldn't say an item, we've spent some time together and he took me on a date, then he had to go away for some work thing and that's it. Nothing more to tell." I shrug.

"Yep you're full of shit right there, burning daylight, now get to the good stuff." Suellen demands.

Evelynn nods enthusiastically. I laugh at the pair of them.

"Fine but I'm not going into details. But I will say he stayed over, and it was amazing, we talked a lot as well as other things. It feels like I've known him longer which sounds like a cliché. But I am normally quiet and shy around guys and withhold who I am. But with Blake it's different I can relax and be me. He makes me feel good about myself. He's listened and comforted me when I told him about something bad that had happened to me when I was younger. I can honestly say I don't know if I've ever felt a connection like I do with Blake and it scares the shit out of me." I say biting down on my nail and smiling.

"That's what we wanted to hear. Blake deserves a slice of happiness too, we're pleased for you. You have no reason to feel scared just roll with it and enjoy yourself. But on a serious note, out of 10 how good was he in the bedroom department?" Evelynn asks.

"I'd say way beyond ten out of ten. Best I've ever had, I know that." I reply smiling.

"That is sweeter than stolen honey what you're feelin' right there.
Now where's my damn lunch I'm hungry."
I smile big learning that Suellen comes out with the best saying's I've ever heard. And knowing that in the short time I've been here I've made two really good friends.
We are tucking into our lunch when Jeanie come's over to our table.
"Y'all enjoying your food?" Jeanie asks.
We all nod smiling with mouthfuls of food.
 "And just to say honey I couldn't be happier That Blake stopped dilly dallying around and took you out. We all could see it, it was just a matter of time."
I pause look up at Jeanie and see her kind eyes smiling back at me.
"Uhh thanks Jeanie, maybe we can get one of those picnics from you again for when Blake

comes back from being away with work. The food was delicious."

I smile and I watch Jeanie's smile fade.

"Blakes away with work? Are you sure honey?" Jeanie asks.

It's my smile that falls from my face this time I nod in response. I look at Evelynn and Suellen to see they both have stopped eating and are looking between me and Jeanie.

"Why have you seen Blake?" I ask. Dread creeping in.

"Uh-huh, he comes in every morning early for his breakfast. He's here on the dot 6am. He's the only one here that early. Been the same most days."

My stomach drops. Why would he lie to me? Maybe I came on to strong. I should have kept my mouth shut when he asked about Cameron's tattoo. No one likes a crying broken woman.

"Um thanks' for the delicious lunch Jeanie, I have to get going. My article won't write itself."

I shove some dollar bills on the table and get out of that diner as quick as possible.

I walk the long walk back to the farm needing the alone time.

I send Evelynn a quick text apologising then switch my phone off.

I've done it again, I've made a fool out of myself thinking that he felt the connection too. God I am a bloody idiot. The more I think about it the more I realise he didn't really say much about his life. Apart from knowing that his ex-screwed him over I know nothing about him.

He didn't say what the work thing was that he had to go away for. Come to think of it what would he be doing going away for work when he owns the Den? Not only that, he never spoke of his childhood, where he lives. Nothing.

Only thing I do know is his favourite movies and that he doesn't like Country music.

I get back to the farm, pour myself a wine and sit on the back decking. Looking out at the afternoon sun, I let a few tears run. Berating myself for letting myself get to attached too soon.

I switch my phone back on and see that Evelynn had messaged asking if I was okay, and did her and Suellen need to go and kick Blakes ass? That message makes me smile. I text back and assure them that I'm fine, and that I probably just read the situation between me and Blake wrong, but all was fine. There was also a text from Louisa reminding me of her baby shower. It's the last thing I want to go to. But I reply letting her know I will be there.

I am not fine at all, it hurt's that Blake has lied to me, it's hurt that I had been so open with him, that I really didn't know him at all. I have never opened up to anyone like that before, never trusted someone that wasn't my family like that before.

I haven't realised I've been sat out here for over two hours when my phone alerts me to a new message. I pick it up and see its from Blake it reads;

hey beautiful, I should be finished with work tomorrow. Will swing by at 6pm to pick you up and take you out for dinner.

I immediately reply feeling the hurt and the anger building in me.

Don't bother I have Louisa's baby shower, not sure when I will be back and have my article that needs to be finished.

My phone alerts me instantly with Blakes reply.

Okay, I will come over to you after. Around 9.

Groaning I type my reply quickly, wishing he would just take it and leave me alone. I don't want to make things ugly between us as it's a small town and I've already made a fool out of myself, I don't want to do it again.

No it's okay, I will just catch up with you some other time. I need to get my work done. See you around.

I don't know if I get a reply after that I switch my phone off. I get up and I make myself just a sandwich for my dinner not hungry and barely touching it.

Soon the sun goes down, so I decide to crawl into bed for an early night.

I lock up and climb into bed, I wait for sleep to take over. Nothing.

I lie there and all I can think about is Blake. I let out a few tears.

Telling myself I'm stupid I barely know the bloody guy, it's ridiculous that I am as upset as I am. All it could ever be was a holiday fling anyway. At some point I have to go back home, so it's probably for the best.

Curling up, I snuggle down, eventually sleep takes hold of me and I fall into a restless night's sleep.

I awake to a loud crashing sound, I sit up straight listening to see if it was in my dream, its then I hear the floorboards creek outside my room. I quickly grab my phone and pull the cover over me, just peering out slightly. I dial 999 it takes my brain a second to kick in that I'm not in the UK anymore. So I quickly redial 911.

"911 what's your emergency?"

"There's someone in the house, outside my bedroom door, I am in Mufftown at the Merricks farm house. My name is Lily. Please hurry I am on my own." I whisper my heart is beating so fast I feel like it's about to jump out of my chest.

"Okay ma'am a unit is on its way to you, stay on

the line until they arrive."
As the operator finishes talking I see the handle on my door slowly begin to turn.

"Oh shit, oh shit! They are coming into my room. Please hurry!"
I shove the phone under my pillow before the operator can reply. I keep the cover up high, nearly covering most of my face and I close my eyes trying my hardest to steady my breathing and pretend to be asleep. If I'm asleep hopefully they will just come and take whatever it is they want and bugger off without killing me.

I hear the door open slowly, I am praying the darkness will hide the fact that I am not fast asleep.

I hear the footsteps slowly enter the room, I can hear draws being opened and rummaging around.

Its taking everything in me not to scream, this is America after all, and everyone seems to have a gun. In the UK it would be a knife, I can scream and make a run for it with a knife, I can't out run a bullet.

I hear the footsteps come closer to me, I hear them grabbing stuff off my nightstand right next to where I am pretending to be asleep.

Keep calm Lily just slow your breathing keep calm. I slowly open my eye that's closest to the pillow, so they can't see I am awake and all I can see is a bottom half of a man in dark clothing.

The body turns towards me, I quickly shut my eye.

I can feel him leaning over me, his breath near my ear.

I can't control my breathing in the panic that's taking over my body.

I feel him sniff my hair. Then I feel his hand lightly run down from my shoulder to the curve of my behind.

By this point I've got my eyes squeezed shut and I am completely frozen in place my breathing is erratic. He must know I am awake.

Please god where are the police. I pray in my head over and over.

The stranger moves his hand slowly round to my waist. His other hand lifting the covers. I am shaking now he definitely knows I am wide awake. I can feel the tears run down my face. His hand touches my knee, it continues running up my thigh. I let out a whimper and scream crying out for him to stop. Fear taking over, I clench my legs tightly together hoping to stop this monster getting anywhere near me. I feel his hand tighten hard on my thigh, squeezing so hard I know it will leave marks.

I can feel him breathing in my ear.

"stop." I say my voice barely a whisper.

"I know your awake, I'm really guna enjoy this and your guna let me or I will kill you, understand?" He threatens.

Rise Above

I nod tears streaming down my face.

"Please don't, please."

My begging only seems to encourage him more, he bites my neck hard, I cry out from the pain as he rips my legs apart.

I scream, I kick out trying to get him off me. He's so heavy pinning me down with his full weight. I can feel him unzipping his trousers.

I don't give up fighting, I try scratching at his face, but its then I realise he is wearing a balaclava, so I can't even see his face.

I try kicking but it's no use, I scream but I know there's nobody, no neighbours for a good two miles or more. I am alone, no one can help me. My only hope is the police getting here before he can do anything.

I am beyond thankful I can hear sirens approaching, he pauses hearing them too. Leaning down he whispers.

"Until next time, this is for calling the cops." He sneers.

He then rears back and hits me right across the face. I can't protect myself as he has my arms pinned. He hits me at least three more times before I black out.

I don't remember anything after that just me waking up in a hospital bed. I can barely open one of my eyes it feel so swollen. My mouth is so dry. I see a nurse looking at my chart at the end of the bed.

"N-urse." I croak.
The nurse looks up and rushes to me.
"Hey there, you thirsty?"
I nod and try and smile but it hurts to much, so I stop.
The nurse brings a cup with a straw to my lips and I take a long drink enjoying the feel of the cold liquid down my throat.
"There that will help. Listen sweetie is there any relatives or friends we can call for you?" she asks.

"Umm no I'm not from around here, I am staying in mufftown at the Merricks place, but they are away." The nurse smiles a sympathetic smile at me.

"Okay well do you have anyone that we could contact for you? The sheriff brought your phone in with you, we have it in a locker safely kept away."

" Um I don't really know anyone, um Evelynn I guess, she's in my contacts on my phone. Maybe she could come and get me." I shrug.
The nurse gently squeezes my hand.
"Let me go get the doctor and I will contact your friend, while the doctor runs through a few things with you okay?"
I nod tears filling my eyes. I try and blink them away but it's too painful, so I just let them fall.
The kind nurse holds my hand comforting me.
"It will all be okay. We will make sure of it."

Rise Above

With that she turns and leaves. Nature calls so I get up and go to the bathroom. I take care of business, as I go to stand I feel pain and stiff at the top of my legs. I look down lifting the hospital gown up a little to see bruising where he'd gripped and squeezed my legs open. Bile rises in my throat and I quickly turn emptying the contents of my stomach. I go to the sink and cup water drinking it and swilling out my mouth. I wash my hands, I noticed bruising on my wrists too where he had me pinned. It is then I look up into the mirror and see my face.

My right eye is completely swollen shut, black and blue bruises all over it. My left eye is also black and blue but at least I can open it.

There is bruising on my nose too. It's then I notice the mark on my neck. I turn my head to get a better look, I can see dried blood and teeth marks where he'd bit me.

Tears fill my eyes as I take in all what he has done to me. The only thing I am thankful for is that the police turned up when they did.

I walk back into the room and see a middle aged man reading my chart. I stop immediately, he looks up from my chart. And offers a kind smile.

"Hello Lily, I'm Dr Brenan you're in Sampson town hospital. Which is two towns away from Mufftown. Now your suffering from a little concussion, you have no broken bones. It's all just bruising which will go down eventually."

I nod for him to continue.

"Now do you have someone who could stay with you over the next 24 hours to keep an eye on you?" The doctor asks?

"I uhh just have the nurse calling my friend now."

"Great now I have to ask did he force himself on you in any way?"
I shake my head in response.
"Good, right I shall leave you to rest until your friend comes we will need your insurance details or a cheque if you don't have any. And the nurse will be back shortly when your friend arrives."
With that he turns and leaves the room. I sit on the bed staring out the window.

There's a knock at the door a few moments later, I jump startled. Slowly it opens and in walks the Sheriff.
"Hello there ma'am I'm Sheriff Johnson, do you mind If I ask you a coupla' questions?"
"No that's fine."
He pulls out his notebook, he's an older guy with a small pot belly.
"So ma'am did you happen to get a look at the guy?" Sheriff Johnson ask's not looking up from his notebook.
"No he was in a balaclava."
The sheriff nods and jots down my answer.

"Did you recognise his voice, did he say anything that might help us find him?"

Tears feel my eyes, as I shake my head.

"No, he just said until next time. I didn't recognise his voice."

I sniff, carefully wiping my face.

Sheriff nods puts away his notebook.

"He got away before we could catch him, we've checked for prints but we're guessing he was wearing gloves couldn't find nuthin'. He smashed the back window we boarded it up for you until the Merricks get back and can replace it."

I nod as the sheriff continues.

"I don't think it was a planned attack I think it was a burglary that he took his chance with a beautiful woman. Highly unlikely he will return.

My deputy will be round tomorrow morning if you notice any belonging's missing report it to him." With that he nods lifting his Stetson slightly and leaves the room.

I stare at the back of the door, not believing how cold the sheriff was and how matter of fact he was. No reassurance of we will catch him, no comfort, not a single apology of I'm sorry you've been treated this way in our little town.

I really want to go home. Maybe if I video call my boss he will feel guilty and let me go home?

It is crazy that I feel safer in a huge city which will have a bigger crime rate compared to a small town in Texas.

Sighing I shuffle to the arm chair next to the bed. And sit and wait for Evelynn to turn up staring out of the small window, planning on calling my boss or at least emailing him pictures of my face and getting him to send me home. If I didn't need the money I'd tell him to stick his job and get on the next bloody flight out of here. I'm sure he will let me go home.

I can stay in touch with Evelynn, Louisa and Suellen. As for Blake, well he will become a memory of a brief but good for the most part holiday type romance.

I don't know how long I am sat there, planning my escape back home. But the door opens and in comes the nice nurse from earlier.

"I got hold of your friend, she was out at a bar and was over the legal limit to drive so she's getting a lift to come and get you. That was a good forty minutes or so ago so I would imagine they will be here by 2 am."

The nurse says looking at her watch. I look up at the wall for the clock and sure enough its 1:30 am.

"Oh I didn't realise it was the middle of the night. I've not really been paying much attention. How long have I been in here then?" I ask confused.

"You came in around 11:30pm."

"Oh, I went to bed early, had a bit of a crappy day. And well it obviously didn't get any better."

The nurse's kind eyes give me a warm smile.
Suddenly we can hear a commotion outside the door. The door burst open and Wes is stood there with another nurse holding on to his arm.
"sorry Sandy I tried to stop him as he's not family, but he wouldn't listen." The other nurse says angrily.

"No worries Linda, I think this is the lift for our patient anyway."
 The nurse who I now know is called Sandy says with a smile.

" I will just go get your meds sorted for you to take home and give you guys a minute."
with that Wes walks into the room right up to me ignoring nurse sandy leaving the room.

"Fuckin Christ Lil'!"
He cups my face, looking at my wounds. His face becomes angry and his jaw set.
"Who the fuck did this to you Lily?"
I shrug, looking down at my hands fighting the tears that are building because I know once the dam breaks I won't stop and I sure as hell don't want to break down here in hospital in front of Wes.
I turn and look out the window, at nothing because its pitch black. how did I not realise it was the middle of the night?
"Jesus fuckin Christ Lily what the fuck did he do?"

Wes gently runs his finger over the bite mark on my neck, I hiss in pain even the light touch hurting Wes quickly pull's his hand away and he goes to put his hands over mine which is when he notices the bruises on my wrists too.

Wes jumps up stepping back running both hands through his hair gripping it tightly. He looks beyond mad now.

"Wes it's okay , he .."

I swallow the tears as Wes need to know that I'm okay , I don't want him doing anything stupid or getting into trouble for me.

Taking a deep breath I try again.

"He didn't , he didn't get that far. I heard him breaking in I rang the police, he just roughed me up a bit that's all." I say on a shrug, like I'm totally fine. Wes looks at me like I'm full of shit, but thankfully doesn't ask me any more questions.

Nurse Sandy knock's at the door, she sticks her head in and says

"Your friend Evelynn is just outside is she okay to come in?"

I nod. And the door gets pushed open with force Evelynn storms in.

"Hell boy you took off running like a damn race horse, leaving me to find my way around this darn hospital. Your truck is still out front, I aint moving it. So if you don't get your ass out there and move it. It'll get towed. Plus I need to help

Lily get dressed. So go on and I'll bring her down you get the truck ready."

Wes looks like he wants to argue back with Evelynn but she just raise's an eyebrow daring him too. I giggle. Thankful for Evelynn making the situation less tense and more normal.

Wes lets out a long sigh. And nods.

"Fine I will be waiting out front with the truck I will meet you down there. If you need me call me."

Wes walks over kissing the top of my head.

And quickly leaves the room.

"You have a very good boyfriend there obviously cares a lot about you." Nurse sandy says stripping my bed.

"Oh that aint her boyfriend honey, that's the brother of the guy she's seeing."

Nurse sandy looks over at me, I nod.

"Well not really seeing his brother either. Think I might keep clear of men for a while."

Both Evelynn and nurse Sandy share a look and keep quiet.

Evelynn hands me my bag of clothes to change into thankfully it's my comfy clothes. Long vest top and black stretchy leggings I pile my hair up loosely on my head and walk out of the bathroom. I slip on my flip flops, as nurse Sandy tells me my dosage for my painkillers and I take a couple now, so they kick in for when I go to sleep.

I sign the forms and thank her for her care.
Evelynn and I get the elevator down to the ground floor.
"I'm sorry I ruined your night, and thanks for coming to get me." I apologise.
"Oh shut up honey don't talk crazy, of course you haven't ruined my night. You sure you're okay though?" Evelynn asks concern in her voice.
I nod and swallow the lump in my throat. Not yet tears.
We walk out of the entrance and find Wes stood leaning on his truck looking angry talking on his phone.
"Yeah okay, got it ,call you later."

I smile up at Wes as much as my face will let me.
"Thanks for coming out all this way to get me. I appreciate it."
Wes guides me to the front passenger seat and helps me in, Evelynn hops in the back and I rest my head on the window. Feeling so drained I just want to crawl into bed. But maybe not the bed where I'm staying, I don't think I could face going back there right now.
"Um Wes could you drop me at the nearest hotel? I don't think I'm up to staying at the Merricks just yet." I plead.

"I'm not taking you to a god damn hotel and there is no way I'd let you stay at the Merricks place with what's happened darlin'. Don't worry

I will stay with you." Wes states.

I let out a long breath that I didn't realise I was holding and feel myself relax a little.

"Thanks' Wes. And thanks' Evelynn I don't know what I would have done without you guys tonight." I say on a yawn.

I rest my head against the window and drift off to sleep. Soon I feel myself being lifted. Panic hits me and I wake, I let out a scream and struggle against the arms that hold me.

"Shhhh Lily it's okay it's me, Wes, calm down darlin, its only me, deep breaths." Wes reassures.

I grip Wes's t-shirt with my hands tightly. Taking in deep breaths trying to calm myself down.

"I'm sorry Wes."

"Don't be sorry darlin, I should of woke you, but I didn't want to disturb you."

Wes carries me into a large ranch like house. Wes puts me on my feet in the entrance way and switches on the lights.

"Thanks' for letting me stay Wes."

"No problem let me show you to where you'll be sleeping."

I follow Wes up the stairs he opens the door to a bedroom and flicks on the lights.

The room is huge and decorated with a blue/grey colour on the walls and deep dark wood furniture. It's a manly bedroom. Not a guest bedroom.

"Is this your room?" I ask.

Wes walks in closing the curtains. And switching on the bedside lamps.

"No darlin this is Blakes room, I don't think he'd be so happy if I had you in my bed." Wes says with a wink.

"Umm Wes I don't want to be rude, but I don't feel comfortable sleeping in here."

Wes stops and looks at me, raising his eyebrow in question. Luckily he doesn't press any further. Just nods and walks past me and down the hall.

"This is the guest bedroom, the bathroom is just across the hall, are you sure you're okay in here?" I nod.

"Thanks' Wes this is great. Sorry to ask but I don't have any clothes with me is there something I could borrow to wear to bed?"

Wes nods disappearing and coming back with a t shirt.

"It's Blakes he won't mind I will be sleeping across the hall and I will set my alarm for every couple of hours to come check on you, what with your concussion and all."

I give Wes a hug thank him and go to the bathroom and get changed into the t-shirt Wes gave me. Its big but just comes to the bottom of my behind. Good job I've got my cotton French shorts on and not my lace ones today.

I walk across the hallway and into my room for the night.

Rise Above

I close the door and walk to the bed and climb in. I switch off the lamp, panic kicks in as soon as the room fills with darkness. I quickly switch the lamp back on again. I turn facing away from the door and curl my knees to my chest. Unable to hold back the tears anymore I let them fall.

I cry and let out the violent sobs rack my body. The nights events replaying in my mind, the thought of what nearly happened, his breath in my ear. I feel so alone, so helpless.

I'm so consumed in my pain I don't hear someone come in, I feel the bed dip and I immediately scream and lash out. Strong arms circle me holding me tightly.

"Shhhh baby shh it's Blake it's guna be okay. I've got you. No one is guna hurt you, I promise."

Blake turns me so I'm facing his chest, I continue to cry while Blake just holds me and strokes my hair. Eventually I cry myself to sleep in Blakes arms.

My dreams plague me, he's there in my dream's, he's got me tied down I can't move no matter how much I try. I scream for help, but no one comes.

I awake suddenly on a scream, I'm covered in cold sweat and I'm panting like I've just run a marathon. I sit up, my hand on my chest trying to calm myself down. I turn and see the beds empty.

The bedroom door bursts open, I jump a mile

and scream.
"Shit darlin', I'm sorry I didn't mean to scare you. I was downstairs having a coffee and heard you screaming. You had a bad dream?"
Still breathing heavily I nod.

Blake climbs into bed and pulls me to him. Cradling me in his arms wiping my damp hair from my face. Why is it I feel so safe with Blake? The only other time I've felt this safe is with Ax or my dad.
"Come on darlin', let's get you in the shower."
I nod against his chest.
Blake takes my hand and leads me down the hall into his bedroom. I hesitate and Blake notices.
"It's okay darlin', the shower in my on suite is better that's all."

We carry on through to his amazing on-suite bathroom with a beautiful walk in shower with a huge shower head. It looks heavenly.
Blake switches on the shower and pulls off his t-shirt, leaving him in just some low sitting black sweat pants.
Even in my unstable emotional state I still admire how bloody perfect his body is.
Blake turns to me and walks towards me. Cupping my face, I can see the emotions in his eyes, the anger he's holding back.
He reaches for the hem of the t-shirt and slowly lifts it over my head.
I'm standing in front of him in just my knickers.

He gently grips my chin and moves my hair away from my neck, he leans forward and kisses over where I was bitten.

He crouches down and pulls down my knickers. I feel his hand gently trace the bruising on my thigh.

I keep my eyes focused on the wall, blocking out my emotions.

Blake leads me to the shower, I step in and soon feel Blake behind me. He reaches for the shower gel and lathers up his hands and he washes my body gently. The shower gel smells of him, the smell calms me. He also carefully washes my hair.

Blake kisses my shoulder in feather like kisses.

"Come on darlin let's get you dried and fed. You need to eat, and you need more pain meds."

I nod and follow Blake out of the shower. He wraps me in a big fluffy towel. And gently kisses me on the lips.

I try and keep the tears in, but one slips out, Blake catches it with his thumb.

"Blake, thank you for helping me and being so caring, it's really meant a lot. And I know you just wanted rid of me and I've been thrown back at you through this. But I didn't ask for you I asked for Evelynn, and she brought Wes. Please don't feel obligated. I will soon be out of your hair and back to the Merricks. I just don't feel safe right now." I rasp holding back my tears. I look up at Blake, as best as I can with one eye,

he's still holding my face looking confused.
"What do you mean I wanted rid of you?"
I retell him what Jeanie had said.
"I went for lunch with Evelynn and Suellen at Jeanie's diner, and well she said that you've been in as normal having your breakfast. You told me you were working away. I was pissed off at first and a little hurt, but I realise we hardly know each other and its okay I get it. I will at some point be going back to England. So I get why you wouldn't want to start anything with me." I say calmly trying to keep the emotion out of my voice. but what I am inside is anything but calm. Inside it still hurts but I won't admit that.

"Darlin' listen to me I was working a couple of towns over. It is something I can't talk about to you as it is confidential. But I will say it was a little dangerous, that's why I told you I was working away to keep you safe." He states.

"So you don't want rid of me and that wasn't just an excuse?"
I ask hopeful, looking into his eyes to see if he's telling the truth.
Blake pulls me to him, arms circling my waist.

"Not ever could I want rid of you."
Relief runs through me, but there's still some doubt there for me. With what's happened to me. Its forcing my hand into trusting Blake, probably a lot quicker than I normally would.

And if I'm honest I could do without any more added drama, so all I can do is take his word for it and I really hope he doesn't break my heart.

"Blake I thought you were the owner of the den with Wes, how is that dangerous?" I ask because I know he can't tell me what it is that he's been called away for, but it just doesn't make any sense.

"Come on let's get some breakfast and we will talk, it's a long old story. Now my main priority is making sure you're okay."

I nod and Blake kisses the top of my head.

Blake changes in his room while I go to put my clothes on that I came home from the hospital in.

Blake comes for me when he's done, I'm just about to put my top on when Blake comes over taking it from me and helping me put it on.

"Um Blake I can get dressed you know, it's only my face that's busted nothing else." I assure him.

"Please, just let me help you." Blake pleads.

There's something in his voice that's vulnerable. I nod and Blake gives me a gentle kiss on the lips.

"I swear to god darlin', when I find the piece of shit that did this to you I'm guna kill him."

I don't doubt his words, the emotion behind them, the promise they hold. It scares me, not because I don't want the bastard to get hurt but because I don't want Blake hurt or even in trouble for me.

"Please don't do anything stupid for me, I'd rather have you with me than in prison because of me." I beg.
Blake chuckles like what I said was a joke.
"Blake! I'm serious don't go getting yourself into trouble."

"Darlin' that aint guna happen, I'm not stupid."
His reply doesn't feed me with much confidence.
No one is bigger than the law.
Blake leads me down to his kitchen where Wes is cooking away at the stove.
"Morning Wes."
Wes turns to me, his beautiful smile slipping just a little when he sees my face. I let go of Blakes hand and walk over to Wes.
He stops what he's doing and turns to me.
I wrap my arms around him and lean against his chest.

"Wes I'm okay, I promise. It's just some bruises."
Wes puts his arms around me and kisses the top of my head.

"Seriously beautiful I'm supposed to be telling you it's all going to be okay not the other way around."
I smile and look up at him.
"I'm going to be fine, I have Blake and you watching over me, you guys make me feel safe." I smile.
"Now breakfast smells amazing what are you making me?"

I hear Blake chuckle in the background and Wes smiles down at me.

Job done, I have to be strong for these guys, I don't like the look of worry on their faces. They've both been so kind to me. I don't want to add more to the burden than they already carry from me.

Wes serves up breakfast. Bacon, eggs and toast. I didn't realise how hungry I was, it was just what I needed.

Wes excuses himself to shower and to get ready for work.

"I will clean up in a second Wes, only fair as you cooked." I shout after him all he does is laugh back at me. I look at Blake who's smiling and shaking his head.

"What? it's the rules he cooked so I should clean up."

"Darlin', you aint doing no clearing up, Wes will already have it done. No arguing."

"My face might look like crap and is painful, but my hands, arms, and legs work perfectly fine."

"Darlin, you in pain?"

I groan and look at the ceiling. Out of what I just said he picks up on that.

"I'm fine I will take some medication in a little while first you can pour me another coffee and tell me about this dangerous job, or well what you can tell me about it anyway."

Blake gets up kisses my head and goes to make us more coffee.

He returns and this time sits next to me.

"Right babe, you met the Satans Outlaws when you arrived."

I nod for him to continue.

"Well I sort of do some work for them every now and again."

"Oh my god, do you like owe them a favour? Or are you like their informant? No wait are you a hitman?" I ask.

Blake is full on belly laughing at me by this point.

"Darlin', seriously you need to stop watching so many biker shows, plus I think the term "owe them a Favour" is a mafia term."

I cross my arms over my chest.

"Well sorry I am not down with the biker lingo, I've never met proper bikers before." I huff.

"Right well my dad used to be a Satans Outlaw, many years ago when me and Wes were kids. He was the president."

I know if my eyes were normal and not completely messed up right now my eyes would be huge, I'm sure I'd be doing my best fish impression. I gesture for him to continue.

"Okay well my pa' wasn't a nice guy, he treated my mum like shit beat on her regular, cheated on her with club whores. He never hit me and

Wes though, we were always sent to our room, we could hear her begging him to stop. He never did. He even beat on her when she was pregnant with our baby sister Maggie. She was born two months early luckily she was healthy and okay.
The mornings after the beatings we would see pa's handy work he'd given mum. I wanted so bad to beat the crap out of him, but I was too young to do anything."
I grab Blakes hand in mine.
"God babe I'm so sorry you had to witness that." I say sympathetically.

Blake lifts my hand and kisses it and continues.
"So anyway. He was a shit president of the club and he got them into some serious shit that put a lot of targets on his and our heads. We had been threatened while out at the market with our mama many times.
Pa didn't give a single shit.
My mamas sister aunt Trudy was married to another club member uncle Max. She used to always look out for us, I heard them talking about getting my mama away to some place safe away from my pa.
Anyway a big war broke out between pa's club and a rival club in the next state over, all because pa had to stir shit and throw his weight around. They ambushed Satans Outlaws compound. Many were killed including my pa and mama. I was fourteen when they both died, Wes

was twelve and our baby sister Maggie was just two."

I get up and climb onto Blakes lap and put my arms around him.

"God babe I am so sorry. If your dad wasn't already dead I'd kick his arse, then kill him."

Blake smiles and gives me a soft kiss.

"So there was me left to look after Wes and Maggie. My aunt Trudy tried to have us, but she struggled as it was. She also had to help care for my uncle Max who had lost his leg in the ambush.

So we stayed here, aunt Trudy and the Merricks took it in turns to come by to check in on us and feed us decent meals. The club paid for the house and bills.

It was expected of me and Wes to prospect and for me to one day become president of the club too. But I wanted no part in that. I have seen what came with that club and I didn't want that for my life and neither did Wes. So the club employ us when they need us for certain jobs. And that's the part I can't tell you about.

But I will reassure you that the club is nothing like it once was.

My cousin has turned it in to a good club and every single one of them guys I trust." Blake states, as I process what he has just said to me.

"Wait a bloody second your cousin is Rip the president of Satans Outlaws?!"

Blake smiles.

Rise Above

"Yeah darlin', and I remember you kissing him. And let me tell you it does not make me feel good remembering that. So let's never ever mention that again."

I cannot believe I kissed Rip who is Blake's cousin. Christ talk about keep it in the family. And bloody hell this family has some super-hot genes.

"Is that what he meant when Rip said in a different world you'd be mine?" I ask Blake,

He lets out a growl.

"I think he meant if he didn't have the life he has you'd be his. But he knew just by us first meeting that I liked you. So he backed off because of that. He's a good guy."

I nod.

"I know you said you can't talk about the job you're doing for the Satans, but can you tell me that you're going to be okay. I mean should I be worried about you?" I ask, searching Blakes face.

He gives me a small smile, shaking his head.

"You don't need to worry about me darlin', I'm trained in what I'm hired for. I'm good at what I do, I just like being extra cautious is all. Especially when it comes to you."

I nod, not having much choice but accepting his answer. And trusting him that he knows what he's doing.

"Now darlin', I hate to ask you, but I need you to go over what happened last night, are you okay to do that?" Blake asks.

Sighing, I knew the questions would come but I thought I might have brought myself a little bit of time.

"Sure okay, but promise me you won't do anything stupid?"

Blake nods and gives me a gentle squeeze at my neck. Letting out a long breath ready to off load. Its then Wes walks in.

"I'm sitting in for this."

Wes pulls out a chair and sits down I look to Blake and he nods for me to start.

I tell them everything from going to bed early because I was upset from knowing Blake had lied to me, to the part of me waking up in hospital.

Throughout the whole thing I could feel Blakes body get tighter and tighter. I avoided looking at either of them in the eye. And I'm proud of myself for only letting a few tears fall. When I finish telling them, I sniff back the remaining tears and dare to look Blake in the eyes.

I can see the fury underneath them, the tense muscles in his neck and his jaw is grinding, I'm surprised he hasn't cracked it.

I turn and look at Wes and get much of the same, but with Wes there's a sadness in his eyes.

"I'm sorry guys, you don't need this, and I don't want to be the one making you feel like you're feeling right now, I am not here to cause you hassle. I am certainly not worth you guys getting into any kind of trouble."

That's my main worry is causing them trouble or them getting into trouble for me.

"Is she for real right now?"

Wes states and he looks pissed off.

"Wes calm the fuck down." Blake warns.

"No brother I won't, she's sat there on your lap, trying to hold it all together and reliving what happened to her last night. The fucking horrible shit she went through. She's reliving it in her God damn dreams, so much that it makes her scream at the top of her lungs because she's so shit scared.

Breaking down and crying because of what that son of a bitch did to her. And now she is sat there worrying about us! Us! saying shit like she aint worth getting into trouble for. What the fuck?"

Wes slams his hands down on the table making me jump. Blake puts his hand on my back to reassure me.

"You need to calm down now!"

Blake growls at Wes.

"Please don't fight or get upset over me please. I'm okay, I'm here, I'm breathing. All is good the bruises will fade. Please calm down."

I reach over and rest my hand over Wes's, he looks down at my hand and then back up at me.

"Christ Blake she aint got no clue, glad you woke the fuck up brother. And Lily, you need to learn that Blake will take care of you, that I will help take care of you when he needs me too. If we ever

end up in any kind of trouble for you, for protecting you. Know this, you are most certainly are worth it don't ever fucking doubt it."
With that Wes stands and walks out the room.

I'm left stunned at Wes's words. I turn to face Blake.
"What was that all about? I mean it was lovely that he cares but you guys barely know me."
"What happened to you is a raw subject for us darlin' with what our mama went through. Wes cares about you because I care about you. And one thing both of us hate is the fact that we weren't there for you and couldn't protect you. I just hide it better than Wes does."
Circling my arms around his neck, I gently kiss Blake.

"I'm sorry, I should of thought that this would be a sensitive subject for you both. And there is nothing you guys could have done. No one was to know it was going to happen. Soon the bruises will be gone, and we can all forget this ever happened." I say on a gentle smile. Blake just leans in for another kiss, and again he kisses over where the guy bit me on my neck.
"Why do you do that? Keep kissing over where the bite mark is?" I ask as Blake kisses it again.
"Because darlin', he marked your perfect skin, and I want to take away the bad and replace it with good. I don't want you to ever think of him and what he did to your neck, so I keep kissing

your neck to replace it with good."

A few tears fall and Blake catches them kissing them away.

"No more tears darlin', he aint worth your tears."

Blakes words only make me cry more. I sniff and take a deep breath.

"I'm not crying for him I'm crying at what you said, you've been so caring and so gentle with me. So stop being so nice to me or I will cry again."

Blake chuckles wiping my tears away, he leans in for a kiss.

"Come on let's get you upstairs for a lie down. And you're guna' have to suck it up, because I only ever plan on being nice to you."

I can't help but smile and nod as he leads me up to his bedroom. I get changed into Blakes t-shirt I wore last night and take some pain meds as my face is starting to hurt and give me a headache. I curl up in Blakes bed he tucks me in and kisses my head.

"I've got to go in my office down the hall and do some work and make some calls. You get some sleep. I will leave my door ajar in case you need me."

I nod the comfort of his bed and the pain meds making me feel drowsy. I curl in deeper loving that the pillow smells of him.

I'm soon in a deep sleep.

CHAPTER TWELVE

I'm woken to loud voices coming from downstairs. I yawn and get up to see what all the noise is about.

As I walk down the stairs I can hear a couple voices coming from the lounge area.

As I turn into the lounge Blakes got his back to me and three guys sat around on the sofas. A pair of ice blue eyes I recognise flick to me, doing a sweep of my body. A smile breaks out across his handsome face it soon falls, and a hard look takes over when he takes in my face. I put on a forced smile.

"Um hi guys."

Blake spins round immediately pulling me to him.

"Shit darlin' I didn't mean to wake you, all okay?"

Blake kisses me gently, I nod and smile, I cuddle into him, turn and face the guys.

"Christ, that fucker is guna have to be fed

through a tube by the time I'm done with him!"
My gaze swings to Mammoth who's sat drinking a beer legs sprawled out across the coffee table.
"Thank you Mammoth but I've already told Blake and Wes, I don't want anyone getting into trouble. Sheriff Johnson came to see me in the hospital last night he has it in hand I'm sure."
Although I didn't really believe my own words, as the sheriff didn't seem like it was of any sort of importance to him. Just more of an inconvenience.
"Now listen sweetheart, no one's going to get into any kinda trouble, we're just guna look into some things that's all."
Khan explains giving me a cheeky wink while flashing me his charming smile.
Rip walks towards me never breaking eye contact, he stops just in front of me. He lift his hand and gently holds my chin turning my head. I know he's looking at where the guy bit me.
"That fucker marked you."
Rip growl's out. I grab his hand still holding my chin.
"I'm okay Rip, it's good it will go down eventually I know it will scar but it could be worse right?"
Rip gently rubs his thumb over my lower lip, I feel Blakes hand on my waist tighten.
"Alright that's enough back the fuck up."
Rips hand drops away, but his eyes remain on me. Blake lets out an almost growl, Rip flicks his eyes

up to Blake. Jaw set, Rip and Blake have a stare off. Until eventually Rip nods.

There's tension in the room and I don't like it one bit.

"Alright that's enough alpha macho man shit, I have no bloody idea why you both seem to have your knickers in a twist. But I'm hungry, so I'm going to make some dinner and you're all welcome to stay. Only if you stop this crap." I chastise.

I stand one hand on hip and the other pointing between the two of them, berating them like naughty children.

I hear Mammoth and Khan chuckling.

"Shit she really has no fucking clue does she?" Rip asks Blake smiling.

Blake pulls me back to him, holding me tight around the waist.

"Nope, and it makes it all the sweeter."

Looking back and forth between the two I let out a sigh.

"I have no bloody idea what you guys are on about and to be honest I don't care, at least now your both smiling and not looking like you're going to fight."

I turn and head into the kitchen. I start opening and closing cupboards looking at what food Blake has in.

I find a big pantry cupboard and I bend down looking at all the different tin's and packet's on the shelves.

"Fuck me, that is one fine ass."

I pause what I'm doing, and I turn looking over my shoulder to see Rip, Khan and Mammoth staring at my behind.

Blake walks into the kitchen looking in a folder, not paying attention and walks into Mammoth.

"What the hell are y'all just stood there for?"

Blake look's around Mammoth. He sees me, and my arse apparently. I quickly shoot up to standing feeling the blush hit my cheeks.

"Darlin' , go upstairs and for Christ sake put on a pair of pants."

I just nod too embarrassed to say anything. Head down I scurry upstairs to find my leggings from last night.

I look for a brush or comb in the bathroom cabinet so I can at least brush my hair which is crazy wild. I catch my reflection in the mirror. My face is still swollen, and I have angry bruises. I turn my head and look at the stitched up bite on my neck. Tears fill my eyes. My head down facing my feet I take a few deep steadying breaths . The last thing I want is for Blake and even the guys downstairs to see I'm weak. Blakes seen enough of me like that last night. If they think I'm okay then they will leave getting involved and stay out of trouble.

I look back in the mirror taking a few more breaths. Forcing a smile on my face.

I turn to leave the bathroom but halt in my tracks. Rip is stood leaning in the doorway, arms crossed over his chest. Those eyes boring into me. A deep frown on his face.

"Blake sent me to tell you he's guna order in for food, you're to rest and not cook, so what do you want to eat?"

Forcing a smile I nod, I let out a relieved breath that he hasn't mentioned my mini meltdown.

"Great thanks for letting me know, I'm coming down now so I will just tell Blake." I smile and go to move past him, but he grabs my arm. I turn to face him only being a few inches apart. He leans down and almost whispers in my ear.

"Stop acting like it's all okay, that you're okay. No one expects you to be and you aint gotta worry about no one but yourself we are all big boys including Blake we can handle it."

I bite my trembling lip, to stop more tears flowing. I let out a little sniffle. Rip's hand gently squeezes my arm and his thumb rubs soothing circles.

"Thanks Rip, I appreciate it. Now let's get some food I'm starving."

I smile up at him and I swear even in my messed up state I can see how very handsome he is, his eyes staring into mine. For a second he leans slowly forward, I think he's going to kiss me, but he stops.

"Christ sweetheart, if you weren't Blakes I'd be making my play, even with your face busted up you're still the sweetest, sexiest thing I've ever fucking seen. Darlin' you need my help, you need my clubs help and we are there for you don't ever fuckin' doubt that."

I can't deny the feeling his words have on me, that he and his club are so willing to help me when they don't even know me that well is so heart-warming and overwhelming. I am also beyond stunned that he sees me that way. And as much as he's stunning with his piercing ice blue eyes, I know my feelings are developing more and more each day for Blake.

"Thanks Rip, and um while I don't understand what you see in me, I thank you for the compliment anyway and you're a very handsome guy. You could get anyone you wanted, but my feelings for your cousin are strong and I am not the type to ever intentionally hurt or betray anyone." I finish on an exhale and look up from my twisted hands.

Rip is looking at me with a smile on his face, a smile that would have women dropping their knickers in an instant.

"And there she goes again fucking clueless. C'mon sweetness let's get you back downstairs to your man before he tears me a new asshole."

I smile big, well as big as I can without it hurting too much. Rip drops his arm over my shoulder and guides me downstairs.

As we turn into the lounge Blakes eyes meet Rips and there's an exchange a secret man to man eye conversation. Whatever is exchanged makes Blake smile and Rip let's go of me as Blake stalks

towards me smiling and wrapping me in his arms. He leans in and gives me the sweetest kiss.
"What was that all about?" I ask looking into Blakes smiling face.

"Nuthin' for you to worry about darlin', just like having you close is all."
I curl into Blake further closing my eyes smiling at how good he feels and how amazing he smells. It's amazing how one person can make you feel so safe and cherished in such a short amount of time and it scares the crap out of me.
"So what takeaway are we having?" I ask Blake and the rest of the room.
"That's up to you darlin', what do you fancy? Apart from me of course." Khan says wriggling his eyebrows at me.
I burst out laughing.
"Ah khan, as much as you're a good looking cheeky bugger, I am sure I can resist your charms. I am rather hungry and would love pizza and a lager right now. That good for everyone? Do you have a pizza place nearby?"
"Damn she shot me down, but any women that wants pizza and beer is okay in my book."
Khan replies with a wink.
Blake pulls out his phone and dial's the pizza place ordering a huge amount of pizza and Mammoth run's to the store to get the beers. I wonder into the kitchen searching the cupboards for plates.

"What do you think you're doing?"

I spin round to see Blake with his arms crossed leaning against the worktop, eyebrow raised waiting for my response.

"Um looking for plates for the pizza."

Blake stalks towards me the look he's giving me has me completely immobile.

He stops just in front of me reaches down and lifts me up suddenly. I let out a pathetic squeal as he places me sitting on the worktops. Like I weigh nothing more than a bag of sugar.

"I told you to rest and not lift a finger."

Rolling my eyes I sigh.

"I was only looking for plates, it's not like I was heavy lifting or spring cleaning. Anyway it's my face that is injured not my arms, hands, legs or feet. I can still do things."

Blake leans in his hands circling round my backside pulling me closer to him, my arms and legs immediately wrap around him. Like it's a natural reflex.

"I know but just let me take care of you, you've been through a lot. Just let me do this okay? Let me take care of you."

Looking into Blakes eyes I know he needs this. In some messed up way I can see he blames himself. I lean in and kiss him. Resting my forehead on his. I try to get through to him.

"None of this is your fault, it's just a bad thing that happened. I am alright. I am here in your arms. It's impossible for you to have guessed that something like this would have happened. I would of never of guessed something like this could ever happen to me. No one could of.

So you need to stop this self-blaming crap, okay?" I say with a smile trying to lighten his mood.

Blake gently runs his forefinger over my face, his eyes following its trail gently over my bruises and swelling.

His eyes come to mine, searching seeing if I really am alright.

The truth is I'm not. I'm scared about going to bed in the dark later, and I'm scared I will have nightmare's again. Will they ever catch the guy that did this to me? What if he tries to do it again?

I also miss my family I just want to hug my mum, but at the same time I don't want them knowing and worrying about me.

But with all those thoughts going through my head I try to portray that I'm okay to Blake, for him to stop worrying. And the truth is I know eventually I will be fine with him by my side.

Blake nod's, he leans in and kisses me gently.

Soon the pizza has arrived, and we are all sat outside on Blakes back deck eating pizza and enjoying a few beers. Well Blake cut me off after two because of my painkillers. My face hurts from smiling and laughing so much. These big scary bikers have managed to lift my mood.

"Yo, pres, remember that time you got caught

sleeping with that woman? You were dating her daughter."

Mammoth holler's from his relaxed position sprawled out on the sun lounger.

"Oh my god! You didn't? Did she walk in on you?" I ask chuckling.

Rip give's Mammoth the finger while smiling and turns to me.

"Yeah, I was young and stupid thought I could have all the pussy I wanted without any come backs. Turns out the daughter wasn't too happy I was fucking her mom. She was a little crazy bitch and chased me down the street butt ass naked with her high heeled stiletto shoe as a weapon."

I can't help but burst out laughing at the thought of this big handsome scary guy being chased by a little crazy women with her heels as her weapon.

Blakes arms soothingly rub up and down my back while he lets out his out rumble of laughter. I calm down but can't help smiling.

"So I have to ask was the mum worth the trouble?"

"Yeah she was pretty fit for an older woman. She was only in her thirties at the time, she had her daughter young."

"Ah ok so she was a bit of a milf then." I state with a smile. All the guys burst out laughing around me as I look at them all in confusion.

"What is so bloody funny?"

Khan is the one to finally control his laughter and answer me.

"It's you sweetness, you using the word milf with your cute British accent out of that cute mouth of yours, it's not something that we'd expect to come out of your mouth is all."

I shrug and smile but wince a little at the pain. Blake ever the observer notices.

"You ok darlin'? You need some pain relief."

I cuddle into Blake further resting my head on his shoulder and nuzzling into his neck breathing in his scent, kissing him.

"I'm okay honey don't panic." I mumble, closing my eyes enjoying the comfort and peace he brings.

The guys carrying on grilling each other over embarrassing times I soon find myself drifting off to sleep.

I am woken to movement of Blake putting me in his bed. I immediately reach out and grab his shirt in my sleep like panic that he's going to leave me.

"Shhhh, it's ok darlin' I'm just guna go to the bathroom and wash up for bed go back to sleep I will be with you in a few minutes."

I relax my sleepy eyes falling closed again. I feel Blake kiss my hair then go off into the bathroom. A while later I feel Blake behind me and pull me to him. Letting out a sigh I drift back off to sleep.

The next few days pass by, Evelynn and Suellen come and visit me, and as usual make me laugh. Even Jeanie stopped by with some pie.

Wes was being like an over protective big brother, watching over me when Blake had to run some work errands.

I kept reminding him that it was my face that was busted not my body and even then the bruising was slowly fading, and the swelling was going down I could now smile without it hurting so much.

Sam and Louisa stopped by and poor Louisa looked ready to pop, she only had two more month's left until her due date, and she was counting down the days.

Eventually I had to return my mums video calls, she was getting worried when I hadn't answered, and I was getting bombarded by my sisters and brother too. Who were also worried for me. so I sat down on Blakes back decking with my laptop and took a deep breath and video called my mum, bracing for her outburst I knew she would have when she saw my face.

Mum came into view and I smiled.

"Hey mum!"

"Oh my sweet girl you're okay, you been to a costume party or something? you have make up all over your eyes and face."

Mum leans forward trying to look closer at my face. I give her a small smile taking another deep

breath I tell her everything that's happened.
Finally I finish speaking and look at my mums face she's crying, it breaks my heart that I'm the cause of that.

"Mum please don't cry, I'm okay. I'm being well looked after by Blake and his brother Wes. Even other people from the town have come to check on me and see that I'm okay, everyone has been really kind." I try reassuring her.

My mum just stares at me then shouts.

"Ben! Get in here now and bring your laptop, we are booking a flight out to Texas and we are seeing to our baby girl she needs us."

I hear my dad come storming in with his laptop in hand.

"What arsehole do I need to kick now? Who's hurt my Lily? I shall have to google if I can get a gun licence being a Brit but I'm sure there must be a way I can. Everyone has a gun over there."

My dad's so busy ranting looking at his laptop that he hasn't even looked at mum's computer screen.

I can't help but smile and chuckle at my dad's loving rant, it even brings a tear to my eye at how loving my parents are. That they would drop everything if I needed them too.

"Mum, dad listen to me, I'm okay. I don't need you guys to fly over.."

I don't get to finish what I'm saying as dad looks up from his laptop and gets a look at my face. He irrupts in anger.

" WHAT IN THE EVER LOVING FUCK HAS HAPPENED TO YOU?!"

"Dad I'm okay, I was attacked but it's fine I'm being looked after-"

Again I don't get to finish my sentence.

"YOU WERE ATTACKED?!"

Even my mother tries to calm him down.

"Ben calm down your blood pressure."

"SOD MY BLOODY BLOOD PRESSURE PENN, OUR DAUGHTER WAS ATTACKED!"

Dad carries on screeching and ranting. With me and mum trying to calm him down a little.

I didn't realise that Blake had got back from work and was stood behind me until I felt his hand on my shoulder. I let out a little screech.

"Sorry darlin' I didn't mean to startle you."

Looking up I smile, and Blake leans down to kiss my temple.

It's then I realise that my dad has gone quiet I look back down to my laptop and see my mum and dad both staring at us. My mum is smiling, and my dad has his arms crossed over his chest still looking pissed off.

"Ah mum, dad this is Blake stone we are err, um good friends. He's been looking after me and so has his brother Wes."

I smile tightly at my parents. I feel Blakes hand give my neck a gentle squeeze. I look up and he's smiling big at me flashing me those dimples I can't help but smile big back. He leans in and

kisses me gently on the lips. Blake stands tipping his Stetson to my parents in greeting.
"Oh my!"
I hear my mum breathe. Moment broken I blush and smile at my parents.
I am about to speak but Blake beats me to it.
"Ma'am, sir I am Blake Stone, it's good to meet you and I just wish this was under better circumstances.

As you can see me and your daughter are more than friends, Lily means a great deal to me. And sir, ma'am I can assure you that I will not let anyone harm her again, and I can also assure you that myself, my brother and my cousin and his club are looking for the asshole. And believe me we will bring him to justice."
"Oh my!"
My mum say's again all breathy, I'm just staring at Blake letting his words sink in, I mean a lot to him?
"That's all very well lad, but my baby girl is sat there with her face looking like she's been in a boxing ring with all the heavy weights.
I want to see for myself that she is in fact okay, and I want to find the rat bastard that did this to my baby girl. Do you understand me?"
Oh god my dad is pissed off and he isn't going to let it lie. I love him for it but at the same time I don't want them coming over here.

"Dad I'm good, okay? plus I have no where here

for you to stay. The little motel is in the next town over and it's not sanitary. And-"

Blake places his hand on my shoulder interrupting me.

"I would be exactly the same sir, I have spare rooms for you here. You and your wife are welcome to come stay here and I'm sure Lily would be more than happy to see you, and have you come visit. I know she's missed you a whole lot." Blake states.

I stare stunned at Blake mouth opening and closing I just don't know what to say.

"Oh my!"

There goes my mum again I swear she will faint soon.

"Great I will get on to the airline and book the flights. I will let you know when they are booked."

With that my dad blow's me a kiss and waltz's out of the room. Leaving me stunned.

"So well, isn't this exciting I will have to go pack lord knows how soon your father will want to be out there. You really are okay though?" My mum asks smiling not looking at me but looking straight at Blake.

"Yeah mum I'm good really. Go pack your case and let me know when you guys are landing at Houston. Love you lots."

I love you too sweetie, and I look forward to meeting you in person Mr Stone." My mum swoons.

"As do i ma'am."

Blake smiles and gives my mum another tip of his Stetson.

"Oh my!"

Mum breathes fanning her face.

"Mum will you control your hormones and go pack, I love you bye."

With that I disconnect the call and look up to Blake.

"You know you didn't have to do that. Daily video updates would've tied them over."

Blake smiles and moves the chair around. He crouches down in front of me, placing both his hands on my thighs.

"Video calls are not enough, if you were my daughter I'd want to know that she was in safe hands and see it for myself."

Blake continues to rub circles on my thighs.

God this man is killing me, I'm falling for him more and more each day. All that he's done for me, all that he makes me feel. How can one person make you feel so on top of the world when it's been such a shitty time?

Leaning forward I place my hand on this beautiful man's face.

"You Blake Stone are the most beautiful man I've ever met inside and out. Also you really know how to put the charm on. I thought my mum was going to throw her knickers at the screen for a minute."

Blake throws his head back laughing.

"I mean it you know? You are the most beautiful man inside and out."

I don't give him a chance to reply I lean in and kiss him, ignoring the pain it causes me and trying to show Blake how much he means to me in this one kiss.

Blakes hands tighten on my thighs and both our breathing becomes heavy. I grip his shirt and pull him closer to me.

"Darlin' we have to stop, you're hurt, and I don't want to be the one that will ever cause you any pain."

Stopping I know I could easily carry on, but truth is I know I don't look great at all at the moment and as much as he is such a gentleman to me I get why he wouldn't want to sleep with me, I must look like something out of a horror film. Even if the swelling has gone down around my eyes, they are still bruised in a nice blue green and my eyes are still very bloodshot. How stupid of me to even think that he'd be interested. The negative thoughts keep swirl around my head.

"Hey, you need to stop that. Stop going into your head, overthinking and self-doubting. You are an amazingly beautiful woman. I just don't want to hurt you, when you are well enough and not in any pain, believe me darlin' I am going to take my time erasing any trace of how that asshole made you feel. Do you understand me?"

Tears fill my eyes, at his words. I nod swallowing back the lump in my throat.

Blake wraps his arms around my waist and kisses me.

We are interrupted by my laptop pinging with an email.

I look over at the screen and it's an email from my mum saying that flights are booked, and that they arrive in two days and how dad has left her no time to pack and prep.

Blake chuckles obviously reading my mums email.

"You have no idea what you've let yourself in for you know that?"

I ask eyebrow raised. The poor man is clueless.

"They are your parents, they're good people, stop worrying it will all be fine."

"Ha! Famous last words. You better warn Wes too, or my mum will be setting him up with my sister."

Blake walks off to the kitchen roaring with laughter. Silly fool thinks I'm bloody joking. I quickly reply to my mum. Telling her I will be there to pick her and dad up.

CHAPTER THIRTEEN

The next day went by in a blur I was rushing around trying to make sure everything was ready for my parents arrival, I was also worried that my dad wouldn't like Blake. I didn't have to worry about mum she clearly has her little crush. I contacted the Merricks to apologise for not staying there. They had already spoken to Blake and were more than understanding.

I had also emailed my editor and informed him of what had happened and that I need to take a couple of weeks off. He was not as understanding apparently the world of growing your own veg waited for no one and the news on fruit and veg never slept. I had until Monday to get an article to him or I would be fired.

I kept this information to myself as I knew Blake would be angry and possibly want to contact my boss. So I asked Louisa to give me some small pointers and tip's on what they do at the Merricks.

It would be a small article, but it would have to do. I sneakily wrote that while Blake checked in at the Den.

Soon the morning came, and I was getting ready to go with Blake on the long drive to Houston airport. I stood in front of the bathroom mirror looking at my bruises.

They had gone down more but were still very visible in green/yellow colours and the deep purple was now more lighter blues. I hadn't really left Blakes house, so I was anxious for people staring at me.

I opened my make-up bag in the hope that maybe I could cover them just a little bit. so I set to work.

A little while later I looked in the mirror, make up done you could still see the bruising but not quite as prominent. I felt better about myself, I felt more like me rather than the victim of a beating.

I got up and looked through my bag of clothes for something to wear, I had lived in either my leggings and Blakes t-shirts or my shorts and vest top.

Pulling out my khaki maxi skirt with high splits either side. I paired that with my white deep v neck vest top and tucked it in. And of course making sure I wasn't flashing the whole of Texas underneath I put on black cropped halter neck bikini top. It was so hot I was dressing for comfort as well as trying to look good.

I put on my basic plain black flip flops. Put product in my hair and let it dry naturally in messy curly waves.

Smiling at my reflection I felt good. I felt like I was getting me back again.

With a spritz of perfume I grabbed my bag and phone and headed downstairs.

As I entered the kitchen, my head down I was putting my phone and other bits in my bag not paying attention.

"So babe are we going to stop for a bite to eat on the way back with my parents or before we leave Houston. Also shall I make us some sandwiches' for the journey or are we grabbing lunch on the way there?"

With no answer I look up and see Blake staring at me cup of coffee half way to his mouth, and Wes smiling like a goof ball looking at me then his brother.

I turn and look behind me, then back to facing Blake.

"What? Is it my make up? I know its heavy, but I don't want people staring at me. And I feel good, I feel a little like me again. Rather than just a beaten woman." I state.

Blake growls puts down his cup and stalks towards me his eyes never leaving mine.

His eyes sweep my body in that way he does which gives me goose bumps.

He wraps his arms around me and pulls me in

tight, and kisses me without holding anything back, leaving me completely breathless.

He pulls back slightly, kisses my neck over my bite mark.

"You look so fucking beautiful darlin'."

I smile up at him.

"Well thank you Mr handsome, but we need to get going, am I making us sandwiches' or what?"

Blake smiles and shakes his head.

"No darlin', I will take you out to lunch on the way."

"Great let me just grab us some water to take, its roasting out there today."

I pat his chest and move around him to the fridge bending down I grab us a couple of waters.

I hear a growl and shoot up, looking at Blake. Wes is laughing his arse off.

"What now?" I ask holding my arms out.

Blake looks to the ceiling apparently talking to God.

"Darlin', do me a favour, do not bend over in that skirt ok?"

I immediately spin round trying to look at my behind, which of course has both Blake and Wes chuckling. So I bend over and try and look that way.

"Oh my god is it see through? Tell me it's not see through. I know it's form fitting over my hips and my behind it's why I always wear a thong, so I don't get a knicker line. It's not is it?" I say again bending over slightly like I'd be able to see.

"Enjoy your long ass blue ball car ride brother!" Wes says barely being able to control his laughter giving Blake a slap on the back as he leaves.

"what's he on about?" I ask watching Wes leave.

"Darlin', that skirt clings to that gorgeous ass of yours and when you bend over, it is not see through, but it doesn't leave much to the imagination. And you adding to that fact that you're wearing a thong , means I'm guna have a long ass car journey with blue balls thinking of that fine ass in a thong." Blake informs me.

"Oh, shall I change?"

Blake chuckles and leans in kissing me.

"No darlin' just stay with me, two minutes away from me and you'll have all the men in the airport around you."

It's my turn to burst out laughing.

"you're crazy, it's sweet you see me that way babe but believe me not all guys think the same. Now come on or we will be late picking up my parents."

With that I walk out the kitchen towards the front door. I hear Blake mumble

"Fucking clueless."

Shrugging my shoulders I head for the truck.

Blake stops for lunch at a cute little cafe in the middle of nowhere, yet it was surprisingly busy after eating their sub sandwiches I could see why. Best I've ever tasted.

We get back on the road. As we are nearing

Houston airport I feel I should run through some warnings about my parents with Blake,

"So honey I thought I should just warn you about a few things my parents might say or do. I don't want to throw you at the deep end with them."

I look over at Blake to see him smiling, his eyes briefly meeting mine.

"Darlin' they are your parents, there's nothing I won't like about them you love them so that's good e'nuff for me." Blake states giving my leg a squeeze. My heart swells even more for this beautiful man.

"That's sweet, but you should still be prepared. You wouldn't send a military man into war without warning, training or even advice so I'm going to do the same for you okay?"

Blake bursts out laughing, and boy do I love that sound.

"I don't think comparing your parents to a warzone is a fair comparison." I shrug, he hasn't seen our family parties.

"Maybe it's a little exaggerated but never underestimate my parents. So do you want some advice or not?"

Blake still chuckling nods and gestures for me to continue.

"Soo my mum and dad are a little loopy. We will start with my dad, he will question your motives with me, he will put you down, and he will expect your respect but won't return it you have to earn it with him."

Blake nods.

"Wouldn't expect anything less darlin' he's just making sure his baby girl is safe and in good hands."

I smile because I'm glad Blake gets it, my ex just assumed my dad was an arse. And constantly challenged my dad rather than give him the respect he should have given him. Then he may have gotten it back.

"Okay well if you want to get into my dad's good books, he loves Guns n Roses, as you know, and he loves rock. He also loves motorbikes and always wanted one. But mum never let him for fear of him dying. Mum can be a little dramatic. But we live in London there isn't many quiet country roads for him to ride on. So he wouldn't get full enjoyment anyway."

"Right Guns n Roses and loves bikes. Can your dad ride a bike?"

"Yeah, he used to have one in the seventies, he's always kept his licence. Because in his words you never know."

I laugh because I don't know what the circumstances would call for him to jump on a motorbike randomly.

"Okay so what do I need to know about your mum?" Blake asks, I let out a deep sigh.

"Well she will most definitely embarrass me, you have no worries about mum liking you, she will love you. But she will say something inappropriate and she will probably want to take your picture to send to my nan and aunts. She will clean your house even though it doesn't need it. And liked I warned she will probably size up Wes for my sister Rose, or any other guy she deems acceptable."

Blakes smiling but he doesn't know that she has no boundaries when it comes to her mouth.
"Your smiling now, but don't come crying to me when she asks you about your fertility so at some point you can provide her with grandchildren. Or she will feed you proper English food because Americans have high obesity and English food is better. When we all know it's really not."
I stop talking and Blake is silent staring out at the road. It's then I realise I've probably freaked him out talking about fertility and grandkids.
"Blake honey, I'm not saying I want your babies, I mean I do. I want kid's at some point in my life but what I didn't mean is that is what is going to happen with us, I didn't mean to freak you out. And I mean well erm,it might one day. And I would like kids of my own, I don't mean for us to go there yet. I'm talking way in the future. I mean if you don't want kids, well-"
I didn't get to finish my rambling, as Blake interrupts me his voice is horse.
"I'm not sure on kids."
I sit there in silence because well ever since I was

little I've dreamed of having my own family, of having at least a boy and a girl.

"Do you mean you're not sure you can have them or not sure you want any?" I ask and although I would be devastated if he couldn't have kids, I am hoping it's that rather than him not wanting kid's because at some point that becomes a game changer in a relationship when you both want different things. At least if he can't have kid's there is other avenues to try.

"I can have kid's as far as I know, I'm just not sure I want them."

"Oh." I sigh.

Blake pulls in and parks the truck in the airport car park. I'm silent because I really don't know what to say. My heart is torn between wanting to stay with Blake and knowing at some point if I stay with him and we last, that him not on board with having kids would become a problem and would cause me some serious heart ache.

Blake grabs my hands and pulls me to straddle his lap. I keep my eye cast down as don't want him to see the emotions behind them.

Blake lifts my chin forcing me to look at him.

"Darlin', listen to me, I'm not saying I don't want kid's and I'm not saying I do. I've seen some fuckin' messed up things in my life and I'm not sure I want to bring a kid into that messed up world. Can you understand what I'm saying?"

I nod my face in his hands. I can't help the sinking feeling in my heart. Maybe just maybe I can show him that the world can be beautiful too. Even if we don't go the distance for him not to have babies would be a crime.

"Just to say, and I'm not meaning with me but in the future you should have at least one baby because you'd make seriously beautiful babies and I know you'll be an amazing father."

I smile to try and lighten the mood in the truck. Thankfully Blake smiles back and leans in and kisses me, thing's get a little heated as his hands move from my waist to cup my arse. I moan and can't help my hips grinding down on him. Blake lets out a throaty moan.

Soon we are interrupted by a banging on the window. I let out a squeal, and Blake and I turn our heads to see an old guy and his wife shaking their heads at us. Heat fills my cheeks from embarrassment, and I hide my face in Blakes neck. Blake just laughs.

"How long are your parents staying for?"

I can't help myself, the smell of him I nuzzle into his neck further my tongue having a mind of its own tasting him.

Blakes hands tighten on my arse. And he lets out a low growl.

"They are here for 10 days."

I mumble into his neck trying to control myself and not have another taste of him.

"Don't think I'm guna last 10 more days darlin'."

I smile into his neck because neither can I.

I sit up and look into Blakes eyes smiling as I wiggle down on his crotch to tease him. He lets out a low moan.

I stop and hop off his lap before he can stop me jumping down from the truck holding the door open, I smile big at Blakes face.

"Come on honey let's get going or we are going to be late picking up my parents."

I wink and start to walk away swaying my hips a little more teasing him. Blake growls and jumps down, rounds the truck and catches me before I have a chance to run away, he pins me against the truck I can feel his arousal through his jeans.

I stop laughing as he leans down and kisses me passionately.

His hands slowly slide up my waist to my breasts, he gently runs his thumb over my nipple. I can't control my bodies reaction. I lift my leg around his hip to try and get even closer and to feel him against me.

My breathing is heavy as is Blakes, he kisses my neck. Then suddenly he stops and steps back. I nearly fall forward I'm so caught up in the moment. I open my eyes to see Blake giving me a cheeky smile and a wink.

"Two can play at that game darlin'." He teases.

I cannot believe he did that.

"You enjoyed it just as much as me, so you just wound yourself up too." I state frustrated.

I say this trying to control my breathing and get my hormones under control.

Blake chuckles and walks back towards me, leans down and kisses me lightly.

"C'mon let's go get your folks before I throw you on the hood of my truck and fuck you and we end up arrested."

I clench my legs at the thought. Blake notices and smiles, smacking my arse as we walk toward the terminal to collect my parents.

Blake and I stand in arrivals waiting for my parents. I cannot contain my excitement for seeing them, it's been weeks now and from seeing them once a week to not at all has felt strange. If it wasn't for Blake I think I'd be feeling a lot more home sick than I do.

Finally the people from my parents flight come through the door, I'm standing on my tip toes to try and see them. Blakes hands on my hips standing behind me.

Soon I see the top of their heads.

"Mum! Dad! Over here!"

I wave frantically trying to get their attention in a busy airport.

Mum looks around then spots me, smiling wide she practically pushes every other person out of the way to get to me, leaving dad trailing behind with the trolley of luggage.

"Excuse me, move please , I need to get to my daughter."

Mum continues to not so politely elbow her way through.

"Hey lady watch it!" An angry guy shouts at mum.

"Oh no she's going to go off on one." I sigh placing my hands over my face.

Mum swirls round to the guy that just shouted at her.

"Now listen here young man, I haven't seen my daughter in a long time and in that time she has been assaulted badly. Now stop your whining and let a mother through to see her daughter you moron!"

The bloke just stares at mum stunned. Luckily dad's caught up with her and takes her by the elbow.

"Come on Penn, we've only been in the country five minutes and you're already causing a scene."

I can feel Blake chuckling behind me, I swirl round and give him the death glare, which only makes him laugh more pulling me into him he kisses the top of my head.

"Oh look Ben, how lovely."

I lift my head from Blakes chest and turn to my parents.

Mums smiling huge and dads frowning sizing Blake up.

I open my arms and grab mum giving her a tight hug, we both cry, Then I feel dad pull me out of mums arms and into his. There something about being enveloped in your dads arms that gives you a feeling of protection that no one can ever hurt you.

I pull back and smile at mum and dad, their smiles faulter. I must have cried most of my make of off as they are staring at the bruises.

Mum moves my hair off my neck revealing the now deep pink scar where he bit me.

She covers her hand over her mouth to hold back a sob. Whereas dad looks like he's ready for murder.

"Sir, ma'am I am Blake Stone it's a pleasure to meet you both. I hope your flight went smoothly?" Blakes greets.

I turn and mouth the words 'Thank you' to Blake for distracting my parents.

"Oh please Blake call me Penny, and this is Ben. And I believe we have you to thank for our flight being so wonderful. Thank you for upgrading us. We've never flown first class before it was truly wonderful."

I spin round to Blake

"You had them upgraded?" I ask.

Blake just nods, like it's no big deal.

"I'm glad you had a relaxing journey, it's a long flight."

"Yes well thank you for that son, let me know what we owe you and I will sort that to your account." My dad grumbles he's not one for being treated, he likes to as he puts it 'make his own way in life'.

"No sir it was a gift and anyway it didn't cost me

a dime, I have a contact that works for the airline. Did me a favour."

I know that Blake is lying, he's just saying that to appease my dad.

Come, let's get to the truck and start the journey home, we can stop for some dinner on the way."

I stop and turn when I realise that mum, dad and Blake have stopped. Blake is smiling and so is mum, dad looks like he's concentrating hard.

"What?" I shrug.

"You said home darlin'." Blake informs me still smiling.

I realise what I said, I let it sink in. And then panic that I'm going to be scaring the crap out of Blake again we've already had the kid's conversation today we don't need to add to it.

"Well, it's home from home, Blake and Wes have been very welcoming. You'll see, you will both be calling it home soon enough."

I try to let out a small chuckle, but it comes out like a hysterical laugh of a mad woman instead. I carry on walking to the car, hearing Blake chuckle behind me.

We are soon well into our journey back to Mufftown, mum nonstop chatting. I catch Blakes eye and mouth "sorry" he smiles in return he reaches over and places his hand on my thigh giving a gentle squeeze, then laces his fingers through mine holding my hand.

Mum of course doesn't miss a trick.

"Oh that's sweet, Ben why don't you do that with

me anymore?" mum moans.

"Christ woman, we live in London do you know how many times I have to change the gears stopping and starting through London traffic? Plus this is an automatic Blake doesn't have to change gears, America doesn't have real cars."

"Ben!"
I roll my eyes. Blakes smiling. God this really is going to be a long journey.
"Apologise to Blake, you could have offended him and his country."
My mum chastises.

"Don't be daft woman, stop making a mountain out of a mole hill."
Oh Christ dads going to get an ear full now.

"Benjamin Stewart Rocke! You bloody well apologise, or I won't do that thing with my tongue you like ever again!"
My head is now in my hands and I am starting to curl into the foetal position. No one should ever hear that from their parents mouths.
Blake lets out a chuckle-cough.
"Mum please stop!"

"What sweetie, you should be happy that your parents still love each other and have a healthy sexual relationship. It's important to keep the flame burning. Although if your father carries on I shall be putting the fire out for a month at least!" Mum replies matter of fact.

Groaning into my palms, I feel Blakes hand squeeze my neck while fighting back his laughter.

" Penn, enough your embarrassing Lil, I will apologise to Blake, but you know as well as I do you couldn't last a month without my mouth."

My mum lets out a school girl giggle and I hear kissing noises. I'm too scared to turn around to what my eyes might witness.

Finally dad stops whatever the hell he's up to and apologises to Blake.

"Sorry son, no offence meant. There you happy now woman?"

Mum just giggles.

I gag holding in the vomit.

"Will you two behave we are in Blakes truck act your age." I scold.

They stop, my mum patting my shoulder.

"Sorry sweetie, sorry Blake."

Before I can apologise for my parents behaviour, Blake replies to them.

"No need to apologise Mr and Mrs Rocke no harm done."

"I beg to differ I think my ears are bleeding." I reply to Blake, Blake breaks out laughing. Either forgetting my parents are in the back or not caring he wraps his hand around my neck pulling me to him for a kiss. As soon as his lips touch mine I soon forget my parents are there.

Pulling back to focus on the road, Blake grabs my hand kissing the back of it, I sigh smiling like a love sick teenager.

Still in the moment completely forgetting that my parents are watching everything from the back seat.

An hour or so passes and Blake turns off the freeway.

"Where are we going?" I ask Blake.

"Well the Satan's Outlaws are having a cookout tonight, they invited us. I thought we could stop there for a bite to eat and your dad can look around at all the bikes."

"Umm Oo-kay." I murmur.

I reply, unsure that's such a good idea, I've heard that they can get pretty wild, and with the club pussy hanging around my mum will not keep her mouth shut I'm sure of it.

As if he can read my mind, Blake eases my worries.

"It's a family cookout, club members and family no err others, there will be kids there." Blake confirms.

I smile, and my mum sticks her head in between us.

"Did I hear right you're taking us to a biker club cookout?" Mum asks.

"Yeah mum, you guys okay with that? It's Blakes cousin, he's president of the club, and there will be families there. Plus dad can look at the bikes." My mum bounces back clapping her hands in excitement. Waking up my now sleeping dad to tell him.

"Ben! we're going to a biker club for a cookout! How exciting is that?! Be good to go to one again, it's been what twenty odd years since we partied with the skull splitters." Mum sighs reminiscing.

"Ha yeah good old mad dog, wonder what he's up to these days." Dad comments.

I spin round in my seat to face my parents.

"You guys hung out at biker clubs? You guys were friends with bikers?!" I ask stunned, not that my parents are judgemental or hell they are not like normal parents but still hanging around with a biker club I thought was even a bit too wild for them.

"Don't you remember? We used to take you to the family cookouts, you used to play with the kids there you would have been oh about 3 or 4 I think. Your dad nearly became a member, but the club was getting into some bad stuff and I didn't want that for you kids and neither did your dad. We just lost touch with them over the years."

I can vaguely remember going to barbeques, but I can't remember who or where they were.

"I had no idea, so you would both be good with going to satans outlaws for a cookout?" I ask just double checking I hadn't just dreamt the last few minutes conversation.

"Yes, of course let me just touch up my hair and make-up. Can't go showing up looking like a jet lag mess."

Mum starts rummaging through her bag and starts touching up her make up.

I immediately feeling self-conscious grab my bag and see what make up I brought with me, and to check my hair is ok and not dried into a complete frizz.

Around forty minutes later we are driving down a dirt track and in the distance a building comes into view. It's a large concrete building, it looks like and old factory, surrounded by wire fencing and barbed wire. I can't help the excitement and nerves taking over my stomach, it really looks like something out of a movie.

Blake pulls up to the gates and two guys open up and let us through to park, there must be at least 30 motorbikes all parked up.

Pulling to a stop Blake jumps out of the truck opening the door for my mum helping her down. I jump out and take in my surroundings. The building is big, uninviting, and a little scary. An American flag hangs from a pole on top of the building as well as a flag with the clubs badge.

I can smell the food cooking, it makes my stomach rumble, Blake comes from behind me wrapping his arms around my waist.

"C'mon darlin, let's get you and your parents fed."

I lift my head and smile up at him, he leans in

smiling for a kiss.

"Yo Blake, y'all planning on joining us or y'all guna spend the night in the car park?"

Me and Blake both turn to seen Rip smiling arms crossed over his chest. In a pair of fitted faded jeans, black fitted t shirt and his cut. God he is bloody stunning. My sister would climb him like a spider monkey.

Blake wraps his arm over my shoulder, as we make are way over. My parents following behind.

We reach Rip and he immediately pulls me from Blakes arms to him and giving me a hug and he kisses the top of my head, then steps back holding me at arm's length giving me the once over.

"You looking a lot better flower. My cousin been treating you good?"

He asks smiling, clearly goading Blake. And it works as Blake wraps his hand around my waist and pulls me back to him. Almost growling at Rip. Which in turn makes Rip throw his head back laughing and boy even his laugh is hot.

"Oh my" My mum breathes, I forgot my parents were stood right behind us. I turn around and my mum is fanning her face smiling and gives me a wink. I roll my eyes.

"Sorry mum, dad this is Rip he's the president of Satans Outlaws.

Rip this is my mum Penny, and my dad Ben."

Rip takes my mums hand and kisses the back of her hand.

"Ma'am it's a pleasure, I can see where your daughter gets her beauty from."

"Oh my." My mum breathes smiling so wide, I'm scared her face will split.

"Turn it down man." Blake says smiling shaking his head.
Rip just replies with a wink, he then turns to my dad holding out his hand to shake.
"Good to meet you sir, I hear you have a liking for motorbikes. After we've all had some food, Blake and I can show you around. we have some classics out at the garage." Dad replies smiling like a kid at Christmas, shaking Rips hand with vigour.
"That would be bloody marvellous, lad."
I smile at Blake squeezing his waist, he returns my smile as we make are way around the back of the clubhouse to where lots of club members and their families are congregated.
Children are running around playing, the guys are surrounding the fire with beers in hand. The women either seeing to the kids or carrying out food or sat on their partners laps. Basically looks the same as any other barbeque, men always seem to gather around any type of flame.
Rock music plays in the background.
I spot a few of the guys I've met before, as well as Raven I introduce my mum and dad to them all.
Blake takes hold of my hand and pulls me away.
"There's someone I'd like you to meet darlin'."

Rise Above

I nod following him. We approach a small group of women one stands as we approach smiling, she has the very same piercing ice blue eyes of Rip. I immediately know that this is Blakes aunt Trudy. I become nervous, this lady is like a mum to Blake and what if she knows I kissed her son as well as dating her nephew! She will think I'm a right slapper.

Blake pulls me to him wrapping his arm around me.

"Aunt Trudy, I'd like you to meet Lily, Lily this is my aunt Trudy."

I stick my hand out in greeting Trudy takes it pulling me into her arms for a hug. Shocked I stand rigid. She pulls back smiling looking me over.

"Welcome to the family, I see what's got all these boys chasing their tails. Sugar you are beyond beautiful. And from what I hear a personality that is just as sweet."

I immediately look away blush filling my cheeks, still not used to accepting compliments. Blake pulls me to him and kisses the top of my head. The whole time Trudy is smiling watching us like we are a fascinating new discovery.

"You introduced her to Max yet?" Trudy asks Blake still smiling.

"Nah not yet, thought you'd wana meet her first, is he about?"

Blake looks around to see if he can see him.

"Of course where else would he be he's in the garage, finishing up fixing rex's bike, go see him, he'll be glad you're here and I know he wants to meet Lily."

Blake nods tipping his Stetson, turning to us to go find his uncle.

I turn my head shouting over my shoulder.

"It was lovely to meet you!"

Trudy smiles in return.

Soon we are approaching a large metal out building, we can here banging and clunking coming from inside.

Blake opens the big sliding door a little more as we walk in the smell of oil, grease and metal fill the room. Tools and posters of bike's fill the walls, a few bikes scattered about the place and to my surprise even a car.

"Yo uncle Max it's your favourite nephew." Blake shouts.

"That you Wes?" Max replies laughing, coming from behind the bike at the far side.

"Ha-ha max, I brought someone I want you to meet."

With that a guy, who is incredibly handsome, and Rip is his double. In dark grey overalls he comes out from behind the bike in his wheelchair, which is decorated with different bike makes names on it. For a wheelchair it's pretty cool.

I smile at Blakes uncle Max, he returns the smile while wiping his hands on a bit of rag.

Rise Above

"Well I'll be damned. How did you manage to get this pretty little thing to go out with your ugly ass? Did he bribe you miss? Did he give you a sob story?"

I'm laughing shaking my head, Max just smiles back.

"Leave it out Max, this is Lily. Lily this joker is my uncle Max."

Blake says smiling.

"Nice to meet ya darlin', my boy treating you good? Or do I need to kick his ass?"

Max says still smiling, rubbing his hands together. Chuckling I reply.

"No, he's been a gentleman, treating me very well thank you. No need to kick his arse. But I will be sure to let you know if I ever need you too."

Max winks.

"So you coming out to join in and have some food and fun? Come and meet Lily's parents. Plus I think Wes is guna be getting here soon e'nuff."

Blake asks.

"Will get cleaned up and be out in a bit."

Blake just nods and turns us to leave I wave over my shoulder.

When we are outside and on our own, I ask Blake a question.

"Blake, why hasn't know one reacted to my face? I know I have a little make up on and it hides the worst but it's still visible. I'm not complaining it's nice that it's not the first thing people say when meeting me."

I look up at Blake.

"I asked Rip to give everyone a heads up about your injuries, and he told them not to mention it and risk upsetting you. Let you have an evening of just being relaxed and being you."

Stopping I turn and face Blake leaning up on my toes.

"Thank you."

I then kiss him showing him just what his thoughtfulness has meant to me.

I'm sat with some of the kids braiding the girls hair. Ravens granddaughter Maddie is the cutest. She has jet black hair, with deep blue eyes. Her mum Firecracker had to work so Raven and big papa have got her for a few hours. I braid her hair into pigtails. She's three and has not stopped talking.

"So, are you a pwincess?"

Maddie asks in her cute innocent voice.

"No sweetheart I'm not. Why do you ask that?"

"Well you live with a queen, are you the maid?"

Laughing I reply.

"I live in the same country as a queen, but I don't live in the castle or work for the queen. Sorry. But I do know a princess."

Maddie's eyes get wide, excitement on her face.

"You do?"

I nod. And stand in front of Maddie and I curtsey and bow.

"Your majesty. I believe you are the most beautiful princess I have ever met."

I give Maddie a wink. She bursts out laughing and jumps up into my arms. Placing her little chubby hands on my face.

"You are so silly Lily! We can be bestest fwiends coz nana say I'm silly too. We can be silly togeva!"

Chuckling I blow a big raspberry on her cheek. She squeals with laughter.

Raven comes up to us.

"Come on Maddie, let's get you back to your mama."

Raven holds out her arms and Maddie jumps into them.

Maddie leans forward giving me a big kiss on cheek. I quickly blow a raspberry back on her cheek. She giggles as Raven makes her way to leave.

"Bye pwincess silly!" Maddie's shouts. I laugh blow her a kiss and turn to get a drink. I look across the fire and see Blake staring at me intently. He's frowning. I smile and blow him a kiss. He ignores me and turns to carry on talking to the guy.

Feeling a little stung by that, I pour myself a large drink. And go sit down.

I'm introduced to more of the bikers and their old ladies.

Its soon getting late as the children are taken off to their homes and put to bed, the cookout soon turns into a more adult party. My parents are both laughing and chatting away to Big Papa, Raven, Max and Trudy.

I found out that Max's road name is wheels, and Trudy's is cougar. Max told me it's because she is one a hot mama, even now, and he's 2 years younger than her and he always teased her about it.

Looking around the people now, I would of never in a million year imagined myself here. But I've never felt more accepted and relaxed in myself.

The music is suddenly turned up born to be wild starts booming over the speakers. I smile and look over to my parents. My dad has pulled my mum up to dance.

Wes comes and sits down next to me.

"I think your folks are having a good time. And I can see where you get your wild side from."

Laughing I hit Wes in the arm, he hands me a shot of tequila. We clink glasses and I knock mine back.

"Probably not the best idea drinking tequila, last time I did shots I ended up kissing Rip and nearly doing a strip tease to the whole bar!"

I laugh as Wes pours me another.

"I know, why do you think I'm giving you shots? I know you'll liven the party up."

That earns Wes another thump to the arm. After my third shot, the music changes to ZZ Tops La Grange one of my faves. With the alcohol in my system I jump up and start dancing swinging my hips, I pull Raven up out of her seat to dance with me. Wolf whistles are blown from around us.

We get handed another drink, without looking to see what it is. I knock it back coughing a little and gagging.

"Better get used to our southern whisky flower!" Mammoth yells there's more laughter and whistles. Bad to the bone comes over the speakers.

And I let the music take over, swaying my hips seductively, hands in my hair, shaking my arse. Eyes closed smiling.

Enjoying the buzz of the booze and the music. I open my eyes and see Raven still dancing with me and she's lost in the music too, and boy she looks hot.

I look around and all the guys have eyes on us. My mum clearly very drunk shouts.

"That's my girl Wooooo!"

I burst out laughing as does Raven. At this point we're handed another drink more whiskey this time I hold back the gag, my eyes still watering a little. I put my arm around raven as she does me. Bad company comes on. Raven and I continue dancing together being silly. Dancing seductively, messing around and laughing. We are both in the moment that I don't even realise we now have a crowd around us. I feel hands on my hips and a body press up behind me. I lean back into the hard body still dancing and swaying my hips with Blake.

Completely lost in the moment I grind myself back and feel Blakes hands tighten on my hips smiling I rest my head back on to his chest. Raising my hands up to grab the back of his neck I turn my head to kiss his neck.

As soon as I'm close to his neck my eyes fly open. Blake smells differently, I look through my drunken haze and realise immediately it isn't Blake.

I go to shove him off, but his hands grip tighter.

"Now, bitch I was enjoying that why'd ya have to go and ruin it?"

He drawls into my ear, I shove my elbows into his gut, but he doesn't let go.

I look for Raven, but she is getting hot and heavy with Big Papa. I look around, there are men around the fire pit I don't recognise any of them. Where the hell are my folks and Blake?

I can feel myself panicking I try to shove and wiggle free, but he just chuckles in my ear.

"Now bitch you aint guna tease me and get away, you want it and I'm guna give it to ya. You're a club whore and I'm a club member you serve me bitch." He demands.

My body has gone ice cold fear taking over me. I try and fight him off me, looking around for any kind of help but the club members that are there, have their backs to me or women on their laps and music is loud they aren't paying no attention to what's happening.

"You leave me the hell alone I aint no club whore

I'm Blakes girlfriend get your fucking hands off me." I scream, at him. Suddenly I feel myself stumble backwards and fall to the ground landing hard banging my head. I roll to my side and look up to find Blake has grabbed the guy up by his throat against the building.

Trudy comes running over to me.

"You okay sweetie? Oh shoot you bumped your head, it's bleeding come on let's get it cleaned up, can you walk honey?"

I nod as she helps me to stand Blake has a look of stone cold death across his face, and his squeezing around the guys neck tighter and tighter not letting up.

I go to walk towards Blake and Trudy grabs my arm stopping me.

I turn to her looking panicked.

"I need to go to Blake, I need to stop him, or he will kill him." I plead.

"Come with me honey, he won't kill him. Rip, Max, Wes and the others will make sure he doesn't. Let him get this out of his system, what virus was doing with you was way outta line and he needs to be held accountable for that. Come on now let's clear you up or Blakes guna loose his shit even more if he sees you bleeding all over the place."

I let Trudy steer me into the clubhouse.

I'm sat in a large kitchen area and Trudy has been clearing up my small head cut. It's only a minor cut, nothing a bit of gauze won't fix.

"Umm Trudy where are my parents?"

She smiles down at me.

"Me, Max and Rip took them back to our house to stay overnight, your mum had a bit too much to drink, and your dad had as well. Plus jet lag and you were happy dancing with Raven, so we thought it be a good idea. Rip, Wes and few others went for a meeting about something or another, and well I can only guess that Raven and Big Papa went somewhere private if you know what I mean? So don't worry they are safe at ours."

I smile and grab Trudy's hand giving it a squeeze.

"I'm sorry I caused this trouble, if the guy had known sooner I was with Blake I'm sure this whole matter would have been avoided."

Trudy smiles and squeezes my hand back.

"Honey virus knew who you were, Rip made sure to everyone in the club you were off limits, that you were Blakes. Between us that man makes my skin crawl, there's a reason they call him virus. Because he can infect and destroy people. That man is poison. Rips been watching him like a hawk, since he heard a few things but needs proof before he can act on anything. Now Max hasn't told me what they are or any details as its club business, but I am hoping they kick him out soon I've never liked the guy."

I let out a long breath. And a few tears fall as

Rise Above

I stare at my hands. I can't help but feel that if I hadn't of been dancing or teasing as virus had said then this could of all been avoided. I need to stay the hell away from tequila and whatever else they were giving me I know that.

Trudy gets me to hold the gauze on my wound while she cleans up. As she's gathering the bits the kitchen door flies open in Blake stops looking at Trudy and the blood stained cleaning wipes. Then his eyes swing to me, holding my gauze to my head.

Anger takes over his face as he turns on his heels and storms out the room slamming the door. I look to Trudy wide eyed she stops what she's doing and runs off after him.

"Stay here honey I will go see what that boy Is playing at."

I don't get a chance to reply before she's gone. I can't stop the flow of tears now. Dropping my gauze I get up and walk towards a back door needing to be outside in fresh air. I walk across the yard and sit at the foot of a tree. I look out across fields staring at the stars, I lie down curling into a ball just looking at the night sky. There's no party going on now all music has stopped and just the smell of the fire pit fills the air.

I feel my eyes becoming heavy and slowly drift off to sleep with the help of the bump to the head and the alcohol.

Soon I feel someone move my hair from my face I

open my eyes and see Blake.

"Hey, I must have fallen asleep, sorry." I apologise.

I move to sit up my head throbbing, instinctively I wince I reach for where I bumped it. There will be a nice bruise there at least I have a matching set I suppose.

Blakes eyes follow my hand to my small cut and nice bruised small egg on my head. The anger in his eyes return briefly before he controls it.

"How long have I been out here asleep?" I ask, twisting my fingers together, looking at my hands. So embarrassed by tonight's dramas I can't look him in the face. I am also worried that he did something stupid and he's going to get himself into trouble for it. I seem to be good at that out here in Texas getting myself into situations.

Blake sweeps the hair from my face and gently grabs my chin lifting my face to forcing me to look into his eyes.

"You've been out here for about 45 minutes. Trudy came and found me said you were in the kitchen and when you weren't there I couldn't find you, none of us could, had us all searching for you. We couldn't see you in the dark led down by the tree."

"Oh I'm sorry I didn't mean to worry anyone I just needed some air and I led down looking at the stars and with the bump and alcohol I guess I just drifted off to sleep."

Blake gently runs his thumb along my chin and jaw, he lets go and reaches into his jean pocket and pulls out his phone putting it to his ear.

"Rip, yeah found her by the old tree out back asleep, yeah she's fine. Speak to you in the mornin'."

He hangs up and puts his phone away he moves to sit next me. I go back to staring at my hands, waiting what's coming. The it's been fun, but I like a quiet simple life, take care.

I wipe the tear falling down my face, next thing I know Blake is lifting me astride his lap. I let out a pathetic yelp in surprise and grab his shoulders.

Blake wipes the tears that had fallen off my cheek, wraps his hand around the back of my head and pulls me in for a kiss. A long hard passionate kiss, that leaves me and Blake breathing heavy . I rest my forehead on his, eyes closed still gripping his shoulders tight.

"Wow, I guess you're not dumping me then?" I ask and get no answer just silence I open my eyes looking into Blakes, who is now smiling looking at me.

"What's so funny why are you smiling?"

Blake sweeps my hair behind my ear.

"I'm smiling darlin' because I could have killed virus for what he was doing to you. Don't worry I didn't. While I was searching for you, I thought you'd seen me lose my shit, that had scared you and you ran off. I thought that I'd lost you, that I had screwed up the best thing that's come into my life. You've buried yourself under my skin darlin' from that first night in the bar and I aint letting you go."

I look into Blakes eyes, tears filling mine, I tighten my grip on his shoulders.

"Blake, you don't-"

Blake puts a finger on my lips quieting me.

"Listen darlin' I aint finished in what I need to say. I failed in protectin' you again tonight, I didn't deal with that all too well. I'm sorry darlin' I let you down. But you can't get rid of me yet, I need to make it up to you. I will fight everyone and everything that tries to mess with what we got. Like I said you're in deep and I know what we got its good but without this crap and some smooth sailing I know it can be fucking awesome, you guna give me that chance darlin'?"

Looking into Blakes eyes I see his vulnerability there, his beautiful deep blue eyes staring back at me. I cannot believe this handsome man with a caring protective heart is begging me to give him a chance. I smile at Blake nodding my head.

"Fucking clueless." I say leaning in to kiss Blake, Blake lets out a small chuckle which soon turns into a low throaty growl. I stop kissing Blake breathing heavy staring into his eyes I lean back untucking my top from my skirt, I lift it over my head leaving me in my black crop bikini. I remove it. Sat before Blake myself bare to him, his eyes lazily sweep over my face and chest. The heat and hunger in his eyes makes my nipples hard.

Blake grabs me pulling me forward kissing my neck working his way down to my breasts. I let out a deep throaty moan.

"Blake, I need you now please."

Blake place two fingers in my thong running them along my seam, I suck in a breath.

"You're fuckin' soaked darlin, were guna be quick but only coz I don't want no one seeing what's mine, when we are back in my bed I'm taking my time tasting you."

With that he removes his fingers and sucks on them and pulls me in to kissing him tasting myself on him. I'm shamelessly grinding myself on him desperate for release.

Blake makes quick work unfastening his zipper, he pulls my thong to the side and he pulls me down impaling me on him. I throw my head back letting out a cry.

I start rotating my hips, rising and lowering myself, watching Blakes face as I do. His hands grip my hips tight, as I increase my rhythm, the feeling building within me. Blake pulls me towards him kissing me. I'm trying to hold my orgasm back, Blake kisses and bites and nips at my neck. Whispering in my ear.

"Let it go darlin' come for me."

He then takes my nipple in his mouth and I can't

hold back any longer I shatter apart calling his name.

Blake grabs my hips thrusting himself in me soon letting out a low growl finding his own release. I gently rock my hips, his face nestled in my neck.

Blake slowly kisses up my neck, leaning back slightly, he holds my face, giving me a slow long kiss. It has my nipples hardening and my pussy contracting all over again.

Blake smiles.

"My girl wants more. I didn't think you were greedy darlin'?"

Purposefully tightening my walls around him, making him let out a throaty groan. I smile.

"Only when it comes to you, I want all of you, you can never have too much of a good thing."

I wink, and Blake throws his head back laughing still rocking my hips slowly, I clench my walls around him again feeling him harden. His laughter dies and he grips my hips letting out a low growl.

"Come on darlin' I'm taking you to bed, where I can enjoy taking my time with you."

He leans forward smiling slowly running his tongue around my nipple making me suck in a breath. He lifts me off him like I'm nothing but a feather, and I let out a whimper immediately missing the connection of us.

I stand and Blake hands me my top, I make quick work of getting it back on, it suddenly hitting me that we are not in private.

Blake grabs my hand and starts pulling me in a hurry towards the clubhouse.

"Umm Blake, I'm not in the mood to be social with others I just really want to shag until I can't walk."

Blake bursts out laughing. Stopping and pulling me to his chest, looking down at me smiling. Looking up at him I can the help but smile back.

"Darlin' I have a room here, I don't intend on being social I intend on doing just that. Challenge accepted miss Rocke be prepared to be shagged as you say, until you can't walk."

It's my turn to burst out laughing. Blake smiles kissing me. I've fallen for him, I am totally head over fucking heels in love for this man. And I'm scared shitless. I plan on enjoying every last minute I have with him. Until the time comes that I have to go back home. I won't tell him and make it more complicated for us, for him. I will deal with the hurt and the pain away from him when I get home. I feel a tear slip from the corner of my eye, Blake notices and frowns wiping the tear away with his thumb.

"Darlin' why are you crying?"

Blinking I quickly smile brushing it off.

"Just a happy tear from laughing that's all now come on Mr Stone, you said you have a challenge to conquer."

Blake seems to accept my answer and not push the matter, he leans in smiling giving me a quick kiss, and continues to pull me to his room where Blake proved that Texas boys never shy away from a challenge and he indeed did shag me so much I couldn't walk.

I awake feeling groggy and my body sore like I did a major workout, I smile remembering last night with Blake.
I turn to see Blake isn't in bed, but a note is left on his pillow.

Darlin
you were snoring so loud I couldn't sleep ;) come to the kitchen when you wake up, I'll make you some breakfast. That's if you can walk by now.
Blake
xxx

Smiling I get up and try to find my clothes which I can't seem to find anywhere. I go to a chest of draws to look for a t-shirt or something I can put on. Opening the top draw it has Blakes boxers in, so I grab a pair putting them on. They are a little tight around my hips and bum, but I don't have much choice. I go to close the draw and notice a gun I freeze. I know the laws with guns are extremely different here than back home, but the sight of a gun still shocks me. Apart from a water gun or toy dart gun I've never seen one before. I shut the draw carrying on my search for a t shirt. I find an old Ac Dc top, which is also a little tight across the chest, shrugging it will have to do. I head out to the kitchen.

Finally finding the kitchen after getting a little lost, I walk through the door not paying any attention.

"Mr Stone, your girl is ravenous, you need to fill me.. again! ha-ha and I can walk too, even if I am walking a little like John Wayne."

Stopping dead in my tracks. I soon take in my surroundings and It's not just Blake sat around the kitchen bar. Rip, Khan and next to Blake is Wes. I turn to the stove there is Also a couple of prospects cooking the breakfast both looking right at me.

I feel my face heat with embarrassment. Laughter fills the room. Blake looks me up and down a big smile on his face slowly disappearing. Frowning I look down at myself, I'm not exposing anything I'm covered. Looking back up at Blake I shrug and walk to him still ignoring the looks and laughter from the guys.

Blakes sat on a stall I immediately stand in between his legs putting my arms around him and he grabs my hips pulling me closer. I kiss him long and slow until one of the guys wolf whistles, I pull away a little smiling.

"Morning handsome." I say smiling in a breathy greeting.

Blake smiles.

"Morning flower! It's damn good to see you this morning.

Khan says raising his cup up in greeting I smile. A little confused by his greeting.

"Hey, get back to fucking cooking breakfast." Rip barks his order to the prospects. Frowning I turn and see both prospects spin round to the cooker fast, but both keep looking back at me every now and again. I turn around and find the guys looking at me too. Especially at my chest.

Looking down at myself I check the top doesn't have a hole in it and my nipple has decided to join the morning breakfast. There's no hole. I look up, Khan is smiling I try turning to look at my behind to see if there's a tear. The guys start laughing. I Step back and hold out my arms and spin slowly in a circle getting pissed.

"Okay, what is so bloody funny about me in Blakes clothes. You care to fill me in?"

I stand now hands on my hips needing a coffee this is too much to deal with before my coffee.

"Darlin', not laughing at you, you look fuckin hot." Blake pulls me back to stand between his legs.

Rip speaks up.

"Babe, we aint laughing at you believe me. None of us have enjoyed looking at another guys boxers or reading Ac Dc until now."

The guys start chuckling and I hide my face in Blakes neck embarrassed.

"Don't hide flower, you've made my fucking mornin' and Blake you're a lucky son of a bitch. You ever feel like sharing, I don't mind sharing toys." Khan hollers.

Blakes eyes narrow and he sets his jaw teeth grinding.

Rip smacks khan hard around the back of the head.

"Ow! Motherfucker pres!"

Khan says rubbing his head.

"Listen to me Khan, you'd be better keeping your fucking thoughts to yourself in future or Rip giving you a smack upside the head will be the least of your fucking worries, we clear?!"

Blake threatens in a low almost growl. And boy its fucking hot to watch him being all alpha. It has me clenching my legs.

"Umm babe, can you help me with something?"

I ask Blake as casual as I can, but it comes out all breathy and needy. Blake swings his gaze round to me. And smiles as he sees the desire in my eyes.

Without any warning Blake bends lifting me over his shoulder, I squeal and laugh. Blake slaps my arse. And marches toward to kitchen door.

"I'll catch you guys later Lily needs me to take care of something."

All the guys laugh and whistle. I laugh and cover my face in my hands.

That morning I let Blake get all alpha with me, twice. I now no longer walk like John Wayne more like Bambi.

After the prospects brought us a late breakfast, we curled up and fell asleep, we didn't leave his room until late afternoon.

CHAPTER FOURTEEN

The next few days with my parents were great, I introduced them to Suellen, Evelynn, Louisa and Sam. And took them to Jeanie's diner. Mum and dad loved the food so much my mum begged Jeanie for her recipe's.

I took them to the Merricks to show them the farm, while Blake had to get work done. Sam took them on a big tour, as I grabbed some more of my clothes to take back to Blakes. As I place my bag on my bed I notice a note on my pillow. Frowning I pick it up.

You think you're safe, you think I won't come back and take what's mine, I'm watching you, I will come for you that's a promise.

Shaking I grip the note in my hand, I spin in a panic looking around the room like he's still there. I sit on the bed trying to slow my breathing. I need to decide what to do. If I show Blake there is no doubt he will go ape shit. He

will go all over protective. And so will my parents. As long as I stay with someone I am safe. No one needs to worry about this. They all deserve a little bit of normality at the moment no more of my dramas and craziness. I screw up the note chucking it in the bin and grab my clothes quickly and get the hell out of there. I find Sam and my parents, I plaster on a fake smile.
"Hey honey, this farm is beautiful. You okay you look a little pale?"
Mum asks concern on her face. I nod.
"Fine mum just rushed a little quick in this heat I think. Little light headed that's all."
Mum pulls me to her.
"Let's get you sat down and a nice cold drink, that will make you feel better."
I push the note to the back of my mind and try to enjoy the time I have left with my parents here.

Mum and dad loved the town and the people. It was their last night, so I was taking them to the Den, everyone was coming to join us in their farewell drinks. They had only been there for ten days to check on me and see I was okay, that time had gone by so quick.
Earlier that day my dad had asked Blake to take him to the police station to ask the sheriff about what they were doing in trying to find the guy, I told him he didn't need to go and that he should let the police deal with it their way and not get involved. But Blake agreed with my dad and

said he wouldn't mind having a word with the sheriff himself. My mum said to let them be and suggested we go shopping for a new outfit for tonight. So Blake dropped me and mum at the mall while they went off to the station. I found a killer little black dress and mum treated herself to a new top. Without Blake or one of the guys with us I found myself constantly looking over my shoulder.

I'm not sure what was said at that meeting with the sheriff, but Blake and my dad didn't come back from it in the best of moods.

I was getting ready putting on my new dress which made me feel sexy.

It was a fitted stretchy material with short cap sleeves, wrap over the bust, and ruched all the way down to the knee.

I had also treated myself to new underwear. I paired the dress with gold heeled strappy sandals and gold bangles. I put product in my hair and let it dry natural and wavy down my back.

I kept my make-up light apart from my winged eyeliner and deep red lipstick.

It was a bit dressy for the Den, but it was my parents last night and it's not like I can get dressed up often. So I was making the most of it.

There is a knock on the bedroom door, just as I was touching up my lipstick.

"Come in, I'm decent." I shout.

I carry on applying my lipstick and was met

with silence, I turned around to see Blake stood there watching me. The heat in his eyes as he looked me up and down.

I smiled and walked towards him swaying my hips just a little more than usual.

"I take it you like the dress?"

Blake pulls me flush to him, I can feel just how much he likes the dress.

"I will take that as an affirmative."

Blake runs his finger along the seam of the dress, down to the v of my breasts.

"I want to kiss you right now, but it will ruin your lipstick." Blakes says in a rough low whisper.

I grab Blakes neck pulling his mouth down on mine I kiss him long and hard.

I pull away, smiling.

"It's smudge-proof babe, so kiss me anytime. Also you must stop coming into the room while I'm getting ready. Or we will never go anywhere."

Blake smiles placing a piece of my hair behind my ear.

"I don't mind staying in the bedroom all the time and not going anywhere."

Blake winks and I burst out laughing.

"Come on handsome my parents and your brother are downstairs waiting for us you can rock my world later."

With that I grab my bag and saunter past Blake, adding that extra sway in my hips.

He slaps my arse and I spin around to give him a look. Blake then grabs my hand pulling me to him.

"You sway your hips and that beautiful ass at me like that darlin' you're asking for a spanking. And I fucking promise it will be while I'm buried inside you. I don't give a shit if your parents are downstairs or not."

With that he leans in taking my mouth in a hot and heavy kiss that leaves us both panting. I'm close to saying to hell with tonight take to bed now. But I don't think my parents would like that much.

Walking into the lounge, Wes is knocking back a beer my mum showing him photos of my sister on her phone. I roll my eyes.

"You see Wesley, all my girls are beautiful, and what's even better is that my Rose is a nurse, and already has a son so it's like a little readymade family that you can choose to expand on."

Wes just smiles at my mum politely, giving me the eye to come rescue him.

Laughing I walk over to mum taking her phone off her. Noticing the picture on her phone is of me, Rose, Daisy and Ax, from my leaving party. I smile its rare you get us all together like that.

"Mum, one; leave poor Wes alone, he's quite capable of finding his own woman, two; Rose would kill you if she could hear you right now, three; please send me a copy of this picture. And finally mum stop pimping out my skin and blister!" I chide.

I hand mum back the phone, Wes is chuckling.

"I am not pimping out my daughter! I'm merely showing Wesley pictures of the family, I think he would very much like Rose and her him. There's no harm in that." Mum defends.

Shaking my head, I look to dad who shakes his head holding up his hands clearly stating to not involve him.

"Wait what's your skin and blister?" Wes asks looking confused, my dad pipes up.

"It's cockney rhyming slang son, skin and blister is sister, apple and pears is stairs, jack and danny is fanny and so on. He replies.

Wes still looks confused.

"Why not just say sister? I don't understand." Wes asks confused.

"Wes you don't need to understand it is what it is. Don't worry about it otherwise you'll have my dad explain the history of the cockney's. As for you mum, call him Wes ok it's what he prefers and just ease off, I don't think Rose is really looking for a guy right now." I state.

Sighing my mum finally relents.

"Fine, have it your way. Wes do you mind if I take a picture of you to show Rose when I get back?"

"Oh my god mum!"

Wes is full on laughing now, dads shaking his

head. Wes nods in agreement and mum takes a picture. I put my head in my hands. This woman is relentless. If she had her way we'd all be married with at least two kids each by now.

"Thank you Wes, my, you're a handsome lad aren't you?"

Mum says looking back at the picture she just took.

"Thank you Mrs Rocke, I got the best genes in the family. Poor Blake has to deal with being second best."

Blake looks up from his phone and give's Wes the finger making Wes laugh.

"You just keep telling yourself that, right come on let's get to the Den, I need a drink."

Blake turns grabbing his keys.

When we arrive at the Den everyone is there, even Rip, a few of the guys from Satans Outlaws and his parents Max and Trudy.

Sat on a table with Suellen and Evelynn. Suellen telling us all about her recent date, Evelynn and I are doubled over in hysterics.

"So not only was he dumb as a prairie dog, he was tight enough to raise a blister. I mean who asks a lady to dinner at the fanciest restaurant in town and doesn't make a damn reservation leaving us stood by the bar for over an hour. Then when the waiter asked him how he liked steak his reply was from a cow and flame grilled. I swear the waiter choked back a laugh and looked at me with utter sympathy in his eyes.

Then after a painstakingly slow dinner he asked for the bill. I'm nice and I didn't want to hurt his feelings and run to the ladies and not come back. He took one damn look at that bill and I swear said a prayer under his breath. Then proceeded to tell me he only had fifty dollars that was all his mama gave him! Leaving me to pay the bill."

I'm crying with laughter as is Evelynn.

"I'm surprised his mum wasn't there being his chaperone making sure he's behaving. Christ if you flashed him a boob that poor little mama's boy would have a boner till Christmas." Evelynn says through her laughter.

"His mama did show up! He had an eleven o'clock curfew she was sat outside in her damn truck!" Suellen exclaims.

"Oh my god I'm going to pee myself in a minute! Where the hell did you meet this guy?" Evelynn cries.

"A friend at work set us up believe me that person is no friend any more, they are coming right off my Christmas card list."

Suellen states with conviction knocking back the rest of her drink.

Standing still wiping away the tears from laughing so much, I go to the bar for the next round of drinks.

The place is packed out tonight, they have a live band performing and apparently in Evelynn's words they are 'the shit.' Which I'm told in these

parts means they are bloody good. I reach the bar, and squeeze between the bodies surrounding the bar. Holding out my hand to try and get the barman's attention. Eventually he catches my eye and heads my way.
"Howdy miss Rocke what can I get ya?" The young barman greets.

"Umm hi sorry have we met?" I ask.
Furrowing my brows I try to remember if we've met.

"No ma'am I haven't had the pleasure until now, Mr Stone pointed you out to us staff. Said we are to make sure you are served quickly and to not charge. So what will it be ma'am?"
Smiling and rolling my eyes, I give my order as he trays up our drinks and hands them to me, I force a twenty dollar bill in his hand.
"No, ma'am they are on the house Mr Stone ordered it."

"I know I'm not paying you for the drinks, I'm giving you a tip for your services, Mr Stone didn't say I couldn't tip."
I turn leaving him with a smile and a wink. I place the drinks on our table, needing the ladies.
"Just off to the toilet I'm about to burst, can you give my dad his beer and mum her gin and tonic?" I ask Evelynn she nods, I turn and as quick as I can I head for the toilets.
I swear giving me a couple of drinks seems to

give me the bladder of a toddler.

After I've finished my business, I wash my hands checking my lipstick in the mirror. I turn and walk out of the ladies.

All of a sudden I have my arm grabbed and I'm being hurled backwards and pushed into the wall hard, hitting the back of my head. Before I can even register what's going on, a hand covers my mouth. And Ven leans in close. My breathing escalates and tears fill my wide and frantic eyes, praying for anyone to walk down here. I whimper to try and scream in my throat. I feel him stick something sharp at my side.

"Shut it bitch, I've got a knife and If you scream or try anything I will cut ya. Now listen to me, you think your all high and fuckin' mighty coming to my town. I show you kindness and take you out and you have the fuckin' nerve to deny me. I didn't say I was done with you. I say when I'm done. Teasing me, practically begging me to fuck that fat fucking ass of yours." He spits.

I try shaking my head, frowning. I'm confused I've never led him on in any way. Using his hand with the knife, he runs it down my chest over my breast travelling down to the edge of my dress. I whimper and try kicking his hand and the knife away, I try pulling his hand away from my mouth so I can call for help.

Ven just grips my mouth tighter, and he slams the back of my head into the wall so hard that my vision blurs and it hurts like hell.

I whimper, tears running down my face, I'm begging him with my eyes to please just let me go. Ven's eyes are so wild and cold, and I can see he's enjoying this.

"Shut the fuck up whore, you're fuckin' begging me to touch you, wearing that fuckin' dress! You fat fuckin' cunt." He seethes through his teeth and rears back spits in my face.

Now you listen to what I'm saying. You stay the fuck away from Stone and you leave this fuckin' town, do you hear me? Your ruining the fuckin' town and the order. You tell Stone and them scum bikers to back the fuck off, or I will fuckin' kill em' and their bitches too."

What the hell does he mean? I have no idea, he's gone crazy.

There's people heading this way the noise distracts Ven turning his head in that direction. I kick out as hard as I can making Ven stumble back a step his hand moving from my mouth. I scream for help. But only half comes out before I'm being grabbed by my hair and my head is slammed into the wall.

I hear women's voices scream about going for help.

Dazed I fall to the floor Ven leans over me smirking.

"Don't forget what I told you sweetheart, it's a fuckin' promise."

With that leans back and kicks me hard in my side over and over. I feel a shooting pain through my ribs and hear a crack. I cry out. The sound of my pain spurring him on he smiles. He just does it more, I'm coughing as the wind is being kicked out of me. I hear voices in the distance, Ven kicks me one last time then spits on me again and then disappears. I'm close to passing out from the pain, nausea building along with my vision clouding. I can't make out who's there.

I keep losing consciousness, finally I can hear a familiar voice.

"Shit! Fuck! Flower what the fuck?!"

"Kh-a-a-n" I wheeze.

"It's ok I'm guna get Blake."

He goes to stand but I try my best to reach out and stop him. I'm so scared if he leaves me Ven will return.

"Nn - no pl – ease do - don't go."

I manage to wheeze out. Khan stops, he holds my hand and I hear him pull out his phone.

I feel my eyes getting heavy the pain is too much that I welcome the darkness that's starting to take over me.

"Hold on in their flower. Yeah Wes, emergency get Blake now! And come to the back of the club where the rest rooms are. Its flower, she's been attacked."

I hear him on his phone again, I'm finding it harder and harder to breathe, the pain is like no other.

"Pres, it's flower she's been attacked at the back of the Den, I'm with her now, Wes is finding Blake. I don't fuckin know. Hold on.
flower who did this darlin?"
"V-e-n" I wheeze only being able to take short spurts of breath.

"Shit fuck you hear that pres. Yeah search for that mother fucker."
I try shaking my head.

"Nn-o pp lease." I try and beg Khan I really struggling now to stay awake. Finding it harder to breathe.

"It will be ok flower I promise."
I hear running footsteps approach. I hear my name being called.
"Darlin', shit! What the fuck?"
Its Blake I reach for him as best I can.
"Blake we gotta get her to the hospital, reckon she got a cracked rib or summit."
I hear Khan say, I feel Blakes arms go under me to lift me. The movement causes me excruciating pain. I cry out. Blake halts his movement.
"Sorry darlin' but I gotta get you to hospital." His voice is pained. I nod and tense waiting for the pain. Blake moves me as gentle as he can, but it still causes me to scream out in pain. I'm cradled in Blakes arms my breathing is becoming more strained. I close my eyes finally giving into the darkness, the pain is too much I welcome it.

"Stay awake darlin', show me those beautiful eyes." Blake begs.

I try and flutter my eyes open, but my body just wants to black out. As I fall deeper into darkness I hear Blakes voice.

"darlin'? shit, drive faster Wes her breathing is getting fuckin' worse."

His voice is so strained and in pain I want to wrap my arms around him and comfort him. But soon I can't keep the darkness out and I am out cold.

CHAPTER FIFTEEN

I can hear mumbled voices talking, I slowly open my eyes, the bright hospital lights pierce my eyes. Vaguely I remember the events that brought me here. Squinting I can see my mum and dad at the end of my bed. My dad cuddling my mum rubbing her back neither are looking in my direction. I feel warmth on my hand I look down to see Blake leaning on the bed asleep holding on to my hand. I reach with my other hand to gently stroke his beautiful peaceful face as he sleeps. The pain as I reach across shoots through me causing me to jolt and suck in a sharp breath.

The noise and movement has Blake shooting up and my parents turn around to face me. Blake leans forward stroking my hair from my face. He looks tired his face etched with worry. I smile a small smile.

"Hey handsome, sorry I woke you." I croak still finding it painful to breathe and talk. My mouth feeling like sandpaper

"Darlin'." He rasps leans in and places a gentle kiss on my dry lips. The emotion in his voice brings tears to my eyes. I try blinking them away, but Blakes sees them and wipes them away. He kisses a soft lingering kiss on the top of my head and moves back. My mum comes rushing to my side.

"Oh sweetheart, thank god you're okay. You feel okay? need me to get the nurse? You in pain? Need more pain relief? Need a drink?"
My mum frantically asks, worry in her voice. Knowing my mum it's because she hates feeling helpless.
"For god sake woman, leave the girl be, you okay baby girl?" My dad asks, his face etched with worry too, although he's keeping a better lid on it than my mum.
"I'm okay, could you please get me some water mum?"
My dad lets out a breath, relived I'm alright and a knowing smile on his face. He knows just me asking for water will soothe my mum making her feel like she's doing something to help. I smile a small smile back.
"Come on Penn, let's go get our girl some water."
Mum nods tears in her eyes but puts on a smile anyway.
"Okay, we will tell the nurse you're awake too."
Mum leans in kissing my forehead.

"Love you so much baby girl."

Closing my eyes fighting back the tears at the sound of my mums raw emotion in her voice. I paste on a smile as she stands

"Love you too mum, and you dad." I rasp.

I notice dad swallow a lump in his throat, but he pastes on the same smile back at me.

"Right back at ya baby girl."

He takes mums hand and they leave the room, leaving Blake and I alone.

Blake sits gently next to me and takes my hand in his, kissing it. I smile a wobbly smile, still trying to fight back the tears. Blake not missing a thing notices he doesn't say anything, he just carefully moves to squeeze next to me I lean into him pain be damned. He gently as he can wraps his arm around me letting me cry, he strokes my hair kissing the top of my head every now and again.

Soon my tears subside. Blake starts talking.

"You scared the shit outta me, do you remember what happened?"

I nod sniffing back the tears.

"When you are ready darlin' I want you to tell me everything you remember. That asshole broke three of your ribs, one punctured your lung. You had to have emergency surgery. You were struggling to breathe. You also suffered mild concussion from the hit to the back of your head. Swear to god I thought I was guna lose you."

I thread my fingers through Blakes bringing his hand to my mouth I kiss the back of his hand. Blake kisses the top of my head.

"I'm sorry I scared you. Wait has mum and dad missed their flight?"
I slowly lean back slightly so I can look up and Blake. He looks down at me and slowly runs his finger along the edge of my face to my jaw his eyes following his fingers movement.
"Darlin' shut up apologising and yeah your folks flight was this morning its now nearly 7pm. You've been asleep since you got out of surgery, partly to do with the op and the meds they got you on but also from your concussion. Your folks aint guna be going nowhere. Not until they know Ven is dealt with and they know your safe. That's if you still want to even stay in this god damn town now, if you didn't I want fuckin' blame you. Christ shit you've been attacked twice."
My heart beats fast in my chest, wait does Blake want me to go home? All this hassle and drama following me around has he finally had enough?
"Do you want me to go home?" I ask watching him intently even through everything that's happened it hadn't even crossed my mind to fly back home no matter what happens here. No way would my heart let me just leave like that. I love this man, every inch of him. Even if he doesn't know it yet. The only way I'd leave is if

he asked me to. It would break me but for him I would do it.

"Shit darlin' no fuckin' way, I want you safe, I want you to stay. I didn't mean that. I meant if you said you wanted to go I'd be devastated but I'd understand."

Wincing at the pain the movement causes me but ignoring it and doing it anyway I reach up and kiss Blake with all that I have conveying what I feel for him, pouring all my emotion into it. It's not the right time to tell him I love him yet, not why I'm lying in a hospital bed. I don't want him to feel guilty in having to say it back. And to be honest I'm scared he won't say it back. Pulling back slightly my breathing laboured from the effort that took me. Looking into Blakes eyes as he cups and strokes my face.

"Sorry Mr handsome I aint going nowhere. Your stuck with this annoying brit for a while yet."

Blake smiles and gently kisses me.

"Good to hear darlin' now lay the fuck back down, as much as I enjoy your mouth on me, I'm not enjoying the pain and discomfort your in."

I laugh lightly and regret it immediately the pain it causes has me sucking in my breath and squeezing my eyes shut.

"Shit darlin, you okay?"

I nod as it slowly eases, looking at Blake his worrying face looking back at me.

"I'm fine, since when did your macho alpha

side start coming out more?" I mock trying to lighten his mood again.
It works Blake chuckles slightly smiling back at me.

"Since I have this crazy British girl to watch out for, my macho alpha side as you call it keeps coming out wanting to protect her."
Blake gives me a wink and kisses the back of my hand, standing as there's a knock at the door, my mum and dad come back in followed by a nurse. Mum hands me my water which I sip, the cool liquid feeling amazing down my dry throat.

"I just have to make a couple of calls to Wes and the guys let them know your awake. I will be back in a bit darlin."
Blake leans and kisses my head I smile and nod in reply. Mum and dad watch as the nurse does her checks and gives me my meds. She asks if I'm hungry and would like something to eat, in response my stomach rumbles. Which has the nurse laughing she says she will be back in a minute with some food for me.
Mum and dad come and sit either side of my bed, both taking one of my hands.

"I'm sorry you guys missed your flight, I hope you will get a full refund if not I can reimburse you."
I say looking back and forth to my mum and dad.
"Shut up girl, your mum and me don't give a

damn about the money or the flight. We are just glad that you're alive and breathing. And we aint going nowhere until you either come home with us, or we are 100% sure that you are bloody well safe from that dickhead."

My dad states angrily. My mum nodding in agreement with him. I sniffle back a tear and smile.

"I'm not going home dad."

Dad just nods.

"We knew you wouldn't sweetheart, you love Blake anyone can see that, he loves you too. That of course does mean that me and your dad will be sticking around a little longer."

My head swings to my mum eyes wide.

"How did you know I love Blake? Did I say anything when I was drugged up in here? And mum he doesn't, he hasn't said that he does, and I haven't told him how I feel yet so please keep that quiet." I beg.

My mum smiles huge back at me, my dad just rolls his eyes at her.

" Ha! I bloody told you she loved him Ben. And I know I'm right about him loving her too!" My mum hoots in my dad's face. Then turns back to me.

"Don't worry sweetheart I won't say anything." Mum pats my hand gently.

"Nice one mum, can't believe I walked into that one."

I smile and let out a big yawn. There's a knock at the door and Blake walks back in carrying a tray of food. Immediately my mum jumps to her feet and grabs the table wheeling it up to me. And topping up my water.

"The nurse handed me this saying to tell you to eat what you can. She had to rush off to an emergency"

Blake puts the tray on my table, and my stomach growls loudly. Making the whole room laugh. Its meatloaf, potatoes, veg, and a jelly pot.

Blake perches next to me and starts cutting up my food for me and starts to feed me. I smile.

"Hey handsome my hands aren't broken you know I'm quite capable of feeding myself. We've been over this before remember?" I say giving him a wink.

Blake gives me a small sad smile.

"Just give me this darlin' let me feel like I'm helping you in some way. I failed protecting you let me please take care of you."

My heart expands and I nod. Blake smiles and feeds me my dinner.

I eat about half of the dinner and the jelly pot not managing to eat anymore and I feel exhausted from that and the meds that I drift off to sleep.

Few hours later I'm woken to mumbled voices in my room. I flutter my eyes open to see who's talking.

I see Rip, Wes, and Blake stood in a huddle. None of them noticing I'm awake. Frowning I wonder what they are up too.

A flashback of what Ven warned me to tell Blake

and the others to back off.

"Don't, don't carry on with whatever you guys have been doing or are planning on doing regarding Ven. It's not worth taking the risk. Please just leave it to the police." I rasp my throat dry. All three turn and look at me. Blake moves straight towards me kisses my forehead and hands me my water I take a few sips as Wes and Rip move to stand at the end of my bed. Both arms crossed over their chest looking like a couple of badasses. I smile at them both, my smile isn't returned I just get a manly chin lift.

"How'd you know we been looking into Ven flower'?" Rip asks, never missing a trick. Damn it.

"Blake must have mentioned it to me." I say as nonchalantly as possible. I don't want them knowing that Ven threatened them, it will cause more of a shit storm and from what I know of these boys that won't stop them doing whatever they are doing.

"Darlin'." Blake growls in warning. I look at him his eyebrow raised and he's shaking his head.

"What are you trying to keep from us, you're a terrible liar darlin'."

Sighing my only option is to try my hardest to talk them out of it.

"I can't be that bad of a liar I always managed to lie to my parents perfectly fine in my teens."
I state.

"Stop stalling what is it?" Wes says in frustration.

"Fine, but you guys have to promise and swear on your mum's and aunt's lives that you will stop whatever it is your doing and stay out of it and let the police deal with it. Otherwise I'm not saying a bloody word."

I give them the mum look I've seen my mum give me and my siblings over the years the 'don't even think about it look'. But Wes and Rip just fight back a smirk.

Just that long tirade has me out of breath, I try and calm my breathing, and breathe like the nurse told me to. She said it will be a little easier when the drainage tube is taken out of my lung, hopefully soon.

Blake hands me the oxygen mask concern written all over his face. Shaking my head I steady my breathing.

"Darlin' you don't have to tell us anything right now, we will wait until your feeling more up to it. I want you to be able to tell us everything and if you're not up to it then we will wait." Blake says concerned.

"Wait, I just thought where are the police? Did they not want to take my statement?"

All three of them look at each other words not spoken out loud. I look at all them, somethings up.

"what, what is it? Why haven't the police not come to take my statement? Blake sighs he sits next to me taking my hand in his.

"You know Ven is sheriff Johnsons son right?"

Rise Above

Frowning I nod. Blake continues.

"Well when your mum rang and told them what had happened. They stated that they will not be coming out as what she was saying was untrue and if she continued to make prank calls to the sheriff's office they will arrest her for wasting police time. Apparently you weren't attacked you tripped over from drinking too much. Resulting in banging your head and hitting your side. The call was made to the sheriff's office to report it earlier that evening by a concerned member of the public. Your mum not taking any shit asked who, they wouldn't say. But when your mum said it was Ven that had attacked you they said that was impossible as he was at a family dinner with at least three witnesses that can state he was there. The sheriff being one of those witnesses."

Letting what Blake said sinks in. Holy shit this is crazy. This sort of thing only happens in the movies.

"What the fuck?" I ask, Wes lets out a chuckle. We all look to Wes I raise my eyebrow in question.

"Sorry you swearing like that don't match your sweet English accent and innocent face flower." Wes says smiling.

"Thanks Wes I guess. Back to the point in hand, how could they think I fell to the ground hard enough to fracture three ribs and puncture my lung severely enough for me to need surgery.

Also why not ask the bar staff I only went up once and before that Evelynn and Suellen brought a round in each." I say getting irate its making my breathing a struggle I snatch the oxygen mask off Blakes hand in a mood. Don't get me wrong I'm in pain and very uncomfortable but it's very frustrating that I can't say what I want without struggling to breathe every few minutes.

After steadying my anger and trying to do slow deep breaths like the nurse said to keep my lungs stretching. That hurts like a bitch.

I pull down the mask to finish talking.

"And there was witnesses that saw Ven, I didn't see who, but I heard them. They definitely saw. Two women I think, they would have been the ones that got khan for help surely you can't argue that right?" I ask looking at all three of them. That has to be enough to prove that Ven did what he did to me.

It's Rip that speaks up this time.

"Yeah well no one got a good look at who the women were. We were too concerned with you and finding Ven at the time. We are looking for them though just with no name and no description its proving a little difficult. We've put the word out, offered reward for any witnesses to come forward." Rip says firmly arms still crossed over his broad chest.

Leaning my head back I look at the ceiling and sigh. I know I need to tell them everything I also need to protect my parents they need to go home.

Ven and his father cannot continue to do this I want to stay here as long as I can to be with Blake, I love him, they may have beat me down, but I will not let them destroy me and my first chance of happiness I've had in a very long bloody time.

I didn't realise I had let my tears fall, so shut off in my own thoughts. Blake gently wipes them away.

"Darlin' you alright? Need me to call the nurse?" Blake asks frowning at why I'm crying.

"No babe, I'm fine. I'm going to tell you all what happened last night. And about a note I received. You guys need to listen to everything don't interrupt me please just let me get this out."

"What fuckin' note?" Blake growls.

Fuck! I look to the ceiling. Blake gently grabs my chin forcing me to look at him.

"I asked what fuckin' note darlin?"

I look at Rip and then to Wes. They look just as angry. Bollocks.

"Okay, well you know last time we were at the Merricks and you were working. Sam was showing my parents around the farm while I was packing up some more of my clothes to bring over to yours. I noticed a note on my pillow. It was a threat, no make that a promise that whoever had attacked me at the Merricks place wasn't finished with me yet and that they would be back for what was theirs."

I finish avoiding eye contact with any of them. I jump as there is a loud crash. I look up and Blakes hands are gripping his hair. A vase of flowers is smashed in a pile on the floor.

"Blake calm the fuck down man." Rip warns.

"Calm down?!"

Blake spins to me, pissed off.

"Why would you keep something like that from me or even any of the guys?"

Blake asks anger and hurt in his eyes.

"I didn't want you or the guys doing anything stupid, I didn't want you to worry. I thought I'd be safe at your place and as long as I was always with someone I honestly thought I'd be fine."

Blake puts his hands on his hips and looks to the ceiling.

His eyes come to me.

"Stop. Just stop for god damn once worrying about everyone else and stop trying to protect everyone. For once let me and the guys help you. You have no fuckin' clue what we are capable of. You don't know what's been going down. Fuck Lily you could have ended up dead!"

He snaps.

I straighten my back and my shoulders. Feeling defensive and anger build in me too.

"Well I didn't end up dead and I'm sorry I kept it from you, but I honestly thought what I was doing was the right thing for you and the guys. That's what you're supposed to do when you care about people, you try and look out for them. That's all I was doing. So you and the guys can look out for me, but I'm not allowed to do it for you?!" I shout. I grab the oxygen mask, needing it after my outburst.

Blake just stands there and crosses his arms over his chest. No one saying anything for a moment tension high in the room. Blake breaks the silence.

"Tell us about last night."

I nod and wipe the tears.

"You guys might want to sit down there's a fair bit to get through."

I point to the chair across the room and they grab them and pull them up to the end of my bed. Letting out a slow steadying breath, I tell them everything, from the knife, what he said threatening them and the club and their families. Throughout me telling them I watched as the mask of anger descended across all their faces.

Blake moves to sit next to me and takes my hand his thumb softly stroking my hand comforting me. I let the tears fall and I had to stop a couple of times to steady my breathing. As I finished Blake stands slowly kisses the top of my head and walks out of the room. The look on his face was stone cold. Rip gives Wes a look and Wes jumps to his feet and goes after Blake.

Rip then moves to sit next to me. Tears falling down my face I look to Rip worrying Blake has gone to do something stupid.

"Don't worry flower Wes has him, he won't let anything happen to him and Blake won't do anything stupid either. What you've just told us, well flower that's just a fuck of a lot for any man to hear about his woman. Add to that he was in the same fuckin' building when it happened not only that, but it also happened under his own fuckin' roof. That's a lot for any man to take on his shoulders. He needs a little time to work through that. Hell if you were my woman. Ven wouldn't be fuckin' breathin' he'd be choking on my M-9 his pa too."

My eyes wide looking at Rip I can see he means what he says.

"What's an M-9?" I ask and he smiles.

"Out of what I just said that's what you focus on?" He asks and I nod.

"M-9 bayonet is a type of knife, flower. One of my favourites. It has a 7 inch blade and milled saw teeth along the back. It's beautiful. It's what they used to attach to the rifles in the world war, it has history."

Rip says with a look on his face that is scaring me right now, he has what is definitely love and admiration for this knife.

"You like any other knives Rip?" I ask already certain of what his answer will be.

"Why do you think they call be Rip flower? And it aint just coz' I leave people resting in peace. Piss me off I will bring them anything but fuckin' peace."

He lets out a deep throaty chuckle. Although that statement is terrifying I can't help but smile back. As much as I'm sure Rip can be a scary and no doubt dangerous when you cross him or his family. His road name is Rip for a reason. But there's also a caring protective side to him that when the time comes for him to find the woman he chooses they will be loved and adored I'm sure.

"So while we are on the subject you not found your woman yet?"

I ask Rip smiling raising my eyebrow in question.

"We were on the subject?" He asks in response. I shrug and prompt him to continue.

"Not yet, I had my eye on one, but she turned out to belong to someone else."

"Oh Rip that's never nice who was the girl? Things change she could still be yours one day."

I say placing my hand on his in comfort. Rip bursts out laughing. I'm confused at what is so amusing to him. But I'm not going to lie and say the sound of his hot guy laugh doesn't make me blush.

"Fuckin' clueless, flower it's you, you're the girl."

My heart stops beating, I am stunned. I know we had a kiss and a little bond, but I didn't realise he felt that way.

"Rip I..... I'm sorry I didn't realise. I um, well I really like Blake and I don't want to lose what I have with him."

L G Campbell

I mumble feeling my face flush fiddling with the bed sheet not taking my eyes off the very important bit of thread. I've never had this kind of attention before. It's nice but makes me feel uncomfortable.
Rip gently grabs my chin, forcing me to look him in the eye.

"It's okay flower, you love him I can see that. I respect that. He's one lucky son of a bitch. But you're lucky to have him too, he's one of the good ones. But he screws it up I'm making my play and he knows this. A beautiful woman with great ass and tits, and a smile that could knock any man on his ass. A woman that is also sweet, caring and loyal. Shit.
Women like that don't come around often believe me. So I don't blame my cousin. And in truth I'm glad that bastard has found some good."
Rip finishes. I just stare, tears fill my eyes and one spills over. He leans in. kissing the tear away. The move has me closing my eyes and holding my breath. This stunning man who can be so menacing and scary, yet so incredibly warm and caring.
It takes me a moment to compose myself.
"I'm so stunned and flattered Rip. And believe me you will find your woman one day. She will be so bloody lucky to have you there to care and protect them. If things were different maybe,

but there not. Your cousin has stolen my heart it belongs to him."

I pause.

"Umm listen please don't tell Blake that I love him I haven't told him yet. I didn't realise it was so bloody obvious. But I don't want to put pressure on him to return it or feel obligated because I'm in here."

I finish on a small smile, Rip still holding my chin and still very close proximity returns my smile and leans in kissing my cheek just lingering there for a while.

There's a cough from across the room that has me jolting back and looking towards the door. Blake is stood there his jaw set tight and his arms crossed across his chest. Making the mistake of the fast movement I let out a scream from the pain and partly for Blake making me jump. I hold my side trying to slowly breathe through the pain. I look to Blake he looks so angry he's not even looking at me he's staring at Rip. I look to Rip, and he's now stood giving Blake an angry look back. What he has to be angry about I have no idea. God knows what Blake is thinking after walking in on that.

"Blake, babe look at me."

I wheeze still trying to control the pain and steady my breathing which isn't easy when it feels like you have a heard of elephants sat on your chest.

Blakes gaze swings to me, the anger slipping

from his face replaced with concern.

"It's not what it looks like I promise you, I was upset, and Rip was just comforting me. That's all nothing else."

I plead with him. I don't want him to come to the wrong conclusions.

Waiting for Blake to answer its Rip who speaks up.

"Listen to your woman."

That's all he says, Blake swings his eyes to me.

"I know nothing happened I've been stood there for the last five minutes. Rip leave us alone." Blake growls his eyes never leaving mine. And I know my eyes are popping out of my head and I'm biting my lip anxiously. How much of our conversation did he hear?!

Just as Rip walks past Blake to the door. Blake reaches a hand out and grabs Rip's arm. He leans in and in a low threatening voice he says.

"Don't ever touch or get that close and personal to my fucking woman again. Cousin or not I will fuckin' kill you. Understand?"

Rip just smiles and gives him a nod. Clapping him on the shoulder as he leaves.

Blake turns back round to me, I'm still sat there like a deer caught in headlights looking back at Blake as he makes his way to me.

He sits down on my bed next to me. His face not giving anything away.

"You're in love with me?" Blake asks again his face void of emotion. I have no idea to what he's thinking.

I feel my face heat. Well shit looks like I'm telling him now. I just have to prepare that this will be too soon for Blake and not feel the disappointment when it's not returned. Squeezing my eyes shut I take another slow steady breath, it's all I seem to be doing lately.

"I err ... yes Blake I love you, I've fallen hard for you. But it's okay that you're not there yet or ready for that. I don't expect you to return my feelings we've only been seeing each other a short time. I wasn't planning on telling you for a good while yet, I didn't want you to feel obligated to return it as I'm in hospital."

I slowly re open my eyes to see Blake with the same expression on his face not saying anything. "Blake say something please."

Blake doesn't say anything he just leans forward takes my face in his hands and kisses me in a long passionate kiss. When he stops he pulls back only a little looking into my eyes.

"Lily Rocke, I love you. I love your smile, your mouth. I love the way you can be so sweet and innocent one minute then feisty and not afraid to stand up for what you believe in the next. I love the way you care for others, I love how you act like it's an honour that people want to be friends with you when reality is, it's them that are the ones who should feel honoured. I love your eyes, I love your tits and your ass. I love how your body responds to mine like they were

made to be together. Lily Rocke I fuckin' love you, all of you."
I'm crying I'm beyond overwhelm and bursting with happiness and love.
I grab his face and kiss him until I'm struggling for breath.
Once I've calmed my breathing. I kiss his neck and taking in his smell all that is Blake.
"I love you Blake stone. The girl that doesn't like to stand out and be noticed, the girl that was even scared flying here. The girl that doesn't feel like I deserve your attention or even your love. But you did notice me, and through all this shit you've made me rise above my anxieties and fears. There is no way I would be able to go through this without you, I've grown since meeting you Blake. you took my heart I completely belong to you. I bloody love you Mr handsome."
Blake still cupping my face kisses me once more.

Slowly Blake lays down next to me, carefully pulling me to him I rest my head on his chest smiling. I feel my eyes getting heavy I feel myself drift off to sleep. The smile never leaving my face.

CHAPTER SIXTEEN

I spent another week in hospital. It drove me crazy I just wanted to be with Blake.

Rip, Wes and Blake never spoke of what they were involved in or what they were planning on doing with Ven. Every time I was going to ask Blake, someone else came in. I was grateful to all that came and visited me, even Mr and Mrs Merrick came by. They were back from looking after her sister. She brought me her homemade apple and blueberry pie too. Which was delicious. But I wanted to just be alone with Blake for at least five minutes.

Blake hadn't been to visit me in the last two days. Saying he was busy with work. But I had a feeling it was to do with Ven. I missed him like crazy.

But today was finally the day I can be with him and go home, well to Blakes home anyway.

Mum came and told me she'd spoken to my boss who in her words was a complete shithead. He said I was to call him immediately when I'm out of hospital. He was not happy at all.

To be honest my job was the last of my concerns right now I just wanted to make sure Blake, the Satans Outlaws and all the family were safe, and they weren't going to do anything stupid.

I was in the bathroom brushing my teeth, I was packed and ready to bolt out of here. Well a steady walk was all I could manage my ribs were still tender and I still got out of breath a little.

Just finishing up I walked back out to the room and packed my toiletries away. I tried brushing my hair but apparently even lifting my arm up to do that was too much. So I had to ask the nurse to help me.

There was a knock on the door.

"Come in"

I look up as Wes walks in I smile and frown in confusion I thought Blake was picking me up.

"No need to look so bummed out that I'm picking you up. Blake is at home sorting out a few things." Wes states.

"Sorry Wes didn't mean to seem disappointed. I just miss your brother and I am desperate to get out of here. I missed you too just not in the same way."

I wink at Wes. He chuckles and grabs my bag and flowers and other gifts people have brought for me.

I grab my paper bag of medication the hospital

gave me. Wes holds the door open for me. And I follow Wes, I stop at the nurse's station thanking them and leaving my flowers as a thank you.

Soon we are in the truck driving to Blakes. I can't help but smile I just want to curl up with him and fall asleep with him.

Soon pulling up the drive way, I notice all the bikes and cars parked up. I look at Wes and raise an eyebrow in question.

"Hey, don't look at me or Blake, the club and your friends wanted to throw you a welcome home party. Blake tried to talk them out of it, but Trudy gave him the evil eye, your mum too. So he backed off and let them do their thing."

Wes shrugs. I smile shaking my head. I look down at my clothes it's the first time I got dressed in actual clothes. It's just my simple lemon summer dress and flip flops.

I have no make-up on. Only plus side is at least my hairs been brushed. Also the irony Is my bruising on my face is nearly completely gone, in its place is the nice bruising on my ribs. But at least I can hide those with clothes. Lost in my thoughts I hadn't realised Wes had jumped out of the truck and was opening my door. I turn and smile as he holds out his hand to help me down.

I turn to grab my bag's, but Wes stops me .

"Don't worry about those now Lil' we will grab them later."

I nod as he helps me walk to the house. As soon as we reach the door it's swung open. And we are greeted by Trudy smiling huge.

"Hey y'all she's home!!!!" Trudy hollers into the house. She leans in kissing me on the cheek.

"Glad your home sweet girl, come on everyone is out back. You doing okay?"

I nod and smile. Looking around for the one person I want to see the most. We reach the back patio doors and I'm greeted by coloured lights strung up and the smell of BBQ cooking, rock music playing, and everyone I know here stood in the backyard. They all turn and raise their drinks. I feel myself blush with the attention. But I'm smiling big and give them a little wave.

My mum comes rushing over.

"Oh sweetheart how are you feeling? Do you need anything?"

My mum asks doing the mum thing of putting the back of her hand to my forehead. I smile and kiss her cheek.

"I'm good mum honest. Thank you both for organising this." I say to her and Trudy.

Dad makes his way over and gives me a kiss and asks the same questions. I'm distracted as all I'm doing is looking around for Blake through all the people. I find Mammoth manning the BBQ. I head for him to ask him where Blake is, I can't even see Rip nor Khan and even Wes has disappeared.

"Hey there flower! Good to see you up and out that hospital."

I smile and nod in return.

"Where's Blake?" I ask.

Mammoth pauses for a moment, he looks up to the house, and then back to me. I turn and start heading to the house before he has a chance to answer. Ignoring the pain my quick movement is causing me.

"Flower now wait he'll be out in a sec." Mammoth shouts.

It's too late, I'm a little pissed that he's not here greeting me, that he sent his brother to collect me not because he was sorting out the party but because something else is more important.

I walk passed everyone and into the house, I check the lounge, its empty, I walk upstairs. I can hear mumbled voices coming from down the hall. Blakes office. I creep slowly trying to listen, not that I can move fast at the moment. I stand outside the door and pause I can't make out what's being said.

Having had enough I grab the handle and swing the door open with force. The movement has me grabbing my side and wincing in pain. The sight I'm faced with though is what causes the most pain.

Blake sat at his desk, leaning over kissing him is Elise. I stumble holding my side. The noise of my entrance makes Blake push Elise off him. She just looks over at me with a smirk.

"Shit, flower."

I swing my gaze around the room, only just realising that Rip, Khan and Wes are all there too.

I turn my gaze straight back to Blake. Confusion

at what the hell is going on. Before I can get a word out its Elise who speaks up.

"Oh honey, I'm sorry to say this to you but your guna have to leave, have your little party, then go."

She says as she puts her arm around Blake, smiling.

"See we're getting back together, we are expecting our first baby I'm nearly four months along now."

She states rubbing her stomach. Tears fill my eyes and spill over down my face. Blake at least has the decency to look guilty and pained. But still makes no move to come to me he just sits there.

I'm holding my chest now as the pain of what she just said shatters my heart.

I finally gather my voice.

"Is .. is it true what she's saying Blake? It's been two days since I've seen you. Is this why I haven't seen you?" I whisper pain dripping from my voice.

Blake says nothing. Just grits his teeth hard and nods.

That nod from Blake tears through me. I can't control the tears streaming down my face now.

"But you said you loved me." I croak.

I see the tic in his jaw go, and an anger takes over his face.

"It was just a holiday romance, I just felt bad for

you, being in hospital. I'm guna be a father now. I can't let my kid grow up without his father, I need to give my kid a chance to have a proper family. I need to focus on my future, and you are not in my future. I'm sorry but I think its best if you leave. The threat that Ven made is my main concern, I love my family and won't have them put at risk."

Blake says coldly through gritted teeth. He places his hand on Elise's stomach.

I grab hold of the door frame to keep myself from collapsing, pain like no other ripping through me. He's looking out for his family, not me.

"Your fucking sorry?! All I've been through because of being with you. The risk I put myself in. All along you just used me as a fling because you felt pity on me! I can't believe you would treat me this way."

I shout pain and anger dripping from my voice.

"Oh come on now honey, you couldn't honestly think he'd want to be with you. Look at yourself, I'm four months pregnant and I look better than you and I'm still smaller than you."

Elise points smirking, enjoying my pain.

I swing my gaze to the rest of the guys.

"And you assholes, you all would have known about this all along. Bet I was one good fucking joke to the lot of you. What were you going to do after you were done with me huh? Pass me around like a club whore?!" I screech.

All three of them grit their teeth.

I look back to Blake. Waiting for a response praying he says this is all a terrible misunderstanding.

"Oh my god will you get it into your thick fat headed skull he doesn't want you none of the guys do. Now you heard my baby daddy, you need to leave. Stop making this more awkward for him and the guys, it's embarrassing to watch." Elise hissed.

If it wasn't for my ribs and the fact she's pregnant I'd love nothing more than to smash her face against Blakes desk.

Giving one last look at Blake. I turn and as quick as my broken body will take me, I leave I head out the front door not wanting to see anyone. I just keep walking as fast as I can down the long dirt track to the main road. Not knowing where I'm going to go. I don't even have my purse or passport, nothing.

I hear the rumbling pipes of a bike approach me from behind.

Ignoring it I keep walking.

The bike pulls up in front of me I don't even bother looking to see who it is. I just keep my head down and keep walking.

"Flower, stop."

It's Rip. I don't stop I just keep on walking.

"Fuck off Rip." I shout, trying to pick up speed and trying to ignore the pain its causing.

"Flower stop! Damn it your guna hurt yourself.

Will you just listen to me for one second!"

I stop and spin round to face Rip the movement causing a sharp pain through my ribs. I let out a hiss.

"Shit! What is it you want? To laugh and point at the chubby English girl some more, how I'm so stupid that I trusted every single one of you. That I thought I was your friend. Laugh some more that I fell in love with your cousin? Tell me Rip what the fuck do you want?"

I cry.

Rip says nothing he just walks towards me. Stops in front of me and wipes my tears.

"I aint fuckin' laughin'. And I am your friend. come with me get on my bike I will take you to the club house or wherever you want to go. I will get your stuff. You can't go walking on your own and you have no money or passport. You also need your meds from the hospital. Please flower." Rip says so sincerely and I really don't have a choice. I have nowhere to go. I nod and Rip lets out a relieved breath.

He takes my hand and leads me back to his bike, as we reach his bike I look up back to Blakes house. I freeze he's stood there arms crossed over his chest jaw set staring. Rip feels me freeze and looks up. He puts his arm around my shoulders.

"C'mon flower, let's get you out of here."

Just as I'm about to turn away and climb on the bike as Elise comes out. She pulls on Blakes arm. He breaks eye contact with me and looks to her.

She smiles placing his hand on her stomach. He returns her smile. I let out a sob, Rip turns me and helps me on his bike.

"Wrap your arms around me flower, hold tight. I'm taking you to the clubhouse, unless there's somewhere else you'd rather be?"

"No, not the clubhouse, take me somewhere where I haven't been with Blake. Please." I beg. Rip just nods.

He starts up the bike, I make the mistake and turn around to look back at Blake, he's kissing Elise. I immediately turn back around and bury my face into Rips back.

We arrive at a house I've never been to before. I get off the bike slowly the ride causing pain in my ribs. I look at the beautiful ranch style house, I turn to look at rip.

"Whose house is this?" I ask.

"Mine, flower. I'm in the middle of doing it up its only half done."

He replies taking my hand leading me up the steps to the door.

"Well it's a beautiful house." I say.

Rip gives me a quick tour of the kitchen and lounge, then shows me to the bedroom.

"This is my room flower, you can sleep here, I will take the couch downstairs."

Rip says as he walks across the room opening a draw and pulling out t-shirt and boxers.

Handing them to me.

"Thank you, but you don't need to give up your

Rise Above

bed for me, I can sleep on the couch."
Rip stops in front of me handing me the clothes.
"You have just come out of hospital, from having three broken ribs and a punctured lung that needed emergency surgery. I'd have to kick my own ass if I made you sleep on the couch. Get these on. You want anything to eat or drink?"
I smile a sad smile.
"Just a drink of water and some pain killers if you have them? I'm not really hungry, thanks for this. Means a lot."
He nods.
"Don't need to thank me," Rip replies, he looks like he wants to say more but doesn't, instead he turns and leaves. I sit on the edge of the bed. And slowly start undressing.
Thankfully with my summer dress, I can just slide the straps down my arms, it slides down. I grab the boxers and try to bend down to put them on. I let out a cry in pain, the simple task proving too difficult for me. Giving up on that I grab the t-shirt. I can't lift my arms up straight yet it's too painful, so I try doing it half way instead. Problem is I can't work the t-shirt down enough, to get my head through. Again causing me pain.
"Ow shit bastard t-shirt."
I hiss in pain. I don't hear Rip knock or come in.
"Fuckin' Christ."
I hear him growl. I pause my head and part of my arms still stuck inside his t-shirt, of course I'm in

nothing but my underwear. I have on my lemon lace Brazilian shorts and lemon lace bra. Ironically it was my effort to make myself feel better and a little sexier for Blake too. What a waste of time that was.

"Umm Rip, do you mind helping me? I struggle to bend and lift my arms up to get dressed."

I mumble through the t-shirt. I hear Rip put down the glass of water and walk towards me. He lifts the t-shirt off me. Standing close just in front of me.

I look into his ice blue eyes, they take in my body slowly, his jaw is grinding, his eyes come back to mine. I can't help the blush that takes over my face. I'm stood here in my underwear in front of a very good looking guy with ice blue eyes that any girl can get lost in.

I hold the t-shirt to cover me, embarrassment taking over.

"No point trying to cover yourself now flower, just seen all there is to see."

Rip takes the t-shirt from me. He holds out the head hole for me and helps it over my head. His eyes never straying from the task.

I slowly put my arms in wincing slightly at the pain.

Slowly he pulls the t-shirt down his fingers skimming my body as he does. The touch makes my breath hitch in my throat.

He stops just by my broken ribs, he runs his finger slowly and gently over the bruising. Causing my body to shiver. His eyes return to mine.

As he lets the t-shirt fall to just past my hips. He then grabs the boxers and kneels down in front of me. Again his eyes never leaving mine.

I place my hands on his shoulders to help myself balance. Slowly lifting each leg slightly. He does the same again slowly pulling the boxers up my legs, kneeling in front of me. He stops just as he reaches the bottom of my hips. His eyes break contact with mine as he looks at my lace covered pussy. I hold my breath as I watch him take a deep breath, swallowing and slowly lick his lips.

He shakes his head, to clear his thoughts and continues to pull up the boxers. And he slowly stands.

I can't deny his actions he has had on my body my nipples have hardened and I'm trying to control my breathing. Rip is a stunning man, any woman would have to be dead not to react to his beauty but my heart although its wasted belongs to Blake.

Rip stands in front of me he notices my nipples through his t-shirt. His pupils dilate, he looks to the ceiling muttering curse words.

"Umm, look Rip as much as I find you attractive. In fact I think any woman with a pulse would find you attractive, and as much as I would love to be able to be the type of person to be a bitch to use you and fuck like rabbits to get back at Blake. I can't. I can't do that to you, and I can't even do that to Blake because I love the bastard prick. Plus I couldn't even if I wanted to because of my stupid ribs, that I got for being with the stupid bastard prick."

I finish anger and hurt pouring into my words.

Tears filling my eyes, I smile a sad smile at Rip He takes a step forward so our bodies are flush. I suck in a shuddering breath.

He cups my face, his eyes not leaving mine.

"Flower, I can't help the way my body reacts to you . You're a beautiful woman. And your stood in your fuckin' underwear. I'd love to as you say 'fuck like rabbits' but I love my cousin too. He's my brother and there are things you don't know. I shouldn't have looked at you like I did or even touched you like that. My dick was in full control of my actions. It shouldn't have happened. I messed your head up when you're already feeling vulnerable. That's me being a prick. You have every damn right to be angry at Blake, I'm angry with how he's handled things. But trust me things will be okay."

Tears stream down my face. God damn it, why couldn't I have fallen for Rip instead. I nod my head and he wipes away my tears. He lets me go and moves to the bed side.

"Get into bed flower, take the pain killers. And rest up I will be in to check on you in a couple of hours."

Rip pulls the cover back for me while I climb in,

he hands me the pain killers and water. I take them. He places the glass of water on the side, leans over and kisses me on the forehead. His lips linger there for a minute.

"Get some sleep, I will sort out getting your stuff." Rip says and walks out the bedroom door shutting it quietly, I lie there for a while and let the tears flow. Crying into the pillow I'm not sure how long for, until I finally fall asleep.

I awake and it takes me a minute to remember where I am.

I look to the window its pitch black outside, I look at the clock its near midnight I've been asleep for nearly four hours.

I get up and go to the bathroom to take care of business.

I walk slowly downstairs in search of Rip.

I head for the kitchen, I can hear him talking to someone. I pause and peek into the kitchen, he has his back to me. I shamelessly listen in on his conversation.

"I am watching her, she's not going anywhere, she's not doing so good brother. She aint got a fuckin' clue and its crushed her. I aint fuckin' happy with how you have treated her and with how this is going down, but I get it, it has to be done."

Rip pauses a moment and nods his head.

"Yeah, I know, shit man I just hope it all comes good in the end. I'm guna go check on her. She's been sleeping for hours now. Yeah. No she's not eating. Alright. Catch ya later."

With that he hangs up. I take a slow step back and wait just a second before entering the kitchen. My mind trying to figure out what that conversation was all about. What don't I have a fucking clue about?

I don't have time to process and think about It now. I take a breath. Mask my face and enter the kitchen. Rip turns when he hears me enter the kitchen.

"Hey flower you feel better?" Rip asks. I nod

"I heard voices thought someone else was here?" I question.

"No one here flower I was just on the phone checking in at the club. You want some food?"

I shake my head. Still not ready to eat.

"Can I just get a drink of milk then I will head back to bed. Thanks though, did you manage to get my stuff?"

Rip moves to the fridge and pours me a glass of milk. And hands it to me.

"Yeah darlin' all in the hallway. I will bring it all up for you in a second."

"Um what did you say to my parents and everyone else?"

I ask hoping my mum and dad aren't worried.

"They know, Elise made sure everyone knew. Mammoth had to hold my mom back she was ready to pound Blakes ass." He laughs.

I smile at the thought.

"Your folks are staying at my parents place. Until you decide what you want to do. Your mum said for you to ring first thing in the morning, so she knows you're okay."

I nod.

"Great thanks I'm going to head up are you okay to help carry my stuff?"

Rip nods and follows me, I go to grab my bags and he snatches them off me. Only leaving me carrying my handbag.

Once upstairs I ask for the Wi-Fi code so I can email my boss. He hands me the code written down on a bit of paper. I smile taking it from him.

Rip heads to the bedroom door and stops in the doorway turning to me he says.

"I promise flower, it will all come good. Now if you need anything else just shout I'm guna crash on the couch. Night flower."

"Night Rip, thanks again."

As soon as he has shut the door, I think about the phone conversation I heard Rip on. I can't figure it out. I do know I don't like the idea I'm being watched and that I'm not going anywhere. I don't like being a part of this whatever it is, being played as a pawn in their game. I've been through enough. And all for nothing. I need to get out of this goddamn town.

I open my laptop and send an email of resignation to my boss. No way can I stay here, no way will my boss let me just go back home and carry on working there.

I email my sister Rose, I tell her all that's happened, I tell her I'm alright. That I just need to be alone for a while and can she pass on a message to mum and dad. But not to tell them where I am. I will make contact when I arrive safely.

I book a flight out of Houston. I spotted Rips truck on the drive way and the keys hanging up by the door.

I pack light. I carefully and with a struggle change trying my hardest not to cry out in pain. It's been a good hour now since Rip said goodnight and I can't hear anything coming from downstairs apart from the tv. I check that I have my passport and purse. I leave a note for Rip and one for my parents on the night stand.

I creep slowly down the stairs, I reach the bottom and can see the lounge door is pushed too, I carefully grab the keys off the side unit. Gently I turn the lock and creep out of the door, I shut it quietly behind me.

I move as quickly and as quietly as my body will allow me to the truck. I unlock it and climb in. Gritting my teeth at the pain. My heart is beating wildly in my chest. I feel bad for all that Rip has done for me, but I can't stay here any longer. I have no idea what is going on and I don't want to stick around and find out. The man I love has just crushed my heart. I need to get as far away from here as possible.

I start the engine leaving the lights off until I'm out of the driveway and away from the house. I turn the truck around and slowly peel out the drive. I notice in the rear view mirror the porch light comes on. I put my foot down and switch on the lights. And drive as fast as I can out of there. I keep driving and checking the mirror to see if I'm being followed but no sign. I let out a relieved breath as I take the turning onto the freeway to Houston airport. I hold back any emotion I have. I hear my phone go off on the passenger side I take a quick look and see it's Rip, I grab it and switch it off. I put my foot down on the gas pedal trying to put as much distance between myself and Rips house as I can.

I drive a good few miles when the petrol light flashes and I curse. I see a sign for a petrol station I pull in. Soon I'm finishing up fuelling the truck and go in search for the toilets. After I'm finished I jump back in to the truck and head off. This time I choose to stay off the freeway just in case anyone comes looking for me.

I drive for what must be 20mins, when I notice headlights in the mirror. Of course it could be anyone but there was no one there a minute ago. Or at least I think there wasn't. The car is coming up fast I put my foot down. Now realising that whoever is behind me is chasing me. They are gaining on me. I can't make out the colour of the car all I know is it's a truck.

The truck comes up fast behind me, ramming the back end of the truck. The shove from the truck shoots me forward causing me to cry out in pain. The truck does it again and again, the sound of loud crushing metal, I scream each time fear creeping up my spine.

In a panic I reach for my phone trying to switch it on. I manage to press the call button knowing the last call was Rip. I hear him answer but it's too late, I drop the phone. I try to turn the truck to move out of the way, but it hits the back end, I completely over steer the truck and it flips towards the ditch. I scream as the truck tumbles and turns I crash hard hitting a tree. I'm dazed and barely conscious. I can hear muffled shouting in the truck looking around I spot my phone in the foot well of the passenger side. I try and reach for it. Just as my fingers are touching it the passenger door flies open.

I freeze and look up. I let out a scream.

Its Ven he has a gun and he is covered in blood.

He reaches over and drags me out of the truck. I claw, kick and scream trying to get him to let me go.

"Shut the fuck up bitch." Ven spits, he rears back and hits me with the butt of his gun. My last thought is I'm going to die as my world turns to darkness.

CHAPTER SEVENTEEN

Blake

I sit on my back porch drinking bourbon. Remembering Lily's broken face as she walked in on Elise and me. It wasn't supposed to go down like this. I was going to let her go gently, send her back with her parents so she was safe and out of the way. Until we could sort this shit storm. It's not safe for her here. Fuck and the thought of Elise kissing and touching me brings bile to my throat. That stupid bitch honestly thinks I've fallen for her horse shit. What she doesn't know is that I'm playing along and so are the guys.

We figured out what her, Ven and the sheriff were up too. We just needed proof and we know there's a rat in the club. We don't know who yet but we fucking will.

I sent Elise home telling her it was best while I sort the house out. She brought it.

It gutted me doing that to Lily, I just have to pray

she will take me back after all this shit has died down. If she will even let me explain.

It's a risk I had to take if it means she's safe then it's worth it.

My cell rings its Rip. I look at the time its near 1:30am. This can't be good.

"What the fucks happened?" I growl into the phone.

"She's gone, she's taken my truck and she's fuckin' gone. Left me a note."

I jump to my feet, grabbing my keys.

"I'm on my way over. ring her cell, she will answer if it's you. Be at yours in 5. Call the brothers, Wes too and get them over to yours now." I order as I jump into my truck.

"On it."

I disconnect and put my foot down and head to Rips as fast as I can. Shit. Rip said earlier she wasn't good. That she wasn't eating.

"FUCK!" I punch the steering wheel.

I arrive at Rips in record time I slam the truck in park and jump out. I don't even bother knocking. Rips in the kitchen on his phone rallying his men.

He gives me a chin lift and points to the letter on the kitchen counter.

Dear rip,

       I'm sorry, I can't stay here. I can't be in the same town and watch Blake be with someone else and raise a family. I just can't, it's just

too painful. I need to get away and be alone for a while. I've paid for parking at Houston airport. Your truck will be safe there for you to collect. Will leave keys under back wheel arch. I am so sorry I took your truck. Please forgive me.
Thank you for all your help.
   Love always
  flower
   xxx

Gripping the paper I swallow the lump in my throat. This is all my fucking fault. I was only doing it to keep her fuckin' safe and now she's out there vulnerable and at risk. I swing round and punch the cupboard door. Splitting the wood. The anger, frustrations and emotions building up in me.
Rip spins round.
"Fuck man, I gotta go, get everyone here now."
Rip hangs up.
"You're paying for that fucking door when this is all over. Hitting that aint guna help no one." Rip states opening his freezer grabbing an ice pack and throwing it at me. I look down at my busted hand and put the ice pack on it. I reach for his cell and I hand it to Rip.
"Call her." I demand.
"She's switched it off after I rang man."
Rip states after he dials and puts his phone on speaker. It goes straight to answer phone.
"Fuck!" I roar in frustration.

"Don't worry man, she wouldn't have got that far I didn't have enough fuel in the truck for her to make it to Houston. She'd probably get twenty to thirty miles until the fuel light flashes. We will find her."

Soon all the guys from Satans show up, and my brother Wes too.

We are gathered in the kitchen looking at the road map of where she will be which road we reckon she will take.

"She's not stupid, if she wants to be alone she will use the country road and stay off the freeway."

Wes states. I nod so does Rip.

Khan gets a phone call, he takes it in the other room. He comes back in looking concerned. I pause and so does the others.

"What the fuck is it?" Rip asks.

"That was Ink, had them keep an eye on Ven from a distance. He said they followed him to Elise's house. They heard a gunshot. He came out of there covered in blood, boys did a quick check through the kitchen window. He shot her dead took a bullet between the eyes.

They rang 911 and sped off after Ven but he was to quick they lost him."

"Shit! Fuck!"

I slam my fist down on the counter.

"How long ago was this?" I ask Khan.

"They said they gave up trying to tail him a good

twenty minutes ago. So from him going into Elise's house probably looking at thirty minutes or so ago."

I look at Rip, his thoughts are the same as mine. Elise's house is only a five minute drive from here. He could have followed her. Elise would have told him where she was.

I go to grab my keys not waiting around any longer. The fact that She's out there on her own and I know damn well Ven will be looking for her too.

Just as I'm about to leave Rip's cell rings. I pause and look at the screen. Its Lily.

Rip answers and puts it on speaker the whole room goes silent as we listen in to what is happening.

"Lily!" I shout.

All we can hear is her screaming and the sound of the truck being hit.

She lets out a scream. The sound pierces through me. I look to Wes he's gripping the side his jaw grinding.

There's a loud crash and another scream. I grip my hair. And closing my eyes. Hearing this and not being there to do anything is killing me.

There's silence on the line for what feels like forever.

"Lily! Lily you there? Are you okay? Lily! Where are you?"

I shout over and over into the phone. Briefly we hear movement over the phone then the sound of a car door being opened.

Its then Lily lets out a blood curdling scream over and over.

We hear Ven's voice, we struggle to make out what he's saying. But Lily has stopped screaming, we are met with silence.

"LILY!" I scream down the phone. It's then Ven comes on the line.

"Hello, Blake. Thought you could out play me did you? Having Rips little boys follow me. the Thing is I've taken a liking to this bitch from England. She's been teasing me and begging me for it, finally I'm guna take what's owed to me. I'm guna ruin her especially that fuckin ass of hers. Damn! And there aint nothing you can do about it!

You try and take what's mine, I'm guna take and destroy what's yours." Ven spits down the phone.

"You fuckin' cunt! When I find you I will fuckin' gut you. You lay one finger on her you're a fuckin' dead man."

I roar anger and emotion raging in me.

All Ven does is laugh down the phone and disconnect the call. I don't even wait for anyone I run to my truck and jump in. Wes, and Rip jump in my truck with me.

Khan, Mammoth, Papa, Fury and Crank jump on their bikes.

Rip shouts out orders. I put my foot down, I need

to find Lily before it's too late.

We go the backroads to Houston, I'm convinced she would have gone this way knowing Rip and the boys would have chased her down on the freeway.

Rip sent the rest of the boys to go on the freeway and ordered the families and other club members on lock down.

In the distance I see something that has my blood running cold.

Its Rips truck dented and smashed up against a tree.

Barely putting my truck in park I jump out and run to the scene.

There's blood on the driver's window, where it smashed into the tree. There's no sign of Lily, but all her stuff is there. I see her cell on the ground, I pick it up and unlock it. What comes on the screen has my blood running ice cold.

It's a selfie of Ven smiling with his gun pressed up against Lily's head. Lily is laid on the grass by the truck unconscious with blood pouring from her head.

I drop to my knees, dropping the cell. Placing my head in my hands.

Wes comes over and picks up Lily's cell looking at the picture.

"Fuck! Rip you're guna wana come look at this."

Wes places his hand on my shoulder gripping it tightly.

"We're guna find her brother, I fuckin' promise.

And we're guna kill that motherfucker!" Wes growls.

Rip takes the cell off Wes and takes a look.

"Shit, fuck."

He pockets the cell. And pulls out his own and makes a call.

"Khan, brother yeah we found my truck, back around about five miles from gas station. Yeah, send the prospects to come clear it up and get Lily's things. Also he took a fuckin' selfie of himself with lily unconscious, gun pressed up to her head blood pourin'. I need you to send me all Ven's fuckin' property addresses. Reckon he aint gone far, has he got any properties near here?"

Rip pauses, as Khan relays information back to him. I stand waiting. Ready to go. We have to get to her and soon.

"Gottcha brother, yeah I reckon he's there. Get the rest of the brothers to meet us there we're guna surround that motherfucker."

Rip hangs up and smiles his evil smile.

"We got that fucker he has a fishing cabin on lake condor which is twenty miles north from here."

Before Rips even finished I'm jumping in my truck. I put my foot down. Rip pulls out his M-19 and Wes pulls out his Glock G19.

"This fucker is mine. I want to be the one to take his last breath."

I growl, both Wes and Rip nod. Hang in there darlin' I'm coming.

CHAPTER EIGHTEEN

I awake, I am led down in a dark room, I go to move my arms, but they are tide down. I try moving my legs, but they are also restrained. My head is groggy and sore. I try looking around the room but it's hard to make things out, just by the moonlight coming through the windows.

I pull and struggle to try and free my arms and legs, but the rope just tightens. I let out a frustrated scream.

Suddenly a lamp across the room is switched on. Squinting adjusting my eyes to the sudden light. I see Ven sat in an arm chair.

I scream for help at the top of my lungs.

Ven just smiles an evil smile playing with his gun.

"You can scream all you like, there isn't another house for miles no one can hear you. In fact I like that I'm the one making you scream. Believe me I will be making you scream a lot more."

Ven sneers.

"Fuck you, Blake, Rip and the rest of the Satans

will be here to rescue me soon, they'll kill you. Why did you come after me anyway I was leaving town, that's what you wanted wasn't it?" I sneer.

Ven throws his head back and laughs.

"You stupid cunt! They didn't tell you anything did they? You see my father has always wanted complete control over the town. He's the sheriff and I was set to be mayor. The problem was Blake Stone and the Satans think they run this town. Blakes always taken things from me, always thought he was better than me. Blake and the Satans shouldn't be sticking their fuckin' noses in mine or my father's business." Ven spits angrily pacing the room. He's beyond crazy, mumbling to himself and pulling at his hair.

"You assaulted and kidnapped me all because Blake was stopping you from getting what you wanted? Do you have any idea how fucking insane that is? And anyway he's with Elise now you got the wrong girl if this is payback for Blake. He doesn't care about me he's with her now."

As I say those words my heart breaks that bit more. Blake and Elise are probably cuddled up in his bed now. I'm not his problem anymore.

"I thought you brits were smart. He's not with Elise. They thought they could out smart me the satans. But I played them, I knew they'd fall for it. You see, I sent Elise round there saying she was pregnant with Blake's baby. Of course she jumped at the chance, thinking she could have Blake back. Stupid thick bitch."

Ven continues, pacing.

"Of course Blake and the rest knew it was a lie but thought that they could use it against me. A ploy to get you away to safety. I watched, I watched as you got onto Rip's bike. The way Blake tried to shield his emotions and put on the fake bullshit act. That Elise and you brought. Stupid fucking bitches."

He laughs walking back and forth playing with his gun.

"Elise won't be a problem anymore, she's lying in a pool of her own blood on her kitchen floor. Stupid bitch."

"You see they all fuckin' loved you one way or another. Not the same way Blake does but you have managed to get under all their skin. So not only by taking you have I managed to break Blake but the Satans too. You see having you, I have complete control over the Satans and Blake."

As my mind struggles to process all the information he's telling me.

"Elise is dead?" I ask. Blake did it to get me to go away to keep me safe?

"Hell yeah that bitch is dead." Ven shouts.

I didn't like the woman, but I wouldn't have wished her dead.

I hear a rumble of a bike pull up. Relief and hope fill me as I think it could be one of the satans.

"Don't get your hopes up that's my associate." Ven smirks and panic sets back in when I see who walks in the door.

Its virus from the satans and he smiles an evil smirk and adjusts his crotch when he sees me tied down to the bed.

"I can't believe you would double cross your own club, you're a rat scumbag." I hiss.

Virus walks towards me and grabs my face hard. Leans in close.

"Listen here you prick tease, I look after number one. I had a better offer. All the money, drugs and pussy I want. And no fuckin' cops sniffing around. Having the chance to sink my dick in you was an added bonus."

Virus licks up my neck and kisses me, bile rises up from my stomach. But I'm not giving up and letting anyone touch me. I bite down hard sinking my teeth into his lip drawing blood. He rears back on an angry roar.

"You fuckin' slut!"

He back hands me so hard across the face that my vision blurs.

"Hey Virus! Keep your damn cool, I told you I want her wide awake when I fuck her. She's been fuckin' teasing me nonstop, she fuckin owes me. I want to be imprinted as her final thought before I fuckin kill her." Ven seethes as he puts down his gun and starts to undo his jeans.

"No please, don't do this." I beg and cry.

"Virus pull up her top. I want to be able to see all

of her, while I take what's fuckin' owed."

Ven moves to the end of the bed. Fisting himself through his unbuttoned jeans.

Virus grabs my top by the neck and in a quick hard tug he rips it off me. Causing me to hiss in pain from my ribs.

Leaving me in just my lemon lace bra.

Virus leans over my chest and licks over my nipple. Ignoring the pain in my ribs I scream and buck to try and get him off me. Tears streaming down my face. Without warning he bites down hard around my nipple causing me to scream. He leans back smiling with blood around his mouth. Then spits in my face.

"That's enough Virus, now I'm taking what's fuckin' owed. I'm taking what's Blakes."

Ven climbs over kneeling, positions himself between my legs. He has a sick smile on his face. I scream and I buck but all he does is smile more. He pulls a knife from his back pocket. I freeze instantly. As he starts to run the blade up the inside of my leg towards the apex of my thighs. He lifts my skirt up to my waist. Exposing my lace knickers. I'm shaking with fear, he runs the knife over my intimate area.

"Please stop, please don't, I beg you please." I cry.

I turn my head to see Virus sat on the arm chair he's smiling getting off on what Ven is doing to me. He start's to unbutton his jeans.

A sudden sharp pain across my lower stomach causes me to scream and I turn to look towards

Ven.

"Keep your eyes on me. You understand bitch. You are to watch every little thing I do to you. I don't want you missing a thing."

I look at the knife it has blood on it. I lift my head and see he's slashed me across my stomach.

I look back at Ven and he starts to pull down my knickers. I shout, I beg and try and kick him, but nothing seems to work. He grabs my thighs tight and pulls them apart. The bile isn't staying down I turn my head and I am sick.

Ven leans over me his face in mine smiling. He places one hand around my neck squeezing so tight that I'm struggling for air. His other hand is running along my entrance. Suddenly he shoves his fingers inside me. I buck and I try screaming but my air flow is restricted. He's rough and hurting me thrusting his fingers.

This is it, no one is coming to help me. I need to dig deep I can't give up, I try and fight with all that I've got. I can't die like this. It's enough to make it difficult for him to do what he wants to do to me, it makes him stop.

"Stay fuckin' still bitch!"

Ven punches me hard across the face causing near black out. If this is going to happen to me then I'd rather be unconscious. I use everything in me to carry on fighting. This time I've pissed him off too much. He rears back and stabs me in the shoulder, leaving the knife in there. I scream. The excruciating pain burning through me.

Dazed I notice Ven smirks and starts to pull down his jeans freeing himself. I'm floating in and out of consciousness I don't have enough strength in me to buck. I try but my movements are slow and sluggish. I feel him press himself at my entrance.

"No stop!!"

I try to shout but it's more of a begging whimper. I turn my head, my eyes feeling heavy. I don't have the strength in me to fight it anymore.

All of a sudden the door flies open, I am vaguely aware of Ven being pulled off me. I hear gunshots and fighting I try to focus and see who's here, but I can't make anyone out.

"Fuck! Lily!"

I know that voice, its Blake. He leans over me and strokes my hair away from my face. I try and focus on him, but my eyes keep rolling.

"Blake don't leave me." I whisper.

Then darkness completely consumes me.

CHAPTER NINETEEN

Blake

The whole way there I'm consumed by the thoughts in my head, driving on auto pilot.
What if I'm too late? What's he doing to her? This is all my fault I should have gone with my gut and just told her everything. The files of all the shit we have on Ven and his father. Drugs, guns and trafficking girls. It wasn't safe, I should have forced her to go away from here until we could take Ven and his father down.

If he's hurt a single piece of hair on her head. I'm going to kill him.

We stop just a few minutes away from the cabin so Ven doesn't hear us approach. We run the rest of the way staying low behind the bushes and trees. We are just outside the cabin when we notice a bike parked up with Ven's truck. I look to Rip.

"That mother fucking piece of shit. That's Virus's bike."

Rip growls.

The rat that's how Ven's managed to get to Lily and know where she is all the time.

We hear an ear piercing scream come from the cabin. I don't wait around I run.

"Shit Blake wait, fuck! Come on Wes."

I hear Rip shout to Wes as I kick the door down my hunting knife in my hand. Ready for blood.

Wes and Rip are at my side when we enter. I look to the side and see Lily tide on the bed exposed, blood covering her entire body. And I see Ven leaning over her with his dick out.

Pure rage descends over me, I grab Ven and haul him off Lily and throw him to the floor. I lean over him. I can see the fear in his eyes as I rear back and stab him repeatedly. Leaning back I watch Ven coughing and choking on his own blood, the life leaving his eyes. After I'm certain Ven has taken his very last breath I jump to my feet. I step over Ven's dead body and go to Lily.

"Fuck! Lily!" I cry as I kneel down beside her. Her eyes are rolling and she's in and out of consciousness. She has a knife in her shoulder her face is beaten, her stomach has been slashed. It's her pained distant voice that breaks me to my very core.

"Blake, don't leave me."

Then she passes out cold.

"Darlin', wake up, Lily I need you to stay awake. I

need you Lily."

I croak, my voice breaking with emotion. I feel a hand on my shoulder.

"Stay strong for her brother, come on we need to get her to hospital and fast."

Wes pulls me to my feet, I walk to the end of the bed and untie her ankles. There are red, blooded sore welts where the rope has cut into her skin. I look up and notice bruising at the top of her thighs along with blood. I freeze. I was too late.

I turn and grab my hunters knife. Straddling Ven I stab that motherfucker in his head over and over the sound of my knife slicing through his flesh, the cracking of his skull and the splatter of his blood covering me is music to my ears. I'm hauled off Ven by Rip.

"Enough! He's dead, the fucker is dead. She needs you now get your shit together."

Rip shouts.

"He raped her. He fucking raped her. I was too late."

I rasp tears filling my eyes and clogging my throat.

" It's not your fault, you did what you thought was right. You did it to try and protect her. Now hold it together and let's get your girl to hospital."

I move to go to Lily. Wes has grabbed a blanket and covered her and untied her wrists. I pick Lily up, being careful of the knife and I cradle her in my arms.

Rise Above

"Leave the blade in there, it could have hit a vain or something, plus it has Ven's prints on." Rip states, I nod as we load up in the truck.

All the way to the hospital I pray that she's going to be okay, that there's no permanent damage. And lastly after all of that I pray that she forgives me.

We arrive at the hospital and the nurses come rushing over with a gurney.

"What happened?" A nurse asks.

"She was kidnapped, and I think she was raped."

I rasp. The nurse stops looking over Lily and looks at me. Sympathy in her eyes.

Soon a doctor comes, and they whisk Lily off to emergency.

Rip makes calls for her mum and dad to be brought to the hospital. We sit in the waiting area. And I just stare blankly at the wall.

I've shut off, shut off from everyone around me, I feel numb.

I'm so consumed in my own thoughts I didn't even realise Lily's parents had arrived.

"Blake honey, look at me."

Penny is crouched down in front of me.

I move my gaze to her.

"Tell me, please what did that monster do to my baby girl?"

I swallow the lump in my throat. I look up to see Ben stood behind his wife, his hand on her shoulder. He nods for me to tell them.

"He kidnapped her, beat her, stabbed her and..."

I swallow the bile in my throat.
I look at Penny, tears streaming down her face, her hand covering her mouth. She shakes her head.
"No god please."
I feel a stray tear run down my face.
"We think he abused her." I rasp.
Penny is sobbing Ben pulls his wife into his arms. Tears in his eyes too.
The doctor walks in asking for family of Lily, I jump to my feet, and I rush forward so does Penny and Ben and everyone else in the room.
We wait eager to hear what he has to say.
"Are you all family of Lily Rocke? He asks looking around the room.
"Because what I have to say is quite sensitive."
He continues.
Just as I'm about to say something Penny jumps in.
"Yes this is all her family and yes whatever you have to say is fine for all of us to hear. They are all here for Lily."
she sniffles into her tissue.
"Right ok then. Well there's no easy way to say this but, Lily was abused sexually. She wasn't fully penetrated, but from the lacerations internally, I'd say by hand or object. Also the bruising on her thighs. She was also strangled, and her left breast bitten. It appears she was severely hit in the face. And stabbed to the shoulder and the slash across the stomach, which she is cur-

Rise Above

rently in surgery for now to remove the knife and stitch up the wounds. She will be fine she's very lucky the knife just missed a vain. I will be of course passing all my details on to the police. A nurse will come and get you when she is out of theatre." He finishes.

Its Rip that steps forward.

"May I have a quick word doc, outside."

The doctor frowns and nods.

I turn to Penny and Ben.

"I'm so sorry, this should of never of happened. It's all my fault. I should have done more to protect her."

Its Ben that speaks up.

"Now listen here son and listen well, we were brought up to date last night on what your plan was, and that yesterday at your home was all an act to keep Lily safe. We understood it's the only way to get her to leave town or just be away from you while you went after that animal. You did not do any of this to my daughter, that cocksucker did. You only had her best interests at heart, you tried to protect her. And let me tell you my daughter loves you and she would have stood by your side through all of this. As much as she may have said she would have stayed away until its done she wouldn't have. You rescued my daughter. Did you hear what that doc said? What he said means you got there in time, you stopped that from happening. You! Do not do what I've watched my daughter do for years and that's blame something on yourself that is far beyond your control. These last few weeks I have never seen my daughter so happy, and that's when she's been attacked bloody twice! You are not to blame. He is and his shit bag father are. He made that man the man he is today.

Now by looking at your shirt I'm hoping you killed that cunt?"

Ben seethes, I'm a little surprised from his speech and his broadness about me killing Ven. I look to Penny and I see a similar look.

"Yes sir. Ven is no longer an issue." I reply.

"Good I only wish I was there to help finish the bastard."

With that Ben pats me on the shoulder and turns to the vending machine.

Shocked at Bens reaction, Penny steps forward and wraps her arms around me.

"My baby girl is a strong girl, she will get through this eventually. Be there for her, let her be there for you. She might make you work for it, for a while. You broke her heart and her trust, but you did it for the right reasons. I think she will see that. Plus I know my daughter loves you. You love her. so don't give up on her. Oh and handsome boy do not take this as your fault you already have enough on your shoulders. My husband is right we've watched our daughter for years blame herself for Cameron's death, don't do the same. Now go change your shirt ready for when she wakes up she's going to need us to be

Rise Above

strong and be there for her. You being covered in blood isn't going to help."

Penny kisses my cheek and turns toward the vending machine to be with Ben.

I look down at my hands and my t-shirt are all covered. I need to change and wash this off but I'm not leaving the hospital.

"Honey, here take this."

I turn around and Trudy is stood with a bag of clean clothes.

"Rip said you guys needed clean clothes so here, take these and go get cleaned up."

I smile a small smile and kiss Trudy's cheek taking the bag I run to the men's room.

Coming out I see sheriff Johnson in the hallway. Seeing red I storm towards him. It's too late for him to react. I swing back and hit him straight in the face knocking him on his ass. His deputy grabs my arms.

"You son of a bitch I'm arresting your sorry ass for assaulting a police officer."

sheriff Johnson yells holding his blood splattered nose.

"Like hell you will."

Is shouted from behind us by Ben.

I look up and walking toward us is two guys in suits. They come to a stop.

"sheriff Johnson?"

The guy in a grey suit asks.

"Yeah, who the hell are you?"

"I'm agent Miller and this is agent Spelman,

you're under arrest for distribution of drugs, human trafficking, and suspected murder."

The agent doesn't even get to finish, Johnson tries bolting his deputy too.

They don't make it far and are soon apprehended and taken away.

I turn to Rip who's just leaning up against the wall smirking.

He gives me a chin lift, I smile back and walk into the waiting room with him,

"Those your contacts? I ask raising my brow.

"Yep, they'd been looking into Johnson for a while now, they came to me. I of course was happy to oblige as the law abiding citizen I am. they cut me a deal that the club was left out of it. And also the mess up at the cabin. Sorted. Virus turned on Ven killing him and Ven turned and shot virus.

We get to live our lives in peace and happiness. Just call me the fairy fucking godmother."

Rip finishes on a big grin. I smile.

A few hours pass and finally the nurse comes in saying Lily is out of surgery. And two people can go visit. It kills me but I hold back knowing that Penny and Ben need to be with their daughter.

"Excuse me sweetie but that man there is her boyfriend and the one who rescued her, he needs to come in too." Penny says to the nurse.

The nurse looks up from Penny to me and gives a gentle nod.

Rise Above

"Fine but just this once. Follow me I will show you to her room"

we walk down the corridor the nurse opens her door and walks in.

I stop dead in my tracks, seeing her lying there looking so small and helpless, endless amount of cables attached to machines, and the tube down her throat has my heart lurching.

"Why is she like this? The doctor said that she was going to be fine."

I ask I'm afraid to touch her in case I knock something.

"The doctor will be in to speak with you in a moment."

The nurse smiles and walks out the room, Ben and I exchange a look both of us anxious and worried for what the doctor is about to tell us.

The doctor walks in formally greeting us.

"There is a slight swelling on the brain, we initially didn't notice the wound to her head where she must have been hit over the head with a blunt object, or was she in some form of accident? We know already about the hit to the face on top of that. We also found some glass remnants in her hair."

I interrupt the doctor before he can finish.

"She was rammed off the road, smashed into a tree. She hit her head on the driver's side window. This was before everything else."

I rasp.

The doctor nods and continues.

"Well that would have been the initial trauma. All her other injuries have been stitched and treated, I am afraid it's a waiting game now. We have put her in induced coma to rest the body and hope the swelling on her brain goes down. We will re scan in the next twenty four hours. Please feel free to hold her hand and talk to her, some say they can still feel and hear while in an in a coma. I'm sorry I couldn't provide you with better news. The nurse will come around every few hours to check her stats. I will see you tomorrow when we come to do her scan."

Before the doctor leaves, It's Ben that asks the question we are all thinking.

"Will she wake up and will she have any brain damage?" Ben asks his voice raw with emotion.

"I'm afraid we won't know anymore until after the scan, it really is a sit and wait game I'm afraid. I'm sorry."

The doctor shakes mine and Bens hand and then leaves closing the door.

Penny walks up to Lily and kisses her cheek. She sits and holds her hand. I'm still frozen to the spot. My heart feels so tight, the fear of if she never wakes up. Or if there any brain damage. It's all too much I need air, I turn and storm out of the room. I make it out through the double doors to the hospital garden. That's where I break. I crumble to my knees, tears falling down my face.

I feel a hand on my shoulder I jolt and turn to see

Rise Above

Rip. He sits down next to me.

"Ben, he told me. Said to come find you. Shit I'm sorry brother. But she's strong, she will be ok, hell she's one of the strongest women I've ever met." Rip states looking out across the garden.

"I should have never let her leave my side, I should have kept her safe. It's all my fault , if I'd just kept my distance from her and never started anything. she would be safe, she wouldn't be led there now fighting for her fuckin' life." I rasp swallowing back my tears.

"Listen to me brother, she chose you. Anyone could see from the moment she gave you sass on her first night in the bar, the connection and the pull you two had towards each other was fuckin' bigger than both of you. Like either of you even had the choice to walk away. Every fucker that night and from then on could see how much she loved you. And you her, even if you were a stubborn asshole in the beginning."

Rip smirks and nudges me with his shoulder.

"Didn't stop you wanting a chance with her though did it?" I return. He shrugs.

"I'm not stupid like my shithead cousin." Rip chuckles as I thump him in the arm.

"She's a damn good woman, fuckin' hot too. Can't blame a guy for trying."

Rip continues rubbing his arm. I chuckle.

"Thanks for coming out here man, trying to make me feel better. But I don't think that tight heavy feeling will lift until I know she's guna be okay." I say rubbing my chest.

"I know what you've been through and what I've seen today is enough to break any decent man. It has been a day from hell that even Satan himself couldn't conjure. That tight heavy feeling will go because she's guna wake up and she's guna be just fine. You've had your moment, now man the fuck up and be strong for her. She needs you. You need to stay strong brother."

Rip slaps my shoulder and stands holding out his hand. I grab it and he pulls me to my feet. I pull him into a tight hug.

"Thanks man." I whisper.

Rip pulls back and claps my shoulder.

"Don't thank me we're family after all. Now come on your lady Is awaiting."

We walk back into the hospital, Rip walks back into the waiting area where the rest of the guys, Wes, Trudy and Max wait.

Trudy walks towards me.

"You doing okay honey?"

I nod.

"I'm alright, aunt Trudy."

I lean in and kiss her cheek, I give Wes and Max a chin lift and walk back into Lily's room. Penny and Ben are by her side their heads turn as soon as I walk back in. Penny walks towards me, kisses my cheek and pats my chest.

"Go be with my girl, she needs you now more

than ever. We're going for coffee. Come on Ben."
She walks out the door, Ben finally follows and stops by my side.
"Go be there for my girl, she can be stubborn when it comes to me and her mum. You tell her to get better and wake the bloody hell up, she might listen to you."
I chuckle.
"You laugh now son, but just you wait. When you have kids of your own, especially daughters with strong minds and they will be because they will be just like her. It will be me laughing then, believe me."
Ben finishes on a rasp emotion clogging his throat. Trying his hardest to believe that she will wake up and live a long happy life.
I nod my own emotion clogging my throat.
Penny sticks her head round the door, wiping away tears from her face.
"Come on Ben, stop scaring the poor lad talking about children, they need to get married first."
Penny gives me a smile and a wink. I return the smile and head over to sit down next to Lily.
I grab her hand in mine, it's cold and lifeless as I lift it kissing her palm. Holding her hand to my face.
"Darlin' if you can hear me, I need you to know I'm sorry. I did what I did to try and make sure you were safe. That you were away from the danger. But it backfired and you paid the fuckin' price for my mistake."

Taking a deep breath my throat burning with emotion. Tears I can no longer hold back now falling.

" I need you, I can't live my life without you. You belong with me. I need you like I need my next breath. So you need to get better and you need to wake up. So we can live our lives together. I promise no one will ever hurt you again."

I close my eyes just holding her hand to my face.

" Ven is dead, he can't get to you anymore. I love you so much Lily. Please god wake up."

I don't leave her side, until the next day when they take her for her scan and tests.

We all sit in the waiting area, as we await the news from the doctor.

Few hours later the doctor walks in.

I stop standing still. Waiting for the words I'm dying to hear from his mouth.

"I can confirm the swelling has gone down very slightly, and there is brain activity. But she will still need to remain in a coma until the swelling subsides more. But these are promising signs."

The doctor smiles, I let out a breath. Penny lets out a sob as Ben pulls her into his arms.

The doctor continues.

"Now, she still has a long road to recovery but like I said its promising signs. We will re-scan in forty eight hours from now. The nurses will continue to monitor her stats in the meantime."

The doctor shakes hands then he's gone.

Rise Above

I resume my position next to her bedside holding her hand. I stay there for the next two days until her next scan. The nurses try to get me to go home but I'm not leaving her side, I am never leaving her again.
Two days later they come and take her for her scan and tests. I'm in the waiting room, Wes and Rip have come to hear the update.
"You need a break man, you need to go home shower, sleep and change. You've been here for four days straight."
Wes says passing me a coffee.
"I'm not leaving her. She needs me I'm not going anywhere. I don't want her to wake up and for me not to be here."
I say drinking my coffee not taking my eyes off the door, waiting for the doctor to return.
"Come on man, you can take couple of hours that's all."
Rip tries to convince me.
I swing my gaze to both of them.
"For the last time I'm not fuckin' goin' anywhere, I'm not leaving her god damn side."
I snap. I take a deep breath to calm down.
"Sorry, just leave me be yeah? I'm not leaving and that's all there is to it." I apologise.
With that the doctor walks in, I jump to my feet we all wait on bated breath.
"It's good news the swelling has gone down nearly fully, brain activity is great, we are bringing her out of the coma today. She won't wake

immediately it can take hours, days or even weeks. It is down to when her body is ready. Keep talking to her and let's hope she wakes sooner rather than later."

The doctor smiles as the room erupts in hoots and hollers celebrating. I look up and release a long breath, feeling some of the heavy weight leave my chest.

I immediately return to her bedside where I stay holding her hand and talking to her for the next five days.

CHAPTER TWENTY

I can hear a mumbled voice, I'm in complete darkness. The voice gradually becomes clearer and I recognise it.

"Come on baby girl, you need to wake up now, we miss those beautiful eyes. Plus if you don't wake up your sisters and brother are threatening to fly over and tease you out of this coma. Rose actually said she would bring old family photos of your Michael Jackson phase and show everyone."

Mum? Coma? Rose better not or I will show everyone her gothic phase. My mum continues.

"She said she would even show Blake."

Mum chuckles. Blake, I want Blake. I try to talk but nothing is working, nothing is moving. I want to wake up, why can't I just wake up? I don't want to be in darkness anymore. I can hear my mum still talking.

"Although I don't think your sister could show him any photo of you that would scare him off, he is a good guy. He hasn't left your side even now we have had to force him to go to the hospital canteen to get some food, he can't be apart from you."

I'm in hospital? My memory slowly comes back to me, Ven, Virus. And finally Blake rescuing me.

"Me and your father wish you would wake up soon, each day that passes that boy looks more and more disheartened. I keep telling him that you will wake up when your good and ready and not a moment before. You are a stubborn girl and if your body isn't ready then it's better that you sleep until it is."

I can hear the emotion in my mums voice as she breaks. I want to hug her to tell her I am okay. But I feel the darkness taking over again the sound of my mum crying is fading. I try to wake up, I try to move my body to stay with my mum, but the pull is to strong, the darkness swallows me.

I don't know how long passes I can hear a machine beeping, but no one is speaking, there is only silence. I feel a heat and weight on my hand. I try to open my eyes, they slowly start to flutter open. It takes me a moment to bring my eyes into focus. The room is dark apart from a small lamp, I look down and see Blakes hand on mine, holding it close to his mouth, his head leaning on the edge of the bed. I try lifting my other arm, it shakes from being weak and feels stiff. But I manage to lift it. I touch and run my fingers through Blakes hair. He looks so beautiful and peaceful while he sleeps.

He mumbles in his sleep, I smile, tears running down my face. I continue stroking his hair. Just watching him not wanting to wake him. He looks drawn out and he hasn't shaved in what looks like weeks.

Blakes eyes flutter open. My hand pauses. I smile at him watching as the realisation hits his face and he jumps up.

"Lily! Your awake, thank fuckin' god darlin' ."

Blakes says kissing my hand. I cup his face and he leans into my hand. A single tear leaves his eye, I wipe it away.

"Babe." I rasp.

Blake leans forward and kisses me.

"I thought I'd lost you, I wasn't sure you'd ever wake up. I'm so sorry darlin'' so, so fuckin' sorry." Blake begs. I try to reassure him, but my throat is so dry and sore I need water.

"You need water? Here darlin take slow sips."

He holds the cup for me while I take small sips, the cold wet liquid feeling like heaven down my throat.

Blake places the cup down and turns to leave to get the nurse.

"Blake!"

I try and shout but it's still raspy and croaky. It's enough for him to stop in his tracks and turn around.

"Don't leave me please?"

I say tears filling my eyes the fear of him leaving

taking hold of me. Blake walks back to my side and kisses me holding my face in his hands stroking away my tears.

"I won't ever leave you I promise."

Blake rasps emotion clogging his throat.

"Listen to me, don't ever blame yourself okay. I love you Blake stone."

I let more tears fall as I smile at Blake. Gently resting his forehead on mine he whispers, voice raw.

"I love you Lily Rocke, so much."

Soon Blake leaves to get the nurse. They call the doctor and they run their checks. Blake calls my parents and even though its two in the morning my mum and dad are coming to see me. As apparently my mum said hospital visiting hours can kiss her arse!

The on call doctor comes and checks my vitals, asking me questions like who I am and where I am. The only thing that threw me is that I've lost nearly ten days. I'm also asked if I remember anything from the event that put me here. Unfortunately I remember most of it. It comes in flashes in my mind. I'm offered counselling for when I'm up to it.

The doctor is just finishing off as my mum and dad burst through the door.

"Now please this isn't visiting times it's the middle of the night you need to leave."

The doctor tries to stop my mum and dad.

"Now listen here doc. We are here to see our

daughter who has been in a coma for near ten days. And believe me we will. And If you get in our way I will shove my size ten English foot so far up your arse, you will vomit my bloody shoelaces. Are we clear?"

My dad threatens.

My mum just smiles up at my dad and pats his chest. The poor doctor just doing his job swallows nervously, nods and leaves.

My mum comes running over.

"Oh my baby girl, I'm so happy to see you're awake. I knew you would fight and wake when you were ready."

Mum rambles while showering me with kisses.

I'm smiling huge while also crying.

My dad comes up to me wipes my tears.

"Now come on Lil' no tears this is a happy time. I can't handle you crying.

Your mum and me love you so much sweetheart and I can't tell you how it feels to know you're going to be okay. You scared the shit out of us for a while."

Dad says emotion thick in his voice. Which of course just makes mum and I cry more.

"Christ you two, I need a bloody pint."

Dad mumbles secretly wiping away his own tears.

"Where's Blake?"

Mum asks.

"I'm not sure he left to get the nurse and doctor. Maybe he's gone to ring Wes or Rip? Or gone to get something to drink?"

I shrug and let out a yawn. I can feel myself getting tired again. Who knew being in a coma would take it out of you.

The nurse sticks her head in asking if I would like any toast, my mouth waters at the thought. I nod eagerly.

Blake walks back in with coffees and muffins for mum and dad.

"Sorry there just from the vending machine, that's all there is open in here."

Blake hands the coffee out, I yawn again and immediately Blake is at my side.

"You feeling okay?"

Smiling, I nod.

"Yep, this is normal for me to feel weak and tired apparently being in a coma makes you tired."

My mum opens her muffin and takes a bite, my stomach rumbles.

"Also being in a coma makes me hungry."

I laugh but stop as I get a sharp pulling pain in my stomach, I pull down the cover a little and pull up my gown, to see the large dressing covering my stomach. The flash back of Ven slicing the knife across my stomach hits me. Looking down I also notice welts on my wrists. I close my eyes as various memory flashbacks hit me.

I feel strong arms go around me, it isn't until that moment I realise I'm sobbing and shaking.

It's Blake who pulls me to him comforting me, holding me close. Until I feel myself drift off to sleep.

I awake the next morning, and I'm curled into Blake who is led on his back fast asleep. I try to move so not to wake him, but my body is still weak. Blake wakes and I smile. He just frowns.
"Darlin' you okay?"
Blake cups my face. Concern in his eyes.
"I am okay. Promise."
I smile, Blake looks intently into my eyes.
"Promise me you will talk to someone and get help, stop acting like you're okay. You've just woke from a coma, you went through hell. Don't worry about anyone else ,you don't have to be strong for them. I'm here to be strong for you, please darlin' do that not for me or your family but for yourself."
I close my eyes, and nod Blake kisses my forehead.
"I love you Blake, don't ever leave me."
I cling to Blake as I let the tears flow, Blake just holds me.
"I love you too, and I aint goin' nowhere darlin'."
We stay like that for a long time until the nurse comes in to do my obs.
The next few days I'm bombarded with visitors. The doctors do more tests, and I'm getting my strength back more and more. I have a therapist come in to start my sessions. Paid for by Blake.
Evelynn and Suellen come to visit bringing me champagne bottle balloon and some books to

read.

"The balloon is a promise for when you get out of here, we are doing a drinks night and we will come to you. Blake will have to make himself scarce."

Suellen organises a date in her diary that I should be out, and they are both free, she also texts Louisa too.

"So what you both been up too? I don't have any exciting news apart from my catheter been removed and I'm able to pee on the toilet again."

Both Evelynn and Suellen wince and cross their legs.

"Nothing new, only I'm looking after my niece's devil creature. I swear its plotting at night how to attack." Evelynn shudders.

"Why what is it? Snake? Tarantula?"

Suellen is laughing and snickering. Evelynn turns and glares.

"That's it laugh it up, you won't be laughing when the little bastard escapes and kills me in my sleep. It smells my fear. It stares at me watching my every move, waiting for the right moment to attack."

"Evelynn calm your tatas, it's a darn Guinea pig! Ignore her honey, she's got too many cobwebs in her attic."

Suellen pats my leg. I'm crying with laughter.

"A Guinea pig?! Really Evelynn?" I ask wiping the tears from my face.

"You both laugh all you want. Yes it's a damn

Guinea pig, you don't know them they are organised, I swear Mr nibbles is going to go for my jugular. He's just waiting for the perfect time."
Evelynn holds her throat. Nodding eagerly trying to convince us of the uprising of the plague of evil Guinea pigs that are going to take over the world and kill us all.
We spend the next hour talking away and I laugh a lot. I let out a little yawn.
"Come on Evelynn , let's leave Lily to get some sleep she looks as tired as a boomtown whore." I cough out a laugh.
"She don't mean you look like a whore just you look as tired as one."
Evelynn snickers and pats my leg, laughing.
I wave them good bye and open one of the books they brought for me. I start reading but soon my eyes are heavy and I'm drifting off to sleep.
I'm dreaming again reliving it all. But in my dreams Blake can't save me, he tries to get to me but Ven is too powerful and kills Blake right in front of me. I'm still tied down and I can't get to warn Blake I try screaming and shouting but no sound is coming out.
I am woken by Blake shaking me calling my name. I open my eyes realising it's all a dream, I grab Blake and hold on to him tight I cry a stream of tears. Blake soothes and rubs my back.
"It's ok darlin' I'm here, it was a dream it's all over now."
Blake kisses the top of my head.

"Blake, I was back there, you came, but instead of you saving me, I watched Ven shoot you dead right in front of me and no matter how much I screamed and shouted to try and warn you, nothing came out. I lost you, god it felt so real." I sob.

Blake continues to comfort me, there's a knock at the door and Rip sticks his head in.

"Not a good time?"

He asks looking at the scene in front of him. I immediately turn.

"No don't worry Rip I'm okay, let me just go get cleaned up. Just excuse my little meltdown."

I smile, I kiss a frowning Blake as I move to get off the bed, Blake grabs my hand.

"Darlin' it's okay Rip can come back later."

I smile, lean in and slowly kiss him.

"It's okay babe, I'd rather it all be normal, and I can forget about that awful dream."

I walk to the bathroom and splash cold water on my face taking in deep breaths. I look in the mirror, taking in my injured face the finger marks on my neck from where he strangled me. I close my eyes, fight back the memories. Taking a few more deep breaths. I plaster on a smile. Acting like everything is alright, its what I've done my whole life and its what i will continue to do. I head back into the room.

Both turn to watch me walk back in. I sit on the bed and Blake pulls me to him, kissing the top of my head.

Rise Above

"We are talking about this later darlin' you are not okay."

He mumbles into my ear. I just nod.

"So Rip how are you? All good with the club?" I ask

Rip smiles and shakes his head.

"Christ woman you're the one in hospital, I'm supposed to ask how you are. Also I'm not stopping I just came to pass on a message from your mum and Trudy."

Blake groans I look to him and smile.

"What's the damn message then? What are those two plotting now?" Blake asks irritated.

"You know what ma is like and now she's found a buddy, there's no stopping her. I'm here to check that your being discharged tomorrow right?" Rip asks me.

"Yep, hopefully out of here after lunch when the doctor has done his rounds. Why?"

"I'm not at liberty to say and if I did my life wouldn't be worth livin'. And you're bringing her home?"

Blake nods.

"Good text me when you're leaving the hospital. Make sure you do, or it will be your life that aint worth living."

I laugh, Rip smiles.

He turns to leave but stops at the door and turns back around.

"Flower, I'm glad you're getting better. But you don't ever have to pretend in front of family how you feel. Listen to your man, let him help you heal."

I nod swallowing passed a lump in my throat. Rip just gives me the cool guy chin lift and leaves. I've managed to fool and act okay to my family and friends nearly my whole life. But apparently here i am completely transparent.

I curl up in Blakes arms, not saying anything just lying there.

It's Blake that breaks the silence.

"That night when you went missing was the longest most painful night of my life. I thought I'd never see you again that I would be too late. I screwed up massively, I should of never of played it like that. You aren't the only one, being haunted by images of that night darlin'. When I saw you tied up to that bed and the blood. I swear my heart shattered into a million pieces. The only good from that night is that I killed that mother fucker. And that virus is dead too, that double crossing rat."

I sit up looking into Blakes pained face. He takes a deep breath and continues.

"What I'm trying to say darlin' is if me seeing you like that, broke me and I am struggling. Well it actually fuckin' happened to you so fuck knows how you're feeling about it all. I know one thing and that is, you aint guna be coping and dealing with that by yourself. You feel like shit, you want to scream, cry, or hit something then do it. Don't hold back. Don't keep it locked up darlin'. Or Ven fuckin' wins. I love you, hell everyone fuckin' loves you. Like Rip said They are your friends and family you don't have to pretend in front of them. Let them worry about you for a change, you need to worry about yourself. It's not a bad thing being selfish sometimes." Blake cups my face and wipes my fallen tears.

"Babe, I'm not going to stop seeing the therapist, and I will try to lean on you and the family more. It's going to take me a while, but I won't let Ven win. I love you too much. And I haven't said thank you to you yet for saving me and for hunting me down to find me, for killing that evil bastard. Thank you for waiting by my side for me to wake up, thank you for never giving up on me. I love you and you know the same goes for you. I'm here for you too Blake."

Blake kisses me with every bit of feeling and emotion poured into it.

We spend the rest of the day just lying there. I fall asleep this time no bad dreams. And I know it sounds like a cliché but it's because I'm safe in Blakes arms. I know he will always be there by my side to protect me.

The next morning I'm excited to leave. The doctor does his final checks.

"Now miss Rocke, you will still be in some discomfort. There are pain meds for you in the bag, please follow the dosage. Also any concerns please come back. Your stitches have healed nicely the rest will fade, we wish you well and in the nicest way I hope we never see you again."

Blake and I thank the doctor and staff and head to his truck to head home for god knows what his aunt and my mum have organised.

CHAPTER TWENTY ONE

We pull up to Blakes house and its much like last time, cars and bikes fill the yard.

I turn to look at Blake smiling. Blake just rests his head on the steering wheel muttering about his crazy aunt not listening.

I chuckle rubbing his back.

"Come on babe, it's nice that she cares so much and plus it's not just her. My mother loves to organise a party at any opportunity she can. Just a few hours and it will all be over."

Blake kisses my hand and hops down, walks around the truck and opens my door.

We walk up the steps to the porch, Blake opens the front door, and we are assaulted with cheers, hoots and hollers. The room is filled with everyone, and my mum and Trudy stand at the front.

Mum and Trudy don't give us a chance to even greet everyone, they pull us both in for a hug.

"Aunt Trudy I told you not to go crazy. To keep it small."

Blake grits through his teeth.

"Oh shush! It's just family and friends. Plus we didn't go crazy we just ordered in a shit load of pizza, a few kegs of beer and a few bottles of wine. I've made a couple of my pies for dessert and Penn made an English apple crumble."
Trudy pinches Blakes cheek.
I'm soon pulled away from Blakes hand, chatting to everyone. Mammoth pulls me in for a big hug.
"Good to see you're okay flower, you scared us all there for a while. Khan here even cried a little." Mammoth teases khan.
"Ahh khan is that true, I didn't know you cared for me that much."
I join in the taunt.
"Fuck off Mammoth, I didn't cry, I'm all man. Just ask your mamma."
Khan retorts smiling. Before Mammoth can speak Khan continues.
"Seriously though flower I'm glad you're okay, we all are. It would have been a tragedy if I couldn't look at your fine tits and ass again."
khan chuckles and kisses my cheek. I feel Blake come up behind me his hand going around my waist. I laugh.
"Khan will you stop teasing Blake. And babe ignore him he's only winding you up. Now boys play nice I am going to speak to Louisa." I kiss Blake and pat Khans cheek.
I sit next to Louisa on the couch and gently rub her big pregnant belly.
"How you doing Louisa? You counting down the

days?"

Louisa nods enthusiastically.

"Hell yeah, this little thang is constantly dancing on my bladder. My due date is only three weeks away. And Sam is driving me insane, he won't let me walk to the shop. Not even letting me pot some plants for fear I will hurt myself or over do it."

I chuckle and feel the baby kick.

"Oh wow that's awesome, I used to feel my nephew kick when my sister was pregnant with him, it's the most out of this world feeling. As for Sam he's just being over protective. Make the most of it enjoy and put your feet up."

I feel eyes burning the back of my head and turn and see Blake watching me intently. I smile and give him a wink. I'm rewarded with a dimpled grin.

"Y'all be next I give it six months."

I turn back to Louisa shaking my head.

"We've only been together a short while, that's way, way down the future."

I can't deny the thought of being pregnant with Blakes baby makes me all warm and gooey. But I don't want to jump the gun.

"Oh shush, you two have been through more than most couples that have been married thirty years. I'm telling you six months."

Evelynn and Suellen sit down and join us.

"What's happening in six months?" Evelynn asks looking back and forth.

"Louisa thinks that I will be pregnant within six months."
I reply rolling my eyes.
"Aint no doubt, you'll be storked in the next six months."
Suellen agrees and Evelynn nods
"Hey rubble! The barn doors open, and the mules tryin' to run!"
Suellen shouts across to rubble.
Confused I look across the room to see him, salute and do up his fly.
I burst out laughing.
"You're going to have to write me a notebook of these Texan sayings and their meanings. They are hilarious."
The rest of the afternoon continues much of the same lots of laughter. I'm gasping for a glass of wine but can't because of the pain killers. I start getting discomfort and I'm in a little bit of pain. I go to find my bag and get some painkillers. Stood in the kitchen taking five minutes to myself.
"You're feeling it now huh?"
I turn and see Raven. I walk to her and hug her.
"Hey, I wondered where you were? I'm okay just in a bit of pain that's all. Painkillers will kick in soon. Just don't tell Blake or he will kick everyone out and put me to bed."
I chuckle.
"I had a delivery at the bar so had to wait for that before I could come here. God honey Its good to see you. When you're up for it party at the bar

or clubhouse. You, me the girls too and lots and lots of tequila."

Raven pulls me in for another hug.

"I'm sorry I can't stop long honey, I came to pick my old man up and get my ass back to work. But I had to come and see you. I'm glad you're ok. I'm here if you need anything especially tequila."

"Thanks that means a lot to me. Might stay away from the tequila for a while though."

I wink at Raven.

"Sorry to say Hun but I think Big Papa, has had a few too many beers, so good luck with that, I'm glad you stopped by.

You are on for that night. Wait until I tell Evelynn and Suellen. A night with bikers I think they might pee their pants with excitement."

Raven laughs, as we walk into the lounge and I help her round up Big Papa.

Few others from the club start to leave, so does Louisa and Sam. Soon it's just me, Blake and family.

We are all sat around eating pie and my mums crumble.

"So come on Mrs Rocke what other British food can you cook for us while your here? Because damn that crumble was the shit."

Wes compliments my mum, as Max clips him around the back of the head.

"Ouch what was that for max?"

"Watch your mouth when speaking to a lady. Did

I not teach you nuthin' boy?"

Blake and Rip both laugh.

"Oh Wes sweetheart call me Penny or Penn, we are pretty much family now. And don't worry about the language my daughters foul mouths would shock you. They get it from their father."

Mum points to dad. My dad just shrugs and carries on eating his pie.

"But I could make you lots of things, like toad in the hole, sherry trifle, shortbread, stew and dumplings. You just tell me what sort of things you like."

Mum pats Wes's knee.

"I don't like toads." Wes states gagging slightly.

Mum, dad and I burst out laughing.

"It's not toads, it's sausages in Yorkshire pudding. It's just called toad in the hole don't ask me why, it just is."

I tell Wes.

"You brits are weird. Why not just say sausage pudding then?!"

I smile, shrugging and curl up into Blake after finishing my delicious chocolate pie. I let out a big yawn.

Trudy stands.

"Right come on y'all let's leave Lil' to get some sleep, give these two some peace."

Mum and dad nod getting up clearing the plates.

"Don't worry about clearing up I will get those in the morning. Mum, dad where are you going you not staying here?"

I say on another yawn.

"Don't be daft love, you rest. No Trudy and Max kindly offered to put us up at there's, give you guys some peace together."

I smile at Trudy and she gives me a wink.

"Well sorry you two but you still got me here." Wes says smiling.

"Don't be a plank Wes this is your home too. Would be weird if you weren't here."

Wes gives me a kiss on the cheek.

"Right come on then aunt, unc and British people I will drive you back as you all can't handle your drink."

Wes grabs his keys. As we say our goodbyes, Rip comes up behind us.

"I'm off, flower take care of my cousin, Blake I will catch you later."

Giving Rip a hug goodbye we turn, and Blake locks up.

I have a long hot shower, washing away the hospital smell off me. I use Blakes shower gel. Loving the smell of him on my skin.

I get out and towel myself off. I just stop and stare at my reflection. The marks caused by him. The bruising on my ribs has died down significantly, there is a fresh scar across my stomach close to my tattoo for Cameron. I trace the scar with my finger. The one on my shoulder is thicker and slightly raised. I look to my breast the bite mark around my nipple still there.

I quickly cover myself not wanting to be reminded of what happened anymore. I just want to forget that Ven and virus ever touched me.

I pull on my satin black night dress that sits mid-thigh. I walk into the bedroom and see Blake shirtless in bed sat up leaning against the headboard. Working on his laptop. I stand there just admiring him.

"Did you mamma ever tell you that staring is rude?"

Blake says without looking up from his laptop.

"No my mum told me to always appreciate what I have, that's all I'm doing." I retort.

Blake looks up, he does a head to toe sweep with his eyes, as I walk toward him. I pick up and move his laptop to the nightstand. I straddle his lap I lean in close until our lips are near touching.

"Now who's staring?"

I whisper, I then kiss him long and passionate. Until we are both breathing heavy.

"Darlin' stop I don't want to hurt you, there's no rush, just take all the time you need."

I lean back slightly and grind my hips. I can feel just how hard he is.

I grab the hem of my nightie and lift it slowly over my head and throw it to the floor. Blakes pupils dilate as his eyes take me in. I see anger cross his face as he takes in my breast where Virus bit me.

Taking a deep breath I take Blakes hand in mine

and place it on my breast.

"Make me forget, make them go away please. I need you to make me feel good Blake. My body is yours they tried to take it, take what is yours back. Please."

A single tear slips Blake catches it.

His thumb rubs slowly over my nipple I groan and grind down.

Blake carefully flips me over to my back cocooning me with his arms. He leans in kissing me slowly.

"Darlin' they never had you, you were always mine. They made the mistake to touch what's mine. I'm going to erase their touch. You want me to stop at any point you just say. I love you and I'm guna' show you just how much."

Blake kisses my wound on my shoulder kissing down to my bite mark, he carries on his journey south kissing over my slashed scar. My skin pebbles, as he carries on traveling further south with his mouth. Until he's kissing up my inner thighs, then his mouth is on me. I moan as he licks and sucks. I'm soon coming apart.

"Blake I'm coming"

My body bucks as my orgasm takes hold. Blake moves over me.

"You sure you're okay ?"

I smile and cup his face.

"I'm more than okay, make love to me Blake." I plead.

Reaching down I hold him, stroking up and

down watching as Blakes jaw tightens. I position him at my entrance and he slowly glides in.

We both let out a moan.

Blake slowly moves rocking in and out circling his hips. Kissing my neck and my breasts. He takes my nipple in his mouth and sucks. My hips buck wanting and needing more. Blake picks up the pace, but still being careful not to hurt me. Both of us panting and our bodies begin to sweat.

I can feel my climax building, my legs tighten around his waist.

"Babe, I'm close oh god!"

I throw my head back as Blake continues drive into me. Ecasty hits, taking me over the edge, I cry out. Blake continues finding his own release groaning deep in his throat.

Both of us try and steady our breathing Blakes head buried in the crook of my neck. Tears sting my eyes I sniff and Blakes head snaps up.

"What's the matter did I hurt you?"

He asks concern and worry in his eyes.

I smile shaking my head.

"No you didn't hurt me, I'm just overwhelmed with emotion. I love you so much Blake Stone. Thank you for erasing the pain, making me yours again."

Blake smiles leans in kissing me.

"I love you Lily Rocke, marry me."

My whole body freezes and my eyes are wide

"Are you serious?" I ask stunned.

My heart is beating a million times a minute.

"I'm deadly serious, I love you, you love me. We've been through hell and back together. I know I am never letting you go, you belong with me."

Blake leans in kissing me, he circles his hips still inside me. Making me moan.

"Say yes, say you'll become Mrs Stone."

Blake whispers as he kisses my neck.

"Are you trying to play dirty to coerce a yes from me Mr Stone?

I pause briefly.

"Because you really don't need to."

Blake stops kissing my neck and looks at me smiling.

"Is that a yes miss Rocke?"

Tears sting my eyes as I am smiling.

"Yes! Yes I will marry you, I bloody love you Blake stone."

Blake wastes no time and kisses me.

"God I love you Lily."

Blake shows me just how much he loves me. Making love to me again until we fall asleep in each other's arms.

That night no nightmares plague my dreams. I sleep feeling safe, free from worry, free from my anxieties. From all that had been thrown at me I was finally free. I had risen above.

L G Campbell

The End

EPILOGUE

I drive as fast as I can. Swerving in and out of traffic my heart beating a thousand beats a minute.

"Lily, aarghh. Mother fucker!" Louisa screams at me from the passenger seat. Her head tipped back with her face scrunched up in pain.

"Don't worry Louisa I will get you to the hospital in time I promise. Just concentrate on your breathing, try to relax and all will be okay."

I try to reassure her. But inside I'm panicking, I really don't want to deliver the baby on the side of the road in Blakes truck.

"What if, if... arrgh fuck wankering asshole. What if Sam doesn't make it on time? What if he misses the birth?" Louisa cries next to me. I never heard her swear in the time I've known her. Yet apparently when in labour she swears like a sailor.

"He won't I promise I will call Blake on the hands free now. Didn't really have a chance until now honey with trying to get you out of the library and into the truck. Have to say I've never had a priest drop to his knees and start praying for me before." I shrug.

"That's because you were yelling at him to move out of the fucking way or you'd send him straight to hell, that Satan himself was your friend and you have him on speed dial." I giggle. As I press the call button for Blake it ring's and I wait for him to answer.

"It was a bit dramatic Louisa he didn't need to drop to his knees and pray for me."

I hadn't realised Blake had answered.

"Darlin' what fuckin' bloke was on his knees for you?" Blake growls through the car speakers.

"Oh calm down it was a priest, anyway that's not why I am calling I've got Louisa in the truck with me, we are on our way to the hospital she's gone into labour you need to get hold of Sam and bring him to the hospital." I finish, before Blake has a chance to speak Louisa shouts out.

"Aarghh shit me, twat waffle, fuck! Owww! Blake I need my hospital bag. Hoo-hee-hoo-hee ."

Louisa continues to breathe through her contraction.

"Jesus fuckin' Christ. Is she possessed?" Blake asks.

I can't help but laugh.

"No babe, she's just having a baby. Now go and get Sam I am about five minutes away from the hospital."

"Right darlin' we will be with you soon."

Blake disconnects, and soon I'm pulling up to the hospital car park.
"Right honey, wait here I'm going to get you a wheel chair okay."

I run to grab a wheelchair and run back to the truck Louisa is leaning against the truck, holding her stomach breathing through a contraction.
The next thing her waters go. Louisa looks at me panic in her face.
"It's okay honey, sit in the wheelchair still loads of time."
I try to reassure her. Louisa sits in the wheel chair and I walk briskly but it's more like a jog to the hospital entrance.

Soon we are up on the delivery ward, Louisa toking on gas and air like she needs it more than her next breath. I keep checking my phone, where the hell are Blake and Sam?
"Shitting cocking hell! Oi! Lily where is Sam? Are my lips big? They feel big." Louisa says while pouting like a fish trying to look at her own lips. She's off her rocker high off the gas and air.
"Gas and air good?" I ask laughing.
"They are on their way, Blake will make sure Sam gets here don't worry." I soothe.
There's a knock at the door and the doctor walks In.
"Hello, I'm doctor Harry Minge."
I choke on my water he's got to be having a laugh

surely.

"I'm sorry what did you say your name was? I ask.

" I'm doctor Harry Minge, and you are?"

I'm trying my hardest not to laugh.

"Ahem, I'm Lily a friend of Louisa's."

I shake the doctors hand.

I'm wiping Louisa's forehead while doctor Minge checks to see how far along she is.

"Good news Louisa it's time for your baby to enter this world."

He smiles up at Louisa. But Louisa doesn't return his smile.

"No-no it can't happen now Sam isn't here. He can't miss this."

Louisa begins to cry, trying to cross her legs.

"Shhhh, honey let me quickly ring Blake see where they are okay."

I quickly move to the corner of the room and call Blake. He answers in one ring.

"Darlin' we are here, what floor? We've just pulled up."

I sigh in relief.

"Thank fuck. She's ready to push, the baby is ready to come now. So you need to run. It's the third floor room 223."

I disconnect and walk back over to a grunting Louisa.

"He's here honey, they are running up as we speak."

I smile. As Louisa whimpers.

There's a loud commotion as the door bursts open to reveal a frantic Sam.

"Don't just fucking stand there. Get over here and hold my god damn hand. What a fucking cock womble!" Louisa shouts.

Sam's panicked eyes come to me. I'm just silently laughing and shake my head in warning not to say anything. He moves quickly to her side and grabs her hand.

I kiss Louisa's head.

"Good luck honey, I will be in the waiting room with Blake okay."

Louisa just nod's putting the gas and air tube back in her mouth

I find Blake in the hallway, I smile as he pulls me in to his arms and kisses me.

"All good?" He asks and I nod.

"Come on let's grab a coffee, who knew Louisa has the pottiest mouth on her when in labour? Oh and you'll never guess what the doctor is called."

Blakes smiling.

"Yeah I heard a snippet of the foul mouth, what's the doctor called?"

Blake asks as he puts his arm around me as we head to the canteen.

"Doctor Harry Minge!"

I burst out laughing. Blake just looks at me clueless. And shrugs.

"Really? Minge, as in vagina ,beaver, snatch, pussy, twat the poontang!?" I say just a little too loudly getting a few looks from people. I blush and hide my face in his chest. This just makes Blake laugh harder.

"No darlin', we don't use that name for a vagina over here but thank you for clearing that up for me, and the rest of the hospital."

Blake smirks.

About an hour later we are called in to see Louisa and the baby.

Louisa is sat up beaming, looking down at the tiny bundle in her arms.

I lean over and gently hug Louisa.

"Congratulations guys."

I whisper not wanting to wake the beautiful little bundle in her arms.

Louisa hands me the baby.

"Auntie Lily, I would like you to meet Eliza Lily Merrick."

Shocked I feel tears sting my eyes. As I look to Louisa and Sam.

"Really you named her Lily?"

Both Sam and Louisa nod.

"Yup, we named her Eliza after my dear nana and of course what better name to give our daughter than Lily. Someone who is so brave, strong, loving and loyal."

Louisa sniffs back her tears.

"Oh you guys, you're making me cry."

I sit down with Eliza in my arms and take in her beautiful little face. I gently stroke her cheek. And kiss her little nose. I smile down at her.

Soon I will have my own perfect little bundle. I did a pregnancy test this morning. I actually did about ten pregnancy tests, all came back positive. I wanted to wait to have a baby with Blake. At least until after we are married in three months. But obviously my body had other plans. I'm so happy but nervous of telling him. Especially what he's been through. I can't bear the thought of him not being happy about the baby. That thought has my gut twisting I feel my nose sting and my eyes swell with tears.

I feel hands on my thighs I look up.

"Darlin' what's the matter?"

I plaster a quick smile on my face.

"Oh nothing babe, I'm just so happy for Sam and Louisa, and it just reminded me of when my nephew was born. Makes me realise how much I miss them." I dismiss, looking down at the cute little girl in my arms and I hand her to Blake. He takes her in his arms and smiles down at her. My chest warms and feels like it could burst at the sight before me. I can't help the big smile on my face.

"It will be you guys next."

Sam says grinning, me and Blake look at each other.

"Steady man, let me make her my wife, then maybe down further down the line." Blake replies.

My heart sinks a little and my smile wavers.

He hands Eliza back to Sam.

I stand and give Louisa a quick hug.

"Come babe, let's leave them to it, all your family will be arriving soon. Congratulations again guys."

We say our goodbyes and head to the truck. Blake drove Sam's truck as apparently he was in too much of a panicked state to drive himself.

I am quiet on the journey home, trying to process my thoughts and when will be a good time to tell Blake.

When we arrive home, I go to walk upstairs. Blake grabs my hand and pulls me to him.

"What was that all about in the hospital darlin'?"

I rest my forehead on his chest looking down at our feet. Taking a deep breath. I decide there's never going to be the right time to tell him so I'm just better off getting it out of the way now.

"Umm here's the thing, well I know you didn't want this, and I certainly didn't want this just yet, but well its happening and I am happy about it so I hope you will be too."

I am stopped mid speech as Blake gently grabs my chin and tilts my face up, so I am looking into his eyes.

"Stop babbling darlin' and just tell me what it is you need to tell me."

Blake demands holding my face in his hands stroking my cheeks.

I close my eyes. And say on a rushed breath. My heart beating fast in my chest.

"I'm pregnant." I blurt.

Blakes thumb stops stroking my cheek, and he says nothing I peek open my eyes to look at his reaction. He's frowning looking off into the distance.

"Babe." I whisper.

His gaze swings to mine.

"Say that again." Blake demands his voice gruff.

"Umm I'm pregnant." I repeat.

Blake still says nothing. My heart plummets.

"It's okay, um, I know this is a lot to take in. we can talk more when you're ready."

My voice wavers, I try to swallow back the tears. I go to remove Blakes hands from my face, but he holds on. I look up into Blakes eyes.

"You're pregnant?" He asks and I nod.

Blakes surprises me and drops to his knees, he holds on to my waist and places a kiss on my stomach. I smile, my tears falling freely now.

"Fuck, darlin' you're carrying my baby. You're fuckin' pregnant with my baby!"

Blake hollers smiling.

"I love you so fuckin much darlin', you've made me the happiest man in the entire fuckin' world you know that?"

I'm smiling so big my face hurts. Blake gets to his feet and kisses me long slow and passionate.

"I love you too handsome." I rasp emotion clogging my throat.

At the doctors we find out I'm further along than I thought. We decide to tell the family. If what has happened to us in a short space of time has taught us anything it's that you don't know what can happen and to grab the good, share and enjoy it while it lasts.
I am sat on Blakes lap at his desk as I video call my mum knowing that Rose will be there.
My mum, Rose and Caden fill the screen.
"Oh lily sweetie! CAN YOU HEAR ME?!" Mum shouts at the top of her lungs.
"Christ old woman, Beethoven can bloody hear you! I think you burst my ear drum." Rose grumbles wiggling her finger in her ear. Blake hides his face in my back chuckling quietly.
"Old? who are you calling old? And stop the stupid comments Rose I'm sure Beethoven's hearing is exceptional all dogs hearing is, but I doubt he can hear from across the Atlantic. Really Rose use your brain."
All of us burst out laughing this time.
"Mum, Rose means Beethoven, the deaf and also very dead composer. Not the St Bernard dog from the movie." I clarify. As mums does she quickly brushes it off and moves swiftly on to the next topic.
"So Lily, Blake how are you?"
I turn looking at Blake and smile.
"Actually mum could you call dad in as well?" I ask .

"Of course honey, BEN! Get in here and come see your daughter."

Mum hollers. Soon dad walks in paper under his arms doing up his trousers.

"Christ what did you put in that chilli, my colon is doing the bleedin' conga. Might want to give the downstairs toilet a wide berth for a while."

Dad wafts his paper around just to emphasise and continues.

"Right I'm ready to call Lily, let's go."

Caden sat holding his nose face scrunched up.

"Grandad Lily is already on the screen." Caden points out. Dad turns to see us on the screen and laughing I give a little wave.

"Hi dad." I wave.

"Christ woman you could have warned me that they were already on there. I've just been talking about my bloody colon for crying out loud."

Dad rants before mum can retaliate. I jump in.

"Guy's, shut up and listen. Blake and I have something to tell you."

all their faces turn to us. I take a deep breath.

"I'm pregnant."

Before I even finish mum is letting out a full blown scream as is Rose. Poor Caden just smiles covering his ears.

Its dad he's just stood there not saying anything no facial expression nothing.

"Dad?" I ask worried he's not happy for me.

"Your pregnant? I'm going to be a grandad again?" Dad asks. My brows furrow as I nod. Confused by his reaction.

It's then dad takes us all by surprise. And throws his newspaper in the air.

"Hell yeah I'm going to be a grandad again! I'm so fucking happy for you sweetheart. And congratulations to you too Blake."

I laugh and smile tears of happiness fill my eyes, my mum and rose are crying too.

"You weren't this happy when I told you I was pregnant."

Rose states to dad.

"I was over the moon for you honey, I just never liked that p-r-i-c-k."

He replies.

"Dad Caden can spell." Rose points out.

Mum ignoring them leans forward.

"Have you told Daisy yet?" She asks, worry on her face.

"No I haven't, do you think she will take the news okay?"

I've been nervous about telling daisy as I know it's all she's ever wanted and it's just not happening for her.

"Truth is sweetheart I don't know, she hasn't come over in weeks and only sent us a quick text. I am worried about her. We've tried turning up, but Tony answered and just said she was laid up in bed asleep. Not like our Daisy at all."

Mums right it's not like her.

"I will ring her straight after I get off the phone

to you, its Sunday Tony will be at the golf club she might answer for me."
Mum gives me a small smile and a nod.
We all say our goodbyes.
I make quick work of trying to ring Daisy.
She doesn't answer at first, but I persist. Finally she picks up.
"Daisy you there?" I ask worried. Blake gently squeezes my neck.

"Lil' oh Lil'." Daisy sobs down the phone.

"Oh my god daisy what is it what's happened?"
I feel Blake freeze behind me.

"Lil', he, he hit me. Please help me."
I completely freeze.

"He what, he fucking hit you?!"
I whisper angrily down the phone.
Blake grabs the phone from my hand and places it on speaker.
"Daisy this is Blake. Listen to me and listen good. Do you have a passport?" Blake asks.

"Yes." Daisy sniffles.
"Right go and find your passport and give me your details I will book you on the next available flight to us. You need to get to the airport now. Take your phone. Lily will call you back with the flight information, pack quick and light."
Daisy moves around finding her passport and

433

reads out her details over the phone.

"Please don't tell mum and dad." Daisy begs.

"I won't, I will think of something to keep them quiet for a while. Go get to the airport. Ring me when you're there and email me when you're on the plane. Get here safely, we will be waiting for you. I Love you skin and blister." I say my voice wavering.

Daisy cries into the phone.

"Thank you, I love you too."

She disconnects, I turn to Blake who is ready to comfort me in his arms.

"She will be okay, I fuckin' promise. She will be safe with us soon." Blake states.

My heart breaks, I wasn't there for her. Anxiety and guilt knots in my stomach and I know that won't ease until I have her safe in my arms.

COMING SUMMER 2019 WALLFLOWER BOOK TWO IN THE ROCKE SERIES DAISY'S STORY.

To keep up to date on upcoming releases, news and giveaways follow my page on Facebook and Instagram.

Printed in Germany
by Amazon Distribution
GmbH, Leipzig